BETH BOLDEN

Chapter 1

"So you figure out where you're signing yet, bro?" Aidan asked as he and Landry sat down in their seats.

For reasons Landry Banks had never quite figured out, Aidan Flynn was his best friend. They'd been best friends since they'd met in college twelve years ago. He was just as much family as his own two brothers were. They'd made it onto the starting roster at Michigan, then onto the NFL Combine, and finally, they'd been both drafted into the NFL.

Aidan had been selected by the Toronto Thunder early in the first round, and he was still their very popular, very successful starting quarterback. Which, in Landry's opinion, hadn't helped his friend's arrogance and occasionally annoying swagger in any way whatsoever. In Toronto, he was practically revered as a god. But still, even now, despite all his obnoxiousness, Landry loved him. There was so much good—so much loyalty and kindness—buried under Aidan's brash exterior. Landry wished more people could see it.

But not today. Because Aidan knew very well Landry hadn't decided yet if he was going to stay with the Bills or take one of the other offers he'd received—and yet Aidan had poked him about it anyway.

"No, which you know," Landry said, elbowing his friend in the side. "God, you kinda suck."

Aidan just grinned. "Hey, what's that saying? You gotta make hay while the sun shines? You eliminate any of the teams that've offered for you yet?"

"I think..." Landry hesitated. This decision was all he'd thought about over the last few weeks. Over and over, round and round, all the pros and the cons. He was pretty sure Elliot, his agent, hated him because they'd had three conference calls and so many texts Landry couldn't even dream of counting them all. That didn't count all the ones he'd sent to Logan and Levi, his two brothers, who also played in the NFL. "I think I want to leave Buffalo, at least."

"Really?" Aidan looked surprised.

"Yeah." Landry was grateful to the team that had drafted him eight years ago, but he was ready to move on. Maybe move somewhere where it wasn't negative eleventy-billion below and didn't snow buckets every winter.

"Well, see, you made *some* progress," Aidan teased. "So you gonna take the Falcons contract or the Condors?"

"The Falcons low-balled me, so probably not them, but..."

"The Condors are a garbage fire?"

Landry made a face. "That was last year. Supposedly it's gonna be different this year. Totally different. I talked to Logan. You know he plays for Asa Dawson, who they even brought in to consult on the Condors' rebuild. And I talked to the new owner. I think...it should be better. Honestly, I'm tempted to take the Condors' deal. Their offer wasn't as good as Buffalo, but..."

As usual, Aidan knew what he wasn't saying. "But they're closer to Miami." *Where Logan plays.*

As much as Aidan pretended not to understand how close the Banks family was, there was a reason they were both here to watch Aidan's little brother, Riley, in his debut today.

"Yep," Landry said. "Charleston's closer to Miami." He was tired of being so far from his brothers. Charleston wasn't necessarily *close* to Miami, but it sure was a hell of a lot closer than Buffalo had been.

Aidan waved out at the field, changing the subject. "You think the kid's gonna play today?"

Landry rolled his eyes. *I love my best friend. I really love my best friend.* "First off, you shouldn't call him the kid, you know that drives Riley nuts. And he's what...twenty-four? Twenty-five?"

Aidan shrugged like he didn't know. He knew.

"And," Landry continued, "we're here because he's the starting quarterback. So yeah, he's gonna play. I don't know why I came all the way out here to Pittsburgh if he isn't."

"You came because I asked you to," Aidan reminded him. "For moral support. And to help me convince Riley to give it up."

Landry winced. "Maybe don't phrase it that way, okay?"

The Pittsburgh XFL team had just taken the field—for many years, so many organizations had tried to get a second professional football league started, but none of them had lasted very long. This was just the newest iteration, and Landry hoped they succeeded where everyone else had failed because it was a real chance for players who hadn't made NFL rosters to shine.

Riley Flynn could've been on a roster as a backup, but he'd chosen, stubbornly, to join the XFL because he wanted to play. Aidan had said it best when he'd called up Landry to invite him to Pittsburgh. *"Nobody's gonna take a shot on someone to start if he stands on the sideline the whole season, holdin' a fucking clipboard, so that's his big plan."*

That was true, though it wasn't like NFL backups weren't well paid. But Riley clearly didn't give a shit about the money. He wanted to play. He wanted to grab everyone's attention, and then he wanted an NFL team to sign him as a starter.

Landry gave him a lot of credit; he could've done exactly what Aidan wanted him to do and *given up.*

But he hadn't.

"I just wish...damn it, I wish he was like five inches taller and like forty pounds heavier." It was rare to detect any regret in Aidan's voice, but Landry heard it now.

"Probably not as much as he does." Landry didn't know Riley all that well. He'd been "the kid" for as long as he'd known Aidan. Since he was so much younger than both of them, Landry barely noticed him when they'd met in college and gone home with his friend for the holidays. Then Landry and Aidan had been drafted to the NFL, and eventually, Riley had gone to college too, and there'd been no reason to connect with Aidan's little brother.

But he did know Riley was undersized for a quarterback.

He'd had great stats in college, but everyone said it was the system, not the player, which had killed his draft stock. Then he'd sat on a practice squad for a year before finally deciding to take the job in the XFL.

Landry knew Aidan wasn't very happy about it.

"I told him to come live with me in Toronto. There's lots he could do for me there."

Yeeaaaah.

Landry could imagine the last thing Riley ever wanted to do was go be a personal assistant to his superstar, hot-shot quarterback brother.

That would sting under normal circumstances, but when Riley wanted to be the star quarterback so badly himself?

Yeeaaaah.

"It's a good thing you told me to meet you here," Landry said, taking a long drink of his beer.

"Yeah, why?" Aidan was focused on the field in front of them. He was ninety-nine percent sure his friend was staring at his brother, out on the field, warming up.

Sure, he didn't seem very big. But he didn't seem that small either anymore. From what Landry could see, he was filling out his uniform these days.

"Because you are absolute shit at this," Landry said.

"What?"

"You should be supporting him, not telling him to give up or come be your assistant."

"He's gonna get his ass kicked, get injured way too many times, and not be able to walk by the time he's thirty-five. I *am* looking out for him. I know the job. It sucks a lot of the time."

"And a lot of the time, it doesn't." Every time Landry had met Riley, he'd seemed to have a pretty damn good head on his shoulders. Of course, the last time they'd met had been...well, more than a few years ago. But surely that hadn't changed. "He's smart, he knows what he wants, and he knows the cost."

"Do we ever really know the cost?" Aidan's voice was wry.

Landry glanced over at him. That was a surprisingly introspective thing for Aidan to say.

"You okay?"

Aidan took a long drink of his beer. "Yeah, yeah, I'm fine. Just, you know...another year, another season."

No doubt Aidan thought he'd brushed it off enough to fool Landry, but almost nobody had known him as long as Landry had.

Maybe one of his teammates or one of the acquaintances always clustering around Aidan would be fooled. But not Landry.

The game started.

It had been...well, years again...since Landry had watched Riley Flynn play.

From the first time he took the field, it was clear why he was taking this risk in the XFL.

He was incredibly dynamic, making plays happen out of thin air, pulling out great throws, and even making one or two first downs with his legs. He wasn't fast, necessarily, but he was quick and exceptional at evading defenders trying to bring him down.

The Pittsburgh Defenders went all the way down the field, and Riley threw a beautiful little out pass to the tight end for a touchdown.

When he and Aidan finally sat back down after cheering and screaming their faces off, Aidan looked over at him.

"Don't you say it, bro," Aidan said. "Don't you fucking say it."

"I didn't say anything," Landry argued, but he *was* thinking it.

"I just want what's best for him," Aidan said. "And this isn't it. Football isn't it."

"Yeah, 'cause football's treated you *real* bad," Landry said, a healthy dose of sarcasm in his voice. "Why can't Riley want a piece of that?"

"The kid doesn't know what he wants," Aidan said, and his tone sounded so dismissive. Like Riley actually *was* a kid.

But as the game continued, and Riley threw two more touchdowns—and one interception, which Landry winced at, and Aidan broke down in way too much detail for at least ten minutes—Landry couldn't help but think that at least, at the *very* least, he deserved a shot.

But every time he tried to even *gently* check Aidan's doom and gloom routine, he frowned more, so finally Landry gave up. Just enjoyed watching what he believed might be a star on the rise.

"Come on," Aidan said, rising as the game clock ticked down to zero. "I have a feeling we'll be welcome on the field. Let's go find the kid."

Landry rolled his eyes but naturally still trotted after him. That was twelve years of friendship for you. "I know this is going to come as a real shock but not everyone in the universe thinks you're God's gift to football."

"What? I'm not?" Aidan mocked as they headed down the bleacher stairs towards the edge of the stadium. Unlike NFL stadiums, or even the larger collegiate stadiums, there was access to the field from the seating area. Guarded, of course, by security, but fans were gathered around them, clamoring for autographs and attention from the players.

It was annoying that, just as Aidan had predicted, the crowds parted for them.

Yes, Aidan was super recognizable. He was Aidan freaking Flynn. But it wasn't like Landry didn't get his own share of looks as they stopped in front of the security guard.

"Aidan Flynn," Aidan said, flashing the guard one of those trademarked smiles. "Wondered if we could head down and say hi to my baby bro."

Landry watched as awe washed over the man's face.

He would be surprised if he hadn't been seeing different versions of this for way too fucking long.

The problem was *way* too many people did, in fact, believe that Aidan was God's gift to football.

Including Aidan himself.

"Oh yeah, sure, man," the guard stuttered, standing aside and unlocking the gate, letting them down onto the field.

Landry was a little worried that Aidan's first words to his brother were going to be either some version of the word *kid*, or a painfully accurate analysis of that interception he'd thrown in the second quarter, but thankfully, instead of either of those, Aidan must've dug down and found the good guy Landry *knew* was underneath all his bullshit. As Riley approached them, pulling off his helmet, Aidan pulled him into a big, tight hug.

Landry just had a split second between Riley's helmet coming off and his head disappearing into Aidan's shoulder to really see him again for the first time in years.

He was tan, and his hair was blonder than Landry expected—so much blonder than Landry could remember it being all those years ago, so much blonder than Aidan's own hair, at least when he resisted the urge to put in highlights. Riley's baby blue eyes were startlingly light, especially with all that eye black streaked underneath them. And then there was his face.

God, when had the kid gotten so fucking hot?

Landry was *straight*, but his two brothers were not, which he liked to tell people made him more enlightened. What it really meant was that he noticed attractive men more than he might normally.

And he was totally fucking noticing how insanely attractive Riley Flynn was.

It shouldn't have been a shock.

After all, Aidan's ego was not *only* a result of his prowess on a football field. Lots of people—probably too many people—thought he was good-looking. But the last time Landry could remember seeing Riley had been on draft night, seven years back, and he'd been what? *Sixteen? Seventeen?* Still growing into his frame and his face, and holy shit, both of those had happened in spades.

Aidan was all angsty about his viability as a quarterback, but while Riley didn't have the inches in height, he was built, maybe not as tall as his brother but with shoulders just as wide. And his arms? Big and thick and corded with muscle that told Landry he definitely knew his way around a weight room.

Shit. I'm totally checking out Aidan's little brother.

But Landry shook off the thought. He was *straight*. He was straight as the day was long, wasn't he? Wouldn't he know if he wasn't? Both Logan and Levi were queer, so it wasn't like he hadn't considered it a handful of times. But he'd never once had his head turned by a guy like this.

He told himself it was because he just hadn't seen Riley in so long, and he hadn't expected him to look like this now.

That was all. It was just the surprise of seeing Riley again after so long.

Riley and Aidan broke apart.

Landry's palms were sweating a little as he approached.

God, his eyes were even lighter blue up close, with little hints of green, like the most pristine water in the Caribbean. Did people even *have* eyes like that?

It's just the eye black making them look lighter and...uh...well, something.

Fucking something, that was what it was.

"Hey, Landry," Riley said directly, apparently having none of Landry's problems meeting his eyes. "Been a long time." He started to hold out his hand, and Landry, who was probably the most recognizable of his brothers, who all played in the NFL, and was therefore *used* to greeting people even under incredibly awkward circumstances, found himself hesitating.

He should really hug him, too, shouldn't he?

This was *the kid*. His best friend's little brother.

But he was also Riley, who was now twenty-four or twenty-five, and he'd just made Landry question—for a moment that had lasted far longer than he wanted to examine closely—his sexuality.

"Uh, hey," Landry said. They shook, and Landry pulled him into a weird pseudo-hug.

For a second, he got the impression of a firm, calloused hand and then a much firmer, compact body.

Okay, maybe Riley wasn't big, but every single inch of him was packed with strength, rippling with muscle.

Not a thought Landry needed in his brain right now.

Really, not ever, but *definitely not* with Aidan standing there, currently in the running for the Overprotective Brother of the Year award.

"Looked real good today," Aidan said.

Riley shot his brother a glare like he'd offered criticism instead of praise. "Thanks. Don't you dare add a *but* to that sentence."

Aidan threw up his hands. "I didn't!"

"I could see it in your eyes. You have the shittiest poker face in the world. Doesn't he, Landry?" Casually, Riley slid his gaze right over to where Landry stood, awkward and sweating, trying to pretend that everything was okay.

Totally normal.

No big deal.

The thing was, Aidan's normal poker face was actually pretty good. But when it came to his brother? Riley wasn't wrong; it was total shit.

"I...uh..." God, Landry was not normally this tongue-tied. Aidan knew it because he glanced over at him.

"Tell him all the good stuff I said," Aidan insisted.

Riley pulled his jersey out of his pants, and for a split second, Landry got a flash of chiseled abs, and his mind went white hot supernova. *Jesus*, it wasn't like he hadn't seen hot guys before. He had. He definitely had, and had been informed, at length, about their hotness by his two brothers. He should be totally fucking immune to hotness. Then there were how many sets of abs he'd seen in locker rooms over the years. Way too many to count.

But these abs belonged to Riley Flynn, and apparently, that made all the difference.

"He said lots of good stuff." Lots of shitty stuff, too, but Landry wasn't going to tell Riley about that, not when he'd really played well.

Well enough that some NFL team, weak at the quarterback position, might take a chance on his enormous upside if he kept this up.

But keeping it up, that was the trick.

Every quarterback could have one stellar game. It was stringing together one great game after another. It was never letting the criticism get to you. It was forgetting every misstep you'd made the second after you made it and making that throw again, even though the last one you'd made had been intercepted.

"Don't go into any detail or anything," Riley teased, shooting Landry a fierce smile that probably decimated anyone in its vicinity on a regular basis.

"That first touchdown, it was really sweet." On a regular day, Landry could've gone into detail about why it was so masterful, how he'd drawn off the safety with a glorious pump fake, and then tossed the ball with exactly the right velocity, even though it was a throw across his body. Or how he'd shrugged off two defenders like they were nothing right before he'd done all that.

It was a combination of skills that would have NFL scouts salivating over him.

But the salivating was short-circuiting his brain.

Guess you're not the only one, Banks.

"You just liked it because I threw it to Ross, who's a tight end," Riley joked.

That was *also* true.

"You can't even say anymore that tight ends are underrated," Aidan said, elbowing him in the side. "Especially not tight ends like you."

"Hey, in another life, twenty or thirty years ago, they wouldn't have let me near the ball."

Landry, hyperaware of Riley in a way he didn't really want to be and definitely did not feel comfortable with, noticed as Riley's eyes swept up and down his form. "Six foot five, built like a tank? Yeah, seriously," he said.

Had Riley just checked him out? Or...

Landry still remembered a few years back when Aidan had called him freaking out because Riley was determined to come out of the closet as bisexual. *"Can't he just keep it to himself? He's gonna make himself a target, and it's not like he's got an easy road ahead of him* anyway..." Aidan had said frantically.

To someone else, it might have seemed like maybe Aidan was homophobic, but Landry knew he wasn't. It had just been a slightly different version of Aidan Flynn, Overprotective Brother of the Century, and Landry had told him to stop worrying. Had reassured him in every way he could. Coming out hadn't destroyed Sam Crawford's chances or stopped him from winning not just one Super Bowl but a second, just a few months back. Hadn't stopped Colin O'Connor or Spencer Evans. Or any of the many queer players on the Piranhas.

Hadn't stopped either of his two brothers from being at the very top of the game or from being appreciated for their skill and their dedication.

When Riley had come out a few months later, Aidan had been the first one to post on social media in support.

Then, he'd been so proud of both of them. Riley for taking that step, and Aidan for swallowing his concerns and supporting him every step of the way. But now, Landry wished that was something he didn't know about Aidan's little brother.

Because yes, absolutely, Riley could've been checking him out.

Normally that would just be a thing that happened. But now, it was lighting him up in a way he didn't understand.

"Hey," Riley said. "Couple of the guys are going out after the game. You guys want to come with? Grab some dinner and a few drinks?"

Landry nearly rolled his eyes because when was Aidan *not* up to party?

Basically never.

"Yeah, sure, of course, we'd love to, right, Banks?"

Landry nodded. "Sure. Got nothing else goin' on."

Maybe he could even keep Aidan from detailing, a few drinks in, everything Riley had done wrong in the game.

Keeping that satisfied look in Riley's eyes—the kind of look that said he'd done exactly what he'd set out to do today—shouldn't have mattered to Landry. But it did. Especially when Aidan, no matter how well he meant, had come here to try to tell him he should pack it in.

But Landry had seen enough. He didn't agree—not that Aidan would ever listen to him about it.

Riley Flynn had something, and he deserved his shot.

Riley wanted to kill his brother.

Not for showing up unexpectedly—Aidan hadn't told him he was coming to his debut in Pittsburgh, but it hadn't been difficult to anticipate he might—but for bringing Landry Banks with him.

Of course, Aidan had no idea about the horrible youthful crush he'd had on Landry. Riley would've rather died than tell him because Aidan never would've stopped teasing him about it. Or, even worse, been *nice* about it, reminding him every chance he got that Landry was straight, so his whole crush was pointless.

It was still fucking pointless, even if it wasn't really a crush anymore.

It was...well, Riley thought, glancing over at where Landry stood near the edge of the dance floor, his handsome face thrown into shadow by the flashing lights, just plain appreciation for an incredibly hot guy.

Riley knew he'd grown into his own face, his own body. But he wasn't like Landry, who was built like Thor and could even *be* Thor on his very best fucking day because he had shoulder-length blond hair and those penetrating honey-brown eyes to prove it.

He was gorgeous and didn't even realize it. Or he did, and he just didn't care.

AKA he had no idea what he'd always done—and apparently still did—to Riley's insides.

Then there was the way he noticed Riley was standing alone and immediately walked over, no hesitation in his step whatsoever.

He'd always been nice that way. Even back in college, when he'd come home with Aidan once or twice, he'd always made sure to talk to Riley. Even though Riley had been a skinny, awkward thirteen-year-old kid.

Maybe inside, he was *still* that skinny, awkward kid with the most unfortunate crush in existence.

"Hey," Landry said, dipping his head low so Riley could hear him over the pulsating thump of the bass. "You shouldn't be over here frowning. Did Aidan say something to you?"

Great. The last thing he needed was *two* overprotective brothers.

Because he definitely did not think of Landry Banks as a brother.

"What would Aidan say?" Though he had a pretty good idea of what that might be. No doubt he'd get one of his brother's infamous emails tomorrow, breaking down the few things he'd done right—and the *many* things he'd done wrong.

If he wanted to make it in the NFL even a fraction less than he did, he might tell Aidan to go fuck himself and delete the emails unread, but annoyingly, Aidan was actually *really* good at analyzing play. So he'd swallow his pride and read whatever he sent anyway.

Landry just shook his head, though. "You know your brother," he said wryly.

Oh, he did.

"Actually," Landry continued, "I thought you played really well today. Don't listen to him, whatever he *does* say."

"So you're not going to tell me to quit, too?" Riley asked, grinning. He told himself the flare of interest he kept seeing in Landry's golden brown gaze was wish fulfillment, but even if that was all it was, what would it hurt to flirt a little?

With two queer brothers, Landry was probably comfortable with most anything.

Besides, with the way he looked, he was probably beating people of every gender off with a stick.

"No, not even close," Landry said steadily. "You're good, and you know it. Or else you wouldn't be doing this."

Riley batted his eyes at him. He knew they were his best feature, and he wasn't above using what he had to get what he wanted—that was definitely a Flynn trademark.

"Aw, you think I'm *good*," he teased, nudging Landry's bicep with his shoulder. "I'm touched."

Landry smiled, and it transformed his face from merely handsome to breathtaking. "You aren't what I expected," he said. "I don't even remember the last time we..."

"You've been listening to Aidan too much," Riley said sagely. "And it was draft night, the night you and Aidan went in the first round." He remembered that night so well because he'd been filled with undeniable joy for his brother—and also a fiery determination that someday that would be *him*.

Six years later, he *hadn't* been drafted in the first round, like Aidan—or Landry—but he was still going to make his mark. He'd be the quarterback nobody expected, the one they'd written off, who proved them all wrong. The quarterback who proved all their theories and assessments were full of shit.

"God, has it really been that long?" Landry muttered, and then he tilted his bottle against his lips, and Riley absolutely did not feel his pulse stutter at the sight.

"Yeah," Riley said.

Landry gazed down at him, and Riley just plain gave up on denial. His pulse was definitely racing. Maybe because it felt like Landry—*Landry Banks*—was finally looking at him like he'd dreamed about for so goddamn long.

Like he was really seeing him.

"I'm trying to figure out if you always looked like this. 'Cause if you did, I'm sure my brothers would've both been driving me crazy trying to get your attention."

Riley knew Landry had two younger brothers. How much younger? He wasn't even sure.

"Really?" He raised an eyebrow. "Just the two of them?"

He *knew* Landry was straight; why was he playing with fire like this?

Because when Landry was looking at him with that kind of wonder in his eyes, it was difficult to believe it.

Landry didn't say a word, though. Didn't even try to deny it. Just stood there and stared at Riley.

Here was the thing: Riley knew he'd kicked ass today. He'd come to Pittsburgh to the XFL, hoping he might change some minds, and he'd started that process in a huge way. He'd need to follow through, but the truth was, he was flying high.

Feeling a little reckless, even.

So he leaned in a bit further, gazing up at Landry.

There'd been a hookup in college who'd told him once his eyes were devastating. He pulled on their full power now, barely refraining from fluttering his eyelashes. He could feel the heat of Landry right through his jeans as he shifted even closer and their thighs brushed together. *God*, this was like a combo of pretty much every gay porn he'd ever seen and all his teenage fantasies rolled into one crazy hot moment he didn't know how to resist.

"I swear," Landry said, his voice low and rough, "you didn't...you weren't..."

Riley felt him tremble.

Landry freaking Banks. *Trembling.*

"Probably not," Riley admitted. Though the truth was, he hadn't looked *anything* like this a few years back, the last time they'd seen each other.

He'd still had the same eyes, of course, and blond hair, but he'd been so scrawny. Hadn't grown into himself or his confidence yet.

For an incredibly breathless second, they just looked at each other. Riley *knew* this wasn't going to end in a kiss, but damnit, if Landry didn't look like he might be considering it.

If he'd heard even a *hint*—even a solitary fucking rumor—that Landry wasn't straight as an arrow, he'd have taken the shot.

But at the same time, he couldn't quite look away because Landry was clearly just as into whatever this was.

"There you two are."

Aidan's voice was a bucketful of cold water on every single one of Riley's hopes.

Goddamnit, couldn't his brother have seen what was happening and stayed the fuck away? Given Landry even a moment longer to consider what he might want? Because Riley believed—or hoped—that if he'd had long enough, Landry might have decided the answer was him.

"Yeah." Landry's voice was gravelly. Rough. Took the bottle of beer from Aidan with a grateful smile.

"And your drink, your highness," Aidan said, setting Riley's drink down on the table next to him with a flourish. "Maybe next year you could stop drinking like my grandmother."

"What is it?" Landry asked, and instead of waiting for Riley to answer, without an ounce of shame—because his drink of choice was *delicious*, okay?—he reached across Riley's body, practically pinning him against the half-wall that surrounded the dance floor, and Riley wasn't a saint.

He enjoyed every second of feeling Landry pressed up against him.

Almost missed Landry licking his lips. After taking a sip of *his* drink.

God, he was going to remember this night forever.

He was going to jerk off to fantasies of this night forever.

"Is that...cream soda?" Landry looked puzzled.

"Captain Morgan and ginger ale, like the good *grandma* Riley is," Aidan teased.

Landry frowned. "My grandma doesn't drink rum. She drinks like...gin and tonics and *Bailey's* in her coffee. Besides, it's good. It's like...vanilla." Even though they'd moved apart and were now standing at a respectable distance since Aidan's arrival, there was an undeniable spark now when Landry gazed down at Riley.

Like he wondered if he'd taste like vanilla, too.

"I'll take it, 'cause at least you aren't calling me *the kid*," Riley said, rolling his eyes.

Truthfully, if Aidan didn't give him shit, he'd wonder what was wrong with him.

His teasing was, of course, completely ridiculous, borderline insulting, proved he couldn't identify a single emotion even if his career was on the line, and also, somehow, the way he showed Riley just how much he loved him.

That was his brother for you: a whole shit ton of contradictions.

"So," Aidan said, "you given any more thought to coming to Toronto?"

Riley was still deciding if he was going to finally tell his brother to fuck off when, to his surprise, Landry answered for him.

"No," he said. "He hasn't. And he won't."

Riley raised an eyebrow. "I won't?"

Landry met his gaze straight on, and something in the bottom of Riley's stomach burned. "You won't. You're doing this. And doin' a damn good job of it, too."

"If he's not a kid, then he doesn't need you to defend him," Aidan grumbled under his breath.

Riley knew it was going to take more than one good game to change his brother's mind. In fact, it would sting, but he wouldn't mind if Aidan *never* changed his mind about following in his footsteps.

As long as one NFL team did.

Riley knew what the prize was, and he just had to keep himself focused on that.

"Okay, I gotta go make the rounds, talk to the guys," Riley said. After all, part of being QB1 was being the leader. He downed the rest of his drink, set it on the table, then, because he couldn't help himself, he turned to Landry.

This time he didn't hesitate, didn't hold back—just went for it. Pressed his whole body against Landry's as he hugged him. "Good defense is always appreciated," he said under his breath so Aidan wouldn't hear.

For a moment, he let himself linger. Landry wasn't exactly pushing him away, either. But then he broke off and left because, if he stayed, he was going to do something he'd almost definitely regret later.

Something he'd *really* enjoy, that was for damn sure, but he'd come this far without discovering just how flexible Landry Banks' sexuality was. He'd live without it.

What he couldn't live without was the success under the floodlights of an NFL stadium. The success he'd craved for so damn long and up 'til now had been denied.

But, Riley thought as he walked away, he had a feeling everything was about to change.

Chapter 2

"You wanted to see me?" Landry asked, poking his head into Coach's office.

Coach Kelley, the new head coach of the Charleston Condors, was only a few years older than him, which Landry couldn't deny he'd initially stuck into the *con* side of why he shouldn't sign here. How would he feel being given marching orders by someone his age? But as soon as he'd arrived for training camp, he'd discovered the pro side of the equation—that his coach was understanding and empathetic, and as a result, he actually *liked* his coach for basically the first time ever.

Instead of being tough and mean and committed to every rule, Coach Kelley turned out to be the opposite. He welcomed feedback—positive *and* negative—and seemed to approach coaching not as a dictatorship but a democracy, encouraging collaboration, and Landry thought the whole facility seemed much more relaxed than where he'd spent his whole NFL career.

He'd been unsure of making such a huge change, but in the end, considering the sweeping changes the Condors had made to the team and to their program, Landry knew he'd made the right call.

This was the right spot for him.

It would be a while before Charleston really felt like home, but he already knew it eventually would.

"Hey, Landry, I'm so glad you stopped by," Coach Kelley said, getting up and shaking his hand after Landry approached his desk.

"You heard about Nelson yet?"

Nelson Perez was their QB1. He'd been in the NFL for a few years, bouncing around from team to team, and like nearly everyone else on the Condors' roster, he'd come here because he wanted a real chance, a shot at changing his fortune. Craved a slice of the Condors' redemption for himself.

But in practice yesterday, he'd come down on his leg funny, and almost immediately, it had been clear the injury was serious.

They had a backup, of course, but the backup was actually *older* than their coach and had mostly been there to mentor-slash-coach Nelson—not be the starter.

"Actually," Coach Kelley said with a resigned sigh, "that's why I wanted to talk to you." He waved at the chair in front of his desk, and Landry slumped down into it.

He'd been afraid it was bad news.

"What's the diagnosis?" Landry asked.

An injury this early in the season—before the season had really even started, in fact—to the most important player on the team? Well, you might as well write the Condors off right now.

Not that any of the media hesitated to do that anyway. Landry hadn't been surprised by this—rebuilding was a conservative term for what the Condors were actually doing. Landry could count on one hand the personnel who'd actually been in this building the year before.

The NFL wanted a clean break. And then Grant Green, the new owner, had come in and done some cleanup of his own.

A few people had texted him and told him he was a little nuts for choosing this path, but Landry had come here anyway because he liked a challenge. Thought what the Condors were trying to do was admirable.

His younger brother, Levi, had told him he was crazy. However, Logan, the very middle child of the Banks family, had understood. *"When I went to the Piranhas, it was the same,"* he'd told Landry. *"And it was the right call. We're buildin' something special here. Maybe you'll get a chance to do that in Charleston."*

But without a QB1, they wouldn't be doing much building of anything at all.

"Torn ACL and MCL," Coach said with a resigned sigh. "Nelson's done for the year. And that sucks, it really sucks, I know, but we're trying to find a new option...and that's what I wanted to ask you about. You're close with Aidan Flynn, right?"

"He's my best friend," Landry said cautiously. He felt a spike of...something. Terror? Excitement? An intoxicating combination of both? Because he had a feeling he knew where this was going. "We played together at Michigan."

"So you know his younger brother."

It had been six weeks since that night in Pittsburgh—and there was yet to be a single day where Landry didn't think about it.

Not a single day Riley didn't haunt his thoughts.

Landry didn't understand what had passed between them any better now than he had then, but he did know a few things: they'd been flirting, he'd liked it, and if Aidan hadn't shown up when he had, anything could've happened. And he'd have liked *that,* too.

"I do," Landry said, trying way too hard to keep his voice even.

Coach stood and began to pace behind the desk, then gestured towards the big television screen that stretched across one wall of his office. Landry glanced over and nearly jolted. Because one of those plays from the Pittsburgh game was on the screen, and Riley, blown up larger than life, paused in the middle of dropping back.

"Riley Flynn has tremendous upside. We need a quarterback, and there aren't a lot of options out there right now we can afford, but then Mr. Green suggested we look outside the norm, and Riley was the first player I thought of."

Landry knew he wouldn't be the final say-so on who the Condors turned to next to be their QB1. But Coach had called him in here because his knowledge of Riley was personal. They could talk to Riley in an interview room, call him in for a consult, but nobody would know him *personally,* and for the Condors right now, at this particular crossroads, coming off the garbage dump of their last quarterback, that mattered. Coach had called him in here to give his honest opinion of Riley Flynn.

It should've been incredibly clear-cut for Landry.

Before that night in Pittsburgh six weeks ago, it would have been the easiest thing in the world. He'd have said, "Riley's great. Dedicated. He'll work harder than anyone in the room. And Aidan's his brother, so he knows what it means to lead a locker room."

But the night in Pittsburgh *had* happened, and there was another, surprisingly loud part of Landry that wanted Riley to stay far, far away from him.

That part of him was absolutely fucking terrified that if Riley came here, if Riley was around twenty-four-seven, if Riley smiled all the time at him like he had that night, then Landry might totally lose his mind.

He felt halfway there, and that was a result of only *thinking* about Riley for the last six weeks.

You know what the right thing is to do, and you're gonna do it. It isn't Riley's fault he's got you all tied up. This is his chance, and you're not going to fuck it up.

The voice inside his brain sounded suspiciously like Logan, but it didn't matter who it sounded like because he was never going to kill Riley's dreams just because he didn't understand the hard-on he had for the guy.

Landry took a deep breath.

"Sir, Riley's great. He's dedicated. He'll work harder than anyone in the room. And Aidan's his brother, so he knows exactly what it means to lead the locker room."

"You've seen him play?"

Landry nodded. There'd been the game in Pittsburgh, of course. Then he hadn't been able to stop himself. At first, he'd tried to deny the desire, but finally, he'd given in and watched each and every one fighting his own growing sense of shame, as Riley led his team to a five-and-one record.

"You're right about his upside. But we need to make sure he doesn't have to do too much."

Riley wasn't reckless, exactly, but he wanted to win so badly it burned inside him like a fire, and sometimes those flames pushed him too hard. Landry knew what that felt like. Knew what that could mean. There'd been several games where Riley had tried to do too much and had made mistakes.

"Agreed," Coach said, nodding thoughtfully. "I've always liked him. Didn't mind he wasn't the traditional quarterback."

AKA built like his brother.

But have you seen him, really seen him? He might not be tall, but God, he's something else.

There was that pulse of shame again.

It wasn't because he found Riley so fucking attractive.

If he *was* queer, there was zero shame in that.

The shame stemmed from the worry he'd been lying to himself this whole time. *Had* he been secretly ashamed at the idea of liking men? Even though his brothers were two of the best people he knew, had he, deep down, judged them for their sexuality and decided that *he* couldn't be like that, too?

Landry shook the thoughts clear. He couldn't obsess about this right now.

"Is there even really a traditional quarterback anymore?" Landry questioned. "The new norm is that there *isn't* a norm. Look at Lamar Jackson. Kyler Murray. Patrick Mahomes."

"Right." Coach seemed to be considering that. "But then there's Malik Willis and Trey Lance. They were small, mobile quarterbacks, and they didn't make it."

Landry shoved the consequences of this conversation to the back of his mind. He'd deal with the fact he was likely to be playing alongside Riley *later*. "Riley may be smaller, but he's got an arm like nothing I've ever seen and an undeniable vision of the field. Riley can do this, sir."

Coach nodded. "I think so, too. Been watching his film for hours now, and I can't see another better option." He grinned. "Unless your friend Aidan wants to leave Toronto."

Landry laughed. Aidan would never countenance being traded here to a team people only cared about because they were waiting to see the next episode in the garbage fire. Besides, Toronto would never let Aidan go.

"Doubtful," Landry said.

"Good, 'cause we can't afford him anyway," Coach joked.

That, Landry had a feeling, more than a lack of available talent at the position, was directing the Condors' search. They were still on the hook for all of the old quarterback's ridiculous salary, even though Tom Taylor was no longer even playing in the NFL. Landry had heard a rumor Grant Green—the new owner of the Condors—had his lawyers working on the problem, hoping to wiggle out of Taylor's contract, but it was unlikely.

A reminder that even though the Condors were trying to move on from an owner who'd cared about winning, no matter the cost, a quarterback who'd liked to abuse women, and a defense that, rumor had it, had taken out monetary bounties on the Piranhas in their playoff game last year, they were still hamstrung by the past.

It was unfair, but that was the reality of the NFL for you.

"Just look at this," Coach said, pressing play on the remote, and then Riley was moving across the screen, his legs evading a defender and then another, twisting his body to avoid a third tackle and then sprinting to the left, tossing a beaut of a throw across his body.

No, he wasn't tall.

No, he wasn't the biggest guy on the field.

But, not for the first time, Landry saw the advantage of Riley's smaller stature. He was quick, evasive, almost impossible to bring down because he'd bulked up, working on his strength to compensate for his height, *and* not only could he make plays with his legs, but he could throw on a dime.

It was just as impressive of a display on the screen as it had been in person.

"I saw that play in person," Landry said, trying to keep his voice neutral. But he heard the excitement bleed into it anyway. What would it be like having Riley as his QB?

Remember? You're not thinking about that right now.

But once the thought had popped out of the box Landry had shoved it into, it refused to go back.

Instead, it showed him a half dozen imaginary versions of Riley—Riley smiling, Riley joking with him at practice, Riley on the sideline, Riley in the red and orange of the Condors uniform and how fucking unreal blue his eyes looked behind the visor of his helmet, Riley on the new couch in Landry's townhouse, leaning closer as he laughed—and not for the first time Landry realized just how fucked he was.

Because he *wanted* it...with a fierceness that kinda took his breath away.

Not just because he thought Riley was hot, though there was no denying that either, but because Landry wanted to *know* him. He didn't, not at all, but he'd seen glimpses of who Riley the man was, and just those glimpses were enough.

"He electrified the whole stadium," Landry said. Remembering how excited he'd been watching Riley. Remembering how even Aidan had screamed for him.

"And," Coach Kelley said, a glimmer of amusement in his dark eyes, "he sure does like to throw to a tight end."

"That's…" Landry cleared his throat. "I don't care about that. I care about this team and putting a winning season together, sir."

"That right there is why we like you, Banks," Coach said, patting him on the shoulder. "But it's an advantage, for sure."

"For sure," Landry echoed.

"Well, I appreciate the time. See you at practice?"

Landry nodded and stood up. "You'll let me know what you decide?"

Coach's smile was wry. "Oh, I'm sure the rumor mill around here will know before even I do."

Landry reached inside the fridge and pulled out a beer, juggling it with one hand while he answered his phone with the other.

He'd been expecting this particular call for three days now, and the longer it had gone before Aidan was blowing up his phone, the more he'd believed—relief and disappointment mingling inside him at the thought—the Condors hadn't signed Riley after all.

But now Aidan had called.

Not texted, like he nearly always did, like he'd done a handful of times over the last few days. Actually *called*.

"What's up?" Landry said, setting his phone on the counter and clicking it onto speakerphone as he dug into the drawer, looking for the bottle opener he knew was stashed in there somewhere.

He didn't need a beer after practice, usually, but today? Oh, he needed one. Especially if Aidan was calling to tell him what he thought he was.

Yeah, what are you gonna do when Riley's around all the time? Swap the water in your bottle for vodka?

"I got big news," Aidan said. He sounded so excited that Landry knew what was coming.

"Yeah? You finally decide to shave off that godawful mustache?"

"I'll have you know that's a prime look," Aidan said primly. "But no. Sorry to disappoint. Riley got a starting job in the NFL."

"Oh?"

"Don't play stupid, bro. Not with me."

Landry tapped his fingertips against the side of the bottle. "Am I?"

"There's only a handful of teams he could be signing with this late to be their QB1. And you know it's the Condors because they fucking asked you what you thought of him."

"They did." Landry took a long drink of beer. He'd sorta hoped that Coach Kelley would keep his contribution to the process to himself, but now that Landry thought about it, really thought about, of course that wasn't going to be the way it went down.

Not with what he'd begun to learn about how Coach Kelley ran his football team.

He'd share. He'd tell Riley just what Landry had said so he'd feel welcome. So he'd feel like someone was already on his side.

And Landry *was* on his side.

"You know I'm not happy about him still trying to do this, but...well, it means a whole fucking lot you spoke up for him." Aidan was rarely serious, but he sounded pretty dang serious right now.

"What else was I supposed to say? I just told the truth. The kid's got talent." Landry kicked himself for calling Riley *the kid*. Because that sure as hell wasn't how he was feeling about him these days.

"You vouched for him," Aidan said, sounding final about the subject.

"Well..." Landry hesitated awkwardly. How many times had he and Aidan discussed Riley? More times than he could count. Never before had it felt like a conversation dotted with landmines, but suddenly, it was. *Man, I think your brother's hot. I'm dying a little at the thought of seeing him again. Freaking out, too. What do you think I should do about it?*

Nothing, that was what Aidan would tell him to do about it.

Probably with a threat—implied or otherwise—that if he touched Riley, he'd kick his ass into next year.

Not because Riley wasn't one hundred and ten percent capable of handling his own shit, but because Aidan would never stop seeing him as a twelve-year-old.

Even though...Landry could tell Riley was *definitely* not twelve anymore.

"Well, *what*?" Aidan demanded impatiently. "I know you did. You don't have to pretend you didn't."

"I mean, he's a Flynn, isn't he? He's your brother. He's a good guy." God, this was so awkward. Landry prayed Aidan wouldn't hear in his voice how uncomfortable he was or, even worse, figure out why.

"Yeah, yeah, he is. Which is why I'm calling."

Landry froze. Had Aidan already figured it out and decided to call, knowing Riley was headed to Charleston, figuring it was time to give Landry the shovel talk *already*?

"He's new to the area, and he's got to get situated and everything, and he's gonna kill me for suggesting this, but look out for him, won't you?"

"Of course." Landry swallowed hard. Of course he would. He would not make it awkward by flirting anymore with Riley. If Riley flirted with him...well, that wasn't on him.

"And I've got one more favor to ask," Aidan said. "Again, you better not tell him this came from me."

"Aidan—" Landry warned. "He's a...well, a full-grown guy. He's not twelve anymore."

"Don't you think I know that?" Aidan retorted.

"Well, you don't *act* like you know that."

Aidan grunted. "What I'm *trying* to ask is if you wouldn't mind if Riley stayed with you for a little bit."

Oh, God.

How had Landry not anticipated that? He should have. He really fucking should have. But he hadn't. He didn't have any excuses to give, and it wasn't like a part of him wasn't totally fucking delighted at the possibility of Riley being *right here*.

Close enough to touch.

Then there was the plain and simple fact that before six weeks ago, Landry never would've hesitated. Probably would've been the first one to *offer* a place for Riley to stay.

"Uh, yeah, of course. Of course he's welcome to stay with me. I've got a guest room." *With no bed. Oh, God, I'm gonna have to buy Riley Flynn a bed.* And not fantasize about them together in it. "It's...it's fine." He stuttered over how fine it was. Because it was not fine at all.

Landry scrubbed a hand across his face. How had he ended up here?

Maybe it was karma for giving Logan shit about falling for his teammate *and* roommate, Dylan.

Dylan, who'd believed he was straight before Logan.

The universe, Landry believed, had to be laughing at him right now.

And if—*when*, he mentally corrected—he told Logan, he was probably going to laugh, too.

"Great. I know he's probably going to kill me when he finds out I asked you." Aidan laughed a little self-consciously.

"At least you realize it," Landry said. "I was worried you were completely unaware of what an ass you are."

"Come on, he needs..."

"Aidan, he's twenty-four." He'd looked it up in a particularly weak moment. Why did it matter how old Riley was? It didn't, but somehow seeing his age right there in black and white on his phone screen had made him seem less like a dirty old man. Not that he was going to do anything about it. *He wouldn't.* "Almost twenty-five.

He's a grown person. He doesn't need you to play big protective older brother."

Aidan was quiet for a long time. "I know," he finally said. "I just...this is a big deal for him. He thinks this is it. And we both know how...how these things can go."

"We do."

They'd both been around the NFL for long enough to witness careers begin so optimistically. They'd seen players fail spectacularly and also slowly fade into nothing, into obscurity.

The very obscurity Riley was afraid of. Had worked so hard to avoid.

It could still happen.

This chance was just that—a *chance*.

"Just be there for him, okay, because I can't be, not the way he'll need," Aidan said.

Landry winced because that was the thing he'd hoped, more than anything, Aidan wouldn't ask him to do. Because it meant he wouldn't really be able to keep his distance.

There'd be no way for...well, whatever this was...to fade.

No way to get any perspective at all.

"Yeah, sure, of course," Landry said. Because what else could he say?

First off, Aidan wasn't wrong. Second off, he wasn't so selfish that he'd put his own freakout over Riley's need.

He'd need someone, and it might as well be him. It *should* be him, Landry realized.

"I appreciate it, man. Think he's coming in tomorrow night. Late? You can figure it out with him. You still have his number?"

Aidan had given it to him ages ago, but Landry had never used it.

Didn't want to use it now because he didn't really trust himself to stop at sending Riley his address and finding out what time his flight got in.

"Yeah," Landry said.

"Good." Aidan sounded very satisfied with himself, no doubt because he'd done exactly what he'd set out to do: arrange everything exactly the way he wanted it.

Landry was not nearly as happy about it. He knew Aidan had manipulated him, and he'd *let* him because pushing back would mean revealing all the shit he was agonizing over.

Was he really queer if he thought Riley Flynn was hot?

Why was he freaking out if he was?

"You've been weird the last few days," Aidan continued. "Shit not going well there?"

"Shit's going fine," Landry said dryly. "I like Kelley. He's...not what I expected."

"In a good way?"

"In a good way."

"Ah." Aidan paused. "Well, I'm sure we're still gonna kick your ass when you come to town."

"I'm sure you're gonna try," Landry said.

In mid-September, the Condors would be traveling up to Toronto to play Aidan's team, and they'd been talking trash about the game since Landry had signed with the Condors. But now, the game held a whole new dimension.

Because it was going to be Flynn versus Flynn.

"Something to look forward to," Aidan said smugly.

"You gettin' your ass handed to you? Absolutely. I think Riley's gonna run circles around you."

Aidan scoffed, claiming he wasn't worried, but Landry heard the uncertainty buried very deep in his voice.

Aidan was very secure in the fact that he was the successful Flynn. The established NFL quarterback, the one with the exceptional win-loss record, the one who electrified the entire stadium when he jogged onto the field.

But Landry had a feeling Aidan knew Riley could be all that and *more*.

Maybe that thought didn't keep him up at night, but Landry knew Aidan and knew it would still linger, like a bad smell.

Aidan was used to never being challenged, and there was a possibility he was going to be challenged now.

And for the first time, Landry realized he was looking forward to it—and was actually looking forward to *helping* Riley be that challenge.

"Let me get this straight," Paige said, shooting Riley with the no-nonsense look that had endeared her to him the first day they'd met. "Your brother overstepped *again*, for the millionth freaking time, and arranged for you to stay with his best friend, the guy you've only had a crush on your whole freaking adult life, and asked him to *watch over you* like you're fucking twelve?"

Riley nodded wordlessly.

"Honey, you need to tell him to fuck right off," Paige said it sympathetically, but the steel edge to her voice made it clear what she thought of the whole thing.

"Which one?"

Riley hated that Aidan had intervened, though it wasn't exactly surprising. It also wasn't exactly surprising that Landry had gone along with it.

"Do I have to pick one or the other?"

Paige leaned forward, resting her elbows on the booth table they were sharing. They'd met up at the small bar in her neighborhood in LA, since Riley had come back to Los Angeles to his small apartment after the shorter XFL season had ended.

"Yes, you really do."

Riley had really, *really* hoped he wouldn't have to take Aidan up on his offer of a job.

The last thing he wanted was to be Aidan's assistant and have to be present front and center to everything *he'd* ever wanted, that Aidan had, as easy as fucking breathing.

But then had come the Condors' job offer, and of course, he'd jumped at it. The opportunity was prime, and he'd been ecstatic at the thought of playing for Jonathan Kelley, who was considered something of an offensive innovator. He might actually be able to utilize Riley's particular set of skills. And, naturally, it hadn't been exactly painful to learn he'd be playing alongside Landry.

He still didn't know what to think of what had happened between them that night in Pittsburgh. It had seemed like *maybe* Landry had been attracted to him. He'd certainly not hesitated to flirt back when Riley had stupidly flirted with him. But instead of dwelling on the thoughts, Riley had resolutely tried to push them all away. Landry was straight. He'd been nothing but straight his whole life, and growing up in a family with two queer brothers meant if he'd been queer, too, surely, he'd have known it.

There was nothing to be gained but heartbreak if he started—or *kept*—fantasizing about a guy that was totally unavailable.

"I didn't tell you everything," Riley said. He hadn't even wanted to vocalize what had happened that night. Because then he might think it was real, and it couldn't have been.

Paige didn't even blink. "I know."

Riley should be used to Paige's sixth sense about these things by now, but it still took him by surprise. "What? How did you know? I didn't even tell you!"

Leaning back against the booth, Paige eyed him. "You said your brother and his best friend came to visit during the first game in Pittsburgh. When I showed up the next week for the second one, all you said about it was that they were there, and, I quote, *Aidan wasn't as terrible as he normally is.*"

"So? He wasn't."

"Okay, maybe he wasn't. But all I got about Landry was one brief sentence. No rhapsodizing about how hot he is. Not a word about how you'd love to climb him like a tree. Nothing about how kind and wonderful and amazing he is. Not a single question about how he manages to put up with Aidan."

"I don't do all of that every single time I talk about Landry," Riley grumbled.

"Oh honey, you do. And it's okay. It's a silly crush 'cause, I'll admit it, he *is* hot. Total Thor material. But you didn't do any of that this time, so I knew something was up. What happened? Something happened, right?"

"I realized later that we hadn't seen each other, like in person, for a while. Years, I think? Before I went to college."

"Ah." Paige managed to imbue a whole lot into just that one sound.

"What?"

"So he hadn't seen you like this. Like you are now."

"Like I grew up, you mean?" Riley asked dryly.

"Don't play dumb. That's something we've never done, so don't you fucking start now. Don't let Aidan diminish that part of you, too."

"Aidan doesn't—"

Paige waved a hand. "Yes, yes, I know. Aidan saved you. Aidan protected you. Aidan watched over you. *When you were too young to take care of yourself. Now,* he needs to cut it out."

"Probably," Riley said lightly when what he really meant was, A*bsolutely, yes. As soon as possible.*

"What I mean is, maybe Landry's not straight. Then, he saw you, all grown up, and maybe it was different. Maybe he was interested. And if he is, then living together is gonna be real fun for you. 'Cause we *both* know you're interested in him."

"Landry's straight." If he said it enough times, maybe he'd really believe it.

"And if he isn't?" Paige raised one flawlessly plucked black eyebrow. "If he *is* interested?"

Riley didn't even know what to think about that.

"He did flirt with me. Well, he flirted *back*."

Paige nodded. "Okay, but you could make a fence post flirt with you."

"I thought you were supposed to be convincing me Landry's interested in me," Riley retorted. He picked up his drink and took a sip. Normally, he didn't drink much during the season, but after the infuriating call with Aidan he'd just had, he'd needed something so he didn't call his brother back and start screaming at him.

"I am, but I'm also the best devil's advocate in the freaking universe, which is why you love me."

"That's only *part* of the reason I love you," Riley said with a grin. He could tell she was hooked now. But this was Landry, after all. They'd been talking about him for years, now that he thought about it. The first time he'd ever gotten drunk with her, he probably told her all about his big brother's best friend and the most unfortunate crush in the entire freaking world.

"So what else happened?"

"Well, uh, like I told you, we flirted. And then he said something like, if I'd always looked like this, his two brothers would've been all over him, trying to get my number. And I asked him if it was just his two brothers."

Paige shot him one of her patented looks. "You did not."

"I was...I don't know, feeling reckless." Riley shrugged. "I was riding high from the good game, and then he flirted with me."

"Which, we already established you could do with an inanimate object."

"And he didn't answer the question," Riley said in a rush before he could decide it was better *not* to share.

"He didn't answer the question?"

"No, he sort of stammered some stuff, but then he leaned in, and I swear he was *shaking*, Paige. And then…"

"And then?" Paige asked archly.

"And then Aidan showed up."

Paige made a frustrated noise that echoed pretty much how he'd felt at that moment. How he *still* felt. Had Landry been about to kiss him? He would never know.

"Your fucking brother," she said.

"Seriously," Riley said, finishing his drink.

Paige took a small, measured sip of her wine. "And now you're going to live with him."

"For a little bit. Until I find a good rental."

"No," Paige said steadily. "Until you're sure you're going to stay on the team *and* you can find a good rental."

"God, you are so painfully practical."

She tilted her wine glass at him. "Takes one to know one, honey."

It was true. That was another reason they'd always gravitated together; they were both clear-eyed and realistic about life.

It was why they'd never dated after that one disastrous blind date. It was hard to feel romantic about someone who routinely stripped the stars from not only your eyes, but their own.

Plus, Paige was his best friend, and Riley knew plenty about people who didn't stick, so the fact that she always would was more important than anything else.

"So what, a few months then? Maybe half a season?"

"Are you really trying to figure out how long I'm going to be staying at Landry's house?"

Paige shot him a look. "Riley, you need to think about this. Something's gonna happen between you."

"You don't know that."

"Does he or does he not have two queer brothers?"

Riley nodded.

"Then he's not going to have the standard, *oh my God, I'm attracted to a guy* freak-out. I give you two weeks before you're fucking."

"Paige!"

"What?"

"I'm not going to have sex with him."

Paige leaned forward with that dangerous gleam in her eye that usually meant she knew she was right and he was wrong and that time would eventually prove it. "Honey, you've only wanted to have sex with him since you were *sixteen*."

"Yes, I know," Riley said primly. "But I'm going there to make it. To *finally* be QB1 in the NFL. I can't...I can't let myself get distracted. Or carried away. Football, that's what's important."

"Right, of course." But she didn't sound like she believed him, which was annoying.

Not as annoying as Aidan constantly hovering, but annoying enough.

"You don't think football's important?"

"No, I know it is," Paige said. "You've only wanted this your whole life. You've done everything you possibly could to make it. Nobody else could have done more."

"You and Aidan," Riley grumbled, "you both say shit and I always know there's a *but* on the end."

"There is," she said with a firm nod. "But here's the thing. Yes, we're both practical. For me, it's in my blood and my bones. It's who I am. But for you, it's different. You still *want* to be silly and get carried away and to have a little romance in your life. You're scared of it because of how you grew up, but that doesn't mean, deep down, you don't want it. You still crave it. And Landry Banks is all those stars, all those wishes and dreams and hopes, in one person."

Riley stared at her from across the table. "I hate you," he said.

"Because you know I'm right."

"*Not* because you're right. Because you *think* you're always right."

She just laughed. "Well, I guess one of us is going to be, huh? Also, if I wasn't one hundred percent, totally, completely right, would you have noticed how much the bartender was checking you out?"

"No," Riley said, even though he knew better.

He hadn't even been tempted by another man—or another woman, for that matter—since that night in Pittsburgh.

Because he finally believed he might have a chance with Landry?

Riley pushed the thought aside. "Maybe I just didn't feel like flirting tonight. I met you for a drink, not to find a hookup."

"But hookups always find you everywhere."

"You say that like it doesn't happen to you." Paige was certifiably gorgeous. They drew attention wherever they went. A lot of people believed, at least at first, that they were together. But while they were both bi, they both tended to stick to their own sex.

Paige liked to say, *"Men are more trouble than they're worth. I don't know how you do it, honey."*

How he did it was by never really making it a relationship.

There was no time, and he rarely had the inclination.

I give you two weeks before you're fucking.

With anyone else he was this interested in, who'd given him even a fraction of the looks Landry had that night, he'd have closed in and made sure they left together—Aidan or no Aidan.

He didn't want Landry to be special, but maybe he was.

CHAPTER 3

It was pouring rain when Riley landed in Charleston.

He'd gotten exactly three texts from Landry.

The first had been an awkward offer for Riley to stay with him, stilted and formal. Riley had stared at the message on his phone for ages, remembering what Paige had predicted—*I give you two weeks before you're fucking*—and decided, finally, to accept because Aidan wouldn't let him live it down if he declined, and also because if Landry continued to be this awkward maybe Paige would be wrong after all.

Don't be stupid. You don't really want *Paige to be wrong.*

He didn't. But if they did end up fucking, Riley didn't know what he was gonna do about that either.

Landry's second message read: **Glad you're coming here.**

Still painfully awkward, Riley decided. Were things going to be this difficult in person? He hoped not. He had a feeling Landry's awkwardness wasn't because Riley had flirted with him but because he'd *liked* it.

When do you get in? The next sentence read. **Aidan says late tomorrow night, but I thought I'd check with you.**

Riley sighed. Paige wasn't wrong about needing to tell Aidan to fuck off, either.

He did. But the funny thing was, he could tell just about anyone else to take their bullshit and shove it up their ass, but not Aidan.

Something like that, Riley texted back.

Landry's answer showed up almost immediately. **Should be back from practice by then. But here's the door code, just in case.** A string of digits followed.

Riley, who actually hadn't booked his plane ticket yet, decided then he wouldn't be showing up late.

Instead, he'd show up earlier, while Landry was at practice, and get settled in to save them both the painful fumbling of Landry trying to show him around the house.

He pulled the hood over his head and shifted his big duffel on one shoulder as he pulled out his phone and typed in the code Landry had sent him into the panel in the front door.

Over the years, Riley had gleaned a lot of info about the Banks family from shit Aidan had said and some very ill-advised *Google* searching when he couldn't resist the urge any longer.

He'd heard plenty from Aidan about how they'd grown up lower-middle-class in Texas. That their family was tight-knit, even now, living on opposite sides of the country.

He knew Logan, the middle brother, played for the Miami Piranhas now and had bought a house just outside of downtown, and he lived there with his boyfriend, the Piranhas' kicker.

So Riley wasn't surprised when he saw the townhouse Landry had rented in Charleston. It wasn't downtown, but close enough to both the practice facility and the stadium, tucked into a homey-looking neighborhood, with basketball hoops next to driveways and bicycles abandoned in front yards.

Maybe the NFL life was, by definition, temporary. But Landry, with his family background, would want something semi-permanent. Thus, this well-maintained but still clearly lived-in townhouse, not the flashy sort of penthouse apartment downtown you might expect someone pulling in his kind of salary to rent.

The foyer was hardwood, polished, and shiny under the light Riley flipped on. He slipped off his shoes, wet nearly all the way through, keeping them on the mat by the front door.

The walls were painted a soft creamy yellow, and Riley passed by the staircase that rose from the foyer and headed towards the back of the main floor. There was a kitchen with ivory cabinets and stone countertops, a single light burning over the sink.

A quick look in Landry's fridge proved he lived pretty much the same way Aidan did. There was a stack of prepared meals on the right, and on the left, eggs and milk. And on the counter, ingredients for protein shakes sat next to a high-tech blender.

Riley, whom everyone was sure was built too small and had spent the last two years bulking up his frame, drank his own share of protein shakes. But he liked to cook, too.

He'd have to figure out grocery delivery here and soon, or else he'd be starving.

The living room had the requisite enormous TV and a big couch stretched out in front of it. The only personal touch was a framed picture on the coffee table of the Banks family. Even though it felt like he'd nearly memorized their faces by this point, Riley leaned down and peered closer at the photograph.

With his long blond hair and enormous frame, Landry didn't quite look like he belonged to the rest of the family, but Riley kept looking and realized it was the combination of Landry's shoulder-length hair and his lack of tattoos. With shorter hair, he'd look like a mix of Logan and Levi. Landry's twin, Lyla, older by mere minutes, had darker hair and a smile Riley recognized all too well.

Feeling caught by his intense study of the photo, Riley backtracked and went up the stairs, pulling his duffel back over his shoulder.

The first door was a bathroom, gleaming and neat, probably unused since Landry had moved in. Which meant that the door next to it was probably his room. But he skipped it and walked to the open door at the end of the hallway.

If he didn't want me to see his room, he should've closed the door, Riley reasoned, even though he knew that was a shitty excuse.

But there wasn't anything in Landry's room that told him anything at all. It had a big bed—understandable considering Landry's height—covered in a stone-colored comforter. The furniture was dark wood, clearly quality pieces despite their stark lines. He flicked on a lamp by the bed and stared at it for longer than he felt comfortable admitting, even though that was only between him and the empty charging station sitting next to the lamp.

Landry's bathroom was also spotless and had not only a huge freaking shower in the corner of the tiled room but an even bigger bathtub. Two people—*him and me*, Riley's brain whispered—could fit into that tub.

Which was how he knew it was time to move on.

His own room was spacious, too, and if Riley wasn't mistaken, he caught the scent of a brand-new mattress the moment he opened the door.

Something in his insides cramped. If he was right, Landry had bought him that bed.

It wasn't the money. Landry had more than he knew what to do with. It was the fact Landry had taken time out of his schedule to go mattress shopping and then had picked this one just for him.

Riley unpacked his duffel. There was a spacious walk-in closet and even an unopened pack of hangers in it.

Then he went downstairs, pulled out his phone, and found a grocery store that delivered, even in the middle of a late summer rainstorm.

While he waited for the groceries, he flicked on the lights in the kitchen, opening a few random drawers and cabinets, taking stock of what Landry had and what he didn't. The bare minimum was the answer. Well, Riley would have to invest in a few pots and pans if he intended to cook the way he wanted to.

His stomach grumbled, and the grocery store app predicted the groceries were still an hour out, so he decided Landry wouldn't mind if he made himself a shake.

Riley found the straws in a drawer near the blender and laughed out loud as he grabbed one. They were all brightly colored and had little sayings engraved in gold on them. One said, *You go, girl!* And another, *Conquer today!*

He picked out a bright yellow one emblazoned with, *Love life!*

If Riley had to bet, these would be Lyla's contribution to his brother's household.

After sucking down half the shake, he set the glass on the counter. It was so quiet in this house, except for the rhythmic pitter-patter of the rain on the roof.

Glancing at his smartwatch, he knew it would still be at least an hour before Landry was home, and spotting the bluetooth speaker tucked away behind the salt and pepper shakers on the kitchen table, he hooked his phone up and pulled up his favorite playlist. Beyonce was always the answer when it was way too quiet.

The first sign Landry had that something wasn't right was the fact his townhouse was freaking *lit up* like it was the middle of the day. The second was the music pouring out of the kitchen.

The third?

Had his back to Landry, wearing a pair of old, worn-out athletic shorts that were at least a size too small, clinging to his hips and the curves of his ass.

The ass that was currently grinding and flexing to the heavy bass of the music.

Landry's mouth went totally dry.

He'd come home early to *prevent* things from being awkward between him and Riley.

One side of his brain wondered, *what's Riley doing here already, and why is he dancing in my kitchen?*

Riley raised his arms, and his t-shirt, already cropped short, rode up, exposing the smooth, muscular planes of his back.

The other part of his brain—the *uncooperative* part—insisted it didn't matter *why* Riley was doing it, only that he *kept* doing it.

But then Riley turned around, and Landry was caught staring.

Not just staring, but plain-as-fuck *gawking*.

Yeah, he definitely hadn't intended to kick off this roommate situation by shamelessly ogling Riley Flynn.

"Oh, you're here," Riley said, and even though his hips had stopped making that sinuous movement that had every single one of Landry's good intentions short-circuiting, there was no denying they swayed as he walked over to his phone, and the music didn't cut out, only became much quieter.

"You're here," Landry stuttered. Sounding like a total idiot.

He'd come home early from practice so he could make sure his plan was in place for Riley's arrival. So he'd be composed and pre-pared. So he'd be *controlled*.

But he didn't feel controlled at all.

Especially not now that Riley had turned around and he had an unhampered view of Riley's abs on full display, his shorts slipped low, and his cropped t-shirt providing a spectacular view of the muscles rippling as Riley leaned against the counter.

You're not queer. Anyone would look at this guy and think, maybe I should give it a try.

Maybe I should give him *a try.*

Maybe Landry wasn't bisexual; maybe he was just Riley-sexual.

Honestly, nobody who could see him like this, eyes as blue as a summer's day and skin tanned and totally fucking gorgeous, would ever doubt that was a real thing.

"Yeah," Riley said casually. "Flight got moved up."

"Oh. Oh. *Oh*." So much for his carefully constructed plan.

Riley shot him a lopsided grin. "Guess I should've texted. But I thought you wouldn't mind, so I got settled in."

"Settled in," Landry croaked.

"How was practice?" Riley looked completely unembarrassed and totally comfortable, like he belonged in Landry's kitchen.

It was *Landry's* kitchen. He should be the one feeling at home. But instead, he felt like an interloper in his own house, too many troublesome and aggravating thoughts and feelings crawling underneath his skin.

"It was...uh...fine." There was one more preseason game before the regular season kicked off. It wasn't much time to get a new quarterback on board, but Coach Kelley, along with Oscar Reynolds, the offensive coordinator, had started tweaking their offense play schemes to compensate for Riley's particular skills.

But without Riley, Charlie Nichols, the backup who'd originally been brought in, partially to coach Nelson, had been forced to run the offense himself.

To say it hadn't gone well was an understatement.

Charlie was thirty-five and trying to get one or two more years under his belt before retirement. He was *not* Riley Flynn, but they'd done the best they could with Charlie under center.

"Would've been a lot better *with* you," Landry added, trying to ignore the lightning streaking through him at Riley's smile.

"Really?" Riley said, looking both surprised and pleased.

"Well, we're tryin' to run the new offense with Charlie Nichols, and you can imagine how that's going."

"Yeah, I can," Riley said, his smile deepening, and *God*, he even had a dimple in his cheek. Landry fought the urge to lean over and press his lips to it.

This was his teammate. His roommate. His freaking best friend's little brother.

He should be totally off-limits, even in Landry's thoughts, but the truth was, it was impossible to shove all these non-teammate, non-roommate, non-little brother thoughts back into their boxes.

It had been a problem ever since he'd flirted with him. But the more Landry considered the situation, maybe it was actually before that. Ever since he'd gotten his first good look at the man Riley had become, the hope of controlling those thoughts had been lost.

He'd been lost.

"Charlie's good people, though," Landry said.

"Aidan already sent me an email about him," Riley said, rolling his eyes a little. "But Coach Kelley gave him my number, and we've chatted a bit since I signed yesterday. I think we'll be good."

Some backups wouldn't take to the role so naturally, but Landry knew Charlie had initially taken the job because he'd wanted to transition to coaching. He wasn't interested in being QB1—and that was all Riley wanted.

"I think so," Landry said. He dropped his bag on the seat of one of the barstools. "You eaten anything yet?"

"No, but I'm about to," Riley said. "Groceries should be here in a few."

"Groceries?" Wow, when Riley said he'd settled in, he hadn't been joking.

"Yeah, groceries. You know those things you buy at the store, so you can make food?" Riley teased.

Somehow Riley's teasing—or was it flirting?—unlocked his brain. Maybe this wouldn't be awkward after all. Wasn't the only awkward one here him?

"I do know what groceries are," Landry said gruffly.

"Shockingly," Riley said. He gestured towards the fridge. "You weren't exactly stocked up."

"I—"

"Don't cook?" Riley finished for him. "Yeah, I know. Don't worry. That's one thing I do really well."

"Cook? You cook?" Why had Aidan never mentioned that to him before? Or maybe he had, and like so much shit Aidan talked, maybe it had gone in one ear and out the other.

Riley nodded. "You know Aidan doesn't know everything about me. He's...well, you know he's pretty busy with his own life."

Landry knew. That didn't surprise him at all.

"Isn't it a little hypocritical of him to try to big brother you all the freaking time while living his own life in Toronto?"

Riley grinned. "You said it, not me."

"Maybe someone *should* be saying it to him," Landry muttered. He'd known forever that Aidan was way too overprotective of Riley, but this was even more ridiculous than he'd imagined.

"Hey, you want to tell him to fuck off, I'm not gonna stop you," Riley said lightly. "But you want dinner? I can make it for both of us. Keep up my end of the roommate side of things."

Landry almost said, *you don't have to do that,* but there was a burning fierceness in Riley's gaze. A determination that he wouldn't be a burden. So Landry nodded instead. "Sure," he said. "And you said you got all settled in? Is the bed okay? It's—"

"New?" Riley finished for him. "Yeah, it's great. Thank you. Really. I didn't realize until I came here that I didn't want to stay in one of those live-in hotels or rent some soulless box. So I'm grateful for the invite."

"Yeah," Landry said. Wondering, because he couldn't seem to help himself if Riley would be so grateful if he knew just how much Landry liked looking at him.

If he knew just how much Landry would give to touch.

If he knew how selfless he *wasn't* being.

The front doorbell rang, and Riley shot him a grin that lit him up inside. "There's the groceries."

Landry followed him out to the front door, partly because he was curious and partly to help Riley carry everything back to the kitchen.

There were a surprising number of bags. "You really weren't kidding," Landry said, lifting three with one hand and grabbing the last two with his other, leaving Riley with nothing to do except sign the delivery guy's tablet.

It was still raining, and he looked like he wanted nothing else but to get dry, but he did give the two of them a second look.

Was it because Riley looked like that?

Or was it because he'd recognized one or maybe even both of them?

"I think you might come in handy," Riley said as they walked back to the kitchen.

"As a pack mule?" Landry asked, setting the grocery bags on the counter.

He slipped onto one of the bar stools, watching as Riley began to unpack what he'd ordered.

Tons of protein, which wasn't a surprise considering the amount he'd probably consumed over the last few years to bulk up.

"I'm just gonna throw a quick marinade together for this chicken and then do a big salad. You good with that?"

Landry raised an eyebrow. "Are you feeding me?"

Riley nodded.

"Then I'm fucking grateful for whatever you put in front of me," Landry said.

"Was that the rule you had when you were growing up?" Riley asked casually as he dumped various bottles and containers into a dish Landry hadn't even known he'd owned, not measuring a single thing.

There was a casual confidence in his movements that told Landry he knew exactly what he was doing, and whatever they ate was going to be delicious.

"Yeah, basically."

"Mama Banks always struck me as someone you don't fuck around with," Riley said.

"This is true." Landry looked back and realized that the only way the four of them hadn't destroyed both the house and their parents was the firm discipline they'd insisted on. At the time, he'd hated it, had not only chafed under the restrictions but had felt the inevitable weight of being the oldest. The *responsible* one.

Lyla, of course, would have a lot to say about him claiming the title, as technically she was a few minutes older, but he'd been the eldest boy of three, and it had fallen to him regularly to control the other two. And Logan and Levi had needed a *lot* of controlling.

"It's weird," Riley said, as he set the dish aside and pulled out veggies from the crisper drawer, "that we don't know each other very well, isn't it?"

That wasn't the first time Riley had cut through the polite bullshit and pointed out the blunt truth. Landry had a feeling it wouldn't be the last.

"How many years do you and Aidan have between you?" Landry answered Riley's question by asking one of his own.

Riley leaned against the counter, clearly at home with a knife in his hand. Even a big shiny chef's knife. If Landry tried to use that, he'd probably accidentally cut off a finger. At the very least, an emergency room trip would've been in his future. But not Riley. And more than anything else, that confirmed what Riley had just claimed.

They *didn't* know each other very well, despite the fact Aidan had been his best friend forever.

"Almost eight years," Riley said. "So yeah, when I wasn't the annoying little brother anymore, you guys were gone and busy with your own lives. I get it." He shot Landry a look. Were his eyes full of heat, or was that just Landry's currently overactive imagination? "I guess we're gonna be making up for lost time now."

Landry swallowed hard. "Guess we are."

"Don't sound like I'm gonna march you down to the cliff and push you right off," Riley said, laughing. "I promise it won't hurt too much to get to know me."

Oh, it wouldn't hurt at all.

What was going to hurt the most was keeping his hands off.

"Is that what all the boys say to you?" Landry teased before he could reel the words back.

Riley fluttered his eyelashes. God, he was temptation incarnate. "The girls, too. I don't discriminate, baby."

"Right." Landry wanted to say, *me too, as long as the guys look like you*, but he didn't because what if this wasn't what this was? What if he was wrong?

Then there was the fact he knew enough about coming out that it wasn't necessarily right to do it just because he enjoyed flirting so much with Riley—and wanted him to keep doing it.

"Though," Riley said, shooting him another look from underneath those killer lashes, "I *do* tend to prefer the boys, so you're not entirely wrong."

Landry swallowed hard. "Is that...is that a thing? Can that be a thing? A preference even if you're bisexual?"

"Of course it can. Sexuality is a pretty fluid thing when it comes down to it. Surely I don't have to tell you that." Riley had gone back to chopping lettuce, like their conversation wasn't sending shockwaves through Landry.

He means: surely, your brothers explained that to you. Not that you personally are...well...fluid.

But maybe he was. More than he'd ever imagined he was.

"Logan and Levi are less on the fluid side of things," Landry explained.

"Ah yes, your brothers. The ones who would've apparently found me irresistible." Riley grinned.

They wouldn't be the only ones.

Landry flushed. The way Riley was looking at him with those gorgeous eyes, like he could see right through him, down to the place where he was questioning everything, and unlike Landry, it was like he *knew* exactly what all this meant.

Even if he couldn't possibly.

"Don't tell me that isn't normal for you," Landry said, trying to equal Riley's casual approach to the subject of just how fucking hot he was.

But Riley just shrugged. "Don't tell me you wouldn't love it if, every once in a while, people saw you as more than a pair of pecs and a head of blond hair? I kinda liked it better when I was that scrawny kid nobody paid attention to."

Even if Landry ignored how he looked, giving his looks the barest attention in the mirror every morning, he knew people still watched him. Approached him. Felt like they deserved a piece of him.

"Yeah, I get that," Landry said quietly.

Now, suddenly, it was hard to see Riley as *just* his abs and his biceps and those dreamy eyes.

"Thought you might," Riley said, the edge of his mouth quirking up. "I just gotta get the chicken grilled, and then we can eat."

"I have film from practice if you wanna watch it while we eat," Landry offered.

"Oh, yeah, that would be great. Coach sent me the playbook, and I've been going over it, but to see it in action? That would help."

"Thought it might." Landry slid off the stool and stretched, headed into the living room, flipped on the TV, and grabbed his tablet, connecting the two devices so he could beam the practice footage to the much bigger screen.

Fifteen minutes later, they were side by side on the couch, chowing down on salad and chicken, watching as Charlie led the first team offense that tomorrow would be Riley's.

"I like that double-crossing pattern," Riley observed, gesturing at the screen with his fork. "I saw that play in the book. But what if we brought you into it, ran a reverse with it, added another wrinkle."

Landry could see it and could see it working as he envisioned the play unfolding in his head.

"Yeah, yeah, you might have something there," he said. He should've predicted that Riley would be as good at cooking as he was at football. Clearly, he intended to excel at anything he tried.

"I don't know if..." Riley hesitated. It was the first time since he'd arrived—really, the first time since he'd met him again, as a man, not just as a boy—that he hadn't been one hundred and ten percent confident.

"If what?"

Riley sighed. Set his plate down. "I'm not a rookie, necessarily, but I'm a rookie in every way that matters. I spent a year on a practice squad, and then I played in the XFL. I don't know if...contributions are encouraged here. Or if they'd be encouraged from someone like me."

"Not always, not on every team I've been on, but on this one? Yeah, absolutely. Coach Kelley is great. You met him. You must've gotten the impression he's not the typical coach."

"Yeah, I did. Obviously, that made this job even more attractive even though..." Riley hesitated again, then plowed ahead, like he had to get this out before he changed his mind about saying it at all. "Even though I didn't have a lot of choices."

Landry heard what he wasn't saying: *I didn't have any other choices.*

"Whatever choices you did or didn't have," Landry said gently, and before he could stop himself, his hand was on Riley's bare knee, and a jolt of electricity seared him. But he didn't move it. Because what he was saying was important, and again, it wasn't Riley's fault Landry was so goddamned attracted to him. "We're goddamn lucky to have you. And this is a good spot for you. A great spot, even. We're...we're all kinda feelin' our way here in Charleston. I can say this, you're going to be more than welcome to speak up, give your two cents. More than any place I've ever played, this is a level playing field."

Landry squeezed his knee and then moved his hand away before it decided to take up a permanent home attached to Riley's skin.

His knee was still a little knobby, like it hadn't quite caught up to the rest of the bulked-up frame, and Landry shouldn't have felt his heart squeeze at the realization, but it did.

Riley had worked so hard to get here. That went without saying. The least he could do was be a support system. Even if he hadn't promised Aidan he would be, Landry knew it was absolutely the right thing to do.

"We're all looking for our own redemption, huh?" Riley asked.

"Yeah," Landry said with a nod.

Riley picked up his food again. "We know what mine is, so what's yours?"

"Maybe not *redemption*, necessarily, but...a chance to prove I can play someplace else."

"A chance to prove you can catch passes from someone who isn't Josh Allen?"

Landry smiled. "Yeah, I guess. And a chance to be closer to my brother."

"That's why you took this job, isn't it? To be closer to Logan?"

"And...there was a lot he kept telling me about Miami, things that happened there, a feeling they had in their locker room, in the facility, on the sideline, that I'd never had in Buffalo. I don't know if we can find it here, but I wanted to try anyway."

"You know," Riley said mischievously, "you're not just a pretty face, cither."

"Thanks," Landry said dryly. Ignoring the way his pulse sped up at Riley admitting he found him pretty.

"I guess we *are* doing this," Riley said.

"Doing what?"

"This getting to you know you thing. Aidan's kept you to himself for way too long."

"Aidan can be a selfish ass."

"Hey, you're telling me," Riley said lightly.

Landry had thought it earlier, but now he said it. "You've got no issue cutting through the bullshit with anyone else. But not with Aidan."

"There a question in that?" Riley asked, glancing over at Landry.

"You don't tell him off."

"I do, sometimes."

"No, you don't," Landry corrected gently. "Or I'd never stop hearing about it from Aidan."

Riley sighed. "You don't need me to tell you why."

Landry didn't. He knew how the Flynns had gotten divorced when Aidan was twelve, and Riley was five. And how in the midst of a very acrimonious divorce, they'd sort of lost track of their own children.

How, for years, it felt like it was Aidan and Riley against the world. Against their own parents, sometimes.

How Aidan had felt responsible for his younger brother. How it had, Landry liked to remind him occasionally, exacerbated his own worst protective instincts when it came to Riley.

"You don't need to explain," Landry agreed. "It was more an observation than anything else."

"It's just not that...easy, I guess...to tell him to fuck off. Not when I get why he's the way he is. When I know he means well. When I know it's all he knows, protecting me."

"What if you don't need protecting anymore?"

Riley shrugged. "We'll figure it out sometime. It helps I've got my own life now, and he's got his."

"Even though he wanted to reel you into his?" Landry didn't know why he was pushing this way. Riley was smart, and he knew exactly what he was about. He'd done all of this, hadn't he, despite all of Aidan's reservations?

"I never would have gone to Toronto," Riley said, rolling his eyes. "Never."

"I know."

Riley shot him a look. "You do?"

"You might not say it to his face, but your actions say it clearly enough." Landry finished the last bit of his salad and refrained, barely, from licking his plate. Sure, he'd been raised to eat everything put in front of him, but this had been a step above the usual.

Riley was quiet for a long moment. "Not everyone sees that," he said.

"Well, maybe there's less getting to know each other than you thought," Landry teased. Except he could think of all kinds of ways that *would* be new. Like if he slid another few inches closer on the couch. If he leaned in. If he tossed all his reservations to the wind and let himself touch Riley the way he desperately wanted to.

"Maybe," Riley said, his tone amused. "Or maybe not." His gaze was glued to Landry's face, then it flicked lower, down to his mouth, and oh yeah, it was entirely possible they were thinking the exact same thing.

Landry quaked inside.

"Come on, let's watch the rest of the plays," he said, clearing his throat and trying to change the subject.

Get back on the plan, he reminded himself. *You had the plan for a reason. Doesn't matter if Riley demolished it without even knowing it existed. You can still drag you two back onto the right path.*

The path of least temptation.

CHAPTER 4

Riley didn't sleep well.

There was the fact it was a new bed and a new house, and he never slept well in a brand-new place the first night. Then there was the additional wrinkle of Landry being just down the hall in his own bedroom.

But the real problem was the nerves skittering through him at the thought that tomorrow morning would be the first day of his *real* NFL career.

The first day he began to prove that Aidan wasn't the only Flynn worth having on a roster.

He tossed and turned, anxiety spiking inside him with every passing thought of everything that could go wrong.

But after finally falling into an uneasy sleep, he'd had uneasy dreams. He'd woken twice, startled awake. Finally, the third time, Riley rolled over and glanced at his phone. Five-forty-three. His alarm was set to go off in about an hour.

With a groan, he dragged himself out of bed and nearly stumbled downstairs in just his boxer briefs, but then he remembered he was staying with Landry, and while feeling the warmth of his appreciative gaze on his body was intriguing, it was *very* distracting, and Riley didn't need any more distractions. Not today, anyway.

So he threw a t-shirt on and headed downstairs.

To his surprise, the kitchen light was already on, and there was Landry, slumped at the table, a cup of coffee steaming in front of him and a protein shake in his hand.

Unlike Riley, he hadn't put a shirt on, and Riley wasn't proud of it, but he nearly stumbled over the threshold at the sight of big and broad Landry—there was a *lot* of bare skin to admire, never mind the trail of golden brown hair that led down to the waistband of his boxer briefs. Landry glanced up, and their gazes caught.

I give you two weeks before you're fucking.

Ugh. What was he supposed to say? *Sorry, but it seems you might be queer after all? You wanna talk about it? You wanna not talk about it at all and roll around in bed instead?*

"Couldn't sleep?" Landry asked.

"No," Riley said. He made a face as he leaned against the counter. "I shouldn't be because I'm ready for this, but I'm nervous."

"'Course you are," Landry said matter-of-factly. "This is a big deal. But you said it, you're ready for this."

Riley headed to the coffee machine and grabbed a mug stacked next to it, filling it nearly to the brim. He kept meaning to quit caffeine, but how did you quit something that smelled so goddamn good?

Normally, Riley wouldn't have admitted to nerves about today.

But this was *Landry*. He knew just how hard Riley had worked to get here—or he had to have a pretty decent idea. He knew what was riding on the next few weeks.

He also had to know just how much Riley did *not* want to go to Toronto, depressed and defeated, and deal with his brother.

Aidan would be nice. Nice and so fucking patronizing. Riley would want to punch him, repeatedly, and Riley didn't want to do that. He loved his brother.

The best thing for both of them was to make separate lives.

"Coach Kelley told me he talked to you," Riley said, hating the uncertainty he heard in his voice. He was confident; he *was* confident. He just wanted to get on that field and throw his first pass, and then maybe he'd settle down, wrap the belief he could *do* this around himself like a warm, fuzzy blanket. "I...I really appreciate that you did that."

Landry's gaze was just as warm. And it bolstered him before he'd even had a chance to get on the field. "I just told the truth," he said. Then he grinned. "Rest is up to you."

It was. He *could* do this.

All those people who believed he couldn't, even his brother, the person he loved and trusted more than anyone else, didn't matter.

Their chatter at the back of his mind faded until it was almost silent.

He believed—and Landry believed, too.

Coach Kelley. Coach Oscar, too. Hadn't they spent the last two days coming up with plays designed especially for him and his particular skill set?

They were on his side and wanted him to succeed maybe even more than he did because if he did, they'd get another year to rebuild.

Riley would continue getting chances, too. Enough that maybe he wouldn't constantly feel like he was trying to prove himself.

Maybe enough that he could finally *relax* and just enjoy himself on the football field again.

"I'm gonna make some breakfast."

Landry raised one golden brown eyebrow. God, he was so gorgeous like this, even sleepy in the early morning light. *Especially* sleepy in the early morning light. Riley could feel his crush nearing non-crush-like proportions.

Could feel himself imagining what it would be like waking up next to him in bed, looking just like he did right now.

"You really don't have to cook, you know," Landry suggested. "Not that I'm gonna turn breakfast down."

"It actually helps," Riley said, straightening and heading towards the fridge. "Relaxes my mind. Besides, I have a feeling I won't be doing much cooking the rest of the week."

There was a lot he needed to do to get ready for the game on Sunday. And he *would* be ready, hell or high water.

After eating Riley's unsurprisingly delicious pancakes, Landry put his bag together, and he and Riley headed into the Condors' practice facility together.

Riley had made noise about renting a car while he was here, but Landry had just shaken his head. "I've got two," he said. "Feel free to borrow one of them whenever you want."

"Really?" Riley looked surprised, glancing over at the *Mercedes* convertible sitting next to the Range Rover they were taking in.

"Seriously, it's just a car," Landry teased. "Doesn't Aidan own like fifty of them?"

Riley rolled his eyes. "You know he does. And he'd smack me if I borrowed one of them."

"*Brothers*, right?"

Riley's laugh echoed through the car, and Landry felt his heart rate speed up right along with the car as he hit the accelerator.

"Right," Riley agreed.

The drive to the Condors' practice facility was quick, less than ten minutes, which was why Landry had been so excited to find this rental in an area that still felt like a neighborhood, as close as he had.

As soon as they parked, he looked over at Riley. He looked pale and a little apprehensive. "You good?" he asked.

Even though he knew what this felt like. Remembered what it had felt like six years ago when he'd first started in the NFL. He'd been fucking terrified, and while he'd certainly had his share of expectations, his share of people to prove wrong, it was nothing like it was with Riley.

"Yeah, yeah..." Riley hesitated. Shot him a smile, not nearly as bright as so many of the others Landry had seen. "I will be."

"Yeah, you will be," Landry said, not only believing it himself but hoping that Riley would, too.

"Well," Riley said, pushing the door open, "I guess no time like the present to get started."

"Hey, wait a sec," Landry said, hopping out and following him, fumbling for the keys to lock the car.

Riley turned, an expectant look on his face.

Landry pulled him into a tight hug, feeling, for that brief second they held each other, the way Riley's body melted into his.

He'd meant it to be a friendly kind of hug, the kind of hug that said, *yep, you got this, dude,* but in reality, it was nothing like any kind of bro hug Landry had ever experienced. It felt hushed, intimate, Riley's chin hooking over his shoulder and staying there.

It was Riley who pulled away first.

He didn't say anything, but there was an expectant question in his eyes.

"I...uh...just wished someone had given me one of those on my first day," Landry said. Meaning it.

"Not my first day," Riley teased lightly.

"First enough it still counts," Landry insisted.

Riley turned to walk across the parking lot towards the front door, and Landry followed, his big strides eating up the head start Riley had gotten in seconds. "Seriously, though," Riley said, not looking at him, which Landry decided was a good thing because if he looked at him again, with those big, wide, blue eyes, he might do something even stupider, like kiss him instead of hug him. "I appreciate the faith. Hope it's not misplaced."

"It's not," Landry said with finality. "It's definitely not."

Practically the moment they walked through the door with Landry pulling out his badge, even though it wasn't like he wasn't distinctive enough to be recognized easily, Riley was whisked away by an assistant waiting for him to arrive.

Landry knew he should be heading down to the weight room, getting his morning workout in, but he hesitated, watching as Riley's back disappeared through the other doorway.

"You look lost."

Landry glanced over and realized Deacon had come in behind him.

Deacon Harris was a defensive end and was one of the very few players on the team this year who had been on the team *last* year.

He was a quiet guy, who didn't talk much unless he had something to say, but Landry had liked him right away. Maybe because the first time they'd met, and Landry hadn't known what to make of someone who'd been on the team the year before, Deacon had announced in a wry voice, "Don't worry, I kicked the ass out of Taylor every chance I got. As far as I figure, it was his turn to be the punching bag for once."

It had been clear then Deacon hadn't liked Taylor anymore than anyone else. That the ex-Condors quarterback had been the choice of the ownership, who hadn't cared about what kind of precedent they set as long as they won.

Then they not only *hadn't* won, losing to the Piranhas in the divisional round of the playoffs, but the NFL had swooped in and, in an unprecedented move, forcibly brokered the sale of the Condors to Grant Green, a thirty-four-year-old tech billionaire who'd not only never owned a football team, had zero experience owning *any* sports team.

But Green had one advantage that the old Condors ownership hadn't had: he wasn't willing to sacrifice moral high ground to win football games.

Deacon had made it through all the house cleaning Green and the NFL had done, so Landry had expected he'd been at least a decent enough guy.

Turned out he was more than decent. He was steadfast and loyal and spoke out and up when something wasn't right.

When Landry had wondered how he'd survived under the old ownership and all their questionable decisions, Deacon had just grinned. *"It was a good thing not too many guys felt like they could take me on,"* he'd said.

It was true, Landry thought as he turned towards Deacon now. The man was big, bigger even than Landry. Just as tall and built, not just like a truck, but a freaking eighteen-wheeler.

Nobody would look at Deacon Harris and think it was a good—or particularly *safe*—idea to confront him.

"You need help finding the weight room?" Deacon teased, nudging him on the shoulder as they headed down the hallway.

"Nope, I'm good," Landry said with a grin.

Deacon eyed him up and down. "Well, not *good*, maybe, but you're tryin'."

Landry laughed. "Not everyone can be you, Harris."

"Damn straight."

They were quiet for a moment as they waited for the elevator to take them to the basement and the weight room.

"Did I see you and the new QB come in together?" Deacon asked.

"Riley Flynn," Landry said, nodding. "Yeah, he's stayin' with me for a bit. I'm good friends with his older brother."

"Aidan, right?" Deacon rocked back on his heels, considering this particular fact. "I've sacked him at least a dozen times. That guy's tough to take down."

Landry considered how many sacks he must have on quarterbacks who were easier to take down than Aidan. It was impressive, but then Deacon had been in the NFL for over ten years and had racked up some crazy stats.

"Well, maybe you can do it again when we play them in a month," Landry said as the elevator arrived and they stepped in.

"He's your best friend, and you still want me to annihilate him?" Deacon asked, raising an eyebrow. No judgment in his tone, but genuine curiosity instead.

Landry hit the button for the basement. "I still want to win," he said. "Besides, Aidan's tough. He can take it."

"What about Riley? He tough, too?"

Landry considered this question. Deacon wasn't normally this interested, but the fact that he asked meant something. He didn't want just a *rah-rah Go Condors* answer; he wanted a *real* answer.

Which, actually, made a hell of a lot of sense. Because he was one of the only holdovers from the year before, Landry had gotten the impression that Deacon was personally vetting everyone they signed. If they didn't make his cut, then they weren't worth it.

"Tougher, actually," Landry said.

Deacon looked surprised at that. "But he's..." *He's smaller.*

"Yeah," Landry said. "He's had to fight for every single fucking thing."

"Hmmm." Deacon rocked back on his heels again, considering Landry's argument. "I can see it."

"You think Aidan's tough to bring down? Riley's gonna be twice as tough because he's got moves."

Deacon raised an eyebrow. Now he looked surprised. "He does, does he?" His deep rumbling voice was amused.

Landry told himself not to blush. Ordered himself not to blush, in fact. Wasn't quite successful. "Uh, well, yeah, you seen him play?"

"A few times," Deacon said. He didn't just put hours in on the weights but also in the film room. "Gonna be fun."

"Maybe don't make him a punching bag," Landry said, suddenly concerned. Yes, Riley was tough mentally and tougher physically than he'd been before, but Deacon Harris was still Deacon Harris.

"He make other people punching bags?" Deacon wondered out loud, though Landry had a feeling he already knew the answer to that question because if Deacon even suspected Riley was that kind of guy, he wouldn't currently be in the building.

"You know he doesn't," Landry said quietly. "He's a good guy. A great guy."

The elevator dinged, and the doors opened. "Figured as much," Deacon said. "He's got nothin' to worry about from me except me making him a better football player."

After a quick stop at the locker room to stow his bag and change, Landry headed towards the weight room. It was half full, a lot of the other Condors players putting in their time.

When Landry finished up his workout, there was still no sign of Riley.

He joined the other wide receivers in their room for the first meeting of the day, and Carter Maxwell, their first leading wide receiver and a bit of a diva, said as he sat down, "So tell us all about this new QB, Banks. He gonna be able to throw alright, or are we gonna be spending every play protecting his ass as he runs for the first down?"

Landry rolled his eyes as he took his seat. He kind of wanted to dislike Carter, who had a high enough opinion of himself it didn't really matter what anyone else thought, but the man was a freaking beast on the field, at least ninety percent of his ego fully deserved.

Plus, he was built a bit like Landry, so they'd already been trading tips since camp had started.

For someone who had such a healthy ego, it surprised Landry how Carter was actually willing to take suggestions.

Whether he *liked* it or not. Landry had always suspected he was listening, not because he wanted to, but probably because he'd been told that he *needed* to. And yeah, the guy had a bit of a reputation as a wild card, with an attitude and a temper to match. He'd been through three teams in three years already, and there was a possibility if he struck out with the Condors, maybe he wouldn't be signed by another team, despite his absolutely outrageous skills.

"He can throw," Landry insisted. "If you watched any film of him, Maxwell, you'd know the answer already."

Carter just grinned. "Watch film? Why would I need to do that?"

Coach Oscar, their offensive coordinator, rolled his eyes as he walked into the room. "Jesus, Maxwell," he said, "I can smell your ego a freaking mile away."

But Carter just shrugged, like he wasn't particularly concerned. "I can back it up," he said.

And wasn't that the biggest problem? Because he fucking *could*. It would be annoying, but Carter made the most impossible catches look easy. Landry knew they were going to win games just because he was on the roster. That certainly made swallowing his attitude a hell of a lot easier.

"Your new QB1 is meeting the media now, but he'll be on the field for practice this afternoon," Coach said. "Then you'll see. Flynn can throw. Good enough for anyone, but especially good enough for you, Maxwell."

"Excellent," Carter said, leaning back in his chair. "He puts it up, I can catch it."

"Let's go over some plays," Coach said. "As we talked about yesterday, the offense is changing to more of an RPO with the signing of Flynn."

It would be completely stupid to try anything other than the run-pass option offense with a quarterback with skills like Riley.

"Yuck," Carter inserted.

"That doesn't mean we're gonna be running the ball more. I still want to keep things sixty-forty, pass to run," Coach said, sounding like his temper was currently being tested. And with Carter, that wasn't much of a surprise.

Sometimes Landry thought he *lived* to test the temper of everyone around him.

"I don't know why you'd want anything less than seventy percent pass with me on the field," Carter said.

"For the love of God, shut up," Nick Williams, another one of the receivers, said. "You're makin' me want to commit a felony."

"Seriously," Landry chimed in.

"Just offering my opinion," Carter drawled, looking uncon-cerned that Nick wanted to demolish him.

"Noted," Coach Oscar said testily.

"More than once," Nick added.

Coach pulled some plays up on the screen then, and at least that quieted Carter for some time because he found studying film excruciatingly boring, and Landry wouldn't have been surprised if he used the opportunity during meetings to take a nap.

If anyone could sleep with their eyes wide open, it was probably Carter Maxwell.

After going over at least twenty plays, Coach finally let them go for lunch, with practice to follow after.

The cafeteria at the practice facility was actually pretty decent, with them providing not only well-balanced and nutritious meals but tasty ones, as well. Although, would it be as delicious as what Riley had cooked him last night? Landry doubted it.

He grabbed a salad as well as a healthy serving of grilled chicken to top it and Gatorade from the drinks case and headed towards the seating area.

He found himself scanning the tables, looking for a head of blond hair and that gorgeous smile, but he didn't find Riley anywhere.

"Lookin' for someone in particular?" Landry glanced over and saw Jem Knight, who, other than Deacon, had been one of the few Condors players who'd been around last year.

"Uh, well…"

"Riley, huh?" Jem grinned at him. "You probably promised Aidan you'd look out for him, didn't you?"

It was annoying being so obvious. Was his attraction written all over his face, too?

"It's not that surprising," Landry argued. They settled down at one of the other tables.

"Considering what I know of Aidan, not even remotely," Jem said, digging into his own salad.

Landry had forgotten Jem had played for the Toronto Thunder before he'd come to the Condors a few years back, so he actually *knew* Aidan and not just by reputation.

"I didn't think he even wanted his brother to play football," Jem continued.

"He doesn't," Landry said flatly.

Deacon approached their table and slid into the seat next to Jem. "Missing your boy already?" he teased.

"Riley's not my boy," Landry said.

"Aidan sure wants him to be," Jem pointed out.

"I don't know about that," Deacon said. "I saw you two hugging in the parking lot. And seriously, no judgment, but that didn't seem just friendly."

"It was," Landry said, hating how defensive his voice had become.

"Hey, like I said, zero judgment. Then I heard in the press conference Riley gave that he was staying with a *good friend*. That you, Banks?"

It was impossible to deny it, even though he wanted to, for no good reason other than it would cut off Deacon's speculation at the knees.

Why did it even matter to him if he did? There was nothing wrong if Riley *was* his boy, even though he most definitely was not.

"You know we don't give a shit here, right?" Jem said. "We're both..." Jem grinned, shooting Deacon a glance. "Very open to that, right?"

Deacon nodded.

Landry wanted to ask them both how long they'd known they didn't care which sex they were attracted to, but honestly, he was afraid of the answer. What if they said, *forever, pretty much my whole damn life*? Where would that leave *him*?

The weirdo who hadn't even suspected he was queer until he'd become painfully, undeniably attracted to his best friend's little brother, that's who.

"You know about my brothers, so you know I don't give a shit, either," Landry pointed out. "It's just...it's not like that with us. Not like that at all. He just needed a place to stay, and Aidan asked, so of course I said yes."

"Course you did," Deacon teased.

"Hey, you don't know Aidan like I do," Jem pointed out. "It's amazing he didn't go AWOL from Toronto just to make sure Riley's hand was held the whole damn way to Charleston."

"He really like that?" Deacon frowned.

"Yes," Jem and Landry answered together.

Deacon chuckled under his breath.

"Well, don't worry, your boy is eating lunch with Mr. G, and I'm sure he's plenty safe with him. Now, when he gets to the field?" Jem shrugged. "All bets are off."

"He can take it," Landry said. "And he needs it. The experience." He hesitated. "And you could use it, too, old man."

Jem stared at him, but Deacon was laughing. "Oh, man, I can't wait for this afternoon," he said. He elbowed Jem. "Not too many can keep you on your toes like this one."

"Need it," Jem said with a grunt. The only acknowledgment that he *was* one of the oldest players on the team.

"No kidding," Deacon teased.

The next time Landry saw Riley, it was in the locker room after lunch and another interminable round of meetings.

You weren't worried about him, not even a little, Landry tried to tell himself, but the truth was so much more complicated. He knew Riley could hold his own. Was smart as a whip and freaking *good* at this, but he remembered the nerves and the vulnerability Riley had shown to him last night and this morning. Landry knew his worries were born out of just how much Riley wanted to succeed at this.

How much he wanted to be the Condors' answer to their quarterback question.

Landry had almost managed to convince himself by the time he showed up at the locker room that the constant litany of *Riley, Riley, Riley* in his mind was because he wanted this for *him*. Nearly as much as Riley wanted it for himself.

But then he walked into the locker room, and Riley was shirtless and laughing with Carter, who was probably flirting with him, and Landry realized with a sinking feeling at the base of his stomach, attraction flaring hard and fast as he took in Riley's chiseled stomach, chest, and arms, he wasn't so selfless as he wanted to believe.

Because what he wanted was not just for Riley to succeed beyond his wildest dreams, but he also just plain *wanted* him.

Whether it was because Riley was the one guy on the planet who did it for him or because he'd apparently been bisexual this whole goddamn time and Riley was the key to unlocking that realization inside him, the sheer fucking *want* was undeniable.

Then Riley saw him, framed in the doorway, and the way his smile brightened, the way it deepened into something so much more genuine than whatever he'd been giving Carter, told Landry maybe he wasn't alone in this.

"Hey," Riley said as Landry approached. He wanted to have words with the equipment manager and also fall on his knees and thank him because Riley's locker was right across from his own, with an absolute prime view.

"Have a good day so far?" Landry asked, pulling his pads out of his locker.

"Yeah, it's been great. Crazy busy, but good. Got to talk to the media some. Meet with Coach Kelley and Coach Oscar. Worked on some film with Charlie. And now my absolutely favorite part of the day...practice."

"Nobody should look this excited to get on the field and get their ass handed to them," Carter grumbled.

"The key is not gettin' your ass handed to you," Landry teased. He turned to Riley. Pinned his gaze just above Riley's shoulder. *Do not look at his naked body. Absolutely do not look at his naked body.* "Heard you had lunch with the big shot today."

"Yeah," Riley sounded excited about it. "Mr. G isn't what I was expecting at all. But he's nice. Really nice. Honest, too. I think he's gonna make this team a success."

"I liked him when I met him," Landry said.

Riley dropped his voice and took a few steps closer after Landry pulled off his t-shirt. Tried valiantly to ignore the possibility that their bare skin might touch. "Was he...I don't know...younger than you imagined?"

"Yeah. Way younger."

"And way hotter, too," Carter inserted. "Bless having a sexy young billionaire buy your team."

Riley turned back towards his number one receiver. "You ever have a thought that isn't basic, Maxwell?"

But Carter just grinned. "Guess I'm just a basic bitch."

"Guess you are." Riley rolled his eyes but also looked amused, which was generally Landry's impression of Carter, too. God, he could be annoying, but in a way that made you want to toss him some balls, see what he could do, more than you wanted to actually punch him in the face.

"Anyway, yeah, he was nice." There was that hope flaring in Riley's eyes now. "Think this is gonna be a good spot for me."

"Me, too."

Landry turned back towards his locker to finish getting dressed. Yeah, NFL teams were more accepting these days, but it wasn't a good look to be caught checking out their brand-new quarterback on his first day.

"See you out there," Riley said, picking up his helmet and tossing Landry one last smile before he turned to jog onto the field.

Landry nodded, taking a sharp, deep breath as he faced his locker. It was just that all this was so goddamn *new*. He'd never been attracted to a guy before, and therefore, it had never intruded into football.

But it was threatening to intrude now.

"Yeaaah," a clearly amused voice behind him called out, as Landry couldn't stop himself from watching Riley leave. "He's not your boy *at all*."

It was Deacon again, and he was grinning.

"I don't know what you're talking about." Landry knew how defensive he sounded.

"You just keep tellin' yourself that," Deacon said, patting him on the shoulder and then turning to head out towards the tunnel that led to the practice field.

A few years back, the Condors' ownership had built a new field with a retractable roof. Because while Charleston had plenty of good weather even late into the fall, being on the coast, they had a tendency towards thunderstorms, especially in the summers when nobody could afford to miss a practice just because the weather was bad.

Today the weather was excellent for August—humid and hot, yes—but not a cloud in sight.

They warmed up and stretched thoroughly with the head trainer, Max Salazar.

"This is nice," Carter said as they lay on the grass, Landry trying to level out his breathing. It was fucking *hot* today, the sun shining relentlessly down onto them.

"Roasting alive?" Landry joked. It hadn't been this hot in Buffalo, that was for damn sure.

"Getting enough time to stretch," Carter said.

That got Landry's attention. "You didn't get enough time to stretch..." Right now, he couldn't remember where Carter had played last year. All he knew was he'd made the rounds because nobody wanted to put up with his attitude in the long term.

"I was here," Carter said. "At the end of the season. The Jets traded me here at the deadline."

He'd totally forgotten that Carter had been here last year. Even for part of the year.

"They thought me and Taylor would be a dynamite combo," Carter said. His voice was strangely flat.

"No?"

"No. And it was bullshit here. No time to stretch. Max was rushed through every single goddamn time," Carter said.

That didn't surprise Landry at all. Nobody was blabbing about what it had been like last year, but if even Carter Maxwell hadn't liked it, that said a whole lot.

"I started showing up to practice stretched 'cause I wasn't risking a pulled hammy to run the routes they wanted me to run," Carter finished as they stood up.

"Really?" That *was* a surprise. Not that Carter had finally been forced to be proactive, but that the Condors' coaching staff had cared so little about their players that they'd potentially sent them out onto the field so poorly prepared.

"Yep." Carter sounded very matter-of-fact.

"And you and Taylor?"

Carter looked at him. "You know how everyone thinks he was a serious piece of shit?"

Landry nodded. That did seem to be the unanimous opinion on the Condor's last starting quarterback.

"He wasn't *just* a piece of shit. He was the piece of shit under someone's fucking shoe."

"And here I thought you only gave a crap about a QB who could throw down the field."

Carter rolled his eyes. "He'd overthrow me on purpose, the asshole. And that was just the beginning."

Landry wanted to ask what happened after the beginning, but then Coach Oscar was yelling at them to huddle up.

Yep, they were about to run plays.

With Riley Flynn under center for the very first time.

Landry met Riley's perfect blue eyes across the huddle, and they seemed serious. Focused. Any insecurities were gone like they'd never even existed in the first place when, in reality, he was probably freaking out under his skin.

Or maybe not, because what he seemed was *steady*.

Absolutely fucking rock solid.

Actually...Landry flashed back to when he'd played college ball at Michigan, and who Riley reminded him of most was...his goddamned brother.

Landry recognized it so well because *Aidan* had that same steely, unshakable focus.

Had Riley learned it from him, or was it just a Flynn thing?

Coach called in the play, explaining what they were doing, and then Riley glanced at each of them in turn, making sure everyone was on the same page before he clapped, breaking the huddle.

The play was one of the run-pass options Carter had mouthed off so much about hating, thinking they meant he'd get less playing time and less touches.

But what Landry knew was it was going to give *all* of them a better chance of doing something more with every down.

Landry took up his spot at the line, facing off against Jaden, the linebacker on the other side from Jem, and the moment the whistle blew, he took off, dodging him with a quick side step, cleat digging into the turf and turning on a dime.

Beck, the safety, crossed over far back in the zone, but he was too far back to stop him, and Landry settled into the soft middle of the coverage, his gaze taking in the play as it unfolded.

Riley had dropped back, protected by the center and the left tackle, as he dodged to the left—there was Deacon, coming in like Riley's personal wrecking ball—but Riley had seen him coming and evaded him. For a split second, his eyes met Landry's, and Landry didn't need to be told any more. He shifted over and down, still running, watching as Riley led him to the ideal spot, and then Riley unloaded, tossing the most fucking perfect spiral, arcing above the rest of the field.

Landry made one last adjustment and felt the ball hit him square in the hands.

Beck was on him a second later, hand pressing to his back, letting him know he was down, without actually making the tackle.

He looked back across the practice field, and the look in Riley's eyes was everything.

Elation. Vindication. Delight.

And something else, too.

Undeniably pleasure.

A burning certainty unfolded in Landry that even part of Riley's pleasure was that his very first pass had been caught by *him*.

His fingers tightened on the ball.

You need to tell him. You need to tell him that didn't feel like any other catch you've ever made. That it felt like more.

But Landry didn't know how to do it. Not without confessing everything.

CHAPTER 5

AFTER PRACTICE, WHEN RILEY checked his phone, there was a very unsurprising text from his brother. **How'd your first practice go?**

Did you fuck it up? Riley knew that was what Aidan really wanted to ask.

He supposed he should be grateful his brother hadn't phrased it that way; at some point, that was absolutely what he would have said—no tact whatsoever.

The guys in the NFL aren't gonna be nice, either. He could imagine Aidan also saying if he actually complained about his total lack of diplomacy.

Went just about as I expected it would, Riley typed back. **Really freaking great.**

He wasn't lying.

There was just one thing that surprised him—the way it had felt when Landry had caught his very first pass.

He'd not let himself consider the possibility it might happen, had let his mind take in the defense—their configuration meant handing the ball off to the running back was off the table—then after the ball was snapped, he'd gone through his progressions. First, Carter was covered, and when he switched to Nick, he was, too.

But it had felt so goddamn right when he'd finally turned to Landry, and there he was in the soft part of the zone, almost right where he wanted him. He'd shifted to the right, and Landry had followed like they'd been playing together for years—for *forever*—and then he'd plucked his pass right out of the air.

Their gazes had caught right after he'd come down with the ball, and it seemed he wasn't the only one who was so freaking happy about being able to throw to Landry.

He looked just as thrilled to be catching Riley's passes.

Don't get cocky now, Aidan sent back.

Riley rolled his eyes and tossed his phone down, pulling his t-shirt on. He had hours left of meetings tonight, but he still felt invigorated.

"You get it, too?"

Riley glanced up, and there was Landry again. He was wearing shorts but no shirt, and his biceps bulged as he crossed his arms over his chest.

His broad, gorgeous chest.

Riley hated how his mouth went dry. Loved it, too.

It was hard to ignore what Paige had predicted when it seemed these days that Landry was just as affected by Riley as Riley was by Landry.

"Aidan's bullshit? You know it."

"Was he at least..." Landry hesitated.

"Not horrible?" Riley finished him for him. "Yeah, he was *not* horrible. Definitely not as bad as he's ever been."

"Good." Landry looked relieved, and it touched Riley that he cared.

He hadn't been sure if Landry hadn't been drinking Aidan's *Kool-Aid* all these years or if he was really willing to give Riley a chance.

"I've got a few more hours of meetings," Riley said. "You gonna stick around or... I'm sure I can catch a ride from someone else." Coach Oscar and Charlie had told him they always got together after practice to go over the footage they'd just taped. Breaking it down, looking for opportunities to improve.

It would've been the suggestion Riley made if they weren't already doing it, so it made sense to just join them.

"I'll stick around," Landry said. "Deacon and Jem and Beck said they were going out after to grab a beer. They wanted you to come, too, if you're still up for it."

It had been an undeniably long day, and Riley couldn't say it wouldn't catch up to him later, but he understood because he'd been around teams as long as he had been, what the invitation really was: a gesture of goodwill and welcome. It would be stupid to say no.

Deacon and Jem were the old guard of the defense, the ones who'd protected the good name of the Condors when ownership hadn't particularly wanted it to be protected. And Beck might be a rookie, but they'd taken him under their wing.

"Sure. I'll invite Carter, too, and Charlie."

"You're not seriously going to invite Carter," Landry said under his breath.

"Yeah, I am." He might be brand fucking new. But it was his job to hold this team together. Aidan had beat that idea into his brain often enough that it came as easy as breathing. Did he particularly *like* Carter? No, not really. But he was still a member of this team, one of the more valuable pieces, if he wasn't counting Carter's obnoxious attitude.

Landry just shook his head. "You're more like Aidan than even he realizes."

"Probably," Riley said lightly, knowing Landry meant it as a compliment. His brother *was* incredibly accomplished and respected as a quarterback, and Riley knew he'd taken a lot he'd learned from Aidan to heart. But the rest? Well, Riley wasn't going to ever give up on anyone.

Not the way his brother had wanted to give up on him.

He had no intention now—or *ever*—of grappling with the kinds of issues that he knew haunted his brother, even if he'd never opened his mouth about them.

"I'll see you in a few hours," Landry said. "I'd say be good, but you already know just how good you are."

Riley grinned at him. "Felt like you knew it, too, earlier."

"I really like Charlie, you know. And Nelson, too, obviously, but...felt somethin' special, catching your balls."

"Believe me, I know just how much you like my balls," Riley teased.

God, he just loved the way Landry flushed, the pinkish color rising along his skin, from underneath his chin up towards his hairline, whenever they flirted. It was like he was seeing a brand-new guy—or the guy underneath he'd never gotten to meet before. Somehow, he'd ended up liking *that* guy even more than the one he'd had a hopeless crush on for way too many years.

Wasn't that saying something?

"Well, I guess I'll see you when you're done with your meeting," Landry said.

"Guess you will," Riley said, not bothering to hide his pleasure or the brightness of his smile at Landry's words.

"You sure you don't want to come with us?" Riley asked Charlie as he threw on a light jacket.

"Nah. My wife, Nadia, she gets worked up if I don't come home to tuck the kids in because then they refuse to sleep," Charlie said sheepishly.

Riley could immediately see the problem with that. "How old are your kids?" he asked.

"Nine and four, and before you even ask," Charlie said with a chuckle, holding up a hand. "No, I don't want any more."

"I think two seems like plenty," Riley said. He hadn't even thought about ever starting a family—or starting closer to the beginning and actually finding someone to just *date*. He'd been way too focused on making it in the NFL.

Maybe he was just as much of a Flynn as Aidan and his parents, not constructed to settle down. Because even though Aidan had, without a single doubt, made it, racking up many successful years as an NFL quarterback, he certainly didn't show any signs of committing to anybody.

In fact, Riley couldn't remember the last time Aidan had told him about a *second* date.

"Not for you?" Charlie asked with a nudge as they headed towards the elevator that would take them upstairs, where Landry had texted that he and the other guys would be waiting for him.

"Someday, maybe," Riley said. "This life's hard for a family. Hard to even date." Not that he'd really tried, much to Paige's chagrin. But maybe if the Charleston situation became stable, maybe if he felt like he wasn't devoting every waking second to becoming successful, he'd consider actually finding someone he *wanted* to date.

Don't be stupid. You've already found the person.

But Riley cut that thought off hard and fast. Sure, Landry was looking at him differently these days. But maybe he wasn't ready to admit how he felt, now or anytime soon. And then there was the little, insignificant matter of him being his big brother's best friend.

If he had even an inkling of what Riley was thinking of, Aidan would absolutely lose his shit.

"Tell me about it," Charlie said wryly.

"Well, I'm glad you gave it at least one more year," Riley said, slinging an arm around the older man. "You've got a lot to teach, and I've got a lot to learn."

Charlie looked pleased. "You know, I thought you might be more like Aidan. Pleasantly surprised you're not."

It was funny; earlier, right after practice, Landry had told him he reminded him *of* Aidan, and now Charlie was saying the exact opposite.

"Really?"

"Thought you might believe you were already hot shit. You know, Aidan and I both went to the Pro Bowl a few years. I know him, not super well, but decent enough. Your brother's an amazing quarter-back."

Riley could sense the *but* coming in that sentence, even as Charlie hesitated.

"With an amazing ego to match," Riley retorted, finishing the thought Charlie hadn't wanted to. He'd known his brother knew Charlie because Aidan had told him as much.

"Yep," Charlie said with an amused glance over at him. "Exactly. But you're not like that."

"How could I be?"

How *could* he be when everyone had been lined up from the very beginning to tell him he was too small, too weak, too short, too everything, to make it?

The very opposite of what Aidan had experienced.

"Good point," Charlie said wryly.

When they exited the elevator, Landry, Jem, Deacon, and Carter were waiting for them at the far end of the atrium.

"We're just waiting for Beck," Deacon said.

"See you tomorrow," Charlie said, and to Riley's surprise, he gave him a quick hug. "Don't let these idiots keep you out too late, alright?"

"Yes, Dad," Deacon said, rolling his eyes.

"Hey, I'm *your* age," Charlie argued, a smile tilting up a corner of his mouth. He seemed amused instead of annoyed.

"Exactly," Deacon said.

"Next time," Charlie promised.

A minute later, Beck arrived, apologizing. "Sorry, guys," he said. "I got stuck reviewing some tape with Coach."

"You're so freaking dedicated," Jem teased, ruffling Beck's hair. "I love it."

To Riley's surprise, they all piled into Deacon's big SUV. "I'm not letting y'all drink and drive," Deacon said firmly.

"And you called Charlie *Dad*," Carter teased.

"We've been around too long and seen too much shit," Jem said.

When Riley had first been drafted, Aidan had sat him down and made him promise to avoid a whole laundry list of things.

Drinking and driving was at the very top of the list. Aidan hadn't had to explain that one because even during college, Riley had seen way too many cautionary tales of players ruining their careers before they'd even begun.

Riley had worked too hard, for too long, to let something like that derail him.

"I think you guys are gonna be real good for me. Definitely give my agent fewer heart attacks."

Landry rolled his eyes. "I bet."

"Who's your agent, Carter?" Riley was supposed to be making friends with him, so he decided to play nice.

"It's Scott Boras, but I'm thinking of switching. Any of you use Alec Mitchell?"

Alec Mitchell was the only high-profile queer agent in football. He managed Chase Riley and Spencer Evans from the Riptide, as well as Sebastian Howard from the Piranhas and a whole slew of others.

Riley glanced over at Carter, suddenly finding him marginally more interesting. "No, but didn't realize you were interested in coming out." That was usually why someone hired Alec. He was masterful at handling something that at one time would've derailed an NFL career but now was barely a blip.

Carter shrugged. "I don't know if I care. It's not like it's a big deal anymore. I just sort of do whatever the fuck I feel like, and if people want to infer something, they're free. Why so interested, Flynn?" Carter grinned at him.

This sounded very much like Carter's style.

"Why the switch, then?" Riley asked, ignoring Carter's flirtatious question. Even if he was interested in Carter—and he definitely wasn't—he'd known enough guys like Carter Maxwell to know he didn't really mean it.

"Because I'm sick of my agent's interminable lectures," Carter said. "Maybe Alec wouldn't be so annoying. After all, look at what he did for Chase. He got him that new big contract with the Riptide. And same for Spencer Evans."

"You already tired of being called the new Chase Riley?" Jem teased.

"I'm the new *Carter Maxwell*," Carter insisted. "I'm not a *new* anyone else."

"Then maybe don't act like it," Landry said under his breath.

Riley was pretty sure he was the only one who'd heard that—because he'd gotten stuck between Landry and Carter in the middle row of seats. He nudged Landry. Trying hard to ignore the way his bigger body felt plastered against his own.

"Seems like you already know what you want to do," Deacon said.

"So where's this place you're taking us?" Carter wanted to know.

"Place we like to go. Friendly. Low-key." They'd already driven downtown, but instead of pulling onto the main street where Riley had heard all the bars were, he turned onto a side street and parked behind a small, dark building.

"What's this?" Carter asked as they piled out of the car. "You knew a Tiki Bar here and you didn't take me last year?"

Riley didn't miss the look Jem shot the wide receiver. "We weren't really in the mood to go out last year," Deacon said bluntly.

The reminder of what last year had been like for the Condors seemed to sober up even Carter, but then they walked through the unassuming doorway, and immediately, it felt like they'd stepped right into a tropical paradise.

"The Pirate's Booty? *Really*?" Carter sounded both surprised and also delighted by the name of the bar, written on the wall opposite the doorway, surrounded by what felt like real palm trees. When Riley pressed a hand to the bark of one of them as they passed by, heading towards the main bar, he realized they *were* real.

As were the flowering plants winding their way up the walls of the bar.

"We used to come here all the time when..." Jem hesitated. "Well, back when things were good."

"They're gonna be good again," Riley said, hoping that if he believed it enough, it would be true.

"Yeah, I think so," Deacon said, his solemn expression breaking into a smile. But Riley noticed that Jem's expression didn't change as they approached the bar.

Behind the long counter, there was a full-sized mannequin dressed as a pirate.

"I want something tall and fruity and bright, with an *umbrella*," Carter announced as they leaned against the bar.

Unsurprisingly, it was pretty quiet since it was only Thursday. And, Riley remembered, as he glanced around the handful of occupied tables, Deacon *had* said it was a low-key place.

"They've got karaoke here on Wednesdays," Deacon said. "And Mondays are Disco Night, if we ever want to have a victory celebration..."

"That sounds fun," Riley said, and it actually did.

"You like disco?" Landry sounded floored by that.

"Well, *yeah*. I mean, doesn't everybody like to get down tonight?" Riley wiggled his hips, and it wasn't so dark in the bar he couldn't see the way Landry's golden brown stare heated up.

Reminded Riley of the other night when he'd been grooving to Beyonce in the kitchen and Landry had come home early.

The appreciation in his eyes hadn't just been pleasure at seeing his best friend's little brother. It had been way more personal than that.

Riley knew it.

He just didn't know what Landry was prepared to do about it.

"Personally, I'd *love* to get down tonight," Carter teased.

"Yeah, nobody who knows you at all is surprised," Beck said. "*I'm* getting a beer. Anyone else want to go for a pitcher?"

"Us," Jem said.

The bartender appeared, and his smile widened even further when he saw who was standing in front of his bar. "Hey, guys, long time no see. You're back for the new season?"

"Yep," Jem said.

Deacon turned back to their group. "Kieran here is, hands-down, the best bartender in the city. He's got an extra special skill."

"Being a good bartender?" Beck wondered.

"Nope." Deacon grinned. "He knows exactly what you want just by looking at you."

"Really?" Landry sounded skeptical.

Deacon opened his mouth, no doubt to argue about it, but Kieran just interrupted. "I got this," he said. "You want me to make you a drink, Landry?"

Landry raised an eyebrow.

"You're pretty easy to recognize," Kieran explained. "Then there's the fact your face is plastered all over the season tickets."

He was the easiest to recognize, with his face and his height, and his build. It was a little ridiculous how Landry kept pretending that wasn't true, but Riley would be the first to tell him it was inevitable that wherever he went, people *watched* him. Not just because he was a football player but because of that ridiculous six-foot-five frame with those crazy wide shoulders. Nevermind all those muscles and the shoulder-length model hair.

They probably all looked at Landry and thought the same thing Riley always had: *how good would it feel to climb him like a freaking tree?*

"I guess," Landry said, still not sounding convinced. "And sure, I'll take a drink."

"Great." Kieran started making a drink, Riley leaning over the counter so he could get a better look. He had a decent idea of what Landry liked, at least when he wasn't drinking beer with his brother, but as Kieran grabbed bottle after bottle, every motion filled with confidence, he had no idea if the end result was even going to be something Landry enjoyed.

Kieran set the finished drink on the polished bar top and topped it in a dramatic flourish with one of the brightly colored umbrellas Carter had wanted.

"What is it?" Landry asked as he picked it up.

But Kieran just shrugged, smiling like he was incredibly amused by the question. To Riley, it was a perfectly legit question. Because not only did Landry have no idea what was in the glass, but it was also a murky kind of orange, not the most appealing color of beverage he'd ever seen.

But then Landry finally took a sip, and pleasure transformed his face.

That's how he'd look if he took a bite out of you.

Riley didn't need the buzz of awareness under his skin to want Landry. And it sure didn't help.

"Well?" Carter demanded. "Was he right?"

"It's...it's sweet and sour and tangy...I don't even know what's in it, but it's perfect."

Kieran nodded. "I know," he said, zero trace of ego in his voice.

Riley knew if he'd had that kind of skill, he wouldn't be quite that matter-of-fact about it. In fact, he'd be bragging about it, Aidan-style, every chance he could.

"Do me next, do me next," Carter demanded excitedly.

But Kieran's gaze fell on Riley instead.

"I think it's only right our new QB gets the next drink," Kieran said. He smirked a little, and Riley swore he wasn't just psychic with the drink selections, but he knew exactly what Riley had been thinking.

Compared to the number of bottles employed in the prepara-tion of Landry's drink, Riley's only took two.

He knew what it would be the moment he saw the glass appear on the coaster.

Also knew it was perfect, exactly the right thing for him.

"And for Riley Flynn," Kieran teased. "Because he knows what he wants, and he's just gonna reach out and take it."

But am I?

"Not a surprise," Riley said, after taking a sip, "but you still did good."

"You remember that," Kieran said, giving him a little nod, a knowing look in his eyes.

"Did he really make your drink? What is it? Aidan told me, and I forgot." Landry stole the drink out of Riley's hand and took a sip. Riley's heart stuttered at the sight of Landry swiping his tongue across his lips, chasing the spicey, sugary vanilla taste.

"Yes," Riley said. "Like he said. I know what I want, and I'm gonna take it."

"Hmmm. It's good. Just so sweet. But yeah, it's good. I like it."

I'd taste just like that. And you wouldn't just like it, you'd love it.

"This is a cool place," Riley said, changing the subject because, at some point, the tension between them would stretch so tight, so undeniable, he wouldn't be able to take it anymore.

If it snapped right now, at this bar, in front of all their new teammates, that might be more than a little awkward.

"Yeah," Landry agreed. He settled against the bar. "You wanna go sit down?"

"Riley!" Carter exclaimed, practically crashing into Landry in his enthusiasm. "*Try this.*"

He pushed a glass full of bright blue liquid towards Riley. Not only had Carter gotten the requisite umbrella, but there was also a tiny plastic mermaid figure floating in the glass.

It was sour on his tongue, and Riley made a face. "What is that? It's awful."

"Exactly!" Carter crowed his delight about this particular fact. "I *love* sour stuff."

"Anyone who looked at you would guess that," Landry muttered.

"Jem says there's a whole upstairs that overlooks the courtyard. I guess that's where the dance floor and stage is. The courtyard." Carter fluttered his eyelashes at Riley. "You wanna go check it out?"

Riley wanted to stay here and keep making himself long for things he'd probably never get. But he *should* go with Carter and keep developing a friendship that would probably end up serving both of them *very* well.

"Sure," he said. Not missing the disgruntled look that passed over Landry's face.

Ugh, Landry thought as he tried to give a shit about the conversation Deacon, Jem, and Beck were having.

He couldn't blame Carter for flirting with Riley. Or wanting him all to himself.

If he'd had the balls to suggest going to explore the rest of the bar—all those fucking dark corners where nobody would know exactly what they got up to—then he'd have done it, too.

But Carter had beat him to it.

It was stupid and almost definitely counter-productive to be sitting here, gnashing his teeth over Carter's obvious flirtations.

Especially when it wasn't like Landry had done a single damn thing about the way he'd been feeling.

He hadn't because it was so fucking new.

He was still trying to wrap his head around the fact he was way too attracted to Riley. Who happened to be a guy. Who also happened to be Aidan's little brother.

He hadn't expected to have to power through those thought processes so Carter Maxwell wouldn't make a move first.

Again, who could fucking blame him? Not with the way Riley looks.

"I still feel we could use some extra help in the secondary," Deacon said.

"You don't think Rex and Eric are gonna cut it?" Jem questioned, pouring himself another beer.

"No." Deacon sounded very sure, and Landry felt a little sorry for Rex and Eric, whom he hadn't even met because Deacon had dismissed them so completely.

Even though Landry hadn't known him for very long, from his short experience with the guy, it was unlike Deacon to be so harsh.

It occurred to Landry that maybe his issues with the two starting corners didn't end with their play—but with something else.

The Condors had cleaned house, but maybe they hadn't cleaned house as thoroughly as they could have.

"You still need a shut-down corner," Beck said.

He'd know because he was a safety, already finding his footing in his second year, and if he had to step in and help out more than usual, it was because the corners weren't handling their assignments.

"Yeah, like that guy you played with at Northwestern."

Some indecipherable emotion flashed over Beck's face. "Micah?"

"Yeah," Jem said. "He up for leaving the Piranhas?"

"Would *you* be up for leaving a team on the rise like that? Hell no," Deacon said. "I'd cut off my right nut for a chance to play for Asa Dawson."

Beck didn't say anything else.

Which, he probably thought he was being smart, keeping whatever he felt under wraps, but Landry wanted to tell him that everything he *wasn't* saying was so much louder than anything he could've said.

There was definitely a story there.

"Surprised you didn't go there," Landry said, speaking up. "You could've. Could've picked your team."

"And left Jem here?" Deacon laughed. "No way."

Jem smiled, but there was something empty in it.

That was the thing Landry had discovered about joining a new team. He'd known all about the Bills. How the players fit together, which ones gravitated towards each other, and all the undercurrents playing out just under the surface.

But with a whole new team of players to figure out, he felt lost a lot of the time.

Come to think about it, the only time he hadn't was when he was with Riley.

He made him feel...safe.

And very *not* safe, too.

He stood. Beck looked over at him in surprise.

"I'm gonna go see what Riley and Carter are up to," he said.

"Right," Deacon said, and oh, he knew exactly what the bee looked like that was currently buzzing around Landry's bonnet. "You have fun doing that."

But his knowing glance didn't stop Landry.

No, what stopped Landry was on the second floor of the bar, overlooking the courtyard.

Riley and Carter.

Carter, leaning in and laughing, his handsome face lit up by the flashing lights in the courtyard below.

Riley smiling, too.

They even looked gorgeous together.

The drink that had been so perfect earlier felt like it was curdling in his stomach like old milk.

You know he's not for you.

But he didn't know that. Not really.

Not with as much certainty as he believed Carter would be totally wrong for Riley. He wasn't serious enough, then there was his questionable work ethic, and finally, his wild card lifestyle.

Riley deserved more.

He deserved *better*.

"Hey," Landry said, trying to approach the pair with something other than a thundercloud in his expression, but it was hard to reign all that in, and he thought Carter noticed.

On the other hand, Riley turned to him, his smile brightening as he spotted Landry approaching.

"Got tired of the defensive talk," Landry said, pushing his fingers through his hair. "Thought I'd see what you two were up to."

"Right." Carter didn't look convinced.

"Hey, why don't you go grab us some waters," Riley said to him.

Carter made a face, but he didn't argue either. Instead, he collected Riley's glass and took off for the stairs Landry had just climbed up.

"You're welcome," Landry said as Carter's blond hair disappeared from view.

Riley's expression was inscrutable, though, as he leaned against the railing.

"He's not so bad," Riley said, and anxiety spiked inside Landry.

Did Riley actually *like* Carter?

God, he'd thought the hardest thing he'd face with Riley's arrival would be wrestling with his sexuality. He'd never imagined he'd have to watch Riley fall for someone else.

"You know how sometimes people think any attention is better than no attention?" Riley asked. "That's Carter. He doesn't mean to be obnoxious. He just doesn't know when to quit. Doesn't know how."

"You've got him pegged pretty fast," Landry said. Hating the envy in his voice. Hoping that Riley wouldn't recognize it for what it was.

But Riley just shrugged. "It's my job to know my guys."

"What about me?" Landry should've bitten that question back. But he couldn't. At the last second, it escaped him.

"What about you?" Riley asked, raising an eyebrow.

"I...uh...what do you know about me?"

"You like to keep the peace." Riley made a face. "You and Aidan have that in common."

It didn't sound like something good. Landry pushed down the worry expanding inside him. *Riley doesn't dislike you; remember how happy he was you caught his first pass as a Condor?*

"We do," Landry agreed. Didn't like it, but it was undeniably true.

Probably why they'd become friends in the first place.

"What else?" Riley considered his own question. "You care a lot. Too much, probably. You worried about what Aidan would say to me today. You worried about what he'd say to me that night in Pittsburgh."

"Of course I did," Landry said.

Hoped Riley might think that was him only being nice.

Not because it lit him up inside whenever Riley smiled.

Thinking about that night, though, made Landry *think* about that night.

How Riley had flirted with him, and he'd loved it.

So much he'd only wanted more—but then, with his unerringly terrible timing, Aidan had interrupted them. Now they were back in a bar, in a dark corner alone, and Aidan wasn't anywhere to be found.

Thank God.

"I think about that night sometimes," Landry continued. *A lot. More than I'm willing to admit to you. More than I'm even willing to admit to myself.*

"Yeah?" The corner of Riley's mouth tilted up.

It felt like an invitation.

Landry ignored the way his hands were suddenly damp with nerves and leaned in a little closer. "Don't you?" he asked.

It came out a lot more confident than he felt—but it was the kind of thing he'd have said six months ago to a girl he liked. Riley was definitely not a girl. The fact that he wasn't made his insides tremble and quake like he'd never experienced before.

Not just because of the nerves. Not just because this was all new to him.

That was all Riley.

"I do." Riley paused. "I think about how you never answered my question."

Landry's heart short-circuited. Of course he knew what question Riley was referring to. He'd said his two brothers would've been all over him, trying to get Riley's info, if they'd known how he'd grown up.

And then Riley had turned the tables.

Really? he'd asked. *Just the two of them?*

Landry hadn't answered his question. Because he'd been terrified of the truth.

Was still kinda terrified.

But not for any reasons Riley probably assumed.

"No," Landry said. His voice dropped. He heard how rough and desperate it sounded. Riley's eyes widened, and staring into them was like drowning in the ocean, willingly. "No, not just them."

Riley licked his lips and leaned in another inch. He smelled like the soap they stocked in the showers, and something indefinable, something bright and citrusy, that had to be just *Riley.*

He put a hand on Landry's shoulder. "It's not easy," he murmured.

Riley didn't have to say what wasn't easy. Landry knew what he was talking about.

It's not easy admitting it.

And he hadn't gone nearly as far as he'd wanted to.

"What's not easy?" Carter asked from behind them.

Landry didn't know what they were doing—were they going to kiss?—but he still wanted to scream in frustration at Carter's interruption.

"Playing in the NFL," Riley said, stepping away from and around Landry. His voice was annoyingly steady, and he'd come up with that answer with barely a second of hesitation.

Maybe they *hadn't* been half a second away from kissing.

Maybe Landry was reading all this wrong.

He hadn't thought so. Riley hadn't had to get so damn close, but he had anyway.

Carter didn't exactly look convinced, though. "Does anyone think it's easy?"

"Probably my brother," Riley said, taking the glass of water from Carter's hand. "Right, Landry?"

But Landry's brain was still scrambling, trying to catch up on what had just happened. On what had *almost* just happened. "Uh, yeah, sure," he said.

Carter leaned against the wall. "The guys want to go soon, so I've been sent, officially, to fetch you," he said. He made a face. "Calling it quits so early."

"We have practice tomorrow and a game in two days," Landry pointed out.

"Thanks, *Dad*," Carter teased.

Before Landry could open his mouth and tell Carter he was wrong, Riley elbowed him in the side. "That's Charlie," he reminded him. "*Not* Landry."

"Right," Carter said, his grin widening. "Don't want Landry to be your Daddy, huh?"

Riley rolled his eyes, but as they headed down the stairs, Landry thought he'd seen a spark of heat in those cool, blue eyes.

Chapter 6

They were both quiet on the way home from the bar.

Riley couldn't blame Landry for being quiet. It was a big deal to come out, requiring a lot of re-aligning of your worldview when you finally acknowledged what you'd always believed wasn't necessarily the truth any longer.

Maybe Landry hadn't explicitly said he was queer. But the implication had been there.

Landry pulled his SUV into the garage. "We still good to leave at the same time tomorrow?" he asked as they got out of the car.

"Yeah," Riley said. He hesitated as they entered the house. He wanted to say something. Wanted to say, *it's okay, I know coming out can be tough. You're allowed to struggle with this.* But all his good intentions were tangled up with his crush and the desperate hope Landry might actually feel the same, and he didn't know how to address one without bringing up the other.

You know how we've almost kissed twice?

Let's try that again. With no interruptions this time.

I promise you'll like it. I know I'm gonna love it.

But Landry's expression was closed off, his eyes tired, and Riley felt the pull of exhaustion, too, and he didn't try to stop him when Landry said he was going to bed.

He felt keyed up from the adrenaline and shaky from all the excess desire and an itch he hadn't been able to scratch, not for days, not for *years,* but to Riley's surprise, when he collapsed into bed, sleep took him almost immediately.

When he woke up the next morning, for a second, he felt a pang of disappointment—why *hadn't* he just kissed Landry, damn the consequences, when they'd gotten home?—followed by an inevitable excitement.

Today was the last day of practice before they left tomorrow morning for the last preseason game.

His *first* NFL game where he was listed, officially, as QB1.

It was hard to be disappointed when a lifelong dream was about to become reality.

Tonight, he promised himself, as he got ready to go to the practice facility, *you'll talk to Landry tonight.*

You're at least gonna tell him it's okay to struggle. That he can talk to you.

Landry was quiet when he got downstairs.

Maybe that was normal. Maybe there was nothing unusual about the way he was acting—after all, Riley didn't *personally* know him all that well yet—but there was also the possibility none of this was normal, and Landry was struggling.

"You okay?" Riley asked after he slid onto one of the barstools.

Landry glanced over at him, a crease forming between his golden brown brows. "I'm fine," he said.

But Riley was pretty sure he didn't *sound* fine.

"You're sure you don't want to talk about anything?" *Maybe about how it feels like you came out to me yesterday? We should talk about that. Or not talk at all. That could work, too.*

Landry shot him a look. "What would I want to talk about?" he said.

Riley rolled his eyes as he finished his protein shake. "Nothing," he said.

Unfortunately, they only had half an hour before he needed to be in the biggest conference room for the pre-game offensive meeting.

There was no time to yank that tablet out of Landry's hands as he endlessly scrolled through Facebook and demand that he look at him, that he *talk* to him about what he was going through.

It was frustrating, but after another mostly silent ride to the Condors' facility, Riley forced himself to let it go. He knew it was a distraction, and what he needed, more than anything else, was to focus on the upcoming game. Getting prepared to play in an NFL game was a major undertaking, and he'd only had a few days to do it.

He was running an entirely new offensive scheme, and Coach Kelley and Coach Oscar were putting together new plays as fast as he could digest them.

He'd seen Landry a dozen times: at the first meeting of the day, then at lunch, sitting with Beck and Jem, and then at practice. But only once had it seemed like Landry had even registered his presence.

When he'd come into the wide receiver room and caught Carter grilling him about his crush.

Riley should've been embarrassed. If his crush was obvious enough that even Carter freaking Maxwell could see it, it was *obvious*. But Landry, other than a frown, didn't seem to even notice he was there.

Practice was more of the same. Endless adjustments. Running the same play a dozen times, then two dozen, until they got it exactly right.

By the time practice ended, Riley was worn out, brain buzzing with too much input, and he just wanted quiet for a moment.

"You stayin' after?" Carter asked as they got dressed. "Break down the practice tape?"

He should. He believed that was part of his obligation as the starting quarterback, but he just needed...well, to not prepare for another second.

That was what he needed.

He needed to lock himself in a closet and just not *think* for a minute.

Maybe an hour.

"No," Charlie said, leaning in from his other side. "No, we're not doing that today. We can go over some stuff tomorrow before the walk-through, but I can see it in your eyes, Flynn. You're overloaded. Go home. Try not to think for a while."

There were lots of things he could do if he wasn't thinking.

Make dinner.

Watch a movie where lots of things blow up.

Kiss your older brother's best friend.

God only knew where that last, very rogue thought had come from.

But it had popped into Riley's head before he could stop it.

"Alright, if you're sure," Riley said, even though it wasn't like Charlie was wrong. He just didn't want anyone to get the impression he wasn't putting the work in.

That this game on Sunday wasn't one of the most important in his life, even if it was *just* a preseason game.

But the intentions he set for this week and the way he played during this game and the next few would all have an indelible impact on his career.

If he wanted to make it, if he wanted to solidify his reputation as a starting quarterback in the NFL, playing great during this first month was the best way to do it.

"I'm sure," Charlie said, patting him on the back. "Seriously, I know Coach Kelley, and I think you've come a *long* way, even though it's only been a few days. You've got this."

"Thanks," Riley said, meaning it.

"You've got a big career ahead of you," Charlie said, shooting him a disarming smile. "Remember me when I'm just a footnote, yeah?"

"Well, yeah," Riley said. "How could I not? I...I really appreciate you stepping up and coaching me like this. You didn't have to."

Charlie just shrugged. "I know it's a lot. And sometimes a lot is too much, you know?"

Riley knew.

"Exactly," Charlie continued. "Seriously. Go home. Rest. Do something stupid. Something brainless. It'll help."

Riley was pretty sure Charlie didn't mean, *kiss your brother's best friend,* but somehow his gaze found Landry across the locker room as he chatted with Beck.

"I will," Riley promised.

"Yeah, you will," Carter teased. "I know exactly what's goin' on here."

"Yeah? What's that?" Riley had a feeling he knew where this was headed.

"I mean, yeah, Landry's hot. But he's kinda serious, don't you think?" Carter said, frowning.

He was. Exactly why Riley liked him. You always knew where you stood with Landry.

Except right now, of course.

"We're just friends, Carter. I already told you that." He had, last night when Carter had questioned him about their *room-mate status*.

He grabbed his bag and headed over to where Landry was standing.

"You ready to go?" he asked.

Landry turned, looking surprised. "You're not staying?"

"Nope. Going home. Not thinking for a whole evening. That was Charlie's suggestion."

Landry nodded. "It was a lot today."

"Yeah," Riley agreed. "I'll make dinner, and we'll watch something brainless on TV." *And not talk about the six-ton elephant in the room.*

Landry didn't know why he hadn't texted either one of his brothers.

He knew he should have, especially after he'd spent most of the night tossing and turning, trying to decide what he should do about the growing tension between him and Riley.

He knew Riley was just trying to help—there was no question he'd realized some of Landry's internal strife as they'd sat at the kitchen counter this morning—but the problem was, he couldn't be both the problem *and* the solution.

With that thought in mind, he'd texted his twin sister Lyla right before he'd stepped into the big offensive game plan meeting.

Question of the day: you ever wonder how we ended up so freaking straight when Levi and Logan so aren't?

During the meeting, he'd felt his phone buzz once and then twice. And then a third time.

On his way down to the wide receiver room after the meeting, he glanced at his phone.

Lyla had texted him twice.

No...

And then: **Is there something you're trying to tell me?**

Landry's stomach cramped. It wasn't that he thought his new-found sexuality was going to be a problem—he knew his family would barely blink when they found out—but instead, he felt himself hung-up on the bigger detail of what it was going to *mean*.

He still worried he'd been in denial this whole time. At least until Riley had forcibly pried his eyes open.

The third message wasn't from Lyla, but from Logan.

Do we still need to have the talk?

God, he did *not* want to have a talk—especially *the* talk—with either of his younger brothers.

No, he texted back to Logan.

Seems like we might. You know sexuality's a sliding scale.

That was what he'd always been told, and Landry had thought he'd understood.

But it turned out that knowing it when it was someone else and knowing it when it was *him* made logical acceptance much tougher.

I didn't say anything, Landry texted back.

Logan's answer came through almost immediately, just as Landry pushed open the door to the wide receiver room.

To the image of Riley sitting on the desk, Carter practically between his legs.

He ground his teeth together before trying to marshal his thoughts into something that didn't resemble jealous rage.

"You alright, dude?" Carter asked innocently.

Like the guy had an innocent freaking bone in his body.

"I'm fine," Landry said, trying very hard not to stomp over to the mini-fridge to grab a bottle of Gatorade.

His phone buzzed again, and he glanced down. **You didn't have to**, Logan had replied.

He should be a lot happier that his family was so freaking accepting, and he *was* happy. Relieved and happy. Of course that didn't mean he understood exactly what had happened in the first place. Maybe being Riley-sexual *was* a thing.

It sure seemed to have hit Carter hard.

Landry ground his teeth together. Pulled up his text conversation with his sister. **Thanks for telling Logan**, he sent her.

Sorry, she replied back almost immediately, **but it kinda slipped out. But it's okay, right? We all love you. You know that.**

Oh, he knew it. Lyla knew it, too. Knew he wouldn't *really* be mad.

Yeah, yeah, Landry sent back. **I love you, too.**

"I'm gonna go, but thanks for the advice," Riley said, jumping down from the desk. "See you later, Landry."

Landry had assumed Riley would join the post-practice film session as he had the last few days, so he'd expected to have some time to gather his thoughts.

But then Charlie had canceled it—actually, in retrospect, it was a good idea because the deeper they'd gotten into practice, the tighter and tighter Riley wound himself up.

Riley exploding would not be a good idea.

Not for Landry and not for the Condors.

So instead of getting his time to try to compartmentalize what he was feeling and what they were even *doing,* he and Riley had headed home together.

Now Riley was in his kitchen, in sweatpants that clung to his thighs and ass in a way that Landry was trying—and failing—to ignore, cooking them dinner.

"You're making me nervous," Riley said, chuckling under his breath as he put a pan on the stove. "I promise I'm not going to burn your house down."

"I don't think that," Landry said, embarrassed at how he'd been caught staring.

His phone buzzed again.

He didn't need to look at it to see it was Logan calling again.

No doubt he wanted to talk about what he sort-of-but-not-really had confessed to Lyla earlier today.

But the truth was, he didn't really want to talk to any of them about it.

That was the problem. The person he wanted to talk to most about it was the person who'd unlocked this desire inside him in the first place.

"Oh, hey, someone else who ignores many calls from his brother," Riley said lightly. "It is your brother, right? Which one?"

He was trying to make things normal. Landry knew he was. And what was *he* doing?

Checking out Riley's ass and thinking about pushing him up against the counter.

He should be ashamed, but he wasn't. Instead, he was turned on, squirming on the barstool like the first time he'd ever been on a date.

Even though this was definitely not a date.

For this to be a date, you'd have to tell him you're into him.

"Yeah. It's Logan."

"You don't want to talk to him?" Riley's questions were still light, teasing. Unlike this morning when he'd slid onto the barstool next to him and looked at him like he could see right through Landry. See right down to where he was struggling.

"Not right now."

"Well, you're definitely making me feel less guilty about avoiding *my* brother."

"You're welcome," Landry said dryly.

"You gonna tell me why?" Riley bent down to grab a casserole dish from the bottom cupboard, and the worn, soft fabric of his sweatpants stretched tight across his gloriously curved ass, and Landry had to swallow hard.

How was it that practically every inch of him was covered, and yet he was still salivating?

It was totally unfair.

"I...uh..." Landry hated how he was stammering. This was more than embarrassing. It was *humiliating.*

Man up, a voice inside that sounded suspiciously like Logan ordered him. *Man up and get this shit done.*

"You know a few years ago when, uh...when you came out?"

Riley shot him a look. "Shockingly, yes," he teased. "Not the kind of thing you forget."

"Right, right, uh..." Landry took a deep breath. "I think I might...*also.*"

"Okay," Riley said steadily. His knife, cutting through a mound of broccoli, didn't hesitate even for a moment.

Maybe Landry hadn't been very good at hiding it.

Maybe Riley and Carter had been laughing together about Landry's painfully obvious bisexual awakening for days now.

But that wasn't like Riley, Landry realized.

He wouldn't do that.

"You know I don't care. I'm hardly a person who's going to judge you," Riley said when Landry went silent.

"I know. I just...I'm *thirty-one*, Riley. Thirty-one years old, and I didn't know this about myself until..."

"Until?" One of Riley's eyebrows quirked up.

You are not going to tell him he's the cause of your bisexual awakening. No, you will not.

"Until recently." It was a total cop-out answer. Landry knew it. Undoubtedly Riley knew it, too.

"Okay." But Riley didn't call him on it. "So what does you being thirty-one have to do with any of it?"

"I'm *thirty-one*, and I've just realized this about myself. What if…what if I knew, deep down, and I didn't want that to be me? What if—"

Riley didn't let him get the rest of it out, *thank God*.

"What if you thought you were accepting and open-minded about people this whole time, and you weren't?"

"Yes. Yes, exactly that." Landry chuckled under his breath, unmistakable relief at someone finally saying it out loud.

"Landry, I'm going to be blunt now, okay?"

Landry nodded and braced himself for the worst.

Realized, a half-second too late, he should've been bracing himself for something else entirely because Riley set the knife down and was suddenly in his space, his hands on Landry's shoulders, so close he could practically catalog every shade of blue in his incredible eyes.

"You are very stupid if you believe that," Riley said softly. "You love your brothers. You accept them wholeheartedly. You've never secretly believed you were better than they were because you assumed you were straight. I promise."

"You do?"

"I do," Riley said confidently. "And so would Logan, if you'd take his calls and stop ducking him. This stuff isn't straightforward or particularly linear. It's a scale, yeah, but that doesn't mean it always makes logical sense. You know, I'm bisexual myself, but I tend to gravitate towards men. And that's okay. You're probably the opposite, and that's okay, too. It's all okay. Whatever you feel, it's *okay*."

Landry stared at him, at the earnest look on his face.

The face that had changed everything.

He'd taken his helmet off in Pittsburgh, and Landry's whole life had re-aligned itself.

Maybe Riley could be the problem *and* the solution, after all.

"Okay," Landry repeated quietly.

Riley's fingers tightened their grip on his shoulders. For a breathless moment, Landry thought maybe he was going to lean in and kiss him. Complete the cycle he'd inadvertently begun that day in Pittsburgh.

But he didn't.

Much to Landry's disappointment.

You could've told him it was him, that he was the cause, and then he probably would've.

He could've. But it felt like way too much, way too soon, no matter how much he craved it.

Being the eldest of two adventurous and pain-in-the-ass brothers, he'd had to learn to take his time with stuff.

Riley made him feel like he was careening out of control.

"You better now?" Riley asked, and even though Landry had just told himself he wanted a better handle on the situation before he considered taking it to the next level, he was disappointed when he let go and turned away.

Riley's question had been serious.

It deserved a serious answer, so he considered it for a second. How *did* he feel?

Less conflicted, that was for sure. Still like he was on an out-of-control train weaving its way through the mountains with no brakes, but maybe that was the way everyone felt around Riley Flynn.

Maybe that was the way *Carter* felt around Riley, too.

Landry squashed the jealousy because it wasn't Riley's fault Carter was Carter.

"Yeah, actually," he admitted. "Thank you."

"I'm not gonna promise coming out will always be easy, but it's worth it every single time. For me, it always makes me feel a little bit more myself," Riley said.

It was impossible to believe the confident guy in his kitchen was anything less than that every second of the day. There was the way he'd taken the field like he had no fear.

But Landry knew better.

Knew he was nervous. Knew he was anxious.

He just buried it deep so nobody saw it.

"I'll keep that in mind," Landry said.

"Now, I'm gonna finish this casserole," Riley said. "And you're going to go call your brother."

Landry rolled his eyes. "Really? Do I have to? He's gonna be all...*I told you you weren't straight* about it. And then he's gonna be *nice* about it. Ugh."

"Probably." Riley grinned. "But you know what he won't be? Worried that you secretly judged him all these years."

"I'm going to remember this next time you're ducking Aidan's calls."

"Like Aidan would ever call. He'd just text. And email. God, I wish sometimes I could block his email address."

"Really?" Landry frowned. "What does he email you?"

"Nope," Riley said. "We're not going there. You don't need to get that overprotective look in your eye, thinking about defending me."

"I know," Landry said, but he was still thinking it. He couldn't help himself.

"I can take care of Aidan myself. Been doing it for years."

"You have," Landry agreed. "Still...I could talk to him, reason with him, at least get him off your case."

Riley shot him a look. "Go call Logan before I decide to stop being nice to you."

"Ooooh," Landry teased. "I like the sound of that."

He did. Way too much.

"Yeah, I bet you do," Riley said. But then he picked up his knife again like Landry wasn't balanced on his own knife's edge of desire and restraint.

It was that particular fact—that he *wanted* to damn his concerns to hell and walk over to where Riley was chopping broccoli and kiss him until neither of them could think of why this was a terrible idea—that pushed him to get up and walk out of the room, tugging his phone out of his pocket as he walked towards the front stoop.

There were some things he had a feeling were going to come up that Riley definitely did not need to overhear.

"Hey," Logan said after only one ring, as Landry settled down on the first step. "You ducking me?"

"No." *Lie*. "There was just something I needed to do first."

He could feel Logan's indecision. Call him on the obvious bullshit, or be nice and maybe get more out of him.

"You gonna tell me what was more important than talking to your favorite brother?" Logan asked archly.

"I'm gonna plead the fifth on that one," Landry said, chuckling under his breath. "Only 'cause you'll tell Levi, and then he'll come kill me."

How had the youngest Banks brother ended up the biggest of all three? Nobody was sure, but it was a fact he liked to lord over both his older brothers.

"Maybe *I'm* gonna come up there and kill you. That's a pretty big secret you've been holdin' onto, Landry." Logan's tone was reproachful.

He's not gonna judge you. Landry reminded himself of Riley's speech. *He's not gonna think you secretly judged him, either.*

"It's...it's new," Landry admitted. "I would've told you ages ago if I'd known, but I didn't."

Logan was silent for a long moment. Long enough Landry squirmed internally. Maybe Riley had been wrong. Maybe Logan *was* thinking of exactly what Landry had worried so much about.

"Hey, that's great. I'm really happy for you, bro," Logan said.

"You're surprised," Landry said.

"Well, *yeah*, a little. But not unhappy. I think it's really cool, and I *am* happy for you. You gonna tell me who he is?"

Landry rolled his eyes. "How do you know there's a *he*?"

This was exactly why he'd come outside to talk to Logan. Because, of course, he'd guess. And there was no way he was going to talk about Riley in *front* of Riley, even though he probably suspected he might be the origin of Landry's bisexual awakening.

"Because you're thirty-one, and Levi and I spent enough time talking about hot guys in front of you, there *has* to be one."

Okay, yeah, it was pretty obvious there was one.

"So," Logan continued, "who's the hot guy? He must be *really* hot to turn your head."

"You know that normally doesn't matter to me," Landry grumbled. It was the truth. He didn't get his head turned by looks often.

But then people didn't usually look like *Riley* either.

Or be so confident and capable, either.

The truth was, maybe Riley's looks had clued him in, but it was the rest of him that kept Landry interested.

"I do, but I know it was someone. So just tell me," Logan said. He was being nice. He probably deserved to know.

Frankly, Landry didn't want to resist that much because he *wanted* to talk about Riley.

"He's...well, he's the worst person I could be feeling this about," Landry admitted.

"Isn't that always the case?" Logan sounded amused now.

"Apparently. It's Riley Flynn. Aidan's little brother."

There was silence again on the other end of the line.

Landry laughed nervously. "Was that the final nail in your coffin, bro?"

"No, I'm just...you don't fuck around, Landry."

"Believe me, I *know*," Landry said. "My best friend's little brother. My new quarterback. My *roommate*. It's..."

"No, I mean, *Jesus fucking Christ*. I didn't realize Riley Flynn was all grown up." Logan sounded confounded. "I just googled him and about dropped my phone."

"You're a happily settled man," Landry reminded him.

"I know, I *am*. I absolutely fucking adore Dylan, but *Jesus*."

"Dylan's great." He loved his brother's boyfriend. He was exactly what Logan needed.

"When I said you don't fuck around, I mean, you got good taste. *Real* good taste."

"Aidan's probably going to kill me," Landry said.

"Oh, definitely. But think of how good you're gonna have it before certain death occurs."

That was the rub, wasn't it?

"Nothing...uh...nothing's happened."

"What are you waiting for?" Logan asked curiously. "I mean, clearly you like him. *Look at him*. He's living in your house, *that work of art is living in your house,* and you still haven't made a move?"

Landry laughed because if he didn't laugh, he was probably going to cry. "He thought I was *straight*, Logan."

"Yeah, so did you before you saw him." Logan was laughing now, too, and maybe it should've annoyed Landry because his brother was giving him shit, but it was impossible not to join in.

"I know. I *know*."

"Oh, you do. So, you need advice?" Logan was absolutely rubbing his hands together in metaphorical glee right now.

"Advice on how to make a move? No. *No*."

"I don't know, I kinda think you do. So does he know he's turned you *not so straight?*"

Landry rolled his eyes. "He didn't turn me *not straight*. I'm not Riley-sexual." Except...maybe he was.

"Oh, I like that. Riley-sexual. We're gonna use that."

"Don't you dare text that to Levi."

"I wouldn't dare. It's too lame to be contained in a text message. He's gonna get a full run-down after this. Lyla, too."

"Great," Landry said weakly.

"So does Riley know or not?"

"He knows I'm not straight, yes," Landry said. "Not that he did it. Because he *didn't*."

"If you say so, bro," Logan said. "I kinda think you should've led with that."

"Really?"

"Well, yeah, at least if you're going for the hot gay porn angle."

"I'm not," Landry said flatly. Though now he was thinking about it and sort of hating his brother for bringing it up.

"Okay, alternatively, you could catch him in the hallway right after a shower, you know, when he's wearing just a towel. I'm looking at this picture right now of him in...well, not much of anything, and I'm telling you that's an *excellent* plan."

"Logan!" Landry exclaimed in a strangled voice. "Are you checking out my...my...uh..."

"The love of your life? Oh, don't worry. It's on his Instagram. You can look at it later when you're alone. Make sure you're alone. And?"

"And?"

"And you can thank me for that suggestion. Once for every time you get yourself—"

"You're the worst," Landry interrupted before his brother could continue down that particular path. "Do you have any *actual* suggestions?"

"Yeah." Logan's voice went quiet and serious. "Just tell him. It's a classic for a reason."

"I don't know if he's even into me like that."

"You're his brother's best friend. And let's face it, you've got a whole look of your own goin' on," Logan pointed out wryly. "You're a Banks. You're hardly painful on the eyes. So he probably had some kind of feelings about you back in the day. You just gotta remind him of that."

"Are you saying Riley had a crush on me?"

"I'm saying it wouldn't be an outrageous possibility."

"So you think I should just tell him. Even though he's flirting all the time with Carter and—"

"Carter?" Logan interrupted. "Carter Maxwell?"

"That's the one," Landry said heavily.

"Riley Flynn isn't going to be interested in *Carter Maxwell.* Landry, you are not thinking straight." Logan chuckled. "*Really* not thinking straight."

"Yes, I know. We've established that," Landry said with a wry voice.

"Carter flirts with everyone."

"I know."

"What I mean is...you've got nothing to worry about."

"I'm glad you're so confident about this," Landry retorted sarcastically.

"I am. And so would you if you could hear yourself. Just...I don't know, seduce him in the kitchen or something."

"Or something?"

Logan laughed. "Just saying, it worked out great for me."

Chapter 7

Landry did not seduce Riley in the kitchen.

It wasn't even a near thing.

When he finally finished up with Logan's *advice*, he came back in and smelled something delicious.

It didn't happen to be Riley, but it did happen to be whatever Riley was cooking.

"Perfect timing," Riley said as he pulled a casserole dish out of the oven. "Let's eat."

They ate in front of the TV, but this time, Landry, sensing that Riley didn't need any more football on his mind, put on a mindless movie with lots and lots of explosions.

Then, afterwards, they went to bed.

Separately.

Landry told himself he was not disappointed and meant it.

Mostly.

But of course, instead of actually going to sleep, he lay in bed and played out the conversation he'd had with Logan over and over in his mind.

Just tell him, Logan had said. Except it wasn't all that easy. Because if he told Riley, *I think I like you*, it wouldn't just be a fleeting thing.

Not for him, and hopefully not for Riley, either. It wouldn't just be scratching a convenient itch.

Speaking of itches...well, he was feeling one now.

For Riley freaking Flynn.

What he needed was something to distract him from the burning irritation just under his skin. The one he wasn't going to scratch. Because Riley was just down the hall, and that felt...really not okay. They were *friends*. Even though the image of Riley's sweatpants-clad ass was burned behind his eyelids and he couldn't seem to clear it.

Landry grabbed his phone from the charger, deciding he just needed something else.

Of course that was when he remembered what else Logan had suggested. *You can look at it later when you're alone.*

Clearly, Riley's Instagram feed wasn't going to solve his problem, but then Landry wasn't a hundred percent convinced he *wanted* it solved.

He clicked the app open, and after that, it was easy enough to find Riley's account.

The moment it opened, he dropped the phone, then had to scramble to pick it right back up again.

The last photo Riley had posted was a selfie. He wasn't wearing a shirt—or probably anything else either, if where the photo cut off was any indication—and his entire tanned torso was on full display. Landry's fingers trembled on the edges of his phone.

He wanted to know what Riley looked like just past those insane ridges of his abs. Wanted to see Riley shoot *him* that hungry, hot stare with those incredible sea-blue eyes.

No wonder Logan had just about swallowed his tongue when Landry had told him.

Riley-sexual, that's what you are.

The itch intensified until it felt like a live wire just under his skin.

He shifted uncomfortably in his very comfortable bed. Would it be wrong to just...*try it*? Wrong to just slide his hand down, where his cock was hard and aching, pressing against his briefs?

It didn't feel so wrong right now.

It felt like the most natural thing in the whole fucking world.

And yet, Riley was just down the hallway. Believing he'd helped Landry out tonight, giving him that much-needed pep talk and then cooking him freaking dinner.

He'd been a generous friend, and how was Landry going to pay him back?

By creeping onto his Instagram and jerking off to his selfies.

Landry tossed the phone on the bed and groaned, scrubbing a hand across his face.

No matter how much he wanted it—and he wanted it really goddamn bad, thank you very much—he couldn't.

He just couldn't.

But he just couldn't lay here either and be tempted by it.

He pushed himself out of bed and opened the door into the hallway.

The house felt dark and quiet. Riley was probably sleeping soundly, with no idea of the kind of quandary Landry was going through.

Stepping into the hallway, he thought he was safe.

He'd just go downstairs, have a cold drink of water, and think of anything but the way Riley had looked in that post.

He was so preoccupied trying *not* to think about Riley—Riley grinning up at him, with that knowing look in his eyes, Riley reaching for him, Riley *naked*—that he didn't notice until the last moment the bathroom light was on.

Then it wasn't.

And then Riley was in the hall, too.

Naked.

Okay, with a towel draped around his waist.

But he was naked *enough.*

"Oh, *oh*," Landry stammered, stopping in his tracks.

Fucking Logan.

He'd suggested this earlier, and Landry had thought even the idea of it was insane.

Hot, but insane.

You could catch him in the hallway right after a shower, you know, when he's wearing just a towel.

However, staring at Riley now, it felt a little less insane. A lot hotter, too.

The night light he'd put in next to the top of the stairs illuminated Riley just enough.

Just enough that Landry could see all that bare skin.

The bare skin he'd *just* been attempting to erase from his uncooperative brain.

Riley frowned. But didn't move.

Landry's gaze was stuck right where Riley's hands held the towel closed. If it slid another inch lower, he might see everything he'd fantasized about when he'd stared at that selfie.

"Couldn't sleep either?" Riley asked.

Somehow, it was *worse* that it wasn't just Landry feeling this way.

"Uh, no, not really." Landry wet his lips. Realized, just as Riley's gaze caught on his own body, that *he* wasn't exactly fully clothed either.

They had exactly a towel and a pair of briefs between them and total nakedness in this dark hallway.

Like this was going to help him sleep any better.

He cleared his throat. "Nervous about the game?"

Riley was still staring at his chest.

Did it have *Sorry, I almost jerked off to you* written across it in bright red letters?

Landry wouldn't have been surprised.

"I guess," Riley said. "Couldn't get my brain to settle, so I thought a hot shower might help."

As if he needed any more reminders that Riley was wet and naked and *right fucking there*.

In the semi-darkness, he looked even better than he did in the daylight. That should've been impossible, but maybe it was because right now, Landry could reach out and pull him close. Touch him the way he'd imagined he wanted to back in bed.

"It help?" If he took a shower, it was definitely going to have to be of the cold variety.

Ice fucking cold.

"No," Riley said, chuckling humorlessly.

"Oh."

"What were you doing?" Riley asked.

God, what had *he been doing?*

He didn't know anything. His brain was one long litany of: *Riley, naked, skin, smooth, muscles, touch, want.*

"I...uh...yeah...*water*," Landry croaked.

Riley smiled. "Right. You enjoy that water. I'm gonna..." He gestured towards the bedroom door behind Landry. "Try to sleep, I guess."

"Yeah."

The door to the guest bedroom was behind him, and he realized it a second too late because then Riley was brushing against him as he walked past, leaving every hair on Landry's body raised with electricity.

It was just Riley's arm brushing against his own bare arm, but it not only totally banished the idea of grabbing a cold drink of water, but every good intention he'd ever had.

The moment Riley's door was closed, he moved, heading back down the hallway to his bedroom, feet carrying him fast, every molecule of his body focused on only one thing.

Being alone.

The moment he slammed the door shut behind him, Landry fell against it, and this time, he didn't hesitate.

He reached down and groaned under his breath as his palm rubbed over his cock.

What would it feel like if it was Riley touching him like this?

How would it feel if he got to touch *Riley* like this?

Landry's head hit the back of the door as he continued rubbing himself. He was so worked up, so ready, had been for what felt like *days*, but truthfully, he'd felt this desperate since the moment Riley had pulled off his helmet weeks ago.

But ever since he'd seen that particular picture?

Now, the want was somehow a *need*.

He closed his eyes, and it wasn't difficult at all to remember it perfectly. Every pixel of it was emblazoned in his brain.

Riley had smelled so good as he'd walked past him in the hallway. He'd have smelled even better up close if Landry had sunk to his knees and tugged the towel away and worshiped the cut lines of his abs, then lower, at the crease of his thigh, and then even lower still, where Landry imagined he'd been hard and ready for him.

He'd never been interested in another man's cock before, but there was no denying he was incredibly interested in Riley's.

He wanted to touch it, to smell it, to *taste* it. He wanted to slide it into his mouth and feel the way Riley vibrated at the sheer pleasure of it. He was desperate to know how Riley's skin felt under his tongue, at how he might shake with need if Landry teased him.

As he stroked his cock over his briefs, the fabric making him more sensitive, not less, he imagined Riley surprising him just like this.

The way his impossibly blue eyes would darken and heat up. Just like molten glass. The way he'd reach for Landry.

He'd tremble against Landry as they kissed.

Then shiver as Landry pinned him back against the door and touched him in every way he could imagine.

Maybe he didn't have any experience making a guy feel good, but he'd gratefully learn at the altar of Riley's body. Maybe it wouldn't be so hard; after all, he knew how to make *himself* feel good.

He was doing it right now, stroking harder and faster, and a moment later, thinking of the way Riley might taste ripe on his lips, his orgasm hit him.

Landry's hands shook as he came down from the high.

That had been so good—so goddamn *amazing*, in fact—he couldn't even fathom how much better it might've been if it hadn't just been all his imagination.

Told you so.

Paige's text to the one Riley had sent the night before came through just as they finished the walk-through the night before the game.

His first game.

His nerves vibrated not only with anxiousness at the importance of his performance tomorrow, but at the whole situation with Landry.

He knew what that undeniable tension was between them.

After he'd resisted every urge to just grab the reins on the situation and admit he suspected why Landry was having his sexual awakening.

Touch him the way Landry clearly wanted to touch.

But he hadn't because what if he was wrong?

What if it fucked everything up?

He hadn't worked *this hard* to just throw it all away because his dick was hard for one of his teammates.

After their hallway run-in, he'd returned to his room, hard and aching underneath the towel, and stretching out on the bed, he'd typed out a text to Paige.

The hours she kept meant she probably wouldn't reply right away—working as an assistant to a costume designer on one of the big soaps meant she had late nights and even earlier mornings, and often she was too busy for big stretches to even surface for air. But eventually, she would, and she'd see his message.

I think your two weeks might've been conservative, Riley sent.

And now she'd finally replied.

Told you so.

Yeah, she had. She'd tried, anyway, and he'd brushed off her certainty because he'd still been trying to pretend Landry was straight.

But now he couldn't anymore because *Landry* wasn't pretending anymore.

Maybe it was inevitable something would happen between them.

"You look fucking dialed in. You looking up how to demolish the Commanders on your phone, huh?"

Riley glanced up. Carter was standing in front of him, grinning annoyingly.

"No," he said. "I was texting a friend."

"A friend that's a *girl*?" Carter leaned in, leering a little. "Thought you were into something a little different."

"No, *you* thought I was into Landry." The most obnoxious part of Carter was that he wasn't a total moron and apparently had at least one observational molecule in his brain because he'd guessed Riley's crush embarrassingly quickly.

You can't call it a crush. You had a crush at fifteen. At sixteen. At eighteen.

But he was twenty-four now, and it was definitely not just a crush anymore.

Back then, he wouldn't have known exactly what he wanted to do to Landry—what he'd want Landry to do to him—but now? He was familiar with all the intimate, explicit details.

It wasn't just sex; he wanted more, too. He wanted to sit on Landry's couch and for Landry to put an arm around him, to tug him close, just *feel* him against his side. Big and steady and loyal. Wanted Landry to always have his back. Craved the thought of Landry telling Aidan to fuck off, even though if it ever became one hundred percent necessary, he *was* capable of doing it himself. Dreamed of him just standing there as Riley did it himself, encouraging him with every moment he didn't try to defend Aidan's overbearing behavior.

Imagined throwing Landry a touchdown pass tomorrow and how right it would feel to celebrate in the end zone with him.

Riley already knew it wouldn't feel the same as if he tossed one to Carter.

"You wanted me to be him just now," Carter said. Still grinning obnoxiously. "You know it, don't even try to pretend."

"So you say," Riley retorted.

"You're always looking for him. In the locker room. On the field. The sideline," Carter said.

"I do not," Riley said, even though he had a terrible sinking feeling Carter wasn't wrong.

He shoved his phone back into his pocket. "You feel good about tomorrow?"

Carter shrugged. "I guess. We've won one preseason game and lost another. But this'll be our first with you under center. No idea what's gonna happen."

Riley didn't either, and that was nerve-wracking.

Maybe that was why he kept seeking Landry's figure out today.

He felt like something steady when he'd been dropped into the eye of a hurricane.

But even as he thought it, he knew that wasn't right either. He wanted to see Landry because he was *Landry*.

Yeah, not just a crush. He could imagine Paige telling him that bluntly.

It wasn't like he'd needed her tough love to convince him, but he couldn't deny her words *were* opening up his eyes.

Something was going to happen.

The only question was *what* and *when*.

"You wanna go out with me? Sneak out of the hotel? Find something to take your mind off..." Carter gestured around. "All this?"

"No, no thanks, I'm good." Riley shot him a look he hoped was tough. "And neither will you."

"What?" Carter exclaimed, sounding disappointed.

"Nope. We're both gonna go up to our rooms and stay in them until tomorrow morning."

"You're the worst," Carter said. "I thought, you know, *Riley Flynn*, he's Aidan's little bro. He'll be fun to have around. Not a total buzzkill."

"I'm not here to be fun. I'm here to win football games." It was the truth. And really, it didn't sting that Carter had compared him to his brother. Because winning the game tomorrow would take all that pain away.

"Fine, fine," Carter grumbled. "Let's go up to our rooms then. You think they'll get pissed if I order porn?"

Riley didn't know and decided he didn't want to ask. He shrugged.

"Ah, well, there's always Pornhub," Carter said as they headed towards the elevator bank at the team hotel.

"Right." Riley wasn't going to think about porn or *sex* because if he did, maybe he'd be tempted, even a little bit, to pull a Carter Maxwell and sneak out.

And not just sneak out, but sneak *into* Landry's room.

Landry watched as Riley disappeared into the elevator with Carter and tried very hard not to glower about it.

First, because if Riley really liked Carter, then that was a hard reality he was going to have to get used to.

Second, if he did, someone might see, and they might put two and two together and get four. And while that might be the correct answer, it was already hard enough dealing with Deacon and Jem teasing him.

It certainly didn't help they were *right*.

Landry scanned the dwindling number of players in the ballroom, everyone heading off to do their normal pre-game routine and knew what he should do.

What he *should* do was go to his room, take a long, hot shower, and mentally prepare for the game tomorrow. Visualize himself catching passes. Blocking well and protecting Riley's flank.

What he *wanted* to do was not the same. He wanted to do some visualizations of an entirely different nature.

If he went back to his room alone, it seemed inevitable that he'd lose what was left of his normally strong self-control and touch himself again with a vision of Riley in his head.

Inwardly, he groaned.

He'd worked hard this morning so things wouldn't be awkward after last night.

But still, when he'd faced Riley for the first time after coming his brains out, thinking about touching him, thinking about the way his body might feel under his hands, he'd struggled to not flush bright, screaming red.

He'd expected Riley to ask why he was acting so weird because even though he'd attempted normal, Landry knew he hadn't succeeded. But Riley hadn't. He'd pretended like they hadn't run into each other practically naked in the hallway the night before.

If he can do it, so can I, Landry thought stubbornly.

His phone dinged in his pocket.

Landry had thought the worst thing that could happen tonight was Riley heading off with Carter, but no, this was definitely way worse.

The message was from Aidan and was a bucketful of freezing cold water on his libido.

What was he doing? Fantasizing about Aidan's little brother?

But that was the biggest issue, wasn't it? Riley wasn't just Aidan's little brother anymore. He wasn't the kid. He was *Riley*—and Landry couldn't help the very un-fraternal feelings he was having about him.

However, Aidan wouldn't understand.

He'd be furious.

Take care of him, he'd yell at Landry. *I told you to take care of him, not fuck him.*

I texted you three times, Aidan's message said, **but you keep ghosting me. Are things going that bad?**

Landry leaned against the wall and rolled his eyes. Of course that was Aidan's first thought.

Probably way down on the list—or not on the list *at all*—was the concept that Landry had ignored his texts because he hadn't known what to say.

Oh, yeah, Riley's doing good. He's so fucking good. He's...

Looks good? You better fucking believe how great he looks.

We're getting along awesome. Better than awesome. He keeps flirting with me, and I keep loving it.

No, was all Landry replied with.

What else could he say?

Surely, Aidan wasn't totally in the dark because Landry was certain he'd been talking to Riley. And no doubt Riley could talk to him without feeling like he was hiding something intrinsically important from Aidan. No doubt he could describe how things were going without an added and heaping dose of guilt.

He slipped his phone back into his pocket and decided to focus on that guilt.

Maybe it would help him keep his hands in his pockets and out of his pants. Even when he took that hot shower and…

Just when he hit the elevator bank, the phone rang.

Of course it was Aidan.

"What the fuck," Aidan said loudly as soon as Landry answered the phone. "You duck me for *days,* and then when I ask you why all you say is *no*. No elaboration, nothing. Just *no*."

"No, it's not going that bad," Landry said, focusing on keeping his voice even and casual.

"Well, of course it isn't, Riley might not be suited to this, but he's not an idiot," Aidan grumbled.

"I'm shocked to hear you actually believe that," Landry said, reaching over to hit the button for his floor.

"Are you going to tell me what's going on or not?" Aidan demanded.

"Don't you have a game of your own to prepare for?"

"I'm not playing tomorrow," Aidan said. Which was pretty typical. A lot of existing starters didn't play in the final preseason game. But most of the Condors' offense was because Riley was new, and they were still trying to find their rhythm.

He'd guessed Aidan wouldn't be playing, but Landry had hoped by shifting the topic of conversation back to Aidan, he'd get distracted and forget why he'd really called.

But Riley wasn't the only Flynn who wasn't an idiot.

"And," Aidan continued, "don't change the subject."

"I wouldn't," Landry protested.

"I'm not stupid, and I wasn't born yesterday. You are the most fucking reliable texter I know, and somehow you've just *forgotten* to reply to me *three* times? I don't buy it. Something's going on."

"God, you're the most paranoid person I know," Landry argued. There was no denying the nice healthy dose of guilt currently pulsing in his gut as the elevator stopped at his floor. "Nothing's going on. He came here. He's playing great. We're working hard. Beginning of story and end of story."

"You don't mind having him underfoot?"

The irony of Aidan suddenly caring about whether it was inconvenient for Riley to move in. Landry didn't roll his eyes again. But he wanted to.

"He's not a child, Aidan. He's a grown person who unsurprisingly is completely able to take care of himself."

Aidan was quiet for a moment.

"It's just..."

"You're lagging behind in the running for Overprotective Brother of the Year?"

"No," Aidan said forcefully.

"Then what is it?"

But Landry already knew what it was. He wouldn't have given Aidan so much shit if he didn't.

"You know what it is," Aidan said. "*Annoyingly.*"

"Yes, I think you really regret getting ridiculously drunk during spring break our sophomore year and telling me all about how you two grew up." Landry said it kindly. Because Aidan probably did regret it.

For someone who was always ready to talk himself up and repeat every bit of praise he'd ever gotten and every award he'd ever been given, Aidan was surprisingly close-lipped about the real accomplishment: practically raising his younger brother when he was just a kid himself.

"But here's the thing, the *craziest* thing. You did good with him. You protected him and took care of him when your parents didn't give a shit. And then he grew up, and you freaked and went totally overboard," Landry said sternly, pulling his keycard out of his back pocket and letting himself into his sterile, unfriendly hotel room. At least it was empty. Because he wasn't a rookie, he wasn't required to share.

Of course, how many times in the last week had he considered suggesting to Riley that they double up?

For completely innocent reasons, *of course.*

"I didn't go overboard," Aidan insisted. "He...well, he wants things that aren't good for him."

"Hard disagree," Landry said. "He knows, more than anyone, more than even *you*, what he's capable of. I saw it myself in practice this week. He's got this, and you being a dick about it is only going to drive him away."

"What about me being a dick about other things?" Aidan joked.

"Well, *that's* a given." Landry sat down on the edge of the bed.

"So, there's really nothing else going on? You swear?"

Landry had never lied to his best friend before. He'd never imagined he might be forced into a position where that seemed like the best option.

After all, there wasn't anything to tell anyway, he reasoned. Riley probably didn't feel the same as he did. What was the point of confessing the truth to Aidan if nothing ever came of it? He'd just piss his best friend off for no reason whatsoever.

"Pinky swear," Landry said lightly.

Later, *much* later, when Riley was not living in his house, and Landry had gotten some proper distance from the situation when he'd really begun to realize what his shifting sexuality might mean, then he'd tell Aidan.

He'd never have to know the origin of it was Riley.

"And tomorrow," Aidan said, voice growing hard, "you make sure you block the shit out of anyone who wants to destroy him, okay?"

"As if I'd do anything different." Landry paused, hesitating. "But you know, the guy can practically bench press an elephant. The person who makes it hardest to destroy Riley is *Riley*."

Aidan hummed under his breath. "Yeah, I know he's worked hard to bulk up."

"It's not just bulking up." Landry had a dim idea that his mouth was running away with this, but he couldn't seem to stop it. "The man's pure muscle. Every inch of him is stacked with it."

Landry told himself he didn't imagine the surprised silence coming from Aidan's end.

Then, as bad as this had been, as much guilt as he'd take to the grave over this conversation, it got *worse*. "You checkin' out my brother?" Aidan joked.

But underneath the teasing tone was an undeniable concern.

Jesus, not only had he walked right into that, Landry had somehow managed to re-activate Overprotective Brother Bot.

Shit.

"Oh, don't be ridiculous," Landry said.

"I'm not being ridiculous. It's not...it's not out of the question."

Landry's mind raced. He couldn't tell the truth. But he couldn't tell Aidan a bald-faced lie either by saying he was straight when he most definitely knew he was not. The rest of this would be hard enough, but he could never live with himself if he did that.

"What if someone told *you* it wasn't out of the question?" Landry didn't wait for Aidan to answer. "Now you know how ridiculous it is."

"I..." Aidan stammered. "Well, of course. *Of course.*"

"See? Ridiculous. Now power down, Overprotective Brother Bot."

"I hate you," Aidan said, but it was clear from his tone he didn't. Not at all.

"No, you don't."

Aidan sighed. "Have a good game, okay?"

"Plan on it," Landry said.

When he finally tossed the phone down on the bed, the horrible conversation blissfully over, Landry was at least not in the mood to hop into the shower and lean against the back wall, and let the hot water run over him, dreaming the whole time it was Riley's hands. Or even more...Riley's *mouth*.

At least there was that.

CHAPTER 8

Riley told himself very firmly he was not going to throw up.

He'd come onto the field for warmups early because sitting in the locker room, just sitting there and staring at the floor, imagining the way the game might go, made him nearly sick.

Maybe visualizations worked for some players, but for Riley, they just made him imagine all the ways everything could go wrong.

But then he'd come out onto the field and heard the cheers as people recognized the name on the back of his jersey, and the pressure had hit him like a freight train.

Right to the stomach.

"You good, rook?"

Riley looked up, and Jem was standing in front of him, a wry grin on his face.

"I'm not a rookie," Riley said. But he *felt* like one.

The last time he'd played in an NFL game, he'd been standing on the sideline, holding a clipboard.

He wasn't the one expected to take this team to the field and then *lead* this team. In that respect, he was absolutely a rookie.

"Sure you are," Jem said kindly. "And it's okay to be totally freaking out right now."

"Did you?" Riley bent over and checked the ties on his cleats. He'd probably done it a million times since he was eleven, and he'd demanded he follow in his older brother's footsteps. But it had never felt as vitally important as it did now that his shoes stay firmly on his feet.

"Um, *yeah*," Jem said. "I nearly shit myself every single play. I got bowled over by a lineman half my size because I couldn't get my head in the game. But you—" He paused. "You're not gonna do that, Flynn."

Riley wasn't so sure.

Of course, he'd been in tough, stressful spots before.

That first game in Pittsburgh, when everyone had been expecting him to fail, and he knew he couldn't? He'd been a wreck.

But he'd still gone on the field and done exactly what he'd prepared for.

You can do that again.

"You're not," Jem repeated and reached down, giving him a reassuring tap on his shoulder pad. "You see how many fans are in this stadium sporting brand-new Flynn jerseys? You got this."

"Thanks," Riley said. Stood. Felt reasonably sure he was *not* going to puke this time. "You know, anytime you want a job as a motivational speaker, it's yours."

Jem grinned. "Thanks, rook. That means a lot. We can't play this game forever."

"Hey, at least *rook* is better than *the kid*," Riley said.

"Who calls you that?" Jem looked confused as they headed out onto the field for warmups. "Not Landry, right?"

"My idiot brother." Riley rolled his eyes. "No, *not* Landry."

"Didn't think so," Jem teased.

"It's not—" Riley was going to say *again* that it wasn't like that between him and Landry. But before he could, Jem interrupted him.

"Yeah, it probably is. But hey, that's cool. We told you it was."

"You and Deacon did, yeah. But…" Riley trailed off as they reached the center of the field.

"No buts," Jem said firmly. He patted him on the shoulder again. "You're good, rook."

"I'm…I *am* good." Riley grinned wildly. He did have this. Didn't he have all the tools he needed? Didn't he believe—at one point, more than anyone else—he possessed all the skills he'd need to succeed in the NFL?

He was going to prove everyone wrong.

Starting with his brother.

"You just got this super fierce look in your eye," Charlie said after he jogged over. "Should I be afraid right now?"

"Not you," Riley said. "But the Commanders? Yeah, they should be fucking terrified."

"Yeah, they should be. You've been tearin' it up in practice," Charlie said. "You ready to warm up?"

"Yep," Riley said. "I'm ready now." And he felt like he really *was*.

The nerves hadn't melted away, but he was using them as fuel now.

They finished warming up, Riley tossing passes back and forth to Charlie, and then he joined the running backs for their own drills, making sure his muscles were awake and ready to go at a moment's notice.

Then they returned to the locker room for one last word from Coach Kelley before they entered the stadium.

Riley knew before, during the Tom Taylor era, the Condors had been hard-edged and aggressive, picking the Beastie Boys' *Sabotage* for their entrance music.

It had felt appropriate for so many reasons, considering how many terrible stories had come out of that time.

But Grant Green, the new owner of the Condors, had done a total sweep, changing even the team's entrance to the field.

It had been enough of a spectacle—the lyrics so appropriate to the situation—that even deep in his playing time in Pittsburgh, he'd heard about the change.

After the first game, Green had given an interview, talking about why they'd selected this particular song. "*We have a lot to prove, a lot to overcome,*" he'd said. "*We aren't going to sabotage anyone, not anymore. That's not our new way. Our way is to take a chance and achieve what I believe we're capable of. That's why I changed the music to* We Own It *because we have to own what happened before we can rise above it.*"

The owner's words had resonated with Riley, and when he'd met Green in person—who'd *refused* to let him call him Mr. Green, but suggested Mr. G instead—had insisted that he wasn't just interested in building a winning team but a winning team who took responsibility for their choices.

The Condors couldn't change who they'd been before, just like Riley couldn't change his size—but they *could* rise above it.

As they returned to the locker room, he caught sight of Mr. G leaning against the far wall, looking like one of their younger coaches, or even a *fan*, not like the owner of the team. Riley could sympathize with the way his body looked tense with nerves, his dark eyes intensely focused on the center of the room as Coach Kelley walked in.

"Gather up," Coach said, and everyone did, drawing in closer so they could hear their coach. He wasn't a particularly tough or blood-thirsty guy, which Riley liked. But he *was* competitive. He wanted to win. Just like Riley. "Maybe this is *only* a preseason game, but each time we take the field together, it matters. Your intent matters. Your execution matters. Your play *matters*. So make each down count. Remember, we're rising above it. No matter what crap people say to you, I don't want to see any bullshit penalties, okay?"

Riley leaned over. Carter was sitting next to him, staring at the floor. "That happen?" he asked, surprised.

"Oh yeah," Carter said in a flat voice. "You know, it's all that regular bullshit, plus extra. People really didn't like the shit that came out about the bounties the defense took out on some of the Piranhas players."

"But that's not...that's not *us*," Riley said. He hadn't expected this, but he supposed he should've. The NFL, in general, had turned against the Condors during the last season, and then there had been that last playoff game against the Piranhas when they'd gone after them with a fury that you rarely saw on a football field.

Players had gotten injured. And that, apparently, had been the last straw for the NFL because they'd stepped in. Forced the team to be sold, and then *Mr. G* had bought it, vowing to turn the culture around.

Riley supposed some players didn't want to let go of their anger.

"I thought it would get better this year. Sort of," Carter said with a shrug. "But it's okay. Like you said, it's not us."

In front of them, Coach Kelley was wrapping up. "No bullshit penalties," he repeated. "If you're being targeted, let me or one of the coaches know. We want to know. We want to combat this the right way. And with that in mind, Deacon's going to say a few words to you, too."

The big defensive end took the floor next.

"Coach Kelley is right," Deacon said slowly, his voice carrying in a way that Coach Kelley's didn't. It reached every corner of the big locker room. "Last year was fucked. Not everyone thinks we've changed, but I was here last year. I *know* we've changed. I know it in every bone in this body. Every fucking muscle. I know we've got a ways to go, but that doesn't mean we can give up now. This is the beginning. Let's make it a good one." Deacon raised his fist. Riley's blood pumped harder, faster. He felt the push now, not just the nerves, but the determination that took him over every single game. "Fly Condors!"

Riley had always thought the Condors' catchphrase was kind of stupid, but hearing it in Deacon's voice, the fervent belief in this team's possibilities obvious in his voice, it was so easy to get caught up and chant it right back to the team captain.

When they rushed out onto the field, Riley found himself believing, too. Believing in the idea of redemption.

Of second chances.

Of *first* chances.

Because this was his.

And he was going to make the most of it.

It seemed like Riley wasn't the only one.

When he took the field for the first time, the rest of the offense surrounding him, the sheer noise from the crowd was almost deafening.

They think you can do this, Riley told himself, and then he narrowed his focus on the task ahead of him.

The defense had done their jobs during the first drive, forcing the Commanders to turn the ball over around mid-field.

After the Commanders punted, downing the ball at the fucking two-yard line, Riley eyed the remaining ninety-eight yards to the end zone.

One yard at a time.

That was one of Aidan's favorite sayings, and at least in this moment, it fit.

Coach Oscar called in the play through Riley's headset, and after he listened to it twice, making sure he got it, he leaned into the huddle.

"Hey, guys," he said, and there were a few nervous chuckles around him.

He got it. He was new, and while he might've been running practice the last three days, nobody knew what to really make of him yet.

Riley met Landry's gaze. "You got this," he said quietly with undeniable certainty.

He called out the play. Met every player's eyes one by one, making sure they understood. Because while he might be the newest guy on this team, he was indisputably their leader now.

Something Aidan had hounded into him until he felt like he could repeat it in his sleep.

You run the plays. You run the team. You got this. If you don't got it, then everyone's fucked. So you got this, you hear me, Riley?

He heard.

Challenge accepted.

The huddle broke up and they got set, Riley getting the first look at the defensive scheme they were setting up against him. Not surprisingly, the Commanders were loading the box, expecting he'd hand the football off to Darius or run himself.

They didn't think he had the balls to throw.

And checkmate.

Cole Johnson, the center, snapped the ball, and they'd worked together enough over the last few days that it landed perfectly in Riley's hands, and his mental clock started ticking down.

He only had a few precious seconds to throw.

But right off the bat, the Commanders' defense dug into the trenches, pushing hard, the offensive line moving backwards, forcing Riley to shift to the left, and then the right, eyes scanning the field for his first option, then the second, and then the third. Landry had fallen into blocking coverage. Carter was stuck in a serious double-team, and Nick was only slightly more open, but he was the best choice Riley could see.

He dodged further left, evading a defensive tackle coming in to flatten him like a pancake, and the weird roar of the crowd nearly stopped him up short, but he threw the ball anyway, watching as it arced over the defensive line, falling right into Nick's hands.

"Yes!" Riley screeched, fist-pumping as he nabbed the first down.

But there was something disconcerting in the way everyone's eyes wouldn't quite meet his, and they weren't celebrating.

"Dude," Carter said, slightly out of breath as he ran back towards where all the players gathered after the play, "you stepped right out of the end zone."

Riley stared at him.

Stared at the ref, who was currently bringing his hands over his head in the dreaded position that didn't mean touchdown. Nope, it meant that the Commanders had scored a safety, because Riley had been too fucking stupid to stay in the field.

"What, *no*," Riley said in disbelief, but as he looked upward, towards the huge video screen currently replaying his dumb ass blunder over and over, it was undeniable.

To avoid being tackled by that last defender, he'd stepped a few inches out of the back of the end zone.

Instead of giving the Condors a first down, instead of taking all his nerves and his preparation and all the work he'd done for so many years, he'd made them and *him*, an embarrassment.

"Hey, it's alright, you know, shit happens," Carter said. He shrugged because, for Carter Maxwell, *shit* did happen, and happened regularly.

"I know," Riley snapped, humiliation coalescing inside him in one nauseating ball.

Shit *did* happen, but not now, not like this, not to *him*.

Not when he needed to prove that the Condors had done the right thing signing him.

Not when he was trying to prove Aidan had been one hundred percent fucking wrong about him.

"It's all good," Cole said. "Let's regroup. Come on." The big center led them to the sideline, where Coach Kelley tried to put a good face on it.

"Riley, listen," he said, putting his arm around Riley, who felt torn between crying and throwing up. "It's all right. It's going to be just fine. We're fine. Right guys?"

Riley looked around as the players around him nodded in agreement.

His first NFL pass, and he'd stepped out of the back of the end zone, not even like a rookie might...like a freaking *idiot* might.

He was going to be on every Sports Center highlight reel from now until the end of time. He'd be the laughingstock of every late-night show and sports podcast. And then there was the inevitable email from Aidan...

Riley drew in a deep, shuddering breath. He was *good* at brushing things off. He'd had to learn to be. But this felt different, so much bigger than him, much too big to simply let go of.

"Hey," a voice next to him said, and it was sharper than he'd expected.

He looked up, and Landry was there, and he'd pulled his helmet off. "Hey," he repeated, reaching out and gripping his arm. "I need you to focus on me right now."

"What?" The crowd's screams nearly drowned him out, but Riley was pretty sure he'd heard him right.

"Focus on me," Landry said.

Riley did, and the look in his brown eyes felt like a hand reaching out. There was sympathy there because Landry didn't have a mean bone in his body, but also, there was an undeniable intensity.

Focus on me. What Landry had really meant was *we need to focus on the game. Don't let this overwhelm you.*

It nearly had.

He'd just been about to head down a black hole spiral, and Landry reaching out made him realize it.

"Right," Riley said and turned back to the players gathered around him. "We've got this. *I've* got this. Let's get some work done."

They only had a few moments to talk about adding in another tight end to help with blocking the defense, and then it was time for them to take the field again.

Landry watched as Riley shook off his frustration and anxiety and re-focused on the game.

It wasn't easy to do that.

In fact, he didn't know any quarterback who could've done what Riley had done and dealt with it so quickly.

Of course, he'd helped. He'd seen the panic and embarrassment in Riley's face, seen the terror that he'd be laughed at forever, and Landry had known exactly what lay at the bottom of that spiral.

Nothing good.

And goddamnit, Riley was not only his quarterback and the de facto leader of this team; Landry *cared* about him. He wanted him to succeed, not just because his success was tied, inevitably, to the Condors' success.

He wanted Riley to be able to shove his achievements into the faces of everyone who'd doubted him.

Even his brother.

Okay, who was he kidding? *Especially* his brother.

Riley called out the play, voice steady and eyes calm.

Landry took his position down the line and decided that, in some ways they were better off now, even though they were down by two points. The Commanders had pinned them to the two-yard line before. This kickoff hadn't been nearly as successful as their prior punt, and the Condors were beginning this drive on the twenty-five-yard line. With lots of room for Riley to make some magic happen and *not* go out of the field of play.

Not that he'd ever do *that* again.

Cole snapped the ball, and Landry pushed forward, at first using his big frame and strength to block one of the defensive ends coming for Riley.

Then when the end was shuffled off, away from Riley, Landry planted and took off in a quick sprint down the sideline, crossing over into the flat, and he had a fraction of a second to position himself after his turn before Riley threw the ball.

It was a tricky play to call so early on in their relationship because it depended almost entirely on timing, and they hadn't had much practice time together yet to develop that, but Landry already had an instinctual feel for how Riley played.

He turned, and then the ball flew through the air, one of Riley's fucking perfect spirals, and he caught it.

Turning up field, he shucked off the safety and, out of the corner of his eye, saw the corner change direction, and begin to cross over.

Ten yards. Twenty. The distance ticked off in Landry's head as he pushed his legs hard. He wasn't the fastest guy on the team—not even close—but he could make it happen when it counted, and he wanted a big play here to prove to Riley he could *do* this.

Sure, the stats were nice for him, too. And he wanted to see the Condors win, but this play mattered so much more than that.

This was Riley's pride on the line, and Landry discovered as he faced off with the corner coming for him that, in this moment, nothing was more important to him than that.

He shoved out an arm, hoping to stiff-arm the corner into submission, but the guy took a different angle than Landry had anticipated. Instead of being able to deal with him from the side, he was coming from the front, and he grabbed Landry by the middle and brought him down.

Still, Landry thought, trying to catch his breath as he lay on the turf, that was a fifty-yard play, *easy.*

A hand reached out to help him up, and to Landry's surprise, it wasn't the corner, but Riley, grinning wildly. He must've run all the way down the field to be the first one to celebrate with him.

"That was unreal," Riley told him as they huddled up again. "That stiff-arm was *sick.*"

"Could've been sicker," Landry said. Didn't say *I think I could've scored if I'd gotten that guy the right way.* Because it wasn't like a fifty-yard gain was anything to sniff at.

But he'd done what he'd intended, and those shadows, hiding in Riley's gaze, were gone.

He was clear-eyed and confident again.

Ready to take the Condors into the red zone and score.

Landry watched him as the huddle broke up.

This is just the beginning of the Riley Flynn era.

Three plays later, as Riley threw a gorgeous fucking pass to Carter in the back corner of the end zone, every player on the team and every fan in the stadium believed it.

I believed it first, Landry noted with satisfaction as they headed back to the sideline after the touchdown.

"Sorry," Riley said to him as they reached the bench.

"What? Excuse me?" Landry couldn't believe he was *apologizing.* For the safety, still? Or something else?

Riley shrugged. "I wanted to throw it to you. Get you the touchdown you didn't get on that long pass. But Carter was open..."

"Riley." Landry turned to face him and put his hands on Riley's shoulder pads. "No."

"No?"

"You don't get to apologize. Not for that. Ever. Okay? I don't care how many touchdowns I get. Carter was open. Unbelievably. Miraculously. You *should've* thrown to him."

"Right." But there was a glimmer of something Landry recognized in Riley's eyes as he sat down on the bench next to Charlie, who held out his Gatorade with one hand and a tablet with the other, so they could start reviewing the plays on that drive.

It was the same thing he'd felt when he'd caught the ball and had wanted so goddamn bad to erase the bad taste in Riley's mouth.

Not just because it would help him focus better and would help the Condors win.

No, he'd needed it so much more because, more than anything else, he wanted to see Riley's face light up with that smile. The one that said *I did it, even though nobody thought I could.*

Landry never wanted that look to leave Riley's gorgeous face.

I knew the whole time he could. Landry wanted to crow that to everyone on the team.

But he didn't.

Until the final minutes were ticking down in the game.

They were leading twenty-four to five, and Riley was flushed and happy with success. Landry's fingers itched, he was so desperate to reach out and just *touch* him.

Then, finally, after everyone had had their moment with the new star quarterback of the Condors, he approached Landry.

Saving the best for last?

God, Landry hoped so. He wanted to think he wasn't alone in this. But he wasn't *sure*, and that kinda killed him.

"Great game," Riley said modestly, his smile betraying how much of an understatement he knew that was.

"Hey, I'm not the one who threw three touchdowns, passed for over two hundred yards, and ran for another seventy-five."

"Aw, you memorized my stat line," Riley said, his smile so wide it crinkled the corners of his eyes. Those eyes Landry never wanted to look away from.

How had this happened?

Riley had been here in Charleston less than a week, but already it felt like he was personally responsible for every beautiful thing in Landry's life. The reason why he woke up in the mornings. The excuse for his heart to keep beating.

"It's hard to miss with how much they keep flashing it on that board over there," Landry explained, feeling himself flush with embarrassment. Had he been too obvious?

"Oh?" Riley even had a dimple when he smiled that hard.

Landry wanted to trace it with his tongue.

"Yeah," Landry said. Feeling like he'd just been exposed.

Riley put a hand on his shoulder. Tucked himself in close. This wasn't so different than the way he and Carter had embraced earlier, after their second touchdown together. But Riley didn't move away. Instead, it felt like he leaned in closer.

"Hey, you were instrumental today, you know? I couldn't have done it without you." Riley's voice was soft. Earnest.

"Nah," Landry insisted. "This was all you."

"You don't think I saw how many times you blocked guys away from me?"

"That's my job," Landry said. It was.

"But you're great at it. So let me say thank you. You gonna take it, or is this going to be just like my apology earlier?"

"No, I...you're welcome."

It *was* his job. But it had felt like so much more than just a job.

It had felt like his personal responsibility to keep Riley on his feet.

"See?" Riley's dimple deepened. "That wasn't so tough, was it?"

"Tougher than you'd imagine."

"Yeah, I get it. You're just used to being so awesome," Riley teased.

"I'm—"

"Yeah, you *are* awesome," Riley insisted. "Super duper awesome with a helping of awesome on top."

Maybe he wasn't alone in this helpless crush that seemed to take him over whenever Riley was near.

He remembered what Logan had suspected earlier. That way back, Riley had a crush on him. But they'd barely talked recently; he was practically a stranger now. He didn't really remember Riley's behavior during those college years when he'd occasionally come home with Aidan.

Maybe he had *had* a crush on him.

But Landry was hardly as sure as Logan had been.

"Thanks, I think?" Landry said.

Riley laughed. "Geez, take a compliment, Banks."

"Well, you're pretty awesome yourself."

Understatement of the century.

"Come on," Riley said, tucking a hand around Landry's waist like it belonged there, tugging him towards the center of the field as the last second ticked off the clock. Landry could feel the heat of it there, like a brand, even through several layers of pads and fabric. "Let's go celebrate."

Celebrating sounded pretty damn good to Landry.

But then it turned out that celebrating actually meant Riley and Carter goofing off around the locker room, half-dressed and gorgeous like neither of them had any idea the effect they had together, as they danced to the victory soundtrack Deacon had turned on the speakers.

"Hey, we won. You're not supposed to be frowning," Deacon said as he dropped down next to him.

Was he frowning? Were his jealousy and displeasure *that* obvious? Landry felt a pulse of embarrassment at the thought they could be.

Maybe they were written all over his face.

Logan had seemed flabbergasted by the idea Riley could be into Carter Maxwell, but there was no denying he had a certain charm.

And Riley seemed caught by it now as they spun around together, weaving their bodies together as they danced and faux-rapped to the Notorious B.I.G. song on Deacon's playlist.

"I'm not frowning," Landry lied. "It was a great game. Great win."

"Exactly. What's your issue?" Deacon gestured towards Riley and Carter. "You jealous?"

"No," Landry said vehemently. If Riley wanted Carter...well, he just hoped Carter realized how goddamn lucky he was *and* didn't fuck it up. Which, since this was Carter Maxwell, seemed like a highly likely possibility.

How many high-profile hookups had Maxwell gone through?

Way too many.

Riley *should* know better, but then Landry was evidence that sometimes a person yanked off their helmet in front of you, and you just *couldn't* do anything else but want them. Even if it was hopeless. Even if it was a fucking terrible idea.

"Right." Deacon did not sound even remotely convinced.

What would he do if *Riley* discovered his envy and called him on it like Deacon was doing?

God, that would be beyond humiliating.

Landry wasn't sure he'd survive that. Not if he had to continue living with Riley, being in his space all the time, feeling the fire of his casual touches, and eating the meals he cooked for them.

"Well," Deacon drawled, "you think about it, okay?"

"Think about what?" Landry asked, but Deacon had already risen and was heading towards the locker room door.

What had he meant?

Did he mean: *think about you and Riley together? Think about what might happen if you told him the truth?*

Because, frankly, he wasn't doing anything else *but* thinking about it, and it was making Landry a little crazy.

CHAPTER 9

Riley had expected it.

Still, as he sat in the mostly-dark kitchen, staring at his email inbox, at the first email sitting innocuously there, just waiting for him to open it and destroy what was left of his victory high, he'd hoped that maybe Aidan might discover a shred of brotherly feeling and congratulate him instead of criticizing him.

Maybe he had.

Riley wouldn't know unless he opened it and read the contents.

He was tempted to do it. Before, he'd always read Aidan's emails, as shitty as they could be, because there were so many important lessons and bits of advice intertwined between the blunt judgments.

You really should read it, a voice inside him insisted. *What if Aidan has something to say you need to hear?*

"You gonna sit there and stare at the screen for hours?"

Riley glanced up and saw Landry standing at the edge of the kitchen, big, brawny arms crossed over his equally big, brawny chest. It was still hard for Riley to get used to the sight.

At least he was wearing shorts now, not like the other night when he'd been wearing just the briefs that had hugged his thighs and his...well, all the parts Riley was trying very hard not to think about.

Trying and failing, if he was being honest.

Riley sighed. "Welcome to my weekly debate about whether to tell Aidan to fuck off."

"That's up for debate?" Landry came up behind him. Riley could feel the heat of him.

Wanted to lean back and feel *all* of it.

But just because Landry had come out to him and Riley *suspected* that his sexual awakening might've been because of him, he wasn't sure, and it wouldn't be right to just assume he was responsible *and* Landry liked him the way he liked Landry.

Because he did.

It definitely wasn't just a silly schoolboy crush anymore. This was full-blown *like* bordering on obsession.

"Actually, yeah," Riley admitted. "A lot of the time, he has good advice."

"And the other times?" Landry asked archly.

"He's *your* best friend."

"Yeah. Exactly. I know what an asshole he can be. More than just about anyone else," Landry retorted, voice dry. "What do you think you're missing out on by deleting his emails and sending one back telling him to mind his own fucking business?"

"Well, the advice for starters."

Riley glanced back, and Landry's gaze was dead serious. "You really think," he asked slowly, "that you wouldn't get that from someone else? Like Charlie? Or even Coach Oscar?"

It was a decent point. "I don't know."

"And what does this do to you each time?"

Riley frowned. "What do you mean?"

"I *mean*, when you don't read them and just delete them, you're getting rid of an extra negative voice in your head. A negative voice you don't need," Landry said, and suddenly his hands were on Riley's bare shoulders, just below his tank top, and he wasn't just touching him in a reassuring manner, but practically fucking caressing him. Riley's heartbeat accelerated. He really wasn't used to Landry touching him like this.

Would he ever get used to it?

Not likely.

"But what—"

"What if the advice is good?" Landry shrugged. "So what if it is? It's still not worth your peace of mind, Riley."

Riley stared at him. "You are not what I expected."

"What, you thought I'd be your brother's number one supporter? Or even worse, his deputy in trying to terrorize you out of football?" Landry shook his head. "And speaking of not being what I expected…"

Riley knew he was talking about him. He *knew*. And yet instead of turning on the barstool and pressing his lips against Landry's, he stayed where he was.

"No. Yes. I don't know." Riley laughed self-consciously.

"We're friends, aren't we? Don't friends want what's best for each other?"

That got Riley to turn in his seat.

Landry was close. *So* close, he could see all the shades of honey in his eyes, each blade of scruff on his chin, grown in after a few days of not shaving. So close he could see the tiny bit of eye black on his cheek that he'd missed during his shower.

Riley's heart contracted. He wasn't used to this fierce, wild wanting.

Didn't know how to compartmentalize it the way he always had.

Especially not when he could literally watch as Landry's pupils dilated with his own share of want.

That was the problem, wasn't it?

"Landry," he said softly, "we're not friends."

Landry froze. "What?"

Probably nobody had ever told him in his whole life that he wasn't a friend. People gravitated towards him because, even though he wasn't the loudest guy in the room or the most demonstrative, there was a solidness to him. A *ride-or-die* loyalty.

It was why he'd worried, at least at first, that Landry would be exactly what he'd suggested—Aidan's lieutenant first and foremost.

But he hadn't been.

He'd been in Riley's corner from the very first.

"We're not friends," Riley said. Reached up, pressed a palm to Landry's bare chest. Felt where his heart was rabbiting at the same pace Riley's was.

Landry didn't say anything, even though Riley kept hoping he would.

But they'd come too far now to turn back.

Riley could already taste Landry on his tongue, and whatever happened next, he was at least going to experience it for real, not just in his fevered imagination.

"Landry, people who are friends don't want to do this to each other."

Landry wet his lips. "Do what?"

"Oh, come on, Landry, you *know*." Riley tilted his head. Felt that heartbeat quicken under his touch. Spread his palm so he could dig his fingertips into the muscle.

Landry's gaze widened. His breath was coming even quicker now.

"I thought…" Landry took a deep breath. "I thought you and Carter…"

Riley laughed. He couldn't help it. The sound exploded out of him. "Are you serious? *Carter*? Carter Maxwell? That Carter?"

"Yes." Landry sounded annoyed. He sounded *jealous*.

Riley could work with that.

"Trust me, it's not him I'm thinking about alone at night in my bed. In *your* bed," Riley cooed, tilting his head up. Watching as Landry's eyes dilated even further.

Oh yeah, he wanted him. Bad.

Well—the feeling was definitely mutual.

Mutual and inevitable, and Riley was tired of fighting it.

Maybe this had been foretold at the beginning of time.

At least from the moment that Landry had walked into his house years ago, and Riley hadn't been able to do anything but just fucking stare at his brother's best friend. From the moment they'd stood together in that dark club in Pittsburgh and flirted because they couldn't help themselves.

Riley's hand slipped up and cupped Landry's shoulder. Dug in. Tugged him closer.

Meet me halfway, Landry. Please. I'm not alone here. I know I'm not.

"We're friends," Landry said firmly.

Oh God, don't put me in the friend zone. Riley nearly said it out loud. *Not you. Not now.*

"But," Landry continued wryly, "you're right. We're more, too. I want to be more."

Then he dipped his head and gently, carefully pressed his mouth against Riley's.

Sensation exploded inside Riley, and he was aware of each and every one. Landry's dry lips. His slight hesitation. The warmth of his palm against Riley's cheek. The way his fingers trembled.

He's nervous, Riley realized with wonder unfolding inside him. *He likes me enough it's made him nervous. And he wanted to kiss me enough he did it anyway.*

Duh, Riley realized. *This is his first kiss with a guy.*

So even though every instinct he possessed was screaming at him to lose himself in the kiss completely—to lose himself in *Landry*—he kept it polite and conservative. Tried not to push too hard. Tried not to wallow in the desire he was finally indulging in.

The ball was in Landry's court, and Riley needed him to want it just as badly as he did.

Then Landry groaned, tilted his head, and deepened the kiss, shaking Riley's world right off its axis.

Riley scooted closer on the barstool, wanting to get closer to Landry, even though the wooden slats of the back frustratingly kept them separated.

Landry's mouth moved more and more confidently against Riley's, and then he teased his lips open with his tongue, and that was game over.

Riley lost himself. Pressed his fingertips into Landry's skin and hung onto those big, broad shoulders he wanted to see every single morning for the rest of his life.

Before, he'd felt desperate with the craving that spiked between them at so many inconvenient times. But now that desire had claws. It dug at him and worried at him, evolving until Landry was so much more than something he just wanted.

He *needed*.

His cock pulsed in his shorts, hard and aching, and there was a distant part of his brain that knew that wouldn't happen tonight. Not yet. He'd practically had to coax Landry to kiss him.

Anything else was most definitely off the table.

But to his shock, he heard Landry's frustrated groan as he tried again to get around the wooden back of the barstool forcibly separating them, and then he broke Riley's mind apart.

He grabbed him and forcibly lifted him, removing him from the stool entirely and setting him on the edge of the counter.

Landry's eyes were wild. Desperate.

Riley thought they probably looked a lot like his own.

For a second, they stared at each other, then Riley opened his legs and Landry fell between them, pressing against him, legs to legs, chest to chest, mouth to mouth like he was starving.

Landry was going out of his fucking mind.

He'd imagined so many times over the last few weeks what it would be like to cash in on the promises in Riley's eyes.

But he'd never dreamt, not in a million years, that it could feel so good.

That he would be *this* into kissing a guy.

Kissing Riley.

Because Riley was so much more than just a guy, he was *Landry's guy*.

The way Riley went loose and weak in his arms as they kissed and kissed made Landry believe that had to be true.

Riley was *his*, the way he'd so effortlessly become Riley's.

"Wait." Riley's breath was ragged, even rougher than his voice, as he broke off.

Landry's lungs heaved like he'd just run a marathon. He'd never felt this way. Not about anyone he'd ever kissed before. He wanted nothing more than to drag Riley upstairs to his bed and strip all his clothes off and finally get to touch and taste him the way he'd fantasized about way too many damn times.

But Riley was asking him to wait, and Landry would rather set himself on fire than do something he didn't want.

Something he wasn't one hundred percent ready for.

The irony, Landry thought as he tried to get his body under control. He'd thought he'd be the one worried and anxious and ultimately hesitating on taking that final step. But it turned out he was more than ready to shed the rest of his straightness and get down and dirty with a guy.

His guy.

"What?" Landry asked.

Riley pressed his fingers to his lips. They were red and swollen. *Wet.* From Riley's own mouth. Landry shuddered a little.

The look in Riley's eyes was full of wonder.

"I like you," Riley said.

Landry laughed. Couldn't help himself. "I like you, too. Pretty sure I already said that."

"Sorry, my brain sort of short-circuited after you kissed me. Yes, I do remember that now. I just…" Riley hesitated. Like he was choosing his next words very carefully.

Landry didn't enjoy that at all. He wanted to hear the truth, the whole truth, even if it was a truth he hated. He didn't want Riley to hide anything, not from him.

"What is it? Do you not…" Of course, just because he needed to know didn't mean this was an *easy* question to ask. "Do you not want to do this?"

But Riley didn't answer. Not directly anyway. He tapped his fingertips against Landry's lips again. Landry wanted to lick them. Suck them deep. Make Riley think of all the other ways he could use his mouth.

Convince him that way if his words alone weren't proof of his feelings.

"You know, when we first met years ago, I had the most ridiculous crush on you."

So Logan *had* been right about that. Landry was having trouble wrapping his head around that revelation, but before he could, Riley kept going.

"Just absolutely ridiculous. I'm sure you knew. I practically followed you around with hearts in my eyes."

Landry shook his head. He hadn't realized.

"Well," Riley said, chuckling, "I guess that's something because Aidan never guessed either. But then we met again last month, and—"

"And I couldn't stop looking at you. Damn, you grew up good," Landry said. A fucking understatement. "I didn't know what was happening. I just knew nothing was what I'd thought it was. I wanted you, but that doesn't mean I had any idea how to deal with it."

"Do you now?" Riley asked, the corner of his mouth tilting up. He looked amused. And definitely hopeful.

Landry nodded, even though he didn't find it particularly funny. He was dead fucking serious. He'd carry Riley up to his bed right now and show him just how serious, if he'd let him.

But Riley seemed to want to talk.

Annoyingly.

"I just...I don't want this to be something that it isn't."

Landry's heart seized.

He hadn't even realized that particular organ was the one so invested in the outcome of this conversation. He'd thought it was just his cock that craved Riley so much, but it turned out his heart had stealthily been involved from the very beginning.

"What isn't it?"

Riley's gaze was serious. Earnest. "I don't want to just be an itch to scratch because you realized you're attracted to a guy," he said. And Landry knew, instinctually, that *this* was the truth.

"Is that what you think this is? Riley, it doesn't matter what you are. A guy. A girl. Something else. Nothing else. I want you because you're *you*. And what I want, it's not even remotely close to just itch-scratching. Though..." Landry hesitated. Wondering how honest he should be. "I'm pretty ready to get started on the itch-scratching part of it."

Riley stared at him. "You mean that."

Landry couldn't believe he had to convince him of this. Hadn't they just been kissing like the world was ending only a few minutes ago? Maybe they could get back to that, maybe they could do even more...surely there was something he could do to prove it wasn't just his cock that wanted more.

"Riley, I *like* you. I liked you from the moment we met again in Pittsburgh, sure, but honestly, I always liked you. We didn't know each other well, maybe, but Aidan talked about you all the time, and I liked every bit of you that I heard about. I liked the *shape* of you before I got to know the parts inside. And now that I'm beginning to really know you, all those parts you don't show to the world? I like you even more."

Riley didn't answer in words. Instead, he leaned in and kissed Landry this time. The way their kiss turned hot and heavy almost immediately made him think that maybe Riley really was on board with the whole *finally* scratching their mutual itch—after all, Landry could *feel* him hard and ready against his thigh, and it was so hard not to reach down and touch. Then, Riley proved it was true. Not in words.

His hand slipped down Landry's chest, and then it was pressing, firm and warm and perfect against where his cock ached in his shorts, and Riley was definitely smiling against his mouth now.

"I see that you *are* ready for the itch-scratching part to begin," Riley joked. But was it really a joke when Riley's hand was currently on his cock? *Finally?*

"You have no idea," Landry said.

Maybe someday he'd tell Riley about what he'd done alone in his bedroom—*twice*—since running into him in the hallway mostly naked.

"We really doing this?" Riley asked, his voice suddenly going low and uncertain.

For the first time, Landry could really see Riley had not only had that crush on him he'd admitted to, but that there was a part of him that still found Landry returning those feelings unbelievable.

"Oh, we're doing this, baby," Landry said and leaned in to kiss him again.

He'd meant it to be a quick, reassuring peck before they headed upstairs, but Riley's mouth was so addictive, so lush and warm and wet and everything Landry had ever dreamed it might be and so much more that he got lost. Again.

When Riley finally broke the kiss, he was smiling. Grinning, really. Like he'd just won the lottery—or the Super Bowl.

"You keep going like that, we're never gonna make it upstairs."

Landry couldn't help but nod in agreement. But the kitchen was cold and hard, and he wanted a nice big soft bed to lay Riley out on. Take his time exploring every inch of his incredible body.

"Well, then take me upstairs, big boy," Riley cooed with a voice that would've melted a much tougher man. He wound his arms and legs around Landry and scooted closer.

It *seemed* like a very good idea, a very *sexy* idea, to carry Riley up the stairs.

He didn't weigh as much as he might, Landry thought with a pulse of concern echoing so many of the arguments Aidan had made, or else he was just way too full of adrenaline to notice the weight of him in his arms.

He *did* notice the way Riley attached his mouth to Landry's neck and his hand to his cock. Couldn't help but notice.

Couldn't help but be incredibly distracted by it. So distracted he nearly tripped on the first stair heading up.

"Riley," he said with pseudo-sternness. "I'm gonna drop you."

"No, you won't," Riley teased. "You got me. I promise."

"Shouldn't I be promising you?"

Riley's fingers did something clever and so pleasurable against his cloth-covered dick that he nearly stumbled on the third step. And then they were delving under the waistband of his shorts, and *God*, that was Riley's touch. Skin to skin. Teasing and stroking, and it felt so goddamn good, Landry could barely handle it.

He pushed Riley's back against the staircase wall and kissed him.

His tongue in Riley's mouth, and Riley's hand on his cock. The pleasure pulsed through him, cycled round and round until he felt dizzy with it.

Weak with it.

Landry maintained he did not *drop* Riley. He wouldn't do that.

But Riley did slide bonelessly to the bottom of the staircase, laughing the whole way, and then he wasn't laughing anymore. Because Landry was on him, kissing him again, his hands shaking as he yanked down Riley's shorts.

"Jesus," he moaned under his breath as Riley's incredible body was revealed to him.

It was everything he'd dreamed of a few nights ago, and *more*.

He wanted to take his time. He wanted to not be on this hard, wooden staircase.

But moving was overrated, especially because of the way Riley looked, and felt, and *was*.

In the end, nothing mattered except Riley's cock, flushed pink like the rest of him, and the way he shook when Landry finally reached out and touched it.

"More," Riley demanded greedily, and Landry wasn't prepared to deny him.

Or himself, either, as Riley reached up and grabbed his shorts, pulling them down.

"If I'd known—" Riley panted as Landry's hand began to move with more and more certainty—he'd worried this would be weird, but it was only weird because of how natural it felt, making Riley squirm—"that you'd be so good at this, I'd never have let you leave the other night."

His eyes were a glorious blue, blurry with pleasure. Pleasure *Landry* was giving him. That was a high he'd never imagined he'd crave, but now he couldn't get enough of. He curled his hand around Riley's cock, and stroked him harder. Wanted to feel every inch of him, every quiver, every reaction.

Felt Riley do the same until it was just one endless circuit of pleasure, back and forth. Landry was aware his mouth was open, and he was probably staring uncomprehendingly at Riley's face.

Wondering: *how did we get here?*

Also wondering: *how can we get back here as soon as possible?*

He was twitching and leaking into Riley's palm, and then he leaned down and kissed him. Riley moaned into his mouth and bit his tongue just a little, and Landry was gone.

Riley strung out his orgasm, stroking him through it with alternating gentle and rough touches, teasing him and satisfying him in a way Landry hadn't ever imagined. He refused to focus on how amazing it felt, though, with his hand still working Riley's cock. He hadn't expected Riley would be close, but then, surprisingly, he jerked and froze as his head fell back, bliss creeping across his face as he pulsed into Landry's hand.

Like Landry's orgasm had pushed Riley into his own, and *God*, that was hot as hell.

"Shit," Riley groaned. "God, you *are* good at that."

Landry laughed. How could he do anything else? They hadn't even made it up the stairs. He'd half-dropped, half-collapsed with Riley in his arms because it had been way too fucking much to even deal with.

With his other hand, he stripped off his shirt and wiped both their palms dry.

"Didn't think I would be?" Landry asked when they were both—relatively—clean.

Riley had settled against the stairs like it was his throne. And as far as Landry was concerned, maybe it was.

He'd be happy to sit here at his feet and worship Riley forever.

"Well, you weren't exactly experienced."

"What I don't have in experience, I'm definitely going to make up with enthusiasm," Landry promised.

Riley grinned back. "Yeah? That your way of promising that the first and last time we have sex won't be on a wooden staircase?"

"Yes," Landry said, nodding seriously. "Next time, I genuinely hope to make it to the bedroom."

"Well, I guess that's one room down," Riley teased.

"One room down?"

Riley leaned in and kissed him, a brief peck on the lips. Landry nearly chased him back and kissed him harder, deeper. Couldn't get enough of him, honestly. "We've christened one room in this house," he said seriously. "One down, the rest to go."

It was only when they dragged their aching bodies off the staircase that Landry realized a basic quandary.

Because they hadn't made it to the bed, he couldn't suggest Riley stay with him.

As a result, he wouldn't be able to roll over the next morning and see him in all that gorgeous dawn light. Might not be able to wake him in the middle of the night because he hadn't gotten enough—didn't know if he could *ever* get enough.

That was sobering and a little bit terrifying, but Landry was going with it.

What else could he do?

"So," Riley said, leaning closer, eyes sparkling as he gazed up at Landry, "what now?"

They shouldn't be awkward anymore. Hadn't they just opened up the front door and booted any awkwardness out unceremoniously? Yes, they had.

Landry could hear Logan's voice in his head. *Just tell him. It's a classic for a reason.* "I kinda hoped we could...uh..." His nerves failed him at the last moment. Landry cleared his throat. "We could go to bed together."

"Didn't we do that already?" Riley asked, but his eyes weren't just knowing; they were practically twinkling.

Heart-eyes, Landry realized. *That's how Riley looks at you. It's how he's always looked at you.*

He realized then that, *yes*, Riley had definitely had a crush on him. Even though Riley had confessed to this less than an hour ago, Landry believed it now.

Could see the seeds of it going back years and years.

Maybe they'd always been heading here.

"We went to the staircase," Landry teased. "Not the same thing."

"You're a cuddler, aren't you? I'm going to sell out to ESPN, and the first thing I'm going to tell them is what a big cuddle monster you are."

"Except you'd have to tell them you love it, too," Landry said, the look on Riley's face—hopeful and a little bit awestruck—bolstering his conviction.

"Yeah," Riley said. "You go. I'll be up in a minute."

Landry raised an eyebrow.

"And *no*," Riley added, "this isn't me brushing you off."

"If you don't want to sleep together, we don't have to. I know having your own space can be important." Landry wanted Riley to have choices, even though they were technically living together already.

Riley shot him an impatient look. "You're fine. I've only wanted to cuddle with you for almost half my life."

"Oh. *Oh.*"

"Right." Riley smiled. Whacked him lightly on the butt. "I said I'd be up soon, and I will be. Have to do something first."

"Tell Aidan to fuck off?"

Riley chuckled but didn't answer. Which, Landry supposed, as he headed up the stairs towards his bedroom, was answer enough.

He got ready for bed. Brushed his teeth again. Plumped his pillows. Put his gym bag in the closet and his dirty socks in the hamper. Set his phone on the charger. Then had a long-ish debate with himself over which side of the bed Riley was going to want.

You don't give a shit which side he takes, as long as he's there, Landry reminded himself as he finally settled in.

A minute later, Riley appeared in the doorway.

He stripped off his tank top and tossed it on the side table so carelessly that Landry wished he hadn't spent the last ten minutes agonizing over whether his socks were in the hamper or on the floor.

"Is this...is that side okay?" Landry hated himself for how much he kept hesitating, for how much he kept stammering.

Riley likes you, too, he reminded himself.

"It's cute you think a side matters," Riley teased as he slid into bed next to Landry. "I guarantee by the time you wake up, we're gonna be sharing whichever side you're on."

Landry couldn't think of anything he'd like better—which was strange because, in the past, he'd always wanted his own space.

Hookups and the one girlfriend he'd had since college rarely stayed the night with him, usually by his choice.

But he couldn't wait to get Riley close.

Riley-sexual, that voice—that reminded him so much of Logan—pointed out with a dry chuckle. Maybe he was because Riley was the exception to so many of his rules.

"Come 'ere," he said and lifted his arm, and Riley slid closer, right into the spot he'd made.

A spot he fit perfectly in.

Landry shifted slightly, turning the light off.

"I deleted that email," Riley said, after a moment, into the darkness. "Without reading it. I didn't need his voice in my head telling me I was stupid. I know it already."

Landry wasn't sure what to say. Maybe it wasn't his business to get between Riley and Aidan, but Riley's reaction to Aidan's bullshit *was* because it hurt him, and what hurt Riley hurt Landry. But he wasn't stupid enough to think Riley deleting one email was enough to solve all the problems between them.

"I'm sure he didn't say you were stupid. We *won*," Landry reminded him.

"Yeah, but he's not used to having a brother who's a sports media laughingstock," Riley said wryly.

"Nobody thinks of you like that," Landry argued.

"Yeah," Riley said quietly.

Landry realized this wasn't the kind of problem he could fix with a timely pep talk. To believe, Riley was going to need more proof to the contrary—and even more than that, he was going to need time to get over it.

It was still too fresh in everyone's eyes.

In the meantime, Landry could just *be* there for him.

"Well, I'm proud of you for not letting Overprotective Brother Bot activate," Landry said.

Riley chuckled. "Thanks." He yawned. "I think…"

"Yeah," Landry echoed and found himself, arms full of the warmth of Riley, drifting off to sleep.

CHAPTER 10

RILEY WAS IN A damn good mood.

Even the text from his agent—telling him not to turn on EPSN—wasn't enough to dim his spirits.

He'd woken up in bed cuddled so close to Landry that it was hard to tell where he left off and where the other guy began. It was every teenage fantasy wrapped into one glorious reality. Landry had rolled over, turned off the alarm, then kissed him.

They hadn't been able to linger in bed—*unfortunately*, because Riley had definitely noticed he wasn't the only one interested in lingering between the warm sheets—but it was enough to see Landry grinning at him over the blender. Enough to have him lean over and brush a quick kiss against his lips after he parked at the Condors' practice facility.

It felt like...well, the beginning of something.

And that particular *something* was so highly anticipated and so longed for, it felt even bigger than it might've otherwise.

The morning meetings had gone well—normally, they'd have Mondays off after a Sunday game—but with the first regular season game coming up in only six days, Coach Kelley had called them all in.

The request hadn't even felt like an overreaction to any flaws in their play yesterday, but instead a fulfillment of a promise that with hard work and preparation, they might actually be able to take everyone by surprise and be contenders.

Riley was willing to grab that possibility with both hands. Landry, too, because he hadn't complained once about heading into the practice facility on a Monday morning.

Unlike Carter, who whined the moment they got into the conference room for the weekly offensive game tape breakdown.

"I was really lookin' forward to sleeping in," Carter complained as he slouched down further in his chair. "I had real good company, if you get my drift."

"Oh, we do," Cole retorted as he took his own seat. "Who'd you pick up?"

"This unbelievably hot chick and her friend."

"Two women for Carter Maxwell, huh?" Landry teased. "Just like florals for spring. *Groundbreaking*." It seemed Landry was in the same kind of good mood as Riley, and even Carter's regular bullshit couldn't dampen it.

"Hey," Carter said, throwing up his hands. "I never said her friend was a *girl*."

"Kudos for your dedication to sexual equality," Cole retorted dryly.

Carter waggled his eyebrows. "I'm an equal opportunity employer."

"Ew, gross, tell the details to someone who cares," Riley said. But he could feel the corner of his mouth tilting up in a smile.

Apparently, finally sleeping with Landry Banks helped him see the silver lining in just about anything.

Even when Coach Kelley and Coach Oscar came in along with Charlie, and they started breaking down film from the game.

Riley hadn't done everything right—even if he wasn't counting the especially stupid mistake he'd made on the Condors' first drive—but he hadn't done everything wrong either. There were a lot of positives sprinkled in-between the criticisms and play breakdowns.

When the meeting broke up and he headed towards the cafeteria, Carter was still bragging about the threesome he'd had the night before.

Yeah, but I had sex with Landry last night. Riley almost said the words out loud. *Sex. With Landry.*

Not only to get him to shut up, but also because, as excited as Carter was about his equal opportunity threesome, Riley knew that no matter what sexual gymnastics Carter had performed the night before, they couldn't possibly measure up to the awkward handjobs he and Landry had shared on the staircase.

He'd had his share of hot hookups over the years, but nothing could be as good as the way Landry had kissed him, like if he didn't, he wouldn't be able to take another breath.

Like Riley was air and water, and Landry would die if he didn't get it.

"...*and*," Carter continued because he never knew when to shut up, "then she said, well, there's a hot tub right here, and it doesn't make sense to let it go unused..."

Riley shot him a look. "Really?" he asked.

Carter shrugged. "She had a good point. Who was I to argue with such unassailable logic?"

Pulling his phone out of his pocket as Carter continued rambling about what had happened in and then *out* of the hot tub, Riley checked his messages.

Three from his brother.

He nearly rolled his eyes. Didn't Aidan have a game to prepare for, same as Riley? How did he have so much fucking time on his hands?

A question Riley would ask him if he decided he wanted to talk to him—which he absolutely didn't.

He already knew what Aidan was going to say. Well, he knew at least *one* thing he was going to say, and while he wasn't one hundred percent sure missing the rest of what he'd tell Riley was worth missing the one very predictable complaint, he was ninety-nine point nine percent sure.

The first message read, **Didn't you get my email last night?**

The second, sent thirty-four minutes later, said, **Are you really gonna ignore me?**

And the third, an hour after that: **You can pretend it didn't happen, but it still happened.**

Actually, Riley thought, shoving his phone back into his pocket, satisfaction spreading through him at his brother's obvious annoyance, he *could* pretend it didn't happen.

He'd deleted Aidan's email from last night, hadn't he? Okay, sure, so it was still in his trash bin, taunting him with its currently unread state, but so far, he hadn't read it, and he didn't think he wanted to.

Especially not after getting these text messages.

"You're distracted," Carter said with an accusatory tone as they walked into the cafeteria.

Riley sighed. His mind felt like a crowded place these days, and none of the issues cluttering him up felt like ones he wanted to share with Carter. "Maybe your story just wasn't very interesting," he teased as he grabbed a tray.

Carter squawked in outrage. "*Seriously,*" he sputtered.

Riley waved a hand. "Maybe you should try something original for once. The hot tub, really?" *How about a staircase?*

"You're *two whole rounds behind*. I'm so hurt; you weren't even listening."

Riley attempted to arrange his features into a sympathetic expression. It was harder than he imagined it would be. "You got something I'm interested in, sure, I'll listen. But your sex life isn't one of those things."

"What about *your* sex life?" Carter retorted slyly.

Riley picked up a bowl of roasted vegetable and chicken salad, examining it. It looked good—not as good as *his*, of course, but beggars couldn't be choosers—and set it on his tray.

"What about my sex life?" Riley said. Trying to keep his tone bland. Not succeeding any more than he had at looking remotely sympathetic to Carter's outrage.

"You make any headway in corrupting Landry Banks yet?" he asked.

Riley made a face as he took an empty table. He didn't need Carter sharing his suspicions—especially since they'd turned out to be surprisingly accurate—with anyone else. Not until he knew what he and Landry were doing.

Maybe not even then.

He was still on shaky ground here. It wouldn't be very hard for the Condors to find a new quarterback, one who wasn't determined to get involved with their franchise's tight end—the one with the face gracing all their season tickets.

As much as he desperately wanted Landry and had wanted him for years, he wasn't going to rock the boat.

"I don't know what you're talking about," Riley said.

"So yes, then," Carter said with satisfaction as he flopped down next to Riley.

"What do you mean, *yes, then*?" Riley demanded. He hadn't said *anything*.

"You had this look on your face. It's the one I get when you finally fucking throw me the ball," Carter said. "Like you finally got something you've been wanting for a really long time."

"I throw you the ball plenty."

"That's a matter for debate," Carter said. "But this isn't. You totally corrupted him."

"A man kisses you in his own kitchen, you're hardly the one corrupting *him*," Riley said before he could think better of it.

Carter dropped his fork and whooped so loudly that every single person in the whole damn cafeteria turned in their direction.

"Oh my God," Riley hissed under his breath. "Stop that right now."

Carter's eyes were gleaming as he leaned in. "Bet you wish I hadn't tormented you till you told me."

"What? Did you even have that threesome?" It suddenly occurred to Riley there was a very good reason—probably more than one—Carter Maxwell had been traded an NFL-high four times. Maybe it was that Carter was a unique and particularly temper-inducing combination of intelligence and, subsequently, painful smugness about it.

"Of course I had that threesome. But you didn't think I *wanted* to tell you about it, did you?" Carter grinned. "Oh, you did. Well, I suppose that's understandable."

"You're..."

"Terrible? Awful? The *worst*?" Carter was still grinning smugly. "I know. But you still told me about you and Landry."

"I did," Riley said morosely. He hadn't meant to. But he was also kind of glad he had. He'd texted Paige, of course, telling her the bare-bones—**Yes, you win**, he'd told her. **We slept together. Literally and figuratively**—but because it was a work day for her, he'd not gotten a reply, and the chances were he wouldn't anytime soon.

And he certainly wouldn't be telling Aidan anything about it.

Maybe telling Carter wasn't the end of the world. After all, wasn't he trying to be friends with Carter?

"Cheer up," Carter said, patting him on the shoulder with an undeniably shit-eating grin on his face. "Weaker men than you have fallen. So you gonna dish all the details?"

"You mean, am I gonna dish on all the details the way you did? Nope."

Carter made a face. "Hey, not fair. At least tell me if he's as hot in bed as he is out of it."

Riley elbowed him in the side. "Hey, that's my..." He hesitated. What *was* Landry to him? He was about to say *boyfriend*, which was not a word he'd ever been tempted to use, but today it had nearly rolled right off his tongue as easy as anything. But it was bad enough he'd told Carter about them without checking with Landry first, so he definitely wasn't going to advertise any possible relationship status without going over it with him.

"Your man, huh?"

"He's something." Riley hesitated. "I know he isn't the kind of guy to do this lightly."

"Especially not swing to the other side, so to speak," Carter pointed out.

"Yeah, maybe normally, but...you know about his two brothers, right?"

"Logan and Levi? Oh yeah." Carter grinned wildly. "I was sort of hoping I could notch the set, but I didn't think that would happen 'til you swooped in and proved not only was it possible, it was *easy*."

"Oh my God," Riley said, rubbing his eyes. "I need brain bleach."

"Remember I played half a season in Minnesota," Carter said. "With Logan. Before he got with his boyfriend. Dylan, isn't it? And Levi? That was at the Super Bowl two years ago."

"Do they—" Riley almost regretted asking the question as he stabbed salad in his bowl with unnatural force.

"Oh yeah, they know. Levi thought it was funny. Hilarious even. Told me I wouldn't be able to get the whole set of Banks brothers 'cause Landry's straight." Carter paused. "Guess you took care of that."

There was nothing Riley could say to that except, "Guess I did."

A few minutes later, Deacon swung by their table and announced they were doing a little victory celebration at the Pirate's Booty tonight. "I knew you two would be up for it," Deacon said wryly. "Especially you, Maxwell."

"My rep proceeds me," Carter said. "I'm in." He glanced over at Riley. "What about you, RiRi? You in? Or are you gonna be busy indulging in a certain someone's continued sexual exploration?"

"Don't call me RiRi," Riley said, annoyed.

Thank God Deacon, like most of the Condors players, ignored three-quarters of the shit that spewed out of Carter's mouth. "So you're in?" Deacon questioned.

It would be way too early to say something ridiculous like, *I'm in if Landry is*—and even worse, there was no way Carter would let that go without making a huge deal out of it.

"I'm in," Riley said.

"Awesome. It's disco night," Deacon said. "So put your dancing shoes on."

"Yes!" Carter said, fist-pumping in the air.

Deacon shook his head, but as he headed back to his table, Riley could see he was still chuckling.

"Dude," Carter said as soon as he was out of earshot. "I swore you were going to pull one of those high school moments and ask if Landry was going before you said if you'd join."

"What, me? Of course not," Riley blustered. Embarrassment flamed inside him because he'd nearly said exactly that. "I can do things without Landry. We're...well, we're..."

"Fucking," Carter said, biting into an apple with relish. "Totally fucking."

But Riley already knew they were doing a lot more than that.

Landry didn't see Riley again until practice.

Told himself that was totally normal.

Understandable, even.

It was a victory Monday, but in only six days, Riley would be starting his first NFL regular season game, and that was a very big deal.

"Hey," Deacon said as he approached where Landry was standing on the sideline, watching as Charlie and the wide receivers helped Riley warm up his arm.

He shouldn't be staring; except he couldn't stop.

He hadn't been able to stop, not since Riley had pulled off his helmet in Pittsburgh.

"Hey," Landry said, meeting Deacon's fist bump. "What's up?"

Deacon's gaze followed Landry's, took in the view of Riley throwing downfield in Carter's direction as he waved his arms obnoxiously, demanding the ball.

He raised his eyebrow but didn't say anything. At least about Riley. "You think he got dropped on his head as a child?" he asked casually, clearly referring not to their new quarterback, but to Carter.

"Seems likely," Landry said cautiously. Not sure why Deacon had chosen this moment when he was probably more obviously crushing than ever, to *not* tease him about Riley.

"He's fun, though. Entertaining. Never sure what he'll say," Deacon said. "We can use a little of that around here."

"What was he like last year?"

Deacon considered this for a long moment. "He came in during the middle of the most fucked up season ever. And I'll give Carter some credit, he realized it immediately. Kept his head down. Caught the ball when we needed him to. But didn't say a lot. Then he showed up this year, mouth moving a mile a minute, bragging and saying shit, and making everyone laugh, and I realized…" Deacon trailed off.

"Realized what?"

"What a good guy he was because clearly he didn't want to play for Taylor. Didn't want to play *with* him. But he did because he had to."

"None of you enjoyed it."

Deacon rocked back on his heels. "Some of us more than others."

"I know the new owner cleaned house. Coach Kelley, too."

"Grant did," Deacon acknowledged.

Landry raised an eyebrow. "Grant?" He'd not heard a single one of the players refer to their new owner by his first name, only by the nickname he'd insisted they all call him, Mr. G.

Deacon flushed. "Oh, well, you know, I was one of the guys who talked to him upfront before he bought the team, so we're…well, close, I guess. Not close. But…well, you know."

Landry didn't know, actually, but what he did realize was Deacon was undeniably uncomfortable. Which…*that* was interesting.

"Right," Landry said. Looked like maybe he wasn't the only one with a crush—though at least his wasn't hopeless.

Grant Green was notoriously private—and crazy rich—so the fact Landry hadn't heard he was queer might not mean that he wasn't.

"Anyway, came over to see if you wanted to come along with us tonight to the Pirate's Booty," Deacon said, clearly trying to change the subject. His mouth shifted into a knowing grin. "Riley's coming.

"Oh?" Landry was trying to play it cool, but he already knew he wasn't any good at it.

If he was, his gaze wouldn't still be glued to where Riley was finishing his warmup in the middle of the field.

"And it's disco night. Don't want to miss disco night."

"Can't have that," Landry said. "Sure, I'll come with."

"You ask him to come to disco night?" Jem asked, popping up next to Landry.

"Of course I did," Deacon said. "You talk to Beck?"

"Yeah, and he insisted on inviting Rex and Eric," Jem said, rolling his eyes.

Landry wasn't sure he'd ever exchanged more than half a dozen words with Rex and Eric, the two starting corners for the Condors, and he wasn't sure what Deacon or Jem's issues were with them. "Why's that a problem?"

"Oh," Jem said, rolling his eyes, "Deacon here is just ridiculous. He's sure there's something off about Rex."

"*Off*?"

"Exactly. He can't tell you what it is, only that it's going to be a problem."

"He seems to play pretty well."

"He's serviceable," Deacon said in a hard voice that Landry wasn't sure he'd ever heard him use before.

Jem smacked him in the shoulder pad. "Be nice," he chided.

"I could've said he totally blew coverage on Nicholson when we played the Piranhas in the playoffs last year. *Three fucking times,*" Deacon said reproachfully. "There's just...something. I told Grant about it, but he wouldn't listen to me."

"Shocking," Jem said sarcastically, "that *Grant* doesn't do everything you suggest. Especially when it's just a hunch."

"Hey, my hunches are pretty damn good most of the time," Deacon argued.

Landry, who hadn't quite been able to look away from where Riley was finishing his warmups, saw him wave him over and decided to take the opportunity to exit the conversation. It was definitely one Deacon and Jem had had before, but personally, Landry thought Jem had a point.

Deacon didn't even know what his problem was—or if Rex even *had* a problem. What if Deacon had decided on a freaking hunch that *he* wasn't worth the contract the Condors had given him? As he jogged over to where Riley was standing, Landry resolved that he'd go out of his way to be nice to Rex tonight.

He liked Deacon, he really did, but his attitude towards the corner was more than a little unfair.

"Do your magic, man," Carter told Kieran, the bartender at the Pirate's Booty, waving in the direction of Rex and Eric, who were looking around the bar like they'd suddenly been transported to an alien planet.

"It's not magic," Kieran said, laughing. "But sure, come on over, guys. I'll grab you a drink."

Landry had already gotten his drink—the same thing Kieran had made him last time. "You're not so adventurous," Kieran had teased back when he'd wondered about that.

"You'd be surprised," Riley had said under his breath, gazing up at him with those same heart-eyes Landry thought he'd see in every dream from here on out.

Rex raised a dark eyebrow. "You aren't gonna ask me what I want?"

"That's the magic, man," Carter insisted. "He just *knows* what you want."

"So, let me get this straight," Eric said, deadpan, "you wanted us to come to a bar where the bartender's magic and all they play is disco?"

"Yeah," Carter said excitedly. "Isn't it awesome?"

It was something, that was for sure.

"I love it," Riley inserted loyally.

With the revelations of the night before, Landry was beginning to see Riley's overtures to Carter and their easy way with each other for what they really were—a growing friendship. Truthfully, even Carter's more obnoxious traits were beginning to grow on Landry.

"It's definitely...unique," Rex said.

"That's the best way to describe us," Kieran said as he poured different bottles into a large fish bowl. "Unique."

"You guys were around last year, and you didn't ever come here?" Landry asked, remembering his promise to be friendlier to the two cornerbacks.

Eric shot him a look. "Nobody really wanted to do much outside of practice last year."

"No fucking kidding," Carter chimed in.

It wasn't just that he'd learned Carter and Riley's friendship was purely platonic, his opinion of Carter had shifted even further when Deacon had told him about his behavior the year before.

How he clearly hadn't approved of Tom Taylor and his proclivity for violence but had been forced to work with him, just the same as the rest of them had.

Kieran slid the fishbowl over in Rex and Eric's direction. "To share," he clarified. "Y'all do that a lot, right?"

Landry watched as they exchanged glances. "Yeah," Rex said uneasily. "Yeah, we do."

"There you go," Kieran said. "Riley, can I get you anything?"

"Nope, I'm good with water," Riley said. "Not drinking this week. Important game."

"It's against the Falcons," Rex said. "They won *two* games last year."

"Yeah, so did the Piranhas the year before last, and look at what they did the next season," Riley retorted. "I'm not writing anybody off."

Eric nodded in approval. "You're a good kid."

"Uh-oh," Carter teased, "don't call him that."

Eric looked confused. "Why not?"

"It's my brother's favorite nickname for me," Riley explained. "It's entirely possible he's lost track of time and still thinks I'm twelve."

Carter checked Riley out head to toe with an exaggerated leer. Two days ago, Landry would've been pissed off and inexplicably territorial. Now he just took it for what it was—Carter being Carter. "You're definitely not twelve," he said.

"Nope," Riley said. He set his water glass on the bar top. "You wanna go dance, Landry?"

Did he want to dance? With Riley?

Yep—he did. In a bed. With no clothes between them at all.

But he'd take what he could get, which was Riley in a loose blue tank that showed off his biceps and made his eyes glow even bluer and tight jeans that had made his pulse race the first time he'd seen Riley's ass in them.

"Yeah," Landry said, and his voice was full of gravel. Probably everyone here knew the truth of what was going on, and he discovered as he took Riley's hand that he wasn't sure he cared.

After all, hadn't Deacon and Jem guessed almost immediately?

You weren't very subtle. That voice inside him that sounded exactly like Logan reminded him. *And who could fucking blame you? Have you seen Riley Flynn?*

Oh, he had.

The atrium, which had been empty and dark the last time they came to the Pirate's Booty, was filled with flashing lights and bodies, all grooving to the best of the seventies.

Riley squeezed his hand. "You okay with this?" he asked, leaning close so Landry could hear him.

"Why wouldn't I be?" he asked.

Riley shot him a look. "If we dance together the way I want to, you know what it could mean," he said. "Or, if you're not ready for that, we could dance together like two teammates might. I don't care. I just want to dance with you."

"What if I'm not a very good dancer?" Landry joked weakly. He knew what Riley was asking. Maybe he should care more about other people realizing he wasn't straight, but the truth was, he didn't give a shit about anyone else's opinion, and additionally, he felt not an ounce of shame for what he was, no matter what that was.

If that was a guy who was totally into Riley Flynn, then so be it.

But there was another part of him that wondered if maybe he *should* be giving this more gravity than he was. People had struggled with their sexuality for years, and here he was ready to just accept it.

"I don't care," Riley said firmly, and Landry realized he felt the same way.

He didn't care what he *should* feel. He only knew what he *was* feeling.

"Then I don't either," Landry said, and Riley must've understood because he gripped his hand harder and then tugged him in the direction of the dance floor.

"I was thinking," Landry murmured as Riley wiggled to the music in a way that gave Landry undeniably weak knees. "I wanted to go back home and dance with you...in bed."

Riley smirked. "Oh, were you?" He slid closer until his hips were nearly flush with Landry's. "Feeling pretty sure of yourself, huh?"

Landry slid his hands down Riley's sides and tugged him even closer, letting himself begin to sway to the disco beat. "Not just sure of me, but sure of you," he admitted.

He'd never been surer of anyone before. Certainly never a romantic partner.

But Riley made him want to toss all his caution away with both hands and just enjoy the hell out of these new feelings.

"See? You're a pretty good dancer." Riley was grinning so hard his dimple popped, and Landry wanted nothing more than to lean down and explore it with his tongue.

Okay, he wanted to explore way more of Riley's delectable body with his tongue. Their hookup on the stairs had been hot, but next time, he wanted a bed and a lot of light and all the time in the world.

"Pretty good, huh?" Landry teased.

But he'd take that because Riley was more than pretty good, and he'd be happy to embarrass himself seven days out of seven, if he could not just watch Riley move to the music the way he did, all sinuous hips and innate grace, but be close to him while he did it.

"Honestly," Riley confessed, "you could just stand there, and I'd enjoy myself."

But Landry had no intention of just standing there.

He tilted his hips and ground them against Riley, the drag of his guy's body both dirty and delicious.

"Then you gotta go and do that," Riley grumbled, but he kept moving, too, as one song segued into another, the lights dancing across the crowd.

Landry didn't know how long they danced together, but he knew by the time Riley pinned him with a hot look and pushed him towards the darkest corner of the atrium, his blood was pumping like lava through his veins, and his cock was rock hard in his jeans.

Riley must've been feeling the same because as soon as the darkness enveloped them, no lights interrupting their privacy, he pushed him against the brick wall, and suddenly Landry's arms were full of him.

For a second, they stared at each other. Riley's breath was short, his chest rising and falling, and his forehead damp. Landry felt the same desperation surging inside him. His hands shook as he settled them back on Riley's hips. Dragged him even closer until they were pressed together.

It was undeniable; he'd never wanted another person with the same fiery need he felt for Riley Flynn.

"Shit," Riley muttered and then kissed him.

It wasn't the passion tempered by caution and hesitation from the night before. Instead, this kiss was wild, with Riley pushing him and Landry pulling him right along.

A distant voice in the back of his head told him they shouldn't be making out like this or practically humping each other, like they couldn't even help themselves in public.

But the voice was too distant, and the pleasure was too immediate, his sense of satisfaction as Riley groaned into his mouth too complete.

He's just as into this as you are.

"I should've known you two would find the darkest corner in this whole damn place."

Carter's smug voice was a bucketful of ice-cold water on Landry's head—and suddenly, that voice, insisting that they shouldn't be doing this, not here anyway, was screaming loudly.

Riley's mouth moved off his, but he didn't step away.

Protecting Landry's honor and his obviously hard cock from Carter's view?

His heart melted a little at the thought, even as his arousal decreased from a rousing boil to a mere simmer.

"Carter," Riley said flatly. "What are you doing here?"

"Bothering you, what else?" Carter teased. "Also, possibly keeping you from an indecency felony. You're welcome."

Riley rolled his eyes, but he finally stepped away from Landry—who had to curl his fingers in so he wouldn't reach out and just take him back. "Seriously?" he said incredulously.

Carter threw his hands up with mock innocence. "Seriously," he repeated. "Jem wanted to know where you'd gotten to, and I *told* him you were probably way occupied, but he didn't want to listen. Guess I was right."

"Guess you were," Landry said. His voice was rough as gravel. He could still remember the way Riley had felt against him, the helpless way he'd rubbed his cock against Landry's thigh. The little groans he'd made in the back of his throat as they'd kissed.

He was a fucking wet dream, and Landry couldn't wait to strip him down and make him *scream*. But he wasn't going to do that in front of Carter. That particular sight would be for his eyes only.

"Anyway," Carter said. "Jem wanted me to find you 'cause he and Deacon were taking off. And I found you. Good for me."

"Fine, fine, *fine*," Riley grumbled. He turned back to Landry. "You good?"

"Oh, he's more than good, honey," Carter retorted before Landry could answer. "But I bet he'd be even better if I hadn't interrupted you."

It was exactly what Landry had been thinking, but he wasn't going to give Carter the satisfaction, so he just nodded.

CHAPTER 11

Riley's heart was still thumping hard when the Uber dropped them off in front of Landry's townhouse.

It shouldn't have been.

He shouldn't still be feeling the press of Landry's fingertips into his hips, the ghost of his tongue in his mouth. But he was. He couldn't stop feeling it, even though it had been at least half an hour since he'd been caught up in Landry's arms. In the interim, he'd had to make more pleasant small talk with Jem and Deacon and then Rex and Eric and Beck, even though a part of his brain—and all of his cock—had been screaming to get Landry alone again.

But Riley couldn't deny he was still experiencing *all* those things, and from the dark, intense look Landry shot him as they got out of the car and headed up the stairs towards the door, it seemed very likely he wasn't the only one who felt like this.

"You still good?" Riley asked as Landry unlocked the door with his code because if he didn't say something, he was going to go out of his mind. The whole ride home, Landry had been quiet. But then his eyes had said everything he hadn't. Then there'd been his touch. Insistent and warm, his hand pressing into Riley's knee.

He'd never considered that particular place an erogenous zone, but by the time they'd arrived at the townhouse, every nerve ending in his knee had been on fire.

Really, not just his knee.

"Am *I* still good?" Landry asked, chuckling darkly.

They were standing in the foyer. Landry hadn't bothered to turn the light on, so most of his face was shadowed.

"Yeah." Riley was uncertain. He'd been so sure the minute they were alone again—actually alone this time—they'd be all over each other, but so far, Landry hadn't made a move towards him. He'd just stood there and stared at him with an undeniably hungry gaze.

But Landry still didn't say anything.

"I just..." Riley hesitated. "I know it was a big thing tonight. Like dancing with me and...uh..." *Nearly having sex in public?*

"You think I didn't like it?" Landry asked.

"It was just a lot, that's all." It had been. Riley had pushed. He knew he had. Maybe he should feel guilty about it, but Landry had been with him every goddamn step of the way, looking like he'd enjoyed every minute of it.

"Come 'ere," Landry said roughly, and Riley went because there was never going to be a time when Landry wanted him and he didn't immediately feel compelled to go. There'd been too many years wishing and hoping and dreaming about this exact request to turn it down now.

Not when he wanted it so much himself.

But instead of kissing him the way Riley had expected, Landry folded him into a tight hug.

Landry gave the best hugs.

Riley hadn't been lucky enough to experience them that many times, but he'd had enough as a teenager that Landry's big, warm embrace had only fueled his crush even more.

Now, his hug did more than just fuel a crush.

It was like a spark hitting a pool of gasoline.

"You don't have to worry about me or about anything we're doing," Landry said, his voice a deep rumble hitting Riley square in the chest. "I want this. I want *you*."

It was so easy to tilt his head back, and see the desire there in Landry's eyes, obvious and evident, even if he hadn't just said the words, and then reach up and kiss him. Riley's tongue dipped into Landry's mouth, and that was all they needed to re-kindle the lust between them.

"God," Landry groaned as Riley's hands skimmed down his chest, around to his sides. He was so big, so solid. And all Riley's.

"Come on," Riley murmured after he broke the kiss. "Let's go upstairs. As fun as that was, I don't want to fuck on the stairs again."

Landry nodded and let Riley lead him upstairs, and this time they didn't get stuck halfway up.

They made it all the way to Landry's bedroom at the end of the hall before Landry was on him, kissing him fiercely, tugging at his tank, and yanking it off.

Riley landed on the edge of the bed and was surprised to see Landry fall to his knees in front of him.

Not that it wasn't a really great fucking look. It was. It was so many fantasies come to life, and Riley could barely believe how good he looked like this.

Like he was ready to give Riley everything he'd ever wanted.

But instead of immediately reaching for his cock, Landry went lower, carefully untying his shoelaces and pulling them off. Then his socks. It wasn't a particularly sexy striptease, not if Riley was using his normal rubric, but by the time Landry made it to his jeans, his heart was racing. Not just because his fingers were hovering right by where his cock was currently hard and leaking in his briefs.

But because every one of Landry's movements had been so deliberate. Careful. Slow. Teasing. Riley was practically shaking with anticipation.

Maybe Landry was new to sex with a guy, but he still knew what the fuck he was doing.

"You want this? You want me?" Landry asked quietly as he neatly undid the button on his jeans, then slid the zipper down. Somehow managing not to touch anywhere Riley was desperate for him to touch. Not because he didn't want to or because he was afraid.

No, that much was obvious to Riley. Landry was drawing out the pleasure. Taking his time. Enjoying every moment.

"I think it's pretty obvious I do," Riley said wryly as Landry pulled his jeans down. He squirmed a little as Landry folded them and then turned his burning-hot gaze back on Riley.

Taking in every inch of him.

"You are so fucking gorgeous," Landry said, and he touched him for real now, a palm against his chest, fingertips trailing down his pecs and then towards his abs. Then he leaned in and his mouth followed the same path, meandering down his skin, like there was no reason to rush. Taking a minute here to suck a nipple into his hot mouth, then another to trace every place where his stomach muscles flexed.

Riley swallowed hard. "Any time now," he ground out.

"No," Landry said inexorably. "I want this. I've wanted this too long to rush it."

"But—"

Riley didn't get any more words out before Landry finally made his move, his mouth closing quick and burning around his cock, straining against the fabric of his briefs.

"I've never done this before," Landry murmured as he finally pulled the last piece of his clothing off. "So if I do something you don't like or don't do something you want..." Landry trailed off. Curled his tongue around the head of his cock and sucked, and Riley nearly shouted with the sudden wave of pleasure washing through him.

But then he pulled back, Riley wanting nothing more than to chase the intoxicating heat of his mouth, but then he understood.

Not just why he'd said it. But what Landry wanted.

Yes, he *hadn't* done this before, but truthfully, it didn't matter because it was already better with Landry than it had ever been before.

"No," Riley said, shaking his head. "No, I'm good. I'm so good. Please. God, *please.*"

Like before, Landry was slow. Cautious. Gradually sliding Riley's cock into his mouth inch by inch, taking his time. Making a long, leisurely perusal of every bit of it. Cataloging, Riley would guess, every single one of his reactions.

It was the most deliberate and yet the hottest blowjob he'd ever gotten.

His fingers curled into the quilt on Landry's bed, and he tried hard to just hang on and not blow his load all over Landry's face.

Not that that wouldn't be the most ridiculously wonderful outcome possible, but Riley wanted him to want to do it again. Wanted to feel this way again and again and about a hundred thousand fucking times after this.

Not helping was the running commentary Landry was subjecting him to.

You're so fucking gorgeous.

I love the way you taste.

I could do this forever.

You can't believe how fucking hot you are right now.

I'm gonna come just looking at you.

Riley panted, trying to fight for control, as Landry tried his best to take him apart.

Landry slipped his fingers lower, exploring every inch of his balls, and then he went lower still, sliding a thumb wet with spit over his hole, and Riley clenched down hard, hovering right on the edge of exploding with the most insane orgasm of his life.

Only too many years of holding back, and a history of ironclad control, kept him together.

"Landry," Riley groaned, squeezing his eyes shut.

"You practically vibrated when I did that." Landry sounded awed. And then he did it again, this time his thumb slipping in just the tiniest bit, and Riley cried out again.

"Next time," Landry vowed, "I'm gonna bend you over this bed and fuck you until you beg for more."

"You can't...you can't say that shit right now." Riley was at the top of the cliff. Teetering on it. Looking down. Craving the wind rushing by his face when he dove off.

He'd never wanted something so badly in his whole fucking life.

"Why not?" Landry sounded amused. He repeated the movement, the brush of his thumb more deliberate than experimental now, like he knew exactly what this was going to do to Riley.

Like that end goal was one *he* wanted, too.

"I'm gonna—" Riley broke off in a string of curses. "I'm gonna come, goddamnit."

"I know," Landry said and slid his cock back in his mouth. Riley felt it twitch against his tongue, once and then twice, and then he was exploding in a rush he wouldn't ever forget.

He came down slowly, realizing one moment at a time what had happened.

Landry had totally goaded him into coming in his mouth, even though he'd intended to take it easier on him.

And yes, that was totally Landry's mouth swallowing around him as his orgasm pulsed through him.

"Shit," Riley murmured, reaching down and cupping Landry's face with his palm. But his eyes were calm. Unbothered.

Okay, bothered some. Like *hot* and bothered.

Not disgusted or grossed-out bothered.

Finally, Riley's softening cock slipped from between Landry's lips, and it took every bit of Riley's determination to stay upright.

"That was," he said in a hushed voice, "the most fucking incredible..."

"It was okay?" Landry asked, sounding like he actually worried it might not be. Like it hadn't been the most mind-altering orgasm Riley had ever experienced.

"It was *more* than okay," Riley promised. "I wasn't going to...you didn't have to..."

"I wanted to," Landry said with certainty. He rose with shaky knees.

Riley turned to him, pressing a hot kiss against his mouth. "And I want to, too," he promised and reached for the fastenings on Landry's jeans.

"You touch me, I'm gonna come," Landry warned. "I'm..."

"Did that turn you on?"

Landry looked at him with wide, baffled eyes, the pupils almost totally dilated. "Is the sky blue? I had to stop myself from coming when you did."

"Really?" That was beyond hot. Riley couldn't believe how hot it was. If he hadn't just come his brains out, he'd seriously be thinking about getting hard again.

Landry nodded, and Riley didn't waste a moment. He shucked Landry's jeans off, then his boxer briefs, and took him in his hand. Landry was huge and hard, twitching as Riley's hand touched him. He wanted to lean over and finally get a taste, too, but before he even could, Landry was coming, shaking like a leaf as he shot stripe after stripe of come onto Riley's palm.

"Jesus," Landry said on a sharp exhale as he finally finished.

"I don't think he's here right now," Riley said cheekily. Reached over and grabbed a tissue from the box on the bedside table. "But next time, if you ask very nicely, I'll see if he's available to come suck your cock."

"Really?" Landry looked at him with wonder. Like that was more than he'd ever expected.

Riley rolled his eyes as he finished cleaning up. "I've only been dying to get my mouth on you for almost *ten years*. You just beat me to it, that's all."

Landry looked very smug. Like he was undeniably proud of this particular fact. He collapsed backwards on the bed, his gaze fond and affectionate on Riley as he tossed the tissues in the garbage can by the door. "I'm not gonna complain if you want to do that. And I'm definitely not gonna complain if you want me to do it again."

"Good," Riley said. He arranged himself next to Landry. "Good news, we've established we both very much like cock."

Landry laughed. "Yeah, I think that ship has sailed."

"Right out of the harbor," Riley agreed.

For a long moment, they lay there in silence.

It was nice to be able to just *be,* Riley thought, and not have to make conversation. Not have to be clever or witty or on top of his game. Landry just *accepted*.

"I hate to do this," Landry said, actually sounding regretful, "but your brother texted me about you today."

"You mean, you hate to bring my brother into this nice post-sex haze we're enjoying or you hate having to bring him up at all?" Riley joked, even though he had a feeling he knew which it was.

"Both, actually," Landry said reluctantly. "He's worried about you."

Aidan was. That was undeniable. Riley knew it just from the texts he'd gotten and ignored.

"Did you tell him he doesn't have to be?"

"Yes."

"He's just mad I didn't answer his email. Thinks I didn't read it."

"You didn't, right?" Landry reached out and stroked Riley's shoulder reassuringly.

Riley nodded. "But I haven't done that before, and unsurprisingly, Aidan isn't handling that well."

"Well, you aren't required to do anything to make him happy. You're focusing on you, and that's good."

It was. Riley couldn't argue with that.

But he also couldn't deny he'd been thinking about the email all day, not only because his brother had kept texting.

What if he'd said something good? Something helpful? Even worse, what if he'd said something *important* and Riley didn't know because he was too afraid of being chastised?

It was why he'd never deleted Aidan's emails unread before.

After all, his brother *was* a very successful NFL quarterback. He had a lot of knowledge, and it was stupid to ignore him just because he could be an asshole.

"Why do I have a feeling," Landry asked, a thread of dark amusement winding through his voice, "you don't necessarily agree?"

"I do, though. I just think..." Riley licked his lips. "I just worry I'm gonna miss something important because I'm being stubborn."

"Listen, I'm the resident expert on stubborn brothers 'cause I've got two of them—plus a sister, who between the two of us make mules look flexible," Landry pointed out dryly. "Trust me. You're not being stubborn."

Riley didn't say anything. He knew Landry was trying to help. He didn't even necessarily think Landry was *wrong*.

"What else did he say?"

What else did you tell him? was the question Riley really wanted to ask but didn't quite have the nerve to.

They hadn't even discussed between the two of them what was really going on. They'd established this was more than just experimentation or letting off steam. But if it wasn't that, what was it? Was it a relationship? Was it a *serious* relationship? Had they both caught feelings?

Riley didn't think he *could* catch feelings because he'd already had them forever.

Surely they needed to have *that* discussion before they even considered how to tell Aidan what was going on.

Though, he already knew Landry was going to be much more interested in disclosing the truth than Riley was. As far as Riley was concerned, what he did in his personal time was not his brother's business.

"Not much else," Landry admitted. "What if...what if I read the email instead of you? What if I told you if there was something you needed to know?"

Riley stared at him, but Landry's expression was perfectly serious. He meant it.

"You want to read Aidan's email and tell me if it's full of shit or not?"

Landry nodded. "That's the idea. And it's a good one, too."

Except for the part where you'll know all the stupid things Aidan calls me out for.

But he and Landry were on the same team now. He'd been front and center for every dumb mistake Riley had made, and he was still here, standing behind him, supporting him.

"Actually…it kinda is," Riley admitted. "I just can't believe you'd be willing to do that."

He'd always assumed Landry was Aidan's number-one supporter.

But maybe that wasn't necessarily as true as it had always been.

Maybe Riley had managed to steal away a little of his loyalty over the last week.

Maybe more than just a little.

It felt like Landry's gaze grew even more serious. "Riley, I know this has been…quick…but I care about you. I wouldn't be here with you otherwise."

"This is *your* house," Riley tried to tease, but he felt the impact of the words deep down. He told himself to not shy away from the seriousness of them, but he didn't *do* serious usually.

Landry's fingers reached up and stroked his face. Like he knew exactly why Riley was joking now.

"You know what I mean," he said.

Riley did.

"Yes," Riley admitted. It shouldn't be hard to admit it, but it was.

Because yes, while Riley's crush had always been there, lingering in the background, always cropping up whenever Landry came around, the emotions swirling around inside him not only felt new, they were unexpectedly strong.

"Come on, go grab your tablet and let me read it. I'm gonna go get ready for bed," Landry said, the corner of his mouth tilting up in a gentle smile. That was the other thing about Landry; besides his heart-stopping looks and his *ride-or-die* loyalty, when he left the football field, he was surprisingly measured and cautious and gentle. On the field, he was a freaking beast, but off of it, he was the kind of guy Riley had always thought he might end up with someday if he could ever slow down.

The irony was he'd had to speed up, and yet the guy had still showed up right in his path.

No, not right in his path. Not blocking him. *With* him, on the next path over. Encouraging him. Supporting him. Being a friend and now a lover.

Was it any surprise he was a little freaked out?

"Alright," Riley said. He pulled on his briefs and tank and headed out of the room.

After grabbing his tablet from his room, he detoured downstairs, pulling his phone out.

Instead of texting, this time, he called her. It was a risk, but he felt so unsettled it was worth doing.

That shouldn't be the case, not when he was finally getting everything he wanted. Right?

"Wow, hell must've frozen over," Paige said, sounding both amused and distracted when she answered. "You're actually *calling*."

"I need your help," he hissed under his breath.

"Honey, I'm gonna tell you right now I'm not the best person to ask about screens and pass protection and touchdowns."

Riley huffed under his breath. Just hearing her voice made him feel better. Slightly less out of control, anyway. "Believe me, I know that," he said. "I need you to tell me I'm not losing my mind."

Her silence was pointed.

"About?" she finally said. Though he had a feeling she didn't really need to ask. She already knew what his panic was about.

She'd probably known this moment was coming from the drinks they'd shared before he'd ever left LA.

"You know what," he said.

She sighed. "Riley, you've only liked him for what...your entire freaking life?"

"It's not the same," he insisted. "It's...it's..." He couldn't put it into words. Wished Paige was right in front of him so he could make some big wide-spread gesture. Because that might properly convey what he was feeling.

"I told you, you always sell yourself short. Settle for short term, for people you don't really like because it's simpler. It's what you're used to. You're not that involved, so it's easy to extricate yourself. It's *comfortable*, even."

"I didn't know what I was doing, or where I'd be living, or even what job I'd have in a few years. That was kind of necessary," Riley argued.

"Bullshit," Paige said simply. "You were just afraid, and that was a good excuse. But you're right there with Landry now, and you can't get away—and you don't even want to."

That was true. The closer Landry became, the more Riley squirmed uncomfortably, but when he had a chance, he still went to him, as easy as breathing.

"You're the worst," Riley muttered.

"I know, honey, I know. But it's good. This is very exciting for you."

"Don't be patronizing."

"Well, don't be a scaredy-cat, and I won't be."

Riley was silent.

"This is where you insist very adamantly that you're not terrified out of your fucking mind," Paige continued.

But he was.

There was no denying it.

He was scared of what would happen on Sunday when he took to the field.

He was even more scared Landry might see his fear and not even judge him for it.

"I can't," Riley said, and he felt raw admitting it. But it was true.

"Good," Paige said. "Now I gotta go, but you stay in touch, okay? Don't be a stranger just because you're all cuddled up with your own personal Thor."

"I won't," Riley said, and he was chuckling now because that was who Paige was. She could make him smile even when everything felt dire.

She hung up before saying anything else, and he looked up and saw Landry standing in the doorway to the kitchen, naked as the day he was born.

'Course, he hadn't looked that way the day he was born.

Are you ever gonna get used to that?

The answer was no, he never was.

Maybe that was why he couldn't stop squirming.

"I thought I lost you," Landry said as he walked past him into the kitchen, grabbing a bottle of water from the fridge. "Everything okay?"

"Yeah," Riley said. "Just needed to talk to Paige for a minute."

"Paige?" Landry raised an eyebrow.

"She's my best friend," Riley said. "Kinda the mirror I like to hold myself up to, once in a while."

"Ah, the mirror you chose. Aidan's what…the mirror you got saddled with?" Landry was quiet, but he wasn't stupid. Not by a long shot.

"Something like that," Riley said.

"Come on," Landry said. "Let's go to bed, and I'll read that email."

Yes, that was exactly the problem. No matter how scared Riley got, he'd still follow Landry anywhere, anytime he called.

It was a siren song he didn't even want to fight.

They settled back in Landry's bed, Landry with Riley's tablet, and Riley with his phone, scrolling through his *Instagram* feed.

Someday maybe Landry would make a full confession about what had changed his mind about *Instagram*.

But today was not that day.

He found Aidan's email in Riley's trash folder and opened it.

Landry hadn't known what to expect. He'd had some idea, of course, because of the things Aidan had said over the years and references Riley had made since coming to Charleston.

But still, Landry hadn't expected this.

"You know, this would almost be nice if you weren't currently dealing with my brother's crap," Riley said, as Landry was reading the email for the third time, trying to tamp down a spike of sudden temper at the patronizing, blunt way Aidan laid out every single mistake—or even slight *misstep*—Riley had made during the game, starting with the safety he'd given up and even ending with criticism about the way he'd scored the Condors' last touchdown. Aidan hadn't liked the route he'd taken. There'd been a better one, or so he claimed.

Personally, Landry thought that was bullshit.

Aidan ended the email by offering scant praise at the win, adding that he shouldn't get used to relying so heavily on his defense.

Except the Condors had won twenty-four to five.

By *nineteen fucking points.*

That was hardly relying on the defense.

Landry tossed the tablet down to the bed before he did something stupid, like hurling it at the wall.

"How do you do it?" he asked, or really, quasi-demanded.

Riley just shrugged. Like this was normal. "He was probably worked up about the safety and was worse than usual. That's not...that's not unexpected."

"It is to me," Landry said, and he slung an arm around Riley's shoulders, tugging him close. "Why is your brother such a..." He couldn't think of what exactly Aidan was; that was how angry he was.

"Controlling asshole? Total butthead? Unrepentant jerk?" Riley was actually still smiling. Probably because he hadn't read the email, but Landry had.

"Yes," Landry said between clenched teeth.

"So nothing worth reading?" Riley asked the question lightly, but Landry heard the uncertainty in Riley's voice.

The lack of confidence.

"Riley, you led us to a great win," Landry said, trying to find his patience. Not that Riley had tested it; it was Aidan who was making it so hard not to totally lose his shit. "You did that. Not Aidan. He wasn't there. But you were. Just you."

"He kinda was, though. He's given me lots of good advice over the years. I mean, terrible advice, too, in that a lot of it made me want to throw in the towel, but I've learned with him. You gotta take some of the bad with the good."

"No," Landry said. "You don't. You don't have to do that."

"See?" Riley sighed. "This is why I didn't want you to read it. Now you're pissed off at him. I didn't want to fuck up your friendship. You were friends with him first, for a long time, before we even..." He trailed off like he wasn't sure what they were doing.

Landry wasn't sure what they were doing either, but he knew enough to know he wanted to fight for Riley—tooth and nail.

Even against his best friend.

"I mean this with all the love for Aidan in the world, and honestly, I probably love him more than almost anyone else, but he's not only full of himself, he's also full of shit."

"He can be."

"Which is why you need to tell him to fuck off. Which is why I'm thinking *I* want to tell him to fuck off."

"You can't," Riley protested.

He really shouldn't. Landry knew it. The relationship between Riley and Aidan was their own business. Just like his own relationship with Aidan was between the two of them.

And the relationship he shared with Riley was their own business.

He could imagine that was going to make Aidan *really* lose his shit, even though it was absolutely none of his business.

"I know," Landry acknowledged. "I can't."

"I can't believe there was *nothing* helpful," Riley said, grimacing.

"You might want to take a look at the route you took on that last touchdown, see if maybe you could adjust it." Landry hated saying it because the route he *had* taken was good enough. Good enough to score.

But maybe Aidan had had a point—and if he didn't, it would be easy enough to see on film.

"I know which one you're talking about," Riley said, humming to himself as he recalled the play. "I'll take a look at it tomorrow."

Landry buried his face in Riley's shoulder. Feeling more in this moment than he necessarily felt comfortable with. He hadn't realized reading that email was going to be taking a peek behind the curtain. That it would be like seeing right into Riley's soul and what he'd put up with over the years.

That it would make him want to burrow in even deeper.

"Thank you," Riley said softly. "I know that was...weird. But it feels good to actually not have to shovel through all that crap."

"You shouldn't have to," Landry argued.

"Haven't your brothers given you a lot of trouble over the years?"

"Yeah, but...but not like this," Landry said.

It was true. His brothers were seriously going to make him prematurely gray. He'd hated how Logan dealt with the ex-boyfriend who'd outed him the year before. He'd hated how he'd just sat and *taken* all the bullshit the guy had said about him and his friend—at the time—Dylan.

But Logan was a big boy, and he'd handled it, and it had turned out that all the ways Landry had wanted to take care of it would've only made it worse.

It had been tough to acknowledge but necessary to realize that Logan had been right.

And Levi? Landry worried about him being all alone out there in Seattle, with nobody he was close to, sticking just to hookups, the way Logan used to before he'd met Dylan.

Maybe he could use some of what Logan had learned here.

Or maybe he could just call up Aidan and give him a piece of his mind.

"Don't," Riley said, but he was smiling. Landry could feel it. "I know what you're thinking, and don't."

"Alright," Landry said. "But know that I want to."

"I do." Riley's voice was quiet. Serious.

Landry reached over and switched off the light, and it felt so natural to just fall asleep like that.

Chapter 12

Unfortunately, everything returning to normal was easier said than done.

Aidan sent Landry more texts over the next few days. He assumed Aidan was texting Riley, too, but he didn't ask what the messages said because his brain kept filling in the worst possible things. That was no good because he didn't need to go AWOL from the Condors, head up to Toronto, and punch Aidan in the face.

But even if he didn't confront Aidan, he clearly wasn't very happy with Landry.

Probably because Landry had put him off with responses like, **Riley's fine. Stop worrying.** Or: **Don't you have some game to be playing in this week?**

The last thing Landry wanted was to get caught up in an argument with Aidan over what he'd said to his brother.

Because the truth was, he was still way too fucking pissed.

He'd say something he'd regret. Either about what Aidan had said or about what Riley had come to mean to him.

Someday, they needed to have a conversation about that, but right now was the wrong time, even if Landry knew what he wanted to say.

"You're staring at your phone like it's personally injured you," Deacon said, flopping down into the chair next to Landry's.

He'd been hoping to have lunch with Riley, but he'd gotten dragged into yet another video session, and he probably wouldn't see him until practice this afternoon.

Landry told himself he wasn't sulking about that, and he wasn't sulking about Aidan's latest message either, demanding again he interfere and convince Riley to talk to him.

The problem was he'd always taken Aidan's side.

But he couldn't anymore.

"Maybe it has," Landry said morosely.

On one hand, things with Riley were so goddamn good, but on the other, he'd never had any idea Aidan was so brutal with his feedback.

If he'd known, would he have done anything? Would he have convinced Aidan to cut it out? He didn't know because he hadn't known Riley back then, except for what Aidan had told him.

Maybe he'd have believed his best friend. He'd have had no reason to do otherwise.

That thought was certainly not helping his bad mood.

"You wanna talk about it?" Deacon paused. "I can't believe there's trouble in paradise already."

Landry rolled his eyes. "It's not about Riley." That wasn't really a lie, because all of this was really about *Aidan* and the fucked up way he thought he was helping his brother.

It was about their friendship and how to salvage it from this sudden wreck.

He didn't want to hate Aidan; he *loved* him.

"You ever have a friend who you *know* is doin' the wrong thing? And you want to stop it, but stopping it will…jeopardize your friendship? Maybe destroy it forever?"

Deacon eyed him seriously. "This isn't about Riley."

"This isn't about Riley," Landry agreed.

"Huh, well, I don't know," Deacon said. He stared at his chicken sandwich speculatively. "You know, last year was total shit."

Landry was aware, though he had a feeling it was one thing to know most of the details, and it was another to have lived it. He nodded.

"I had friends on the team who didn't have a problem with signing Tom Taylor. Didn't have an issue with throwin' Davis under the bus, even though he'd done everything he could as a quarterback to put us in a position to win. Guys I thought were friends who had no issues going along with all of that. Had no problems with implementing the bounty system they came up with at the end of the season, even though the Piranhas beat us the first time fair and square." Deacon sighed. "I spoke up because I couldn't do anything else. 'Course it didn't do jack shit. I knew it wouldn't. But what else could I do? I couldn't just stand by and say nothing. But I spoke up and said my piece, and then everything they did after that, that was on them."

"You're not friends with them anymore," Landry guessed.

"No. We're not friends anymore. I'm supposing you want to stay friends with this person."

"Yeah. Yeah, I do."

"Aidan Flynn wouldn't be an easy person to be friends with. Not for as long as y'all have been friends."

Landry nearly asked how he'd guessed, but Deacon was smart. He knew his history. He knew some of Riley's history. And Jem had played with Aidan in Toronto for a few years before coming here.

"You'd be surprised, probably," Landry said with a sigh. "He's...well, he's not what everyone thinks he is. And I'll be the first to admit that in the last few years, he's changed. Gotten harder. Tougher."

"The NFL's gotten harder, tougher, too," Deacon pointed out.

Landry knew it. But he also knew that wasn't the only thing.

Aidan had gotten caught up in his own mystique. But lately, it had been even more than that. He'd gotten dissatisfied but refused to talk about it. Kept his distance sometimes. To the point where Landry couldn't get through to him.

Landry knew deep down Aidan was afraid of what Riley succeeding would mean for him, no matter how unfair that was.

But none of that excused what he'd said to Riley in that email—and no doubt in countless others.

"Yeah, it has," Landry said. "But that's not all of it. I just..." He didn't know what to say. He'd told Deacon this wasn't about Riley, and it wasn't.

But it was, too.

"You know he calls him *the kid*?" Landry said.

Deacon's lips quirked up into a smile. "Thought this wasn't about Riley."

"In some ways, everything's about Riley," Landry pointed out wryly.

"I get it. I've been in love before. Didn't work out, but didn't mean I didn't feel it at the time."

Landry opened his mouth to argue he wasn't in love. He couldn't be. But maybe...well, his reaction certainly seemed to prove otherwise, didn't it? He shut it again. Didn't know *what* to say to that. But luckily, Deacon kept talking.

"Riley's got a level head on his shoulders. He can handle himself," Deacon continued.

"Yeah, but—"

"But?" Deacon raised an eyebrow.

"I said it wasn't about him, and I can't say it isn't a *little* about him, but this is also about me and Aidan. Our friendship. I gotta say something. He keeps pushing, and I'm gonna...well, explode. Lose my shit on him. I don't want to do that. That'll drive him away for sure."

"Then tell him," Deacon said bluntly. "Before you do or say anything you'll regret."

Landry knew what he wasn't saying: that maybe the friendship would be ruined, but it would've been ruined anyway if Aidan kept on behaving this way.

He wanted to think Deacon was wrong, overreacting, but he didn't think so, not anymore. Not after reading that email.

Riley would probably argue that some of the criticisms made him a better quarterback, and even helped him end up here in Charleston. But Landry couldn't accept any of that.

The man who'd written that email had taken Overprotective Brother Bot to a whole new level, and Landry couldn't tolerate it, even if Riley found a way to.

It was cruel in a way Aidan had never been cruel.

"You know what you have to do," Deacon said after finishing his sandwich. He pushed back his chair and stood. "I'll see you at practice."

Landry had a spare hour and a half before practice and decided to spend it in the gym.

He didn't typically lift on Wednesdays, but his temper was still boiling away inside him every time he thought of the condescending, patronizing way Aidan had talked to his brother.

The way he still insisted on calling him *the kid*.

How, before this summer, Landry had actually found that sorta *funny*.

Well, he wasn't laughing now.

He was sweating through a series of bicep curls when his phone buzzed in his pocket. Then again. Then a third time.

He finished his set, and checked his phone, hoping, maybe, Riley had gotten out of his meeting early, but no, it wasn't Riley.

It was Aidan.

Calling.

Landry's fingers tightened on his phone. The last thing he wanted was to destroy their friendship, but like Deacon said, if he left things unsaid, all that shit was going to do that anyway.

Maybe he could say some of it. Say the bare bones of it, anyway.

He answered. "You stalkin' me now, Flynn?" he asked, adopting a casual, teasing tone.

"I wouldn't have to if either of you would actually talk to me," Aidan said with undisguised annoyance.

"I responded to every single one of your texts," Landry said, continuing to play dumb.

"Yeah, but not with what I…" Aidan broke off. "Riley's dodging me, and you're not helping me at all with that. What's the point of having him *right there*, in your house, and practicing next to you if you're not gonna help me out?"

"Riley's an adult," Landry said. And, oh boy, was he—but that wasn't the point of this conversation. He dragged his mind back on track. "Riley's a grown person, Aidan. He doesn't have to talk to you."

"What's that supposed to mean?" Aidan sounded pissed off and also borderline panicked now.

"It means I'm not gonna be your errand boy," Landry said firmly. "You want to talk to Riley, then *talk* to him, don't order him or boss him or God forbid, criticize him. I think he'll be a lot less likely to dodge your texts and your calls if he doesn't actively dread everything about you."

"I still don't know what you're talking about." Aidan's tone had morphed again, and now he was sulking.

But he knew.

"I mean, *be nice*," Landry said firmly. "And for God's sake, stop trying to win the Overprotective Brother of the Year award. You've got a whole bunch of them on your shelf already, right next to your MVPs. You don't need one more."

Aidan didn't say anything.

"Personally, I think he's doing great," Landry said. Told himself he'd have said that no matter what. Even if they weren't sleeping together, even if he wasn't crazy about Riley. It was just the truth, wasn't it? "He's a dynamic player. Dynamic like you, but different, too. You can rest easy. You taught him everything you know, and he's gonna be right up there in the future."

"Great." But Aidan didn't sound particularly happy about that outcome.

Landry didn't understand. "You're not jealous, are you?"

"Jealous? *Jealous*? Fuck no."

"Good. Because you've got enough issues already."

"I do not," Aidan sputtered.

But he did—and even if Aidan denied it, he knew fear mingled with jealousy over how Riley might do in the NFL was one of them.

Landry didn't know what the rest of them were, but he knew the man well enough to know they definitely existed. Maybe someday Aidan would choose to confide in him, or maybe, instead, they'd drift apart.

Or even worse, maybe they'd end up fighting over Riley, and their friendship would end up exploding in one big catastrophic argument.

"Yeah, you do, but it's alright."

"Well, thanks," Aidan retorted sarcastically. "I appreciate your understanding."

That prickliness that had been growing over the last few years was what told Landry something was up.

Just not what that something was.

He nearly asked, but he could already tell Aidan wasn't in the mood to share.

Not today, anyway.

"You know I'm always here for you, Aidan," Landry pointed out.

"Yeah, except when I want you to get Riley to talk to me," Aidan said.

"I told you—"

"Yeah, yeah, I know. Riley's his own person, *blah blah blah*. Fine. I'll try to be nicer if you'll try to put in a good word, okay?"

"Alright," Landry said, only because Aidan *had* promised to try to be nicer.

It wasn't going to fix everything, that was for sure. But maybe slowly, it would begin to get better between them. If Riley was honest, and Aidan was nice, maybe.

He hung up the phone and finished his workout, heading down to the locker room to get ready for practice.

Riley and Charlie were sitting on one of the couches in the locker room, absorbed in a tablet, going over some plays, but when Landry passed by, Riley glanced up, and there was a wealth of words in that single look.

Missed you.

Want you.

Hope Aidan didn't piss you off too much.

Have a good practice.

Can't wait to get home with you.

It wasn't nearly as good as hearing Riley tell him all those things—or saying them himself—but it would have to do.

A few of the players they were close to had definitely seen them together at the Pirate's Booty on Monday night, but they weren't officially a couple, and Coach Kelley didn't know either, so this would have to be enough for now.

When they headed to the field, Coach Oscar called out, "Gather up, guys. Let's go over the plan for the day."

Landry jogged over and discovered when he did that the plan for the day was a clinic on route-running.

Something every guy who caught a ball could improve on, even him. Even Carter, who kept making faces about the implication that he wasn't absolutely fucking brilliant every time he set foot on the field.

And in a turn of events he hadn't expected, they'd be running routes with the actual starting corners covering them. "A test," Coach Oscar said, "for both sides of the ball."

Which meant that after the team warmup, Landry found himself lining up opposite Rex, the corner Deacon had said he didn't quite trust.

But Landry himself didn't have feelings about Rex one way or the other.

At least until Coach blew his whistle, Cole snapped the ball, and Riley dropped back.

The play they were running was a button-hook route, where Landry would pretend to sit in the soft part of the zone, then once he was past the safety, he'd curl around, hopefully deep down the field, and Riley would hit him right on the edge.

It was designed, when executed well, to result in a touchdown, or at the very least, a thirty or forty-yard gain, *and* it was typically the kind of route the Carters of the world would run. But Landry wasn't the run-of-the-mill kind of tight end. His ceiling was much higher. He knew it, and he definitely knew Coach knew it, which was why he'd given it to Landry to execute first.

"Gonna make me work for it?" Rex asked, raising an eyebrow, and for the first time, Landry thought he saw something in his eyes, in the smugness of his taunt, that he didn't like either. Maybe it wasn't just Deacon's instincts overreacting.

But before he could look closer, the play began, and he took off, noting his position to Riley, to the safety, hanging back in the zone, and also Rex, who was shadowing him pretty closely.

In a real game, Rex might not be so sure Landry was the targeted receiver, but here, it was obvious enough that he barely gave him any room to maneuver, constantly trying to box him out, make it so Landry couldn't turn around and catch the ball.

It wasn't *quite* playing dirty. Landry had been covered by enough corners playing dirty he could tell the difference, but it was skating right along the edge, and frankly, it pissed him off. This was just practice. Who would be stupid enough to risk injury to themselves or one of their teammates by being so unnecessarily aggressive?

Landry jabbed with his elbow, turning just in time to see Riley releasing the ball. The timing wasn't perfect, but then game timing rarely was, either, so maybe this was good practice.

Still, he wasn't happy about it. Not at all.

But that wasn't the end of being annoyed. Not by a long shot.

Because then, a split second before everything went to shit, Landry felt the pressure of Rex's leg against his own, then they were tangled up, and Landry fell to the ground, unable to keep himself upright, landing with an *oomph,* as Rex batted the ball away above him.

It wasn't the first—and definitely not the last time—he'd been tripped up by a corner. But maybe one of the first times it had happened during practice and definitely the first time during a practice when he was sure it was on purpose.

For a second, Landry lay against the turf. His back ached, understandably, but as he felt his extremities, he was pretty sure other than a few bruises, he'd be fine.

Still. What the fuck had Rex been thinking?

"Landry!"

He glanced over and saw Riley running over. Out of the corner saw Rex, too. Saw the smugness on his face before he turned away.

Yeah, Deacon had good instincts, and Landry didn't think he was wrong.

He hadn't wanted to get beat today, and Landry had been about to beat him.

"Oh my God," Riley said, out of breath, leaning down close to him. "Are you okay?"

He'd gotten here so quick that he must've run full out. The concern on his face told the whole story: he must've gone down as ugly as it had felt.

He was lucky he didn't have a broken ankle or a sprained knee. Or worse.

"I'm good," Landry said, and Riley reached out a hand to help him up. He groaned a little as he stood. "Gonna be black and blue tomorrow."

"Whoops," Rex said with a shrug. "Sorry about that, dude."

But his apology didn't reach his eyes.

"You good to go again?" Coach Oscar said, arriving at their little group.

Landry met Riley's gaze. "Yeah, I'd like to try that again," he said.

This time he wouldn't let some amateur move literally trip him up.

He'd expect Rex to play dirty.

"You sure?" Coach looked worried—but not as worried as Riley, who was still frowning. "Don't need to get checked out or anything?"

"I'm good," Landry reassured him.

He'd noticed this overabundance of caution when it came to conditioning and injuries since coming to the Condors, and based on comments a few of the guys had made who'd been here last year, that was for a reason.

They were actively trying to change the culture of the team, and that wasn't an easy thing to do.

"Alright. But we're gonna give you a play off. Maxwell, you're up next."

Landry considered arguing, but when he started to jog over to the sideline, the leg he'd fallen on was already protesting.

He'd definitely be spending some time in the ice bath post-practice.

Reaching the sideline, he hit the bench, grabbing a cup of Gatorade, sipping it as he watched the same play unfold again.

This time, though, Landry noticed that Coach hadn't put Rex on Carter; he'd put Eric on him instead. The other starting corner.

Carter might not have had Landry's finesse with routes—though Landry had a feeling he'd fight him on that—but he didn't have to because he had a whole new gear Landry didn't have a hope of reaching.

He sprinted past the line, losing Eric in the first few steps, though when Carter slowed down in the zone, past the safety, he did manage to mostly catch up—but, in the end, it didn't matter because then Carter found that other gear again, and Riley's throw found *him*.

And because Carter already had half a dozen paces on Eric, and he was long past Beck, there was nobody to stop him from practically jogging right into the end zone.

On the next play, Landry got back on the field, blocking as Nick was tripped up by Rex just before Riley could throw the ball.

He saw Nick's disgusted expression before he turned his head and wondered if he was mad at himself—or maybe more understandably with Rex.

Then it was Landry's turn again.

"You ready?" Riley asked him before Coach blew the whistle.

"Yeah, I'm good," Landry said.

What he meant was, *I'm not gonna let this asshole play dirty this time without playing dirty right back.*

Rex lined up in front of him again, and for a second, Landry saw the concern flash across Coach's face. But he let it go. It was the right thing to do, to let him work through this, and that he'd decided the same thing made Landry respect him a little bit more.

The play unfolded the same way as it had the first time. Landry found a little extra burst of speed, glad that he'd put in the hard days during the off-season, and managed to put a little more distance between himself and Rex.

But still, Rex stuck to him like glue.

Landry huffed out a breath as he got close again, pushing right into Landry's space.

But this time, Landry didn't give him a chance to stick his feet right into his path, and instead, he shoved hard with his elbow, turning his body so Coach wouldn't see it and call it like the blatant foul that it was.

Rex went down like a sack of potatoes, with an accompanying groan, as Landry's elbow connected right with his stomach.

Angling his arms, he watched as Riley's pass arced towards him, and he caught it mid-stride, covering the rest of the field to the end zone in a few long strides.

Riley's face lit up.

"Touchdown!" Carter hollered, from the other side of the field, miming the ref's action with his arms.

"Great play," Riley said with a smirk when Landry returned to the huddle. "I especially liked that stiff-arm."

"What stiff-arm?" Landry said innocently.

But Rex was glowering as he limped over to the bench.

Served him right, Landry decided.

Later, when practice was breaking up, Carter meandered over to where Landry was standing by the bench.

There was something unexpectedly contrite in Carter's face. An emotion he'd never seen there before.

"Sorry," Carter muttered under his breath. "Should've warned you Rex can't keep his elbows or his feet to himself."

Landry wanted to be surprised, but deep down, he wasn't as much as he should be.

"Seriously?" Landry said. "Why didn't you say something to someone?"

But Carter just shrugged. "It's good practice, I guess. 'Cause it's not like corners keep them to themselves during games. I've gotten better at shrugging him off. But you weren't expecting it. You should've been."

"Still," Landry said, feeling like he should be pushing this. The Bills never would've tolerated that behavior at practice because, like any NFL team worth their salt, they wanted to field a *complete* team on game day. Not lose players to stupid, easily prevented injuries.

"Yeah, who's gonna believe me," Carter said wryly. "I'm Carter Maxwell. I know what they say about me. *Talented guy, but let me tell you all about all his fuckups.*"

"Don't sell yourself short," Landry said firmly, patting him on the shoulder pad. "He pulls that shit on you again, you tell me. One better—you tell Coach."

"Everything okay?" Riley asked as he approached.

"Everything's fine," Carter said cheerfully.

Landry considered disagreeing with Carter's assessment, but if he did, maybe Carter wouldn't tell him the next time.

He'd been around this team long enough to realize there was definitely going to be a next time. Yes, the Condors had significantly cleaned up their act, but there were still residual problems lingering right under the surface. Everything wasn't fixed, and pretending it was, wasn't going to do anyone any favors.

"I think that just about wraps it up," Charlie said, shutting his tablet, scrubbing a hand over his face. He looked about as tired as Riley felt. "I think I'm gettin' too old for this."

"If you are, then so am I," Riley said. "'Cause I'm worn out. But I wanted to go over one more play."

He'd considered watching this particular snippet of film on his own because it was entirely possible Aidan was full of shit.

It wouldn't be the first time.

But it also wouldn't be the first time he was right.

"One more play? Really? Okay, which one."

Riley cued it up on the screen.

"What?" Charlie looked confused. "This one? You scored a touchdown on this play."

"Yeah, I did," Riley said, watching as the play unfolded. It hadn't originally called for him to keep the ball and run for it, but when the defense had rushed, his offensive line had managed to split them, and he'd seen the opening and run right through into the end zone. It had seemed like a pretty easy decision at the time—touchdown or *no* touchdown—but then Aidan had brought it up specifically.

"Why are we watching this again?" Charlie asked, as Riley played the clip for the second time. He sounded mystified.

Riley wasn't sure either. But there was something...the way the defense had shifted in response to their own formation...*yep,* there it was.

He could see it now. Exactly what Aidan had said. There'd been another route. An easier route. And, if he wasn't imagining things, he could've actually gotten Landry the ball. In Aidan's mind, a throwing touchdown was always better than a running one. *You won't be able to keep running the ball the way you are now*, he'd said to him probably a hundred times. *Don't just be a glorified running back. If you're gonna be a quarterback, be a quarterback.*

"I see it," Charlie said. "I can't believe…" He trailed off.

"What? That I didn't see it? Me, either. Well, put something on the weekly schedule…go over all the scoring plays, too."

"Really?" Charlie sounded surprised. "Do you really think that's necessary?"

"We can learn as much from our successes as our failures," Riley repeated, his stomach sinking.

He hadn't wanted Aidan to be right.

It was galling that he could be such a jerk, but what was *most* infuriating was how often he was spot-on with his assessments.

"That doesn't even sound like you," Charlie observed.

Riley began to pack up. He was ready to get home. Hug Landry. Collapse into bed.

Then get up tomorrow and do the whole thing over again.

"It's not me," Riley said matter-of-factly. "That's one of my brother's favorite sayings."

"Ah, Aidan." There seemed to be a wealth of meaning in those two words.

"Yep," Riley said. He really didn't want to talk about it. First off, he was too tired. Second off, he was even more conflicted about his brother than he'd ever been.

If only he'd been wrong.

But he hadn't been.

"He giving you shit?" Charlie asked, waiting until they were in the elevator, heading up to the main level, where the entrance to the parking garage was.

"Aidan? Uh, well, not any more than usual." Riley wasn't sure whether that was the truth or a lie, considering how many unanswered texts were sitting on his phone.

Aidan hadn't taken his silence well at all.

But then, Riley hadn't really expected that he would.

"You should—"

But Riley knew how this went. He'd heard it enough times from enough people. "Tell him to fuck off? Yeah, I know."

"Actually, no, that's not what I was about to say." Charlie grinned. "But yes, that works, too."

His phone buzzed again in his pocket like Aidan had somehow known they were talking about him.

Of course, it could be any number of other people, but at this particular time? When Riley was just finishing up his work day?

Well, chances were good it was Aidan doing the same.

"Why don't you?"

"Because of plays like that," Riley said, gesturing. "Because he was right. He's right more often than he's wrong."

"So are you," Charlie insisted. "You're gonna lead us to another great win this week. I feel it."

Riley knew Charlie meant well. But still. "Appreciate it, man," he said, and the elevator doors dinged open. "Tell the girls hi from me."

"Will do. Natasha keeps telling me she wants a jersey with your name on it. Guess I'm just not that cool anymore."

"Were you ever?" Riley teased.

Charlie chuckled and broke off on the way to his own car.

Riley had finally found the time to grab a rental, so Landry wouldn't have to stick around for him past when he might normally. And as the starting quarterback, that was becoming more and more likely. Landry had grumbled about it, which had touched Riley, but it made sense.

He unlocked the car and slid inside, tossing his bag into the backseat.

Sat there for a long moment, then dug his phone out of his pocket.

He'd been right. The text *had* been from Aidan.

Don't hate me, was all it said.

"Fuck," Riley said, banging his free hand against the steering wheel. It was like Aidan *knew* the only way to get through to him was to be semi-apologetic.

Semi because it wasn't like Aidan ever bothered to actually apologize.

But they both knew this was as close as he was getting.

He pressed call before he could change his mind. "I don't hate you," he said when Aidan answered with a cautious, "Riley?"

Aidan didn't say anything for a long moment.

"I just didn't want you to say anything about the stupid mistake," Riley continued, feeling reckless. "And I knew you would."

"It's what I do," Aidan acknowledged.

Didn't even sound like he regretted it.

Years ago, Riley might've told him that maybe, just maybe, he could try not to do it, but he'd learned there was no point. This was who Aidan was.

He should've spent all those years coming to terms with it, learning to live with it. But he never had.

It still stung every time, no matter how much he tried to fight the hurt.

"You know, you could've just said, *good job*," Riley said.

"What're you gonna learn from that?" Aidan asked, but his voice was as gentle as it got. "That's not gonna help you win *next* week, or the week after, or the week when it really matters. You know that."

Just like that touchdown play, Riley wanted so badly for him to be wrong.

But he knew Aidan wasn't.

Just like he knew he'd never *really* tell his brother to fuck off.

Riley sighed.

"I know, you hate it when I'm right," Aidan said.

"How'd you know about that play?" Riley asked, changing the subject. Because there was no use in going round and round about the same fucking topic. Aidan wasn't going to change, and Riley wasn't going to stop wanting him to.

"I watched it. That's how. You know, I've told you that you shouldn't just be reviewing your fuckups but your successes, too. Learn from them, too." Aidan took a breath, and Riley knew he was going to keep going. Going to keep lecturing, but he was full up with that kind of thing already.

"Yeah," Riley said before he could start in again. "Message received."

"Alright."

"Your practices going okay?" Riley asked into the awkward silence. This was why they rarely talked on the phone. The minefield of things they'd only argue about was too treacherous. Too full of things that *might* make him hate his brother, and he didn't want to.

"Fine, of course."

Of course.

Riley rolled his eyes.

"Charlie workin' out for you okay as a backup? I hear he's kinda taken the quasi-coach role, too," Aidan said.

"Yeah, he's cool. Good at the job. I wouldn't be surprised if he ends up as a coach one day."

"You know what they say: those who can't do, teach."

"Aidan," Riley warned.

"I know, it's shitty. Don't you think I don't know how shitty it is? I *like* Charlie. I want more for him, same as I want more for you. But you know why I say it—I don't want you to end up like him. Washed-up and barely hangin' onto a backup spot. You're worth more than that."

"Even if that's what I want?" Riley retorted.

Aidan didn't say anything to that.

He was probably thinking the same thing: *this is why we don't usually do this.*

"Don't ignore me next time," Aidan said brusquely. *Then we don't have to do this again.*

"I was busy," Riley tried protesting, but he knew it was pointless.

Aidan knew; Aidan *always* knew.

Sometimes he even knew best.

But not one hundred percent of the time.

"Yeah, okay," Aidan said, sounding amused. "Just let me know you're alive, alright?"

"You have Landry for that." Riley had told himself he was not going to bring up Landry because Aidan was weirdly observant, and what if he gave something away before either of them was ready to tell him? Or before they even knew what to say about it?

"Landry's strangely protective of your status." Aidan's tone was frustrated. "Doesn't want to get involved."

"I don't blame him for that. I wouldn't want to get involved between us either."

"Riley."

"Don't *Riley* me."

"Hey, at least I didn't call you the kid. You know I'm trying not to do that anymore."

"Yeah, for good reason 'cause I'm *twenty-four*," Riley retorted.

"Fine, fine, *fine*," Aidan said. "I mean it, though."

"Okay." Riley didn't know what he meant. That he wanted to make sure he was alive? Or that he didn't want Riley to hate him?

Or both?

"Good luck this week."

"You, too," Riley said. "I gotta go." He needed to before he said something he'd regret.

Like that he missed and dreaded Aidan in equal parts.

CHAPTER 13

"You've been quiet," Carter said, pointing his fork at Riley. "Are you stressing about what kind of bill we're gonna run up?"

Riley still wasn't sure how Carter Maxwell ended up invited to his first offensive line dinner.

Actually, that wasn't quite true. He knew. Riley had invited him at the last second because he'd wanted Landry there, and it would seem *less* weird if Carter came, too.

"No," Riley said.

For his first time hosting the offensive line dinner, Charlie had helped him find an upscale steak and fish house downtown, pointing out that they often rented out private rooms. "*We won't want to be bothered*," he'd reminded Riley, for which Riley was grateful. He *didn't* want to be bothered. Especially the last few days.

"See?" Carter gestured again. "You're weirdly quiet."

Boyd, the left tackle, chuckled. "Nobody's gettin' a word in edgewise, Maxwell."

That was *also* true.

But Riley knew he'd been quiet.

He'd been quiet ever since he'd talked to Aidan.

Why hadn't he told him to stop? It had been the perfect moment to really stand up for himself. Aidan might've even listened—or tried to.

But he hadn't taken the step and cut the cord because what if he did? What might happen?

Riley loved Aidan, even when he didn't want to.

Aidan was his brother, even though it wasn't like he felt blood meant anything. After all, how long had it been since he'd talked to either of his parents? He wasn't exactly losing sleep over that.

Something brushed against Riley's foot as he contemplated what to say that would adequately explain his introspection. Then he felt that same touch again.

Riley looked up and saw Landry staring at him from across the table.

"Nervous, I guess, about Sunday," Riley said.

It wasn't like he'd even lied. Of course he was nervous. Whenever he thought about it, what was riding on Sunday's game, all the pressure of his future piling on him, he felt a little nauseated.

Then, inevitably, he thought, *And what will Aidan say if I don't succeed?*

But Riley already knew what Aidan would say. *Hey, why don't you come to Toronto and work for me?*

Hell would freeze over before that happened, but it's not like his complete disinterest in becoming his brother's assistant would stop him from suggesting it.

"You're lookin' real strong in practice," Cole said loyally.

"Yeah, seriously," Boyd agreed.

It was great that the guys on the offensive line had his back—both literally and figuratively—but even that knowledge didn't shake Riley's bad mood.

But then Landry's foot nudged his again, and when Riley looked over at him, the corner of his mouth was quirked up.

"Thanks, guys," Riley said. He *was* grateful this team had already accepted him, and not only that, but that they were already beginning to feel like a family. He'd not expected that just like he hadn't expected Landry to come back into his life like he had.

From what he'd heard his brother say over the years, he might've been successful in Toronto, but Aidan had always been an island.

You're not your brother. You're your own person; your own kind of success.

When he'd come home the night before, frustrated and exhausted, Landry had asked him if he wanted to talk about it. Riley hadn't, but he'd worried turning Landry down on his obvious invitation would upset him.

But the opposite had happened. Instead, Landry had just held out his arms, and he'd held him for a long time. Not asking what happened. Not needing to know what Aidan had said or hadn't said.

He'd just supported him.

The same way the guys around him were doing now.

"I'm proposing a toast," Riley said, raising his water glass. "To turning a new page this Sunday. And to playing the game like it was meant to be played."

"Amen!" Boyd said.

Cole added his own cheer to his fellow lineman's.

"It's gonna be a great game," Carter agreed. "I feel good about it."

"Don't jinx us," Landry retorted, but he was smiling as his foot absently tapped against Riley's.

Reminding him, Riley realized, that he was here for him.

No matter what.

He hadn't said those words. They hadn't even talked about their relationship—even though that was very definitely what they were embarking on—only kept sleeping together in the same bed.

There'd been less of the fun kind of sleeping together and more of the just sleeping together variety because they'd not only been worn out from the long days, but Riley had been understandably preoccupied with his brother's bullshit. But now, staring at Landry across the table, his blond-streaked dark hair resting around his shoulders, the face he didn't even realize was gorgeous and irresistible in the dim lighting of the restaurant, Riley felt that indefinable spark of attraction flare up inside him.

He adjusted in his seat, letting his whole calf brush up against Landry's.

Landry raised an eyebrow, which Riley answered with a grin.

"You two are adorable," Carter said, leaning over so his voice didn't carry across the table. Riley was grateful because he was pretty sure Rex and Cole, along with the rest of the line, didn't realize what was going on between them, and he wasn't really ready for anyone else to find out.

Not until he and Landry talked through what they were doing—and tonight, he wasn't in the mood for conversation.

He was in the mood for something involving a hell of a lot less words.

All it had taken was the realization that he wasn't his brother.

He was his own person, totally unique despite the same last name, and whatever happened, he was allowed to judge his success by a different standard.

By his own standard.

He knew better, but he'd been letting Aidan's own mile-high requirements color what he believed he was capable of. He'd been letting *Aidan* set the standard. But no more.

Aidan had helped him, no doubt about it, but Riley didn't need him.

Sure, there'd been another path to that touchdown, but he'd still scored, hadn't he?

He'd made that happen. Not Aidan. He and his team.

"I don't know what you're talking about," Riley teased, pretending innocence, even as he slipped out of his shoe and let his sock-clad foot caress Landry's leg. Watching as Landry's eyes darkened with undeniable desire.

"Yeah, no clue whatsoever," Carter said sarcastically. "You're only eye-fucking each other across the table."

"Feeling jealous?" Landry spoke up.

Which was so freaking ironic Riley couldn't help but chuckle. Because, from Landry's own confessions, *he'd* been the jealous one.

"No, of course not. I could pick up anyone I wanted to," Carter boasted smugly. "Could have super hot sex any night of the week. *Every* night of the week."

"Yeah," Landry agreed, but then he leaned forward, and the heat in his gaze licked right up Riley's spine. "That sounds fine and all, but what about cuddling?"

Carter shot both of them an incredulous glance. "That what you're tryin' to convince me you're doing? Bullshit. I call bullshit."

"Bullshit, huh? That's rich coming from you, Maxwell," Riley teased. "But yeah, we're all about the cuddling. Landry's my own real live teddy bear."

Landry grinned at him.

"Gross," Carter said. "You two aren't just fucking. You're *in love*."

Riley's insides froze. He had a crush. That was all. Of course...he'd had a crush *before*, hadn't he? This was so much more than that. He'd be the first to acknowledge that. But love?

Was he in love with Landry?

Landry didn't seem particularly perturbed by Carter's accusation.

"Can you imagine?" Landry asked casually. "Aidan would take me apart. Slowly. Painfully."

"Like he could," Riley retorted. "You're bigger than he is."

"Yeah, but he's craftier," Landry pointed out.

"In that asshole, pull-the-wool-over-your-eyes kinda way." Aidan would never play fair. It wasn't in his DNA. He played to win, always. No matter what it cost.

"Exactly," Landry said, flashing him a flirtatious smile. "You think I wanna take that risk?"

But from the look on his face, it was clear he was prepared to do it.

For *Riley*.

Riley had known it, of course, had known from their first kiss that Landry wasn't just experimenting or fucking around or hooking up with him because he was conveniently right there.

But he hadn't put two and two together and gotten four until now.

He's falling in love with you.

Same as you're falling in love with him.

Well, shit.

"I gotta...uh...bathroom," Riley stumbled.

He pulled out his phone before he even made it there because there was no telling what excuse Landry was going to pull out of his ass just so he could follow him back here.

SOS, he typed to Paige. **I think things just got serious.**

She responded right away because he'd used their special code word that meant *answer me now, not later.* **You two finally talk?**

Not even that, Riley typed back. **We didn't say a word.**

But they hadn't had to.

He'd seen it, clear as day, in Landry's eyes.

Maybe they were still getting there, but someday, if they kept going like this, they were going to reach that point. It was inevitable.

Then why are you freaking out? You've only wanted him forever.

That was the question, wasn't it?

Because he *knew* Landry. Knew he'd be steadfast and loyal and the best partner he could ever hope to have. Why else had Riley had such a hopeless crush on him for so many years? Yes, he was hot, but lots of guys were hot, and he hadn't been carrying a torch for them. He'd been holding out for Landry.

You're the worst, Riley typed out. **I hate it when you're right.**

Paige answered almost instantly: **No, you don't. Not about this.**

And goddamn it, she was right, *again.*

"You alright?"

Riley looked up from his phone, and Landry was standing in the bathroom doorway.

He'd totally been caught.

"Oh, yeah, I just..." Riley took a deep breath. "I'm sorry I've been weird the last few days. I think...I think I'm going to be okay, though."

"I know you are," Landry said with absolute certainty.

Of course he did.

"I realized I'm not my brother."

Landry laughed and leaned back against the wall, letting the door shut behind him. "I could've told you that. Trust me—I never wanted to kiss your brother. But you?"

"It's not just that," Riley said, not wanting to get distracted by the idea of kissing Landry—which was inherently *very* distracting. "I realized...we're not the same. I can't use his standards when I think of who I am and what I'm doing."

"Is that what you were thinking?" Landry asked softly. "You're not him, Riley. I know that better than just about anyone."

"I didn't even realize I was doing it. I just thought, for so long, he was...I don't know...the gold standard, you know? And it doesn't help that everyone else thinks that, too. He's Aidan Flynn. *The* quarterback for the Toronto Thunder. Three-time league MVP. Super Bowl winner. He's what everyone wants to be. Is it so crazy I wanted to be like him, too?" It hurt even saying it, but it was undeniably true, and it was time he owned up to it.

He'd spent too long living underneath Aidan's long shadow; if he didn't step out of it soon, he'd be stuck there forever. And that was the last thing he wanted.

He didn't want to be the best version of Aidan Flynn. Not any longer.

What he wanted—what he *needed*—was to be the best version of Riley Flynn.

"And," Riley added quietly, "Aidan was your friend. He'd won you over. Won your loyalty and your affection, and you saw underneath his asshole behavior and saw him for who he really could be, same as me, and well...that certainly didn't help."

Landry's bone-deep conviction morphed into something resembling concern. "Riley—"

"No," Riley interrupted and reached up and kissed him. Briefly, even though tearing his lips away from Landry's was harder than he'd ever imagined it could be. "I don't want you to worry."

"I'm not *worried*. I'm just..." Landry took a deep breath. "I know you've got a lot going on. You're trying to figure out your way apart from your brother. You're starting your first NFL game on Sunday. And..."

"And I have you. Yeah. I know. I'm crazy about you, Landry." It was easier to say than Riley had anticipated. "I don't want you to decide this is too much for me because I'm here, standing in front of you, telling you that you're not too much. In fact, you're just enough. You're perfect. You're everything I thought I wanted for so freaking long. Then you showed up, and you were even more."

Landry tipped his head against Riley's, resting their foreheads together. His gaze was warm and—Riley couldn't deny it any longer—*loving*.

He'd fallen in love with Landry Banks.

Yes, it'd only been a little over a week.

But the truth was, he'd been falling for Landry Banks for most of his life.

How could he not?

It turned out the actual *falling in love, you're-the-man-I-want-to-be-with-for-the-rest-of-my-life* part wasn't like a big crash, but a slow, inevitable slide.

"I like you, too," Landry murmured. "So much. I can't stop thinking about you. Even when you're right there."

"Even if eventually Aidan wants to kill you?" He hadn't meant to bring his brother up, but that *also* felt inevitable. They were going to have to talk about Aidan eventually.

Apparently, eventually was right now.

"He'd try, maybe," Landry said, smirking. "But you're right. I'm bigger than he is. And he's also what...a thousand miles away?"

"Convenient," Riley said.

Landry could probably see right through him, could identify the love in his eyes. Riley couldn't deny he was pretty much heart-eyes personified right now and wasn't even trying to hide it. Couldn't bring himself to do anything other than enjoy it.

"It is," Landry said softly. "But you know, we can't hide this from him forever. Even if I want to."

"Why do you want to?" Riley wasn't bothered by that particular instinct of Landry's; hadn't he had the exact same thought? But he *was* curious.

"Uh, well...self-preservation for one. And second, I'm afraid somehow he'll blame you. And he doesn't need more reasons to give you shit."

"You really think he'd blame me?" Riley was surprised. He'd been pretty sure Aidan would give *Landry* shit because he'd been the one to supposedly seduce his younger brother. Like Riley hadn't used every single goddamn tool he owned to entice Landry over to the queer side of the fence.

"He's too hard on you," Landry said, frowning. "And it's not cool. It makes me want to punch him in the face. I mean...I never liked it. I always tried to tell him he was full of crap, but he never listened, and at the time, that didn't matter as much. But now? I can't stand it."

"Aw," Riley said. "Did I win you over to my side?"

He'd been teasing, but the look in Landry's eyes was dead serious.

"Yes," Landry said.

With no qualifications, no explanations, no sidebars. Nothing. Just *yes.*

"Oh." Riley was floored. Didn't know what else to say.

Landry reached up and cupped his cheek. Slid his hand back until it reached Riley's neck. He squeezed. His touch felt warm and loving and like the most reassuring thing Riley had ever felt. "If you believe anything," he said. "Believe that."

Riley's confession was right on the tip of his tongue: *I think I might love you, and that terrifies the fuck out of me—but it also feels like the most natural thing in the whole world. Explain that to me, please.*

But before he could, the door swung open to the bathroom, and suddenly Carter was there, arms crossed over his chest.

"Really?" he said, sounding unamused. "You two, again?"

"Us two, again," Landry said wryly.

"Boyd was wondering where you'd got to. Personally, I said to just let you drown, but that might make things hard on Sunday."

"Thanks, we're touched," Riley said.

"Seriously, though, you might want to stop ducking out on team events, freaking disappearing *together* if you don't want anyone to know what you're up to," Carter pointed out.

"How do you know we don't want anyone to know?" Landry asked slowly.

Carter looked surprised, his mouth dropping open.

"We're not you," Landry continued very earnestly. "We're not fucking around. This is serious. People are gonna know, eventually."

"Oh. *Oh.*" Carter snapped his jaw back up. "Well, in that case, go back to staring soulfully into each other's eyes. Because that'll definitely give anyone who comes in here exactly the right idea."

He marched over to the urinal, did his business, and after washing his hands, he shot them both another baffled look and exited the bathroom.

"Did you know what that was about?" Landry asked once he was gone.

"Not really, no," Riley said. He knew Carter wasn't entirely wrong, though. He should move away from Landry, from where they were pressed so closely together. Anyone might come in. But he didn't really want to.

"Well, I suppose it's Carter so that's to be expected." Landry took a deep breath. "But the thing I wanted to say before he came in...I know we did this kinda backwards."

"We did?"

"I know we're both crazy busy these days. Barely a moment to ourselves, but...I still want to do this right. Do right by you." Landry's expression was so earnest it made Riley's heart beat faster. Somehow, him being seriously romantic was even sexier than when he was trying to seduce Riley. How was that possible?

"You *are*, Landry," Riley promised.

"Then let me take you out on a date. A real date." Landry suddenly looked worried. "You do that, right? It's okay to ask?"

Riley was both touched and amused. He really was crazy about this guy. *Everything you ever wanted in one impossibly hot package. Of course it's okay to ask.*

"Landry, for you, *yes*," Riley said. "Not sure when we can do it..."

"I'll figure it out," Landry said. "You can count on me."

"What about, uh...the rest? About..." He wasn't naive. Not a prude by any stretch of the imagination, but somehow saying the word *sex* to Landry made him squirm.

Was it the thought of having it?

That might be it.

Was it just how much he really, *really* wanted more of it with Landry?

Definitely possible.

"About?" Landry raised an eyebrow.

He knew, but he was going to make him say it.

Riley made a face. "Sex, okay? *Sex.* S-E-X."

"You want to have sex right now? In this bathroom? Okay, we can do that. Does this door..." Landry trailed off, glancing behind him at where Carter had so rudely interrupted them.

"No, no," Riley said, laughing. "Tonight. Later. At home. In a bed. Not a staircase. Not a bathroom. In a *bed*. In fact, I think you made a promise last time..."

Landry's eyes darkened. He looked intent. *Hungry.* "Anything you want," he said, "and it's yours."

Riley was a freaking work of art like this. Landry could look at him, just like this, for the rest of his life.

Golden skin, a sharp contrast against the blue of his comforter. Slim hips. A perfectly curved ass. Back muscles rippling under Landry's touch as he ran a light but possessive hand up his spine.

"Gorgeous," Landry murmured under his breath.

He'd been keyed up—well, basically since the moment Riley took off his helmet in Pittsburgh, but especially now—since Riley had brought up the promise he'd made in the heat of the moment the last time they'd had sex.

Like Landry hadn't been thinking, every spare moment he had, of the way Riley had shuddered under his touch the moment he'd touched him.

"Are you just gonna stand there and *look*?" Riley complained, his voice half-muffled by the comforter.

"I promised I was gonna bend you over this bed and make you cry with how good it is," Landry said. "I plan to make good on that."

"If you're worried about foreplay, we've had plenty of that. All that footsy under the table at the restaurant," Riley pointed out. "Nevermind the way you kissed me in the bathroom."

That had been a promise, too. A promise that he had every intention of taking Riley home and fucking him so good neither of them would be the same after.

But Landry was so worked up, so incredibly turned on by just the *thought* of it, that he didn't quite trust himself to do it. Not yet.

Which was why he was still just looking.

Oh, he'd touched Riley a little. Hadn't been able to help himself when they'd started kissing the moment the front door closed behind them.

Definitely as they'd stopped every few feet going up the stairs—Riley pushing him against the wall and devouring his mouth like he'd die if he didn't get his lips on him ASAP.

Finally, they'd stumbled down the hallway, Riley shedding clothes insistently until he'd collapsed against the edge of Landry's bed, totally fucking naked and totally fucking gorgeous.

"I'm contemplating how I want to do this," Landry said. He settled his palm on the broad plane of Riley's back. "I don't want to rush it."

"God forbid," Riley muttered. "Meanwhile, I'm *dying* here."

Landry grinned. "You can get real mouthy when you get horny." His hand drifted lower, right over the delectable curve of Riley's ass. He didn't tense at all, just pushed his body right into the touch. Like he was desperate for it.

He wasn't the only one; Landry's hands were still trembling. Riley groaned into the bed. "*Yes.*"

With his other hand, Landry pulled the drawer in the bedside table open. He'd stashed condoms and lube there after their last sexcapade, and part of him had expected, every time they'd gone to bed together—just to sleep—for Riley to discover what he'd bought.

But they'd both been too worn out, mentally and physically, for anything but a quick cuddle before falling asleep.

"You gonna beg me?" Landry asked archly as he opened the lube.

Riley arched against the bed, mumbling something about *please* and *thank you*—or maybe that was something more like *fuck you*. Landry chuckled.

He was pretty sure if he reached around, he'd find Riley's cock hard against his stomach as he snuck in a few little thrusts against the edge of the mattress.

He could do that now, but Landry had every intention of being the one who got him off.

Sneaking a hand around Riley's waist, he discovered exactly what he'd hoped for. Riley's dick twitched as his palm found it and spread the precome leaking out the tip, letting it slide through his fist.

"Fuck," Riley said, trembling as Landry's other hand brushed against his ass, thumb brushing his hole. "God, I'll do anything," he begged as Landry continued to take his time.

As far as he was concerned, anything less than a slow, leisurely exploration of all Riley's many, *many* bodily delights was a crime.

Landry slid his thumb in, mentally cataloging every reaction of Riley's. From the way his body trembled, to the goosebumps dotting the skin of his back, to the way his cock twitched in his hand.

While Riley had been telling him he wanted it, begging and pleading for it, that was the proof he'd wanted. The proof that nearly unwound *him*.

"I'd say you can give me more," Riley begged, wiggling underneath his touch. "But I'm sure you're some kind of ass fucking expert now."

How presumptuous would it make him look if Landry agreed? That he'd spent way too many nights before they'd ever had sex, before they'd even *kissed*, doing his share of research. Making sure that if he ever got the opportunity to touch Riley, he'd do a good job?

Pretty presumptuous.

But he knew it would make Riley smile anyway, so he'd tell him after, when they were cuddling, damp with sweat.

"Wanna be an expert on *you*, what you like. What makes you feel good," Landry murmured, moving his hand around Riley's cock with more purpose, sliding in a second finger to join his first.

Riley was so hot and tight, practically squeezing him, and Landry didn't know how he'd manage to keep his tenuous self-control when he finally got his dick inside him, but he *needed* to.

It had to be good for Riley.

The best he'd ever had.

He cared about him way too much to ever settle for less.

Loved him too much to ever tolerate anything else than his best effort.

Landry's hands froze.

Because he did. He loved Riley.

Since he was pretty sure he'd never fallen in love before, he'd expected the realization to take him by surprise—like a clap of thunder or like being struck by lightning—but instead, he'd sort of slid right into it until he just *knew* it was true.

"It's good, it's so good," Riley babbled. "Keep going, *God*, keep going."

"You're not going to come." Landry squeezed his cock.

"Fuck," Riley said, so much filthier in bed than Landry had ever expected, but he couldn't deny he loved every moment of it.

Leaning down, he pressed his lips to Riley's spine. Couldn't help but start to move his fingers faster and with more purpose now.

He didn't just *want* Riley; he *needed* him.

Slowly, Riley relaxed into his touch. Landry slipped in a third finger, Riley groaning through the stretch, Landry's own moan joining in as he let him in.

Riley's hips were thrusting erratically now, and Landry could feel by the way he trembled at even the minutest push and pull of his fingers that he was close.

Landry was close, too. Just from touching Riley.

If he touched himself, he might explode before he ever got a chance to coax Riley to come around his cock.

"Come on, *come on*," Riley begged. His voice slurred. "I'm good. I'm so fucking good. Promise."

But Landry could feel that he was.

His fingers trembled as he removed them from Riley's body. Tore open the condom.

Gritted his teeth as he rolled it on. Even that touch was almost overwhelming.

He dug deep down for control as he fitted himself against Riley's open hole and slid in.

For a second, everything in his mind went incredibly still and silent.

It was like sliding home, the best fucking thing he'd ever felt.

Riley—the man he loved—all around him, so tight and perfect Landry could barely breathe.

"Goddamn," Riley groaned.

Landry knew his fingertips were biting into Riley's hips, but he didn't seem to hesitate. He just pushed backwards, sliding Landry all the way home, and his self-control snapped.

Not cleanly. Not in half. It just *exploded* everywhere, and Landry barely recognized himself as he took Riley's lead, thrusting forward in the same rhythm as Riley was pushing back, fucking himself on Landry's cock.

Someone was begging—crying, maybe?—and it might've been Riley, or it might've been him. Landry wasn't sure. He only knew it was so good he'd die if he couldn't keep going like this forever.

Sex had never felt like this before, like his head had been blown clean off.

Riley's knees wobbled, and then he collapsed onto the bed, and Landry chased him, trying to make it good, trying to remember everything he'd read about hitting the right spot, but it was so good, it was hard to focus on anything except the overwhelming feeling of *rightness*.

This was how sex was always supposed to be, he realized.

Fucking amazing if it was with the right person.

"God, *harder*," Riley cried, and the order bypassed Landry's brain entirely, going straight to his body. He thrust harder and then harder still, wild with the pleasure coursing through him.

Riley shook underneath him and then went absolutely still.

Landry felt him tighten around him, clenching around his cock as he came, and that was it for him.

He collapsed against Riley's back on rubbery legs as he came in long, shuddering pulses that felt like they'd never end.

But they did, eventually.

Leaving him shaky and suddenly painfully aware that everything he'd wanted this first time having penetrative sex with Riley to be, hadn't quite worked out.

Oh, it had been glorious.

Landry had never had better sex in his whole goddamn life.

But he was filled with a sudden, corrosive worry that he'd not given Riley what he'd intended to.

"You're heavier than you look," Riley said, voice muffled by both the comforter and Landry's bulk. "And you look plenty heavy."

"Sorry," Landry said, scrambling on weak knees to stand up. He pulled out, and Riley folded down like his strings had just been cut.

Then he rolled over, and all that concern swirling inside Landry evaporated.

Riley was grinning. Wildly. Freely. With so much affection and happiness in his eyes there was no way he hadn't enjoyed that just as much as Landry.

In fact, Landry had a feeling there was that exact same goddamn expression on his face right now.

"Yeah?" Riley asked, his mouth widening impossibly further.

"Yeah," Landry said.

He took off for the bathroom. Took care of the condom. Grabbed a washcloth for Riley and helped him clean up, and then nothing on earth had ever made as much sense as collapsing into bed next to him.

"I was worried I was too...uh...rough," Landry confessed as Riley rolled onto his chest, cheek pressed against his pec.

"No," Riley said. "I wanted it. It was...well, you know how it was. You were there."

He had been. It had been like a storm had taken and possessed both of them.

And the honest truth was he couldn't wait to get lost in it again.

That was how Riley made him feel. Out of control with want and need, and somehow, impossibly, he was totally safe and protected in the eye with Riley next to him, Riley's hand tucked inside his own.

"I was," Landry said seriously.

It's way too early to tell him how you feel, he thought.

But that didn't mean he wasn't feeling it.

Acutely.

"We're definitely doing that again," Riley said. "Next time, though, I'm going to pin you down and ride you so hard you see stars."

Landry's mouth went dry. Oh, he wanted that, too. He wanted it every which way. The only thing he absolutely needed when it came to sex was that it was with Riley. Anything else was possible.

"I don't know," he said, trying to keep his voice casual, even though the feelings rushing through him just now were hardly casual. "I kinda thought maybe next time you could show me what all the fuss is about."

Riley pushed himself up on an elbow so he could look right into Landry's eyes. Those wide, impossibly blue eyes looked shaken. "You want me to fuck you?"

"Do you not want to?" Suddenly it occurred to Landry that maybe that wasn't something Riley did. Maybe it wasn't okay to want that.

But before Landry could overthink for even a split second, Riley was reaching out, pressing a palm to Landry's cheek. "Yeah," he said. "I want to. Just didn't think that was something *you'd* want."

"Are we having sex together?" Landry asked.

Riley nodded.

"Then," Landry said, feeling Riley re-settle on his chest as his eyes fluttered closed, "that's something I want."

CHAPTER 14

Riley wasn't just going to puke. Nope, he was way beyond throwing up from nerves. Nausea was something he could handle, *knew* how to handle, but this...this constant buzzing under his skin, anxiety spiking whenever he so much as thought about the game tomorrow?

It was a freaking nightmare.

He was currently pacing in his hotel room, too keyed up to do anything as mundane as sit on the bed and watch TV or read or even scroll through Instagram.

After the walk-through, he'd walked with Landry to the elevator, and Landry had given him a quick peck before anyone else had joined them. "Just in case," he'd said, "I don't get to do that later."

They hadn't talked about sleeping together tonight. Riley wouldn't be surprised if Landry had some idea he didn't want to bother him the night before one of the biggest games of his career.

Because while last week had been undeniably great, everyone had already put an asterisk next to it—it was a *preseason* game and therefore didn't count as much as it might.

But tomorrow was a regular season game. It would matter. There wouldn't be an asterisk next to it. In ten years, most people would believe this was his first game, not the one he'd played in last. And, unlike last week, which didn't count for the Condors' standings, this game would count towards their win-loss record for the season.

Nobody expected them to do anything. The Condors were in something way more drastic than just rebuilding mode. Then, even worse, they'd lost their original starting quarterback to injury before the season had even begun.

If they lost, and then lost again, and lost another ten times, nobody would even be surprised.

But Riley already knew he refused to accept that.

In the last two weeks, he'd gotten to know the team better, the coaches, the staff—and he knew they wouldn't accept that either.

But how to reconcile all that inevitable pressure with his need to shed it like a skin the moment he took the field tomorrow?

He nearly picked up his phone and texted Aidan. He'd know how he felt because he'd been in this exact same spot so many times. Once, he'd even admitted to Riley how anxious he got before games, but somehow, he always managed to shed the nerves the moment he needed to.

You can't call him. You can't call him anymore. You need to learn how to do this shit for yourself.

But even the thought of all that weight on his shoulders made him want to bow to the pressure.

Then, suddenly, it occurred to him that he wasn't alone.

He might not have Aidan in his corner anymore—had he ever really had his brother in his corner? Riley wasn't sure—but he had someone else.

Landry.

He threw on a hooded sweatshirt, tucked his room key and his phone into the pocket of his shorts, and slipped out of his room.

He knew what room Landry was in because he'd passed it on the way to his own after the walk-through. He glanced up and down the hallway. It wasn't like this was expressly forbidden, but leaving your own room after curfew was definitely not encouraged. Especially not if you were doing it for what Riley wanted.

Sex, maybe. If only so he could get out of his own mind, even for a few minutes.

But comfort, definitely.

Riley didn't see anyone, so he hesitated at the door. Then knocked. Softly. And then a bit louder.

A few moments later, the door opened, Landry's face framed in the gap between the door and the doorframe.

"Everything okay?" Landry asked, looking concerned.

Tomorrow, he had to put on a good front. Look like his confidence went bone-deep. That it was unshakable. But tonight, with Landry, he didn't have to be any of those things. He could be himself. He could be vulnerable.

"I wanted to see you," Riley said. Hesitated. "*Needed* to see you."

"Oh." The concern on Landry's face melted into affection. "Come in."

He pushed the door open wider, and Riley glanced down as he passed by him in the tiny hallway leading to the main part of the room.

"You really came to the door like that?" Riley asked, raising an eyebrow at how little he was wearing.

The bed was unmade, and the TV was on, but only on a low volume, like Landry hadn't really been watching it.

Riley pulled off his sweatshirt, and he watched as Landry's eyes dilated as his bare chest was revealed.

"I wasn't expecting anyone," Landry teased. "Though maybe I was hoping for you."

Riley sat down on the edge of the bed. Couldn't deny he was enjoying the view of Landry, too, clad only in his boxer briefs, those thick, muscular thighs, and big, broad chest on full display.

He wanted to nuzzle him like a big teddy bear.

Like *his* teddy bear.

"You didn't say," Riley said reproachfully.

"I know," Landry said, dipping his head down as he sat down next to Riley. "I didn't want to distract you. I know how important tomorrow is."

"For me, yeah, but for you, too."

But Riley knew it wasn't the same. Landry wasn't the leader of the team. Landry was well into his NFL career and would go down as one of the best tight ends to play the game—the fact the Condors had spent so much money on him when they didn't have much, to begin with, and had chosen to put him front and center on their marketing materials said everything.

Landry didn't have to make his career here. Whatever happened with the Condors would just be the cherry on top of all his success.

"Yeah, but I know how nervous you are. I can see it in your eyes." Landry put a hand on his knee. Squeezed it. "And don't worry, I don't think anyone else can see it, but I do. Because I know you. Because I care about you."

It was impossible not to be cut down to the marrow by that look on Landry's face. Impossible not to tell him the truth. "Why do you think I came to you?" Riley said, hearing how raw his voice sounded.

"Come on," Landry coaxed, and a minute later, they were lying in bed, Riley in what was becoming a familiar position, his cheek resting on Landry's pectoral muscle.

It was a surprisingly good pillow.

"You know, you're gonna be okay," Landry said softly. "I know what you're capable of, and you're going to go out there tomorrow and kick ass. I've been seeing it all week."

"Yeah." Landry wasn't wrong; practice *had* gone well all week.

"At the very least, the Falcons don't have a corner as tenacious as Rex," Landry said, chuckling. "We can run that play."

"I'm counting on it," Riley said.

For a long time, neither of them said anything.

Riley had never been with anyone he could just *be* with, the way he was with Landry. Didn't feel pressured to be funny or charming.

"We're really doing this, aren't we?" Riley said, finally breaking the silence.

Landry's arm tightened on his back. Not in panic, because when Riley glanced up at his face, there was no alarm there whatsoever. Instead, all he saw was satisfaction.

"I hope so, 'cause I'm in this," Landry said. "I'm...well, you gotta know how I feel about you, Riley."

He had an inkling. At least if it was anything like what *he* was feeling.

"Same," Riley murmured. "And not just cause you lived rent-free in all my adolescent fantasies."

Landry laughed. "You should tell me about some of those sometime."

"Hell no," Riley said. "They're all super embarrassing."

"Exactly," Landry said.

"It feels good to know it's me and you together...against whatever we're against," Riley finished awkwardly. "I don't know how long we're going to have to keep this under wraps from Coach or from Mr. G. I don't know how we're going to tell Aidan or when, but...it still feels good. No matter what the fallout is."

"I don't know about when we'd tell Coach or Mr. G either, but as for your brother...I was sort of thinking we'd tell him when we saw him in two weeks," Landry said.

Riley was surprised at the certainty in Landry's voice. He'd clearly been thinking about this.

"Yeah," Landry continued. "I've given it some thought." Like he'd read Riley's mind. "I don't know how you feel about it—he's *your* brother, after all, and you've had the majority of the issues with him—but I know I don't want to keep it from him. Not for a long time. This is...well, you're too important for me to keep a secret. Not from someone I care about, too, like Aidan."

Riley didn't know what to say. When he'd said, *I guess we're really doing this*, he hadn't really considered what that meant.

Now he was.

Yes, that meant telling Aidan.

Was it crazy that he was more afraid of his brother's reaction than the one they'd get from Coach Kelley or from Mr. G?

Yes, it was. But then, Aidan was a beast of a whole different color.

"Yeah, he's my brother, but he's your best friend," Riley said cautiously. "We can tell him then, if you want. The only thing that's non-negotiable is that we do it together."

"A united front, maybe prevent him from deciding one of us seduced the other one?" Landry sounded amused.

"I kinda think we seduced each other, though it wasn't like I didn't make a very earnest effort," Riley teased. "And then there's you, who walked around without clothes on every chance you got."

"Maybe I just do that all the time, even when you're not around," Landry protested.

"Hey, if I looked like you, I'd do that, too."

"I wasn't the one in *only a towel* in the hallway," Landry argued, amusement rippling in his tone.

"Oh, you liked that, huh?" Riley's face hurt, he was smiling so hard.

"You drove me insane," Landry said roughly. "Which you probably know. In any case, yes, we'll do it together. And the rest..."

"I don't know how Coach Kelley is gonna feel about it, but I do know Mr. G said he wanted to model the Condors on the Piranhas, and it's not like they ever booted anyone out for being queer and together."

"Hardly," Landry scoffed. "Look at my brother and Dylan. The quarterback and his coach. The *head coach* married a guy. In the middle of the freaking season."

"Exactly." Riley was quiet for a moment. "How about...I just want to have a game or two under my belt. Feel like I belong to this team, make it harder for them to freak out and boot me out."

"Riley, you belong," Landry insisted. "But I get it. I do. We can wait to tell Coach Kelley and Mr. G if you want. However long you want to wait, I'm good with it. I know your position is not the same as mine."

Riley hadn't known beforehand, but he realized how glad he was that Landry had admitted that. If Landry, so far into a successful NFL career, tried to claim he occupied the same semi-precarious position as Riley, he wouldn't have loved him so much. Landry was undeniably kind and fair—but more than anything else, he was *honest*. Even if the honesty wasn't necessarily comfortable.

"I don't want to wait forever," Riley said. "What kind of relationship can we even have if we're keeping it under wraps for months and months? I don't want that."

"Me, either," Landry said.

"Even if it means you're...well, that you're *out*?"

"Riley." Landry pointed out patiently, "Has it ever seemed like I gave a shit if people knew I liked guys, too? If I was queer, just like my brothers? Just like you?"

"No," Riley admitted. If he was being honest, that was *really* attractive. Like Landry needed any more reasons to be insanely, irresistibly attractive.

"I care about you, and I don't care who knows it," Landry said with absolute certainty. "We'll tell your brother when we see him because I do think that conversation is probably better to have in person."

"What, so Aidan can punch you in the face?"

"Hey, I'm not looking for an excuse to kick his ass or anything," Landry said wryly. "But I think...maybe he won't be as pouty about it if he knows how we feel. If he *sees* it."

"He's gonna be pouty about it no matter what," Riley said matter-of-factly. "But that will be one hundred percent his issue."

"Yeah," Landry agreed. "And as for the rest of the team and the coaching staff and Mr. G...that decision is up to you, Riley. I trust you to do what you feel is right for you, and for us."

Riley marveled that there *was* an *us*.

And that the *us* was him and Landry.

He wanted to say those three little words so badly they were right there on the tip of his tongue.

But he didn't.

He wasn't necessarily afraid anymore, but it didn't feel right, yet. And the need to do it immediately, the moment he'd felt it, had passed because now he knew he'd get a hundred chances to say it. A thousand chances to show it.

Landry wasn't going anywhere, and he felt the warmth of his love, even if he never said the words, radiating through him.

"Is it okay if I stay here tonight?" Riley asked, even though he already knew the answer.

"I've never wanted anything else," Landry said.

If Landry hadn't witnessed Riley's nerves for himself last night, the uncertainty in his eyes and in his voice, the terror he might let everyone down revealed just for him to see, he'd never have imagined he was anxious about this game at all.

Today, under the harsh lights of the visiting locker room, he jumped on a low table and addressed the whole team.

"Nobody thinks anything of us," Riley said, "nobody thinks we can win any games. Nobody thinks we're worth the money Mr. G paid for us. That we're just a worthless group of people who aren't ready or willing to give up yet. I don't know about you—but I've heard this bullshit my whole damn life, and not only am I tired of hearing it, I've been ready forever to put it to bed. Let's give everyone who doubted us—me and you and this whole freaking team—a reason to look stupid Monday morning. Let's go out there and show everyone that we're not just untried and undersized and washed-up. That we're not just rebuilding. That we're not just recovering. That we don't need one year or two years or three years. That we're here, *now*."

Deacon clapped and whooped.

Landry gave a shout and pumped his fist. More players joined in, and Riley's face, gorgeous even with eye black smeared over it, broke into a bright, confident grin.

Like he knew, just as Landry had told him the night before, that he *had* this.

Usually, Coach gave a speech, too—at least he had in the preseason games.

But today, instead, Mr. G strode into the middle of the room.

He was unassuming, barely six foot tall, and slender. Pale skin, like he spent too much time inside, with messy brown hair falling across his forehead, as if getting a haircut took too much effort.

But his hazel eyes glowed with as much confidence as Riley had just displayed.

Everyone had said he was crazy to invest all these millions in a franchise that many had claimed was finished, *done*. That the Condors were too broken to ever be fixed. Too broken to ever be redeemed.

He'd been the first to believe that wasn't true.

Now they all believed, too, and at the front of the line leading them was Riley, who believed so much it practically rolled off him in waves.

Whether that belief went deep, Landry wasn't even sure. But what really mattered was that everyone else saw it and fell in line right alongside their leader.

After all, tenacity and determination were highly contagious diseases.

"Riley's right," Mr. G said, raising his voice to be heard over the yells and cheers. "Nobody believes in us. Nobody even gives a fuck about us."

Landry glanced over to where Deacon was leaning against a locker, his dark hair even messier than Mr. G's. There was something there, a look on Deacon's face Landry recognized deep down. A feeling that echoed inside himself.

He likes him, like *really likes him*, Landry realized.

"Here's the thing," Mr. G continued, "we can go out there and limp through the season. Fulfill every prediction they made about us. That we're done, we're finished, that all we deserve is to be put out of our misery. But I'm telling you now, I didn't come here to be miserable. I came here, and I bought this team, because I refuse to accept this team, that *you*, are too far gone for redemption. Now, we've rooted out the worst of the corruption here." Landry watched as the owner's fists tightened at his sides. "Bravery isn't quitting when the going gets hard. It's putting your head down and doing it anyway. I didn't come here to be miserable. I came here to fucking *win*." Mr. G lifted his fist, clenched tight, and pumped it.

The shouts and cheers were deafening.

When he'd come here, Landry thought as he jogged out of the tunnel towards the field, he'd expected his brothers and his family to not understand why he'd made this choice. He could've stayed in Buffalo. Could've gone to Atlanta and played for Arthur Blank and the storied Falcons franchise.

But he'd chosen to join the underdog.

Why? Because he believed the same thing Mr. G did. The same thing Coach Kelley kept reminding them about.

Logan had called him up when he'd texted his decision to the family group chat.

"I knew you'd do it," he'd said. "I knew the instant their offer came in, you'd go to Charleston."

Landry hadn't been able to hide his surprise. "Really?" *He* hadn't even known. Not until he'd sat down and really thought about it.

"Of course. It's the kind of guy you are. You're not the guy who just extends a hand to the kid who just got knocked down. You're the guy who joins that kid and fights back at his side. So of course you'd be nuts enough to go to Charleston."

Logan wasn't wrong.

He wasn't here to offer a helping hand. He was here to get down in the trenches and fight back with these men by his side.

Riley hadn't been voted one of the captains because he hadn't even been around during the vote, but Landry had been, and to his surprise, he'd been asked, even though he was new to the team. So he joined Deacon, the defensive captain, and Ethan Miller, the kicker and special teams captain, at the center of the field for the coin toss.

They won and deferred their kickoff until the beginning of the second half.

Returning to the sideline, Landry stopped in front of Riley, sitting on the bench next to Charlie and Cole, going over the first few planned plays.

Riley glanced up at him. His gaze was steady, even, glowing with confidence.

"Go get 'em," Landry said and reached out, Riley taking his hand and clasping it in his.

Landry squeezed.

"See you out there," Riley said.

It was both a vow and a promise.

For years, Aidan had told Riley that at some point, when you reached a certain level of mastery at the quarterback position, the game slowed down. Stopped racing by like an out-of-control train hurtling down a mountain. That you could control it versus letting it control you.

Riley had felt that once or twice in college. Had tasted tantalizing hints of it when he'd played in the XFL for the Pittsburgh Defenders.

Had even felt it last week.

But he'd never felt as in-control as he did this afternoon.

Ethan, the Condors' kicker, jogged onto the field to kick off the second half.

They were currently up seventeen to seven, which didn't feel like a lot of wiggle room, but the Falcons' only touchdown—really the only time they'd ever moved the ball at all—had come on a very deep pass, Rex losing the receiver. He'd come back to the sideline, surly and angry, kicking some equipment, before Deacon and Jem had pulled him to the side and tried to calm him down.

But on two of their four drives, the Condors had moved the ball really well, methodically marched down the field, notched first downs, and grabbed yardage one manageable chunk at a time.

Most importantly, Riley felt like he was truly leading.

He stood high in the pocket.

Every pass he threw, he was proud of.

He handed the ball off to Darius, who ate up the field, running hard.

He ran himself, but only when the situation truly called for it.

At the beginning of the second half, he didn't feel like he'd done anything Aidan could even criticize.

You're not thinking about him, not right now. Not today.

That was the change, Riley realized.

He'd stopped trying to live up to Aidan's long shadow and focused hard on setting his own path.

He wasn't a second-rate version of Aidan Flynn. He wasn't even a *better* version of his brother. He was the best version of *Riley.*

It was third down and two; they were nearly at mid-field, and Coach Oscar called in the play, and Riley felt a thrill when he heard the words he'd been waiting for.

Of course, he'd thrown the ball to Landry a couple of times during the first half, but this was *the* play.

He loved the hell out of playing football; he wouldn't have worked this hard for so many years if he didn't. Just being on this field, leading this team, was an honor and a blessing. But throwing the ball to Landry? He couldn't deny there was something extra special about their connection.

Riley announced the play to the huddle. Met Landry's eyes across the middle. He nodded, and Riley nodded back.

They'd both wanted this and now they were going to get it.

It was a risk. He could've handed the ball off to Darius and let him get the two yards.

But Coach Kelley had stood up at halftime and announced to the team that they weren't playing this game safe.

"We either win, or we go home just the team they thought we were. I know which one I want," he'd said. "I know the only way I can hold my head up on Monday morning."

Riley knew what he wanted, too.

He not only wanted to hold his head high, he wanted to prove everyone wrong who'd ever predicted he wasn't going anywhere. That he was going to end up a washed-up running back who pretended he was a quarterback.

With Coach Kelley's words echoing in his head, Riley clapped and broke up the huddle.

He leaned down, called out the snap count, and watched as Cole snapped the ball, where it landed in his hands.

Out of the corner of his eye, he saw Landry duck the safety in the middle of the zone, lingering for just a moment.

Don't stare him down, don't even look at him till the last moment. Until you don't have any choice.

The main risk of the play was, of course, an incompletion. But there was a possibility he and Charlie had discussed of the safety guessing the way it would unfold and stepping in front of the ball, intercepting it before Landry could turn and catch it.

Riley had to make sure he didn't give the safety a single goddamn clue so he'd never guess the direction they were going.

He had to hope Landry was going to turn at the exact second. Had to *trust* him completely. In this play, timing was everything.

They'd practiced it relentlessly during the week, over and over again, so Riley knew the way Landry—and the other receivers, Carter and Nick and the others—ran in his sleep. Could feel their footfalls with his eyes closed.

Or with his eyes looking down Carter, double-teamed along the other sideline.

At the last possible second, Riley, giving Landry as much time as he could, threw the ball, watching as it arced through the air. Landry turned, caught it against his body, and turned back towards the end zone. With each driving step, he moved further and further away from the corner.

Until he was sprinting right into the end zone, and Riley was running, too, before he'd even realized it, hurtling himself into Landry's arms, laughing and screeching so loud that he'd done it, probably even the fans in the stands could've heard him.

Landry lifted him up, and he fist-pumped in the air, once, and then twice.

His face was full of joy—and full of love—and Riley didn't think he'd ever forget that moment.

Landry released him and then picked up the ball that had fallen to the ground. "This," he said, over the roar of the crowd, "belongs to you."

It felt like he wasn't just handing him the football, the first touchdown he'd scored in a regular season NFL game, the first, Riley knew, of many. But something bigger, too.

It felt like Landry was handing him his own self-respect right along with his loyalty, his recognition, and most importantly, his heart.

"Riley, how did that touchdown to Landry feel?"

Riley grinned at the reporter who'd asked the question. He knew press conferences weren't always fun. But this one? After beating the Falcons thirty-five to seven, this one was going to be a freaking blast. He could already tell, especially considering the first question.

"Which touchdown to Landry?" he asked impudently.

He'd probably pay for that later, but he was feeling too good to give a shit right now.

Yep, Riley was feeling damn good. Because he'd thrown not just one touchdown but *three*, and two of them had gone to Landry.

The reporter grinned right back. "The first one, sorry. The first drive of the second half. That was a tricky timing play, and you're still pretty new here to the Condors."

"Yeah, I am, but we've practiced a lot together in the last two weeks. Really gotten our timing down. Not just me and Landry, though, but all the receivers. They've put a lot of work in, and it paid off today. That's a tricky route for a tight end to run, but I trusted he'd do it, and he'd do it right."

Another reporter raised their hand, and Nikki, the head of PR for the Condors, called on her. "Could that be because you've known him a long time? Longer than some of the other players on the team?"

"I'm assuming," Riley said, "you're referring to the fact he and my brother are close. Actually, though, I'm not sure I ever threw him a pass before I came to Charleston. So no, it wasn't really because I've known him for a while because he's friends with Aidan—but because of who Landry is and the kind of work ethic he possesses."

Nikki called on a few more reporters, but the questions were all easy lobs. Nobody pressed him, not even on the few bad decisions he'd made. Not bad enough to resort to something like an interception or a fumble, but Riley already knew, despite the amazing win, he and Charlie and Coach Oscar would be back in the film room next week, breaking down everything.

But more importantly, he already knew that whatever his brother said—good or bad or middling—it didn't matter because Riley knew the job he'd done was exceptional.

After the press conference, he followed Nikki out the door and back towards the locker room where the rest of the team was gathered before heading out on the team bus for the airport.

But to Riley's surprise, they weren't alone in the hallway. Mr. G was standing there, leaning against the wall, a soft smile on his face.

"Hey, Riley," he said, pushing off from his spot and joining him and Nikki as they walked. "Great job today."

"Thanks, Mr. G," Riley said. He'd liked the owner from the moment they'd met and even more after sharing lunch together right after he'd been signed.

"Not that I ever doubted you."

"Even though they called you crazy for signing me?" Riley asked archly. He'd heard the talk. He couldn't *not* hear it.

How many times had he been told, *Riley Flynn would be a great backup, but he's not a starting quarterback*?

But Mr. G had bet on him, anyway.

"If they didn't see what I saw when you were in Pittsburgh, they were the crazy ones," Mr. G said, shrugging. "I'm not a *football guy*, as they like to say, so I just take all those assumptions and ideas and throw them away. So what, you're not six foot three or six foot four? Who gives a fuck? Can you throw the ball? Can you run the ball? You proved you can do both of those the last two weeks." Mr. G put a hand on his shoulder. "Remember that if anyone gives you shit about being short."

"Thanks," Riley said.

"And," Mr. G said, grinning wider, "that touchdown you threw to Landry was a work of art. You two together, you're something else."

"I think so," Riley said, agreeing. Hoping that when Mr. G found out just how good he and Landry were together, he'd still be on the same page.

"And," Mr. G said, leaning in a bit closer, his voice dropping, "it wasn't just the way you handled yourself in Pittsburgh, but earlier. Back in college."

Riley raised an eyebrow. He had a feeling he knew what the owner was getting at.

"You mean I could've just stayed in the closet and not hurt my draft stock? When it was already suffering?" Riley questioned.

"Exactly. You're authentic. That's worth more than someone who's six foot three," Mr. G said. "At least to me. And to this team, clearly, because you've already won them over, Riley."

"Glad to hear it," Riley said and then hesitated. Just last night, Landry had told him it was up to him. That he'd get the final say on when they told people. "Between you and me, throwing touchdowns is always great, but to have my first official NFL touchdown go to Landry..."

Mr. G grinned. "Yeah, I wondered."

"Yeah." Riley didn't want to say anything else. Maybe he hadn't really understood. But at least he wouldn't be blindsided when the news came out. If even a fraction of the intelligence gleaming in his light hazel eyes was legit, he wouldn't be surprised at all.

Mr. G patted him on the shoulder again. "Still glad you're our quarterback."

They stopped in front of the doors to the locker room. "Honestly," Riley said, "it's *my* fucking honor, sir."

The corner of Mr. G's mouth quirked up. "You know, I tried to get Davis Abernathy to come back and play for us."

Riley hadn't known that the owner had even approached the former, quasi-disgraced quarterback the Condors had discarded, and then the Piranhas had picked up as their quarterbacks' coach.

"I didn't think he was playing anymore," Riley said cautiously.

"He wasn't. He *isn't*. But I felt with the way this organization treated him under my predecessors, it was only fair I try to make it right. I couldn't in the end, but that was okay because we cleared the air, and that was the most important thing. He's content where he's at, and I couldn't be happier for him."

"He got the raw end, for sure."

"Collateral damage," Mr. G said wryly. "We'll be trying to fix that forever."

"I think," Riley said slowly, "the important thing isn't how long it takes but that you're doing it. Even when it's hard. Couldn't have been easy to approach Davis."

"It wasn't," Mr. G said. "But you're right. It was the right thing to do."

Riley was still turning his conversation over in his head when Landry flopped down next to him on the plane.

"You've been surprisingly quiet," Landry said, smiling as he turned towards him. "Thought you'd be dancing down the aisles."

Riley raised an eyebrow. "I saw you there in the locker room for my victory dance."

Carter had cranked up the music, some old Notorious B.I.G. song, and the whole team had joined in, even Deacon, who'd originally claimed he didn't dance.

But he did when they won.

"Thought you'd still be doing it," Landry pointed out.

"I was, I *am*, just thinking about stuff. Talked to Mr. G after the press conference."

"He happy with you?" Landry asked, then answered his own question. "He better be because you played fucking lights out."

"Oh yeah, he is. Just...I think I might have hinted to him about us. He took it pretty well."

Landry looked surprised. Not upset, though, not at all. "Really?"

"It felt right, and while I didn't say it explicitly, I think he got the point. He'd just pointed out that first touchdown pass to you was a thing of beauty and that we worked really well together."

"We sure do," Landry murmured, dipping his head close. Riley knew he wanted to kiss him, but he didn't.

Yet.

Someday, he could do it.

Maybe even sooner than Riley had imagined he could.

"And I said something about how it meant more, throwing my first official NFL touchdown to you. And he said he wondered..."

"He's a super smart guy," Landry said. "Observant."

"Yeah, I got that vibe."

"And he didn't seem..." Landry trailed off.

"Upset? Not even in the slightest. Then...well, he told me he offered my job to Davis first. Did you know that?"

"Davis Abernathy? Really? I'd be shocked if he hadn't just told Mr. G to fuck off, even if it wasn't him who'd convinced the rest of the NFL he was unemployable."

"I know, right?" Riley reclined in his seat. "But no, Mr. G said they cleared the air. I realized then—I mean, of course I knew before, but I hadn't really put two and two together—that I'm in Davis' old job."

"You're holdin' it up respectably," Landry said loyally.

"Yeah. I think so. I just hadn't thought about it." Riley heard the wry edge to his voice. "Spent too much time obsessing over being the new Flynn on the scene."

"Yeah," Landry said, reaching over and squeezing Riley's hand briefly. "Yeah, but you're handlin' that better."

"I am," Riley agreed. He tipped his head back. Closed his eyes. He was tired. But happy. Really fucking happy.

"Hey, tomorrow night, you think they're gonna hold another victory party at the Pirate's Booty?" Landry asked.

"I'd imagine."

"Huh. Okay. Well..."

Riley heard the weirdness in Landry's tone and glanced over at him. "Everything okay?"

"Yeah, yeah, of course." Landry smiled. "I just thought...wanted to take you on a date before that. If you wanted to go out with me."

"If I wanted to go out with you?" Riley chuckled. "I thought I'd be a pretty sure thing by now."

"Yeah, but...I wanna do right by you," Landry said.

"I'd love that." Couldn't help the thought echoing in his brain. *I love you.*

Chapter 15

Landry told himself he wasn't nervous about this.

Sure, he'd been on dates before, and like Riley had said, he was kind of a sure thing, but it was still really important to Landry that everything go right.

He looked over the table he'd set up one last time and then headed downstairs.

Riley was standing in his bedroom, fixing his hair in the mirror opposite the bed he no longer slept in.

Landry leaned against the doorframe and just watched him unobserved.

It was both unbelievable and also amazing that in three short weeks, Riley had become more than just Aidan's little brother, had become so much more than *the kid*, had become the one person who filled his heart with joy.

"Hey," Riley said, glancing up at him. "You gonna just stare at me all night?"

"You look like that? Yeah, I am," Landry said, wrapping his arm in his hand and tugging Riley closer. Loving the feel of Riley's body against his own. "'Cause you're gorgeous."

"Yeah?" Riley tilted his head up. His impossibly blue eyes twinkled. "Where you gonna take me? Somewhere you can show me off?"

"Not tonight," Landry said. "I wanna keep you all to myself. At least 'til we have to go make our appearance at the Pirate's Booty."

"We gonna traumatize Carter again? Because I'm already looking forward to that."

"The traumatizing part or the part where we get home, and I strip you naked and make you come so hard you nearly forget your name?" Landry had mostly been teasing, but then Riley's eyes darkened with lust and that was definitely the biggest problem. Because he wanted to forgo the date and the appearance at the Pirate's Booty and just stay here in bed with Riley, enjoying the feel of his naked body pressing against his own.

"Why can't I have both?" Riley grinned.

"You can't have everything you want," Landry said firmly, but they both knew he'd give Riley just about anything he wanted.

"Liar," Riley teased. "I know which part you're looking forward to, but that's okay, I am, too. So what's this surprise I had to stay upstairs for?"

"Well...it's actually still *up*," Landry said, gesturing up. "You haven't been up on the roof yet, so I thought this was the perfect time."

"You've got a roof terrace?"

Landry nodded. "And it's all ours for tonight."

"What are you waiting for?" Riley asked. "Come on, show me your roof, baby."

Hand-in-hand, Landry took him to the hidden door, tucked into his walk-in closet, and then led him up the narrow staircase to the roof.

"It's not much," Landry said as they emerged onto the terrace. It *wasn't* very big, but just big enough for the table and two chairs he'd carted up here. And the dinner, resting underneath silver covers.

There was a bottle of champagne chilling in a matching silver bucket and a bottle of sparkling cider next to it because he knew Riley didn't like to drink during the week.

Of course, today was Monday and their day off, but he was still trying to be respectful. Still trying to show he was supportive.

Not because Riley was particularly difficult to please, but actually the opposite. He was easy to please, easy to surprise, easy to appreciate, and that made Landry want to love him that much better, that much deeper.

"Wow," Riley said, clearly not getting the memo that this wasn't much. Because it wasn't. But even he had to admit, despite having trouble tearing his eyes from Riley, the view was pretty damn good. "It's amazing up here. I can't believe you did all this."

Landry pulled him close again. Loved the feel of him. The smell of him. How had he come to be the most comforting yet arousing thing he'd ever experienced? He didn't know, but he knew those feelings weren't ever going to fade. "It wasn't that much," he said.

Riley shot him a look. "It's plenty. Is that dinner? Did you cook?"

"I can't cook like you, not even close, so I had it catered." Landry shrugged. "One of the best restaurants in town, too. Deacon recommended it, so it must be good."

"I'm sure it's amazing. I can't wait to dig in. But first..." Riley murmured and reached up, pressing his mouth against Landry's. It was so easy to fall into the kiss. Easier, somehow, each and every time they did this. "Thank you. For doing this. For being...well, for being you."

They sat down then, which Landry was partially grateful for—because if they didn't, he'd have been way too tempted to drag Riley back downstairs *or* continue their habit of nearly having sex in public—and also partially hated, because how was he supposed to wait when Riley felt that good and tasted that good and made him feel as desperate as this?

The food wasn't fancy because Landry had specifically requested that it not be. He wanted to impress Riley, but at the same time, he *liked* the casual feeling of sharing a regular meal with his guy.

"This chicken is delicious," Riley said as he took another bite and chewed. "You think they'd give me the recipe?"

"After the game you played last week?" Landry smiled. "Yeah, I think so. You're the new miracle in Charleston."

"I'm not," Riley said, shooting him a lopsided smile.

"You told me that just today you caused a sensation in the grocery store," Landry reminded him. "How many autographs did you sign?"

But Riley just shrugged. "I think they were more surprised than anything else that an NFL quarterback buys his own groceries."

"I told you, you didn't have to. We could get delivery again," Landry pointed out.

"Except I like to do it. Reminds me I'm not a god, just a man who needs almond milk and protein powder."

Landry set his elbows on the table, hearing the echo of his mother yelling at him about his manners. "You're definitely a man, no questions. If you ever need a reminder..." He grinned. "Come to me, okay?"

Riley shot him a hot, smoky look. "How about later?"

"When I say anytime, I mean it literally. *Anytime*," Landry teased.

"Now you're just being mean," Riley grumbled, but he was smiling, and his eyes, well...Landry thought they might be full of affection—or maybe it was something even more than that. Something he was feeling, too.

"Speaking of food, you figured out where you want to have the offensive line dinner this week?"

"Actually—" Riley hesitated. He looked suddenly worried, and that worried *Landry*.

"What is it?"

"I thought it would be fun to host them here, and I'd cook. Have a little house party, if you don't mind."

"I love that idea," Landry said, realizing that he actually, really did. Hosting their friends and teammates here, at the house they were sharing? Sounded really fucking amazing. Not something he'd have ever imagined he wanted. Even when Logan had told him about the backyard barbeques he and Dylan hosted for their Piranhas teammates, he'd not felt even the slightest bit of envy. He'd thought, *Wow, that sounds like a lot of work.*

Now what was he thinking?

Where could he sign up, and how quickly could he do it?

"Really?" Riley looked excited. "I wasn't sure, and it *is* your place, but it just feels so much more personal, and I want things to be personal here. Especially after...especially after last year? Yeah, I feel like everyone's still trying to figure out the new Condors, and shouldn't we be setting that example? Deacon and Jem have started it, and Carter too, surprisingly, but I'm the leader, and I should be leading, too."

"You *are* leading," Landry said softly.

"Yeah, but I could do more," Riley said firmly. "I *want* to do more. At first, I didn't really see this as my team. I was coming in late, taking over for Charlie and Nelson's team, but now? Now it feels like mine. I want it to feel like mine."

"Then make it yours, Riley." Landry meant every word. "Just tell me what I can do."

Riley tilted his head. A soft smile graced his handsome face. "You're really great, you know?"

It was Landry's turn to be bashful. He didn't think he was doing anything particularly special. He was just being the kind of man—the kind of partner—he knew Riley deserved.

"Uh, well, I'm just..."

Riley reached across the tiny table and gripped his hand. It wasn't as large as Landry's, but Landry felt the callouses scrape along his own as it fit perfectly into his. "Yeah, you are," he said. "No arguments. Or else I'm gonna tie you up and torture you."

Landry raised an eyebrow, feeling his blood heat again at just the idea of being helpless and totally at Riley's mercy. He'd be a tough but fair captor. "Is that really a threat?" he teased.

Riley grinned. "Maybe not."

They finished the meal and then Landry had reached over, popping the cork on the champagne, preparing to bring out the chocolate desserts the caterers had dropped off when Riley's phone rang.

He glanced at it, then frowned. "I wonder why Deacon's calling me."

"Maybe something about meeting up later at the Pirate's Booty?" Landry poured a glass of champagne for Riley and then himself, setting the bottle back into the ice bucket.

Riley answered the phone with a, "Yeah?"

He nodded at whatever Deacon was saying, then Landry watched as his face creased into a frown, which deepened further at every word Deacon said.

Uneasiness bloomed in Landry's stomach. Something bad had happened, and Deacon was calling Riley as the unspoken leader of the defense to the leader of the offense.

Finally, after a final nod and a, "Yeah, we'll be there," Riley hung up.

"Well," Riley said, setting his phone on the table with a definitive click. "That's not good."

"Seems like a whole lot more than *not good*," Landry observed.

"Rex broke his leg playing basketball," Riley said. "I guess he got tangled up with some people while he was guarding the basket."

"Probably playing dirty again," Landry mumbled, then immediately felt guilt swamp him at the thought. Yeah, Rex had played him dirty in practice a few times, but he didn't deserve a bad injury like that, one likely to keep him out of the rest of the season and, on top of that, put his football-playing future up in the air.

"Probably," Riley said. "He's in the hospital. I said we'd stop by. See how he's doing. I guess he's having surgery in the morning. So we should go tonight."

Landry *did* make a face at that. "Really?"

"Yep." Riley looked regretful. "Deacon says he's bringing over some guys, too. Coach Kelley's gonna be there, and Mr. G, apparently."

"You think they're gonna allow all these guys in the hospital?" Landry questioned. Yeah, he really didn't want to go. Yes, he supported Rex. Hoped he'd regain his mobility and his prowess again so he could play someone else dirty someday. But he really didn't want to go visit tonight.

Tonight, he wanted to dance with Riley and find another dark corner and make out until his knees felt weak and wobbly, then come home and have another round of very excellent sex.

That was how he wanted the night to go, not head over to the hospital and visit someone who Landry wasn't sure would bother doing it for any of the rest of them.

But Riley looked determined, and as the leader, he would be expected to be there.

"I think it's worth trying, and the gesture alone is worth it," Riley said with determination. "Come on."

Landry made a face and downed his whole glass of champagne because if he was going to have to pretend to give a shit about someone who'd essentially tried to put *him* in the hospital, he was going to need some liquid courage to do it.

When they got to the hospital, the nurse led them up to the orthopedics wing, where the surgical group that specialized in the Condors' injuries resided.

Landry hadn't ever been up here—hadn't ever had an injury like this that needed specialist care, and counted himself lucky that was the case.

On their way to Rex's room where he was being kept overnight til the surgery, and, as the nurse said, "Drugged within an inch of his life for the pain," they ran into Mr. G.

"Oh, good, Riley, you're here," Mr. G said, running a hand through his hair. "Deacon said you'd be by."

"Rex doing okay?"

Mr. G didn't look confident. "He looks like he just smashed his leg to bits and like he was out of it from how much pain meds they gave him."

"Ugh," Riley said. "That's terrible. Do you know the details of his prognosis?"

"Not anything specific, just that he needs surgery to set the break," Mr. G said heavily. "It's not looking good for the rest of the season."

"Here he is," the nurse said, stopping in front of a private room. The door was open, and as Landry stopped, he saw Rex lying in bed, his head turned away from them, his leg propped up in a sling to keep it completely immobilized.

"Yeah," Rex slurred into the phone. "It really fucking sucks. Yeah, I know. I know." His words came out even slower than normal, drawn out like syrup, probably from the heavy medication the doctors had put him on. "I know, the bet's this weekend. I *know*. It's not like we were favored anyway, but with Flynn...*I know*. Fucking sucks. We're gonna fucking lose by a million if nobody's coverin' Chase fucking Riley. Won't even cover the spread." He paused. "You're gonna lose a mint? How about me? I'm riding on this one, baby."

Landry froze. He glanced over at Riley, who was equally still.

Betting was one hundred percent not allowed in the National Football League. It wasn't just frowned upon or highly discouraged, it was an enormous offense, and if you were caught, even for a minor infraction, it always meant serious punishment. Calvin Ridley, who'd bet $1,500 on a game he wasn't even playing in, had been banned for a year when he'd been discovered.

Landry had thought Rex was bad news, had believed it when he'd personally gone after him in practice, and even more when Carter had warned him about the corner's typical behavior.

But never in a million years had he imagined this.

Was the guy so arrogant and smug about his position that he thought he could just blab out loud, in the middle of a busy hospital, about blatantly breaking the one universal rule of professional sports? *Don't ever fucking bet?*

He might be, Landry realized.

Next to them, he watched as Mr. G's face morphed into hard, inflexible lines.

On the bed, Rex kept blabbing about how far he'd committed himself with this bet—it seemed like it wasn't a singular occurrence either, but this particular game was a parlay on some other bets he'd lost, including, apparently betting *against* the Condors on several occasions.

Mr. G cleared his throat.

Rex glanced over, and the sudden realization, coupled with the intense regret and guilt blooming across his features, made it clear he knew he'd just been caught.

Even the veneer of heavy-duty pain meds wasn't enough to shield him from the way he must know the shit had just hit the fan.

"Oh, Mr. G," Rex said weakly. "Didn't see you there."

"No, I'm sure you didn't," Mr. G said in a tone forged from steel.

It was worse, Landry realized, than it might've been otherwise because he knew Mr. G had personally conversed with and vetted every player and every coach and every staff member who'd stayed over from the previous ownership. He'd wanted to clean house as completely as he could.

Not only had Rex broken the cardinal rule, but he'd done it while fooling the Condors' new owner. Even if there was room to forgive—and Landry knew there wasn't—Mr. G wouldn't be tempted. He was pissed as hell because he'd personally vouched for Rex, and this was how he'd repaid him.

"We thought we'd come see how you were doing," Riley said hesitantly. Landry had a feeling that no matter how many lessons Aidan had given him on how to be a team leader, he'd never instructed him on how to deal with a player who'd just been caught, right in front of the fucking owner, gambling.

Worse, even, than breaking a leg doing something that wasn't on the football field.

"Like shit," Rex said bluntly.

Landry had a feeling he wasn't just talking about his leg, but probably the money he'd lose on the bet. *And* the rest of the money he'd likely lose because the chances of him being banned for life from the NFL were high.

"I bet," Landry said wryly. *Ironically.*

Rex made a face. Clearly, he hadn't appreciated the joke.

Landry wouldn't either if he was him, but then he also wouldn't be caught dead taking the kind of risks Rex had.

"Mr. G," Rex said, and yes, he was begging. That much was abundantly clear. "You don't have to...it's not what it looks like, I swear."

But Mr. G was still staring at him with an expression that looked like it had been carved from marble. He clearly didn't believe a word Rex was saying.

Landry couldn't blame him. He didn't exactly believe Rex, either.

"Rex," Mr. G finally said, and his voice was gentler than Landry personally thought he deserved, "we all heard what you said. It's my responsibility to report it to the NFL. You know that. They'll conduct their investigation and figure out what's true and what's not true."

"But—" Rex was still arguing. He looked like he desperately wanted to jam the call button and request so many hardcore drugs he didn't even know what was happening. But that wouldn't stop it. Not now.

"No," Mr. G interrupted. "No. We talked about this, Rex. We talked about my responsibility to this team, what I wanted it to be. And instead of listening to me, instead of being the kind of player—the kind of *man*—I know you could be, you *bet* on the Condors. You gambled on us. Which you know full well is forbidden."

"But—" Rex attempted to interrupt again, but yet again, Mr. G wasn't having it.

"No, no, you don't get to try to argue with me. Not now. I'm very sorry you're injured. Sorry for your family. But yes, I will be reporting this. No matter what the NFL finds, the Condors will cover your surgery. Your recovery. Your physical therapy. And that's the last dime you will ever get from this team. Is that clear?"

Rex shrank back into the pillows. Looking pale. "Yes," he said bitterly, like he was being unfairly punished when in Landry's opinion, Mr. G had been more than a little generous, considering what they'd all just overheard.

"What's going on?"

Landry glanced back, and there was Deacon in the doorway, Jem and Beck a few steps behind, looking confused.

"Just more truths being discovered," Mr. G said flatly and turned on his heel and walked away.

Deacon glanced at his retreating back like he wanted nothing more than to follow but felt torn. Like what he really wanted was walking away, even though he knew his obligations were here, right in front of him.

"What happened?" Deacon demanded.

Rex buried his head in the pillow.

Landry felt a pulse of sympathy for him, even though he didn't really deserve it.

He probably didn't even realize the magnitude of what had just transpired, and he wouldn't until tomorrow when he woke up from his surgery and the drugs began to wear off. Then he'd know, and there'd still be nothing he could do.

"Rex was on the phone when we came in," Riley said in a low voice. "And he was talking to someone about...about betting. On the team. On Sunday's game. And how we weren't going to cover the spread, even if we won, because he wasn't playing anymore." He paused. "How much money he was going to lose as a result."

Deacon's mouth compressed into a hard line. "And Grant heard it," he stated rather than asked.

Riley nodded.

"Shit," Deacon said, and then he *did* turn and leave, pushing between Beck and Jem, clearly going after Mr. G, even though Jem held out a hand, trying to stop him.

"He didn't want to be right about you, Rex," Jem said, and he sounded angry. Maybe not just at Rex, who definitely fully deserved it, but at himself, too. At all of them. Because they'd trusted Rex, who'd turned out not to be worthy of any of it.

"You don't know what it's like," Rex said, his voice cracking. "You don't know what it's like to have a *family*, and to have to take care of them. *All* of them."

"You pimp yourself out on Instagram or OnlyFans or, God knows, anything else, but you don't fucking *bet* on anything," Beck said savagely. "You know better."

Rex didn't say anything else.

"Come on," Riley said, putting a hand on Beck's arm. "We don't need to be here for this. We...we're real sorry, Rex."

"Not as sorry as you are, though," Jem said.

Unfortunately, that was probably true.

Riley knew he was quiet on the way home, but then Landry didn't say much of anything.

It was sobering what had just happened in Rex's hospital room.

Not only had he seriously injured his leg, he'd destroyed his future.

"I didn't know what to do," Riley finally said as they walked into the house. "That was…"

Landry turned in the foyer, opened his arms, and Riley fell into them as easily as breathing.

"Awful," Landry finished for him, his voice muffled from the way his mouth pressed against the top of Riley's head.

"Yeah," Riley agreed. His throat felt raw. "I wanted to do something, to *fix* it, but I couldn't. It's not…it's not fixable."

"You didn't do anything that needed to be fixed," Landry said firmly. "That's all on Rex. He chose to make those decisions, to take that path. And you know what? Even if we didn't walk in on him today, the NFL would've eventually realized what he was doing. It was only a matter of time. He was playing with fire, and he knew it, and he just didn't care."

Riley knew he was right, but it didn't stop him from feeling a tiny frisson of guilt deep down. If they hadn't been there today, if they hadn't walked in on Rex's conversation…

But they had.

Wishing wasn't going to change anything.

It certainly wasn't going to go back and convince Rex not to take the worst step possible.

"I really thought things were…I don't know…*better*," Riley said.

"They are better," Landry promised. His arms tightened around Riley.

"Yeah, tomorrow's gonna suck. We've got the Riptide this week, and they just won the freaking Super Bowl, and now we're gonna have to play them without Rex."

They were already a long shot to win.

Rex must've been desperate to bet that the Condors would beat last year's Super Bowl champs—already favored to repeat.

But then, why else would he do it at all if he *wasn't* desperate?

"Yeah," Landry agreed.

"It was always going to be pretty much an impossible task, David versus freaking Goliath," Riley murmured. "And now, we're all gonna be reeling from...well, from this."

Because it wasn't just as devastating as losing Rex to a season-ending injury, though they were. It was also the inherent betrayal he'd revealed on his way out.

Landry didn't say anything, but Riley knew he was thinking the same thing.

"What if..." Riley hesitated. "What if we not only have the offensive line over this week, but...well, the whole team? The coaches, too. And Mr. G."

"You want to host a hundred people in this townhouse?" Landry asked, sounding amused. But then he didn't sound against the idea either.

"It's not that small," Riley defended. "We can manage it. There's the living room, and the kitchen, and the back deck. We can make it work. And I can cook."

"You can," Landry agreed. "But we can also have it catered."

"But—"

"Riley, you can't put on a party for over a hundred people yourself. Let me help."

"Fine, fine, we can cater *part* of it," Riley agreed. He pulled back a little and saw the smile tugging up a corner of Landry's lips. "You're still great, you know. The best, actually."

"Because I'm willing to help you host the entire freaking football team here?"

"Not just that—though that's a big part of it—but because you didn't even blink when I asked. You just rolled with it, you're…" Riley took a deep breath. It felt like the words were tumbling out of him without even trying. Without even meaning to. "You're just what I always wanted and didn't think I could have. But I do, now."

"Yeah, you do," Landry said and pressed his mouth against Riley's. It was a sweet kiss with the barest hint of a promise for more.

Not just the undeniably hot sex, but that he'd continue to be everything Riley had ever wanted and would never stop being the things Riley had never thought he could have.

Chapter 16

"Let me get this straight," Carter said. "You *chose* to host the whole team at Landry's house. Not just the offensive line, or even the offense, but the whole freaking team."

"Yep," Riley said. "You got it right."

Carter shook his head and then lifted the six-pack of beer he held in one hand. "Then I guess you're gonna need this. More than this, I'd guess."

Riley took the beer and gestured towards the kitchen, just visible through the small hallway leading out of the foyer. "Food's through there. It's probably gonna be a tight squeeze, fitting everyone in, but Landry and I both wanted to do this after...well, after Rex."

Something flickered over Carter's expression. "Yeah, he's an asshole," he said.

Riley wouldn't have gone that far—misguided, for sure, and self-centered, to put himself above his team, no matter the consequences—but Rex wasn't a *bad* guy.

He didn't think Mr. G would've ever been willing to forget what they'd heard in Rex's hospital room. It had been way too blatant. But maybe he could've softened the blow somehow.

"Don't tell me you feel sorry for him," Carter said, identifying the hesitation in Riley's reply correctly.

"Not *sorry*, exactly," Riley said. "He did this to himself, but well, it sucks, doesn't it?"

"I don't feel a shred of sympathy for the guy," Carter said, his voice going harder than Riley had ever heard before. "He'd have sent any of us to the hospital without batting an eye. And here's the other thing, some of us get an enormous load of shit even though we didn't ever really *do* anything wrong." Riley heard what he wasn't saying. *Rex was a fuckup, and he didn't get traded to tour different NFL teams, until nobody really wanted him.* "The bullshit he pulled? Totally against the rules. He knew it, and he did it anyway. So yeah, he should pay."

Carter tended to run his mouth a lot, but Riley didn't think he'd ever heard him expound so passionately on a serious-ish topic.

"Alright," Riley said. "I agree."

Carter looked surprised. "You do?"

"Well yeah. Of course I do."

"Huh." Carter plucked one of the beers out of the six-pack Riley was holding. "You know," he said as he popped the top off. "The house I own, it's a hell of a lot bigger than this."

"You own a house? A whole house?"

Carter shot him a look. "Yeah, 'course I do."

"And it's big?"

Carter took a sip of his beer. "Well, *yeah*."

Jem and Deacon showed up then, lingering in the doorway as Carter moved inside. "Have you ever seen Carter's house?" Riley asked. He'd sort of expected Carter to own one of those soulless super-modern penthouse apartments in one of the high rises in downtown Charleston.

An appropriate setting, maybe, for all the hookups Carter was always having.

"Oh yeah," Deacon said. "It's like a fucking mausoleum. All white marble. Cold as hell."

"That's not true at all," Carter scoffed incredulously. "You're making that up."

Riley glanced from Carter to where Deacon was smiling way too smugly behind him.

"Stop giving the guy fits, Harris," Jem said, amused. He elbowed his best friend in the side. "Come on, let's go get some grub. Beck texted me and said he was saving some delicious as fuck ribs."

"Beck texted *you*?" Deacon said with mock outrage. "What is he, *your* protege now?"

"You know he's yours," Jem said, smiling impudently.

"Come on," Carter said, "let's get out of Riley's hair and find some food. I better get at least one of those ribs Beck's saving."

But Riley knew—though he kept quiet—there'd be plenty of ribs for everyone. He and Landry had ordered a ton of food from the barbeque place, and not only were there pans and pans of ribs, but gallons of slaw, macaroni and cheese, and enough hush puppies they'd probably be drowning in them for the next week.

He stayed by the door for the next twenty minutes, ushering in Coach Oscar, Coach Kelley, and a handful of additional players. He was just about to shut it and go find some food himself when someone he *didn't* expect climbed up Landry's front steps.

He'd passed along the invite to the whole organization, of course, but he'd never imagined that Mr. G himself might show up. Landry was going to practically shit himself when he saw that the owner of the Condors was in his house.

"Hey, Riley," Mr. G said, and they clasped hands. "It's good to see you again."

"Better, at least, than the last time," Riley said wryly. Because the last time had been in the hospital when they'd found out about Rex.

"That's true," Mr. G admitted. "It's real nice that you and Landry decided to host this."

"Well, we thought we could all use a bit of a boost. Already a tough game this week, flying to LA to play the Riptide. Harder to do it without one of our starting corners."

"That's for sure," Mr. G agreed.

"Any idea what you're doing about replacing him?" Riley asked as he shut the door, and he and Mr. G headed down the hallway towards the kitchen.

"Ah, well, Desmond will start, of course. He's the backup. But after that...still working on a plan, actually," Mr. G said.

"Well," Riley said, "I plan on putting us in a position where we can win. No matter what."

It was a big promise, especially considering they were going into the Riptide game down a player who might've actually been able to stop Sam Crawford and Chase Riley from blowing up the score-board. Not many teams were as complete as the Riptide—power-houses on both sides of the ball.

But Riley hadn't gotten where he was by giving up before he'd even gotten started. Neither had Mr. G, who he'd read had been born to a fairly standard middle-class family and had earned a billion dollars with his software company by the time he was thirty-five.

If either of them had given up when people had told them to *or* when the cards were stacked against them, they wouldn't be here today, standing in the foyer of Landry's townhouse.

"We'll keep the faith," Mr. G said. "Now, what's this I smell? Barbeque?"

"Yep," Riley said. "It's just this way."

"Desmond can't hack it," Deacon said bluntly. "He's gonna give up three touchdowns alone, two hundred yards *easy*, to Chase Riley."

"Shhhh," Landry reminded him. "He's here somewhere. Probably drowning his pain in ribs and cornbread."

But Deacon's stare was not only steely, it was wise beyond his years. "I know Desmond pretty damn well," he said. "He's a decent backup. But he's not a corner capable of covering Chase Riley. He can't even really cover Carter in practice. Carter runs circles around him regularly."

"That's true," Carter agreed. "And for once, that's not just my ego talking."

"Though it sure likes to," Landry retorted. Were he and Carter ever going to be super friendly? He wouldn't have ever assumed so, but *Riley* and Carter were becoming closer, and Landry had a feeling he was going to be forcibly dragged from the *I'm merely tolerating Carter Maxwell* camp to the *I'm spending time with Carter Maxwell out of my own free will* camp.

It wasn't a camp he'd have normally chosen, but if it meant Riley was there...well, he was on board. If he hadn't been sure before he was in love with Riley Flynn, the fact he was ready and willing to tolerate Carter Maxwell just to be with him...that would've convinced him once and for all.

"You know," Jem said, "I heard Micah Rose is still wantin' to be traded."

The gaze of everyone in their small knot of players, currently conversing where normally Landry's kitchen table sat, swiveled in Beck's direction.

"I don't know why everyone keeps looking at me whenever you bring up Micah," Beck said defensively.

Too defensively, if Landry had to guess.

"Y'all were pretty damn close in college," Deacon said mildly. "That's why. Together, you were The Wall. Seems like a natural thought to bring him here. Recreate some old magic."

"There wasn't any magic," Beck said, which they all knew was blatantly untrue. Beck and Micah had both been nominated for a Heisman Trophy their senior year, which was basically unheard of. Even *one* defensive player making it to the Heisman ceremony was a big deal, and two? It had only happened once before, in 1986.

Of course, neither Beck or Micah had won, but there'd been a lot of talk about them splitting the vote. Maybe, some people said, one of them might've taken the trophy if there hadn't been two of them.

But there had been.

Landry could remember the picture from the ceremony, Micah and Beck, with their arms around each other, huge smiles on their faces. He remembered the quotes, too. About how they were best friends. How they knew they weren't going to end up playing for the same NFL team, but that, to them, that was the ultimate dream.

And now Beck was claiming there hadn't been anything special going on.

Well, that was bullshit if Landry had ever heard it.

"That's too bad," Deacon said. "Because I just told Grant he should reunite *The Wall*."

If he'd expected Beck to react, he didn't. Because his face went cool and remote, every emotion was hidden behind the mask he'd just slipped on. The same mask he always wore whenever Micah Rose came up.

"If he thinks Micah's best for this team," Beck said, "then he should bring him in. I'm going to grab another drink. Anyone want anything?"

The whole group shook their heads because, as Landry had predicted, the moment Beck was out of earshot, Jem said, "What the fuck was that about?"

Landry decided to make a valiant stand—almost definitely ineffectual, but brave, nonetheless—and go to bat for Beck.

"Maybe," he said with a casual shrug, "they weren't really that close. You know how the media likes to create stories out of nothing."

"No. No way." Deacon sounded adamant. "That wasn't just a story. They were real close. I went to the Big Ten Championship their senior year. Stood on the sideline. It wasn't faked by the media. The two of them were thick as thieves."

"Not like you haven't seen good friendships go bad," Jem pointed out. "We don't talk to half the guys from last year's team."

Deacon scowled. "Those guys were assholes."

"Yeah, well, maybe Micah Rose turned out to be an asshole," Carter inserted.

Landry didn't think so, though. Logan knew Micah because they were on the same team, and though he'd clearly been unimpressed with the guy at first, now it seemed he'd gotten a lot closer to the other Piranhas.

Especially, Landry had noticed, the Piranhas players who identified as queer.

But Landry wasn't going to say that now, even though he knew Deacon and Jem were both bisexual, and right after the draft, Beck had come out, too.

It wasn't, Landry knew, his secret to tell.

It was Micah's, if he ever decided to share it.

"He struggled a bit, you know, like most rookies without a real good system to fall back on," Deacon said. "Though nobody was real sure why, 'cause he's got Sebastian freaking Howard, one of the all-time best corners in the NFL to learn from right there on his team."

"Maybe Sebastian didn't love a rookie replacing him," Jem said. "Maybe he was a jerk about it."

"Or maybe Micah was an asshole. Hard to say."

Landry didn't know if he was the only one who'd caught the weird undercurrent with Beck the moment Micah had come up as a topic of conversation but also had an unrelated opinion. One he felt he should share. "I don't think," Landry said cautiously, "that from what I know of Beck, he'd ever be friends with a guy who's an asshole."

"Can't argue with that," Carter said. "Beck's a good guy."

"Yeah," Jem said with amusement. "Too good to even hook up with you."

That was, of course, the moment Riley showed up. "Who's too good to hook up with Carter? Everyone with half a brain?"

Landry had to shove his hands in his pockets; the desire to sling an arm around Riley and tug him close was so strong.

If they'd been at the Pirate's Booty or in a more private setting, he might've just done it. But Coach Kelley and most of the team didn't know about their relationship still, and he'd put the timeline in Riley's lap, not his own.

"Beck. Didn't Landry tell you?" Jem was laughing now. "Carter totally hit on him the first day of camp."

"He doesn't *look* like a football player," Carter complained. "How was I to know he wasn't like a coach or something?"

Riley's eyebrows hit his hairline. "Beck doesn't look like a football player? *Seriously*?"

"Okay, he kinda does now. Maybe he even did then. What's wrong with a guy trying to get some action in close to home?" Carter pointedly glanced from Riley to Landry. "It's not like *some people* haven't already discovered how convenient it is."

"Yeah, but they're not hooking up in a *supply closet*," Deacon said.

"You asked him to hook up with you in a supply closet?" Landry questioned.

"It was handy!" Carter exclaimed, throwing up his hands.

"Your libido is a terrifying thing," Jem said, shaking his head.

"Terrifyingly awful," Carter said, waggling his eyebrows suggestively, "or terrifyingly magnificent?"

"Just plain terrifying," Riley said firmly.

"What can I say? Sex helps keep The Beast at bay." Carter sounded completely unapologetic about that—either that he actually called part of his personality *The Beast* or that he regularly used sex to quell it.

"You mean, your temper," Deacon said.

"Yep. Remember my rookie year? Broke four tablets on the sidelines that year. The NFL fined the shit out of me. Had an orgy, was totally fine after that."

"I think your dick's so exhausted it can't *get* angry," Riley teased.

Carter tilted his head to the side like he was actually contemplating the legitimacy of the accusation. "You know," he said, "I'm not sure you're wrong."

"Hey, you know, whatever works for you," Landry said. Surely Carter hooking up with everyone on planet Earth was better than letting his temper rule him again. As long as that coping mechanism kept working and Carter was happy with it, who was he to judge?

"I'd agree, though I'm not sure Beck would," Jem said, grinning. "He was so scandalized."

Carter rolled his eyes. "He's hot, he's single, and he's a player in the NFL. He should get used to getting hit on."

"You ever get used to it?" Deacon asked Jem, who just shook his head. "Nope, me, either."

"That makes three of us," Landry agreed.

"Except when it's *Riley* doing it," Carter teased, and the whole group laughed. "Seriously, though, it's good you guys did this. We..." He hesitated, which was so unlike the normally confident Carter. "We needed it."

"Yeah," Deacon said, clapping Landry on the shoulder. "Thanks for opening your house up to this rowdy lot."

"The house could be a little bigger, but thanks, it's gone great," Landry said. Some of the team and coaching staff had left after eating, which had helped it not be *quite* so crowded, but they'd definitely been at maximum capacity.

"I thought we could use it, even if it was a tight squeeze," Riley said, and to Landry's surprise, he put an arm around his waist and tucked himself into his side like he belonged there.

He does belong there.

Landry had a feeling that it was only a matter of time—maybe only a matter of days—before everyone on the team knew, including Coach Kelley.

"Next time," Carter said, "we'll hold it at my *mausoleum*. It's got plenty of room."

"Really?" Deacon sounded surprised.

"Yep," Carter said. "And y'all can live in anticipation of seeing what the Maxwell homestead is really like. Don't believe what Deacon here says. It's not cold or ugly, and it definitely doesn't contain any dead bodies."

"For that," Jem said, slapping Carter on the shoulder, "we're honestly grateful."

"No dead bodies, but regularly hosts orgies," Riley teased. "If you ever sell it, you could use that for the sales brochure."

"Not *that* many orgies," Carter argued.

"Landry," Deacon asked very seriously, "how many orgies have you hosted in *your* house?"

"Regular orgies or just orgies for two?" Landry asked instead of answering. "Cause I think I'm gonna have to plead the fifth on both."

Carter scoffed. "You and Riley won't even give me any details. What's the point of two of your hottest friends hooking up if they won't share the play-by-play or take pictures or spontaneous video or *anything*? You two are way too close-lipped for my sanity."

Riley laughed. "Sorry, Carter. It really is your loss."

"It is," Carter said mournfully.

"Wait a minute," Deacon said. "Jem and I aren't your *hottest friends*? I think I'm hurt."

"Wounded to the core," Jem added dramatically.

"Now," Carter said speculatively, "if I considered Mr. G a friend, you two might have competition."

"Ouch," Jem said.

But Deacon, Landry noticed, didn't say a word. Only pursed his lips, like he was annoyed that Carter had noticed how attractive their owner was.

"He's rich, too," Carter observed.

"Probably not as rich as you now that he's bought an NFL team," Landry pointed out.

"Good point! I could always offer to lend him some money."

"And some cock?" Riley snickered. "I know your game, Maxwell."

"Sadly, you don't know it *nearly* well enough," Carter said.

And even though Landry had no reason to be jealous because there was no way Carter even meant half of what he was saying—never mind that Riley had made it plenty clear who he was interested in, and it wasn't Carter Maxwell—Landry's arm tightened around Riley.

"Ooooh," Carter said, "I know that look. Landry wants to punch me for flirting with his guy."

"If Landry wanted to do that," Landry said dryly, "he'd have to punch half the world."

Riley grinned. "Awwww, you're both too cute."

Carter fist-pumped. "I'll take that!"

"You're weird," Jem said, rolling his eyes.

"No argument there," Carter said cheerfully, like he not only embraced being the odd one, but *enjoyed* it.

Landry realized then that he wasn't *eventually* going to end up liking Carter because he was always around, but he already did.

How had he gotten here?

Happy and relaxed, with a team he gave a shit about, and his guy tucked into his side, smiling up at him like he was the most brilliant person on earth?

Landry really didn't know, but he wasn't stupid enough to question it. He was just going to go with it. Embrace it.

Make sure it never changed.

"I'm freaking dead on my feet," Riley said, collapsing onto a barstool he'd just dragged back into the kitchen from the garage, where they'd stacked almost all the furniture from the lower level of the townhouse.

He gazed over where Landry stood by the sink, stacking rinsed serving dishes for the caterers to pick up tomorrow morning. "How are you still vertical?"

"This needs done," Landry said stubbornly. "But I was thinking...you wanna take a soak?"

"Oh, in your tub? *Yes*," Riley said.

"Well, let me just finish these," Landry said, "and we'll go upstairs, forget that we just hosted way too many people in the last few hours."

"I never thought Carter would leave," Riley confessed.

"Maybe he thought if he hung around long enough, he'd see me strip you naked," Landry grumbled.

It was adorable how low-key jealous Landry still was over Carter's flirting. It shouldn't have been endearing, except that it was. Must be because they both knew Landry wasn't actually worried about Riley being attracted to Carter.

"I sure hope so," Riley said. He slid off the barstool onto his aching feet and walked over to where Landry stood by the sink. Wrapped his arms around Landry's waist and rested his cheek against the broad planes of Landry's muscular back.

"You sure hope Carter wanted to see me strip you down?" Landry teased. But there was a rough edge to his voice, like now *Landry* was thinking of getting Riley naked, and Riley approved.

Because he wanted the same thing.

Both of them, naked, in the big tub in Landry's bathroom.

"I hope *you* strip me down," Riley corrected gently. "But if you're too tired, I'll settle for just you cuddling me naked in the tub."

"If either one of us is naked and wet and in the tub, it's not going to end there," Landry said ruefully.

Exactly what Riley had been hoping for.

"Hey, the tub wasn't *my* idea," Riley teased.

Landry flicked the sink faucet off. Turned around, leaned in, and kissed Riley thoroughly. "Maybe it's not just the naked and wet part," he admitted, then hesitated. "Maybe it's 'cause I'm crazy about you."

Riley knew what he wanted to say.

He wanted to say it, too.

"I'm crazy about you, too," Riley murmured back, lips brushing against Landry's.

Most of the time, what he felt was simply too monumental to fit into words. Perhaps it was the same for Landry. Someday, maybe someday soon, the actual words wouldn't be too hard to reach for, for both of them.

How had they ended up feeling this way after such a short time?

Maybe we've just been headed here for a long time. From the moment Landry walked into our house all those years ago. From the moment I took my helmet off in Pittsburgh and Landry looked at me like I'd been hoping he would for forever.

"Come on," Landry said softly. "Let's go upstairs."

Landry took his hand, and they made their way up the stairs to Landry's room and the bathroom.

The first day he'd arrived, he'd snuck a peek into Landry's room and noticed the tub. Had even thought, *it's big enough for two, even for a guy Landry's size*, but Riley had never dreamed they'd end up here, sharing it.

It had felt too big, too monumental to even dream of back then.

Too much everything he'd ever wanted to put into words if it didn't end up happening.

But it did happen.

In the bathroom, Landry didn't turn the overhead light on, but in the shadowed darkness, he reached over and flicked the faucets on to fill the bathtub.

Riley hopped up on the bathroom counter, watching as Landry pulled a few candles out of a cabinet and lit them with a lighter he scrounged from a drawer. "Awww," he said, "candles and everything. Does anyone else know what a romantic you are?"

Landry shot him a look. Affectionate. Sweet. Full of dirty promises. "No."

"Not even Carter?" Riley teased. It was too easy to poke him about Carter, and he knew deep down Landry didn't mind. That was why he kept doing it.

"If Carter was involved, I'm sure I'd have some kind of camera set up to video us," Landry said dryly.

"Seriously," Riley agreed. He reached up and pulled his t-shirt off. Watched as even in the dim light of the bathroom, Landry's gaze grew even warmer, his eyes dilating further. And he definitely did not miss the way Landry's cock was pressing hard against the front of his shorts.

It seemed unreal that after all this time, after so long wanting it, that was all for him. Riley didn't think he'd ever get used to it.

"If you don't stop doing that, we're never going to be able to *just* take a bath," Landry said seriously, as Riley wiggled and slid off his own shorts. He got exactly the reaction he'd hoped for from Landry, which was another one of those addictingly hot looks shot in his direction.

"I'm sorry?" Riley teased. "I kinda thought we had to get naked to get in the tub."

"We do, but you're stripping so...so..." Landry trailed off.

Riley jumped off the counter, sidled up to Landry, and then tucked his fingertips under Landry's waistband. "So?" he questioned, gazing up at Landry. "So...what exactly?"

"Ugh." Landry laughed. "You know what you're doing to me. You always know."

"Maybe that's the goal," Riley admitted. "But it's nice to know it works."

"Every damn time."

"Good." Riley couldn't stop the smile that was spreading across his face. Why had he been freaking out about this? It was so freaking good. It *felt* so freaking good. He wanted to feel this way with Landry forever. "You gonna let me take your clothes off?"

Landry glanced over at the tub, which was only about half full. "Do you ever have to ask?"

Riley didn't think so and took his time, tugging Landry's t-shirt slowly over his head, revealing his broad chest and narrow waist and all the incredible muscle in-between. Pulled down his shorts, listening with satisfaction to Landry's sharp inhale as his palm grazed over his hard cock.

"If you..." Landry huffed out a laugh. "If you do that, I'm not gonna be able to keep my hands to myself."

"Who says I want you to?" Riley discarded the rest of Landry's clothes, and then they were both standing there naked. And the tub was still only half full.

Maybe they wouldn't make it in there after all. Not with the way Landry was eyeing him. Not with the way Riley knew he was eyeing him back.

"Come on," Landry said, "let's get in before we get totally sidetracked."

"Hey, not our fault we look great naked," Riley said as he followed Landry into the hot water.

He had no intention of staying on his side of the tub, and when Landry settled down, back resting against one of the sides, Riley moved over to him, finally coming to a stop between his legs, feeling his still rock-hard cock against his back as he lay back.

Landry settled a warm, possessive arm around his waist and rested a chin on Riley's shoulder.

"This is nice," Landry said after a long moment.

A long moment where Riley nearly said half a dozen times, *screw our sore feet; let's just fuck.* He hadn't even been sure how much he wanted it, that's how tired he'd been—from both the event they'd hosted tonight as well as the long practices they'd endured this week—but now lust was rising in his blood, Landry's bare wet skin slick against his own.

"Just nice?" Riley said incredulously. "It's...well, it's a lot more than nice."

"Okay," Landry conceded. "It's hot as hell, but I'm trying to ignore that. Trying to be a good boyfriend. Not just a horny one."

Wasn't that a fucking trip still?

Landry Banks was his boyfriend—and he was both undeni-ably good *and* perfectly, awesomely horny.

"How about this," Riley said. "Let's talk about telling people. Maybe that'll help us keep our hands to ourselves."

Landry's fingertips dug into Riley's chest, and his cock seemed to do the opposite of pretend disinterest, but Landry said, "Sure. Thought you already told Mr. G."

"Yeah," Riley agreed. "I did. But I thought...I thought we should tell Coach Kelley soon. This week? Maybe after the walk-through on Saturday?"

"Really?"

Riley rolled his eyes. "You're a very dirty secret, you know, but I don't want that. Not for us. Not for you."

"But you said—" Landry started.

Riley knew what he'd said, but well, the more his feelings grew, the more he didn't want to wait, even if maybe it would be smarter. But also, the more he got to know the Condors, both the coaches and the players, the more he felt like they wouldn't judge him for his relationship.

"I know," Riley said. "But...I've changed my mind. I don't want to go into this game without being honest at least with Coach. The rest of the team? Well, a lot of them already know. I wasn't thinking a big announcement or anything, just...being together."

"I'm good with just being," Landry said. "I'm good with whatever you want. You know that."

"So you want to tell Coach with me on Saturday?"

"Do I *want* to?" Landry sounded amused. "I'm still a little worried someone's gonna kick my ass, but for you, Riley, I'll be happy to do everything—and *anything*."

The most beautiful thing was Riley knew he meant it. Knew he meant every single damn word.

Landry Banks, who was the most fanatically loyal person he knew, the most dedicated, the most determined, was *all his*. He was all his, in the same way Riley was *all* Landry's.

Suddenly, he didn't give a shit about this bath or the tub or his feet, which were still aching a little.

He turned in Landry's arms and kissed him. Their mouths slid together, hot and wet, and Riley whimpered in the back of his throat as Landry's hand slid down his chest, down his stomach, and he palmed his cock. Once then twice.

"Come on," Riley said, pulling back. It was definitely his turn to say it. "Let's go to bed."

Landry didn't need any more encouragement than that. He just picked Riley up, and they stumbled into the bedroom, still wet, kissing the whole way, and laughing as they fell onto the bed.

Riley was on Landry almost immediately, knowing exactly what he wanted. "Just like this," he said, leaning down and pressing his mouth against Landry's. "I wanna ride you, look at you when you're about to lose it. Except you can't. You *won't*."

"I won't?" Landry raised an eyebrow.

Riley ground down on Landry's hard cock, gasping a little as it rubbed his own. "You won't, not til I've come so hard I can't speak, I can't even breathe."

"Yeah." Landry's voice had gone gravelly and deep. So deep Riley could feel it way down in the base of his stomach. "Yeah. I won't. I want you to feel good. Want you to feel the best." He was babbling a little now, groaning between each word as Riley kept moving his hips.

"I can't wait any longer," Riley admitted and shifted off Landry, reaching for the lube and condoms in the drawer.

"Do you want me..." Landry trailed off as Riley wet his fingers and, without ceremony, started to circle his hole with them. He wanted Landry *now*. Wanted his big cock deep inside him until he didn't know where Landry left off and he began. "God, that's so fucking hot, you doing that."

"Yeah?" Riley panted a little. Electricity was fizzing under his skin, making him dizzy with how desperate he was for Landry.

Landry's hands were everywhere, touching Riley's chest, brushing across his nipples, framing his stomach and his hips, kneading his thighs, and then finally, when Riley felt like he was about to scream from the stimulation, sneaking back behind, where he was prepping himself and sliding a finger in alongside his own.

Riley groaned deep in his throat at the feel of Landry's fingers brushing right alongside his own.

"Fuck," Landry growled, "you're so fucking hot and tight. I just want..."

"Yeah? What do you want?" Riley knew what he wanted. It was brushing against his own hard, leaking cock right now. If he so much as touched himself, he couldn't guarantee he wouldn't just explode.

"You. Just you. Only you. *Always* fucking you." Landry panted as he tucked his finger deeper into Riley's ass, and Riley couldn't help but grind down on it, the feel of him and Landry together.

Riley twisted his fingers inside, probably rushing more than he should through the prep, but he was so worked up, so ready—honestly about to go out of his mind with the way the need had crept up on him so suddenly.

He'd managed the normal level of arousal buzzing under his skin throughout the day—really, throughout the week, when they'd been busy at the practice facility almost every day until late into the evening with barely enough energy to make out a little in bed and give each other a pair of fairly straightforward handjobs.

Of course Riley had wanted more. He'd wanted to fulfill the promise of the last time they'd fucked. Wanted to lay Landry out and make him beg and cry for it, the same way Riley felt like he was so close to doing himself.

But right now, the urge was too strong, and he couldn't resist it any longer.

He slid his fingers out and moved further down, giving Landry's cock a quick swipe of his tongue as he tore open the condom packet with trembling hands.

Riley made quick work of the condom and then, bracing his hands on Landry's chest, began to sink down onto his cock.

He was big, and Riley had rushed through fingering himself, but the further down he got, the more the urge seemed to push him on and on. He'd thought he'd feel less out of control, but with Landry's gaze burning into him, his hands digging hard into his hips as he sank down, he felt wilder than ever.

"Yeah," Landry growled when Riley finally settled against his hips. He reached for Riley's cock, but he batted his hand away. If he touched him now, this would be over way too fast, and Riley wanted to savor it. Wanted to remember the way this felt days from now, weeks from now, probably even *years* from now.

Instead, he leaned forward and dug his fingertips into Landry's chest, grinding down onto Landry's cock with enough force that both of them moaned.

"Feel good?" Landry's voice was guttural, and even more arousal sparked up Riley's spine as he continued to ride him.

It was better than good; it was unbelievably fucking amazing in the most overwhelming way possible.

Riley nodded, squeezing his eyes shut as he pushed his palms harder into Landry's chest for more leverage and then thrust faster.

He gasped as Landry set his feet and began to move, too, meeting each movement of Riley's with one of his own.

Riley couldn't help it anymore; he threw his head back and wailed at the feel of it, the pervasive pleasure of Landry working deep inside of him.

He hadn't wanted to touch himself, but he couldn't help it anymore. Reaching down, he barely grasped his cock in his hand, ecstasy spiking, and Landry groaned as Riley slumped forward, pulsing between them.

Landry's arms wrapped around him, and he gave one more thrust, and then he was shaking, too, pulsing with his own orgasm.

Riley didn't move for a long time. Wasn't sure he *could* move, honestly.

"Just when I think *wow*, that's some really great fucking sex," Landry mused below him, voice soft and relaxed.

"I know," Riley agreed, with a happy sigh as punctuation.

"You're amazing," Landry said, and Riley felt the honesty of his statement all the way down to his toes.

"I won't be stupid and say it was *just sex*," Riley teased back because it was easier to make light of it than to talk about how deeply, how completely Landry's affection and loyalty resonated with him.

"Don't you dare," Landry said, and then he groaned as Riley rolled off, heading to the bathroom to clean up. To Riley's surprise, Landry followed him in, disposing of the condom and before Riley could even wet the washcloth in his hands, wrapping his arms around Riley's shoulders. "That wasn't just sex."

It hadn't been.

There'd been a way Landry was looking at him right before he'd come his brains out, and Riley knew he'd been looking back the exact same way.

"You know it could be like that?" Riley hadn't. In fact, he'd always assumed people were making shit up about feeling their souls connect or whatever.

But he'd felt it. Not just today. But half a dozen other times, and not only during sex, either.

That was why he was convinced this was love and not just a crush gone completely wild—and why he knew it wasn't just him feeling this way.

Landry was right there with him, every step of the path they were taking, and it felt good to know he wasn't alone.

That he'd never be alone again.

"No," Landry answered, and there was that bare-bones honesty in his gaze. Riley could see it in the mirror as he gazed down at him like Riley was the greatest thing in the whole world, and he couldn't quite believe he'd been lucky enough to find him. "But I'm hoping we keep feeling it for a long time to come."

Forever, Riley thought. *That's what he means.*

CHAPTER 17

Landry didn't think he'd be particularly anxious when he and Riley cornered Coach Kelley after the walk-through on Saturday. He'd come out to his parents over *FaceTime* last night, and that hadn't been particularly terrifying. They'd already done it twice before him, though, so their understanding expressions weren't very unexpected.

They'd been a little more surprised to hear he was dating—or rather *who* he was dating. Riley had given him time in his room to make the call, and even though Landry had thought that was ridiculous at the time, he'd been glad Riley hadn't been present when his father had said with shock crossing over his features, *"You're dating Riley Flynn? That's Aidan's younger brother, isn't it? Really?"*

"Really, Dad," Landry had said with more patience than he'd thought he possessed.

"I always liked him," his mom said. *"And he's a real cutie, Landry."*

"Thanks, Mom," Landry had said, rolling his eyes.

But a few minutes later, he'd called Riley in, and the sweet way Riley had called his father, *Mr. Banks*, and then asked his mom for her famous brisket recipe had made him very certain that all this, no matter the embarrassment or the complication, was worth it.

Coach had seemed like a much less tough nut to crack than his parents.

But then they'd gotten here, to this moment, Riley next to him, wiping his palms on his shorts, and suddenly Landry wasn't sure.

He was sure of Riley, of course.

Sure they were doing the right thing.

But suddenly not quite sure of Coach's positive reaction.

"What was it you two needed?" Coach asked, clearly distracted as he sorted through some papers on the desk, barely glancing up at them.

With curfew coming up, most of the other players had wandered off by this point, and the room was almost entirely empty. There were a few players laughing all the way at the back of the hotel ballroom, including Carter, Deacon, and Jem. They were, Landry was almost one hundred percent sure, aware of what was about to happen and were totally waiting to see if Coach lost his shit at the news.

That realization didn't help keep Landry's blood pressure regulated.

"Well, uh, sir, we wanted to talk to you about our relationship."

"Been great," Coach enthused distractedly, still not really looking at them. "Two touchdowns last week, and I'm sure you'll be just as effective tomorrow."

Landry hoped so, too.

He reached over and grabbed Riley's hand. Squeezing it, not necessarily for Riley's comfort but his own.

Riley started again. There was just a hint of exasperated frustration in his voice. "I'm not talking about our relationship on the field, sir."

Coach looked up then.

"Your relationship on the..." He glanced down, and Landry knew the moment he saw their intertwined hands.

"Oh. *Oh.*"

"Yes," Riley said. "Now you've got it."

Coach didn't say anything, just stared at them.

Landry wet his lips. He'd expected this going...well, differently. Definitely better than how it was currently going. "We're going to make sure to keep it off the field, sir, and not let it affect our practice or our performance on the field," Landry promised. He'd thought that was a given if you knew him or Riley at all, but it couldn't hurt to say it, either.

Coach rested a hip on the corner of the table, and the pinched look on his face relaxed. Sometimes Landry forgot how young he really was. Only a few years older than himself and in charge of an entire football team. The responsibility staggered. Landry had trouble being responsible for ordering the weekly groceries—a task he'd been more than happy to turn over to Riley.

But when Coach didn't look worried or harried or stressed, which was almost never these days, he looked...well, *young*. Understanding, too, now that Landry thought about it.

"I can't say I expected that this would happen, but you've known each other for a long time," Coach said slowly. "I'm not upset about it. I'm just...surprised, I suppose? But also not surprised at all. Anyone with eyes can see the way you two look at each other. I just didn't know it had gotten so serious."

"You *knew*?" Landry couldn't help the question.

He just shrugged. "Well, *yeah*. Like I said, I wasn't blind."

"Oh." Landry wasn't sure what to say.

"But I'm happy for you two. Make sure you just keep it at home. We don't need..." Coach pursed his lips. "We don't need a lot of *additional* distractions, not right now."

Landry knew he was talking about Rex.

"Understood," Riley said.

"Not that I'd have expected anything less," Coach added. "You both work so hard, I wouldn't believe anything would interfere with the effort you're putting in at practice and on the field."

"Thanks," Riley said. "We're not looking to make any big announcements or media pushes or anything. Just...didn't want to live in secret, that was all."

"You tell Nikki yet?"

Nikki was the head of PR for the Condors. She'd been a new hire, apparently because Mr. G hadn't trusted her predecessor.

"Yep," Riley said. "Earlier today."

"Then I'm probably just repeating her, but if you don't want to answer a question about your personal life, then you don't have to. It's not the media's business unless you want to make it their business. I don't care either way, though, of course I'd rather you keep the focus on the football, but you need to do what you feel is right."

"Understood," Landry said. He reached out his other hand. Coach shook it. Then shook Riley's. "We appreciate the support."

Coach's face broke into a smile, dimples emerging on both cheeks. He looked young now, and even though Landry knew he was single, he wondered if Coach had ever wanted something like what he had with Riley. If he'd ever been tempted to just reach out and grab it even if the timing was crap and the circumstances were terrible.

"Well," Riley said as they walked away, "I think that went okay. He was a lot more understanding than I expected."

"You mean, he already knew," Landry corrected. He was torn between embarrassment and relief. Had they really been *that* obvious?

Apparently, yes, if Coach's words were anything to go by.

"Oh," Riley said, grinning, "I didn't even worry about that. I always assumed everyone could see my crush from space. Just considered myself lucky that you didn't."

Landry leaned down and pressed a kiss to the side of his head. "Maybe if I had, this would've happened even sooner."

"Maybe." Riley seemed to be considering the possibility as they approached where Carter and the rest of the guys were loitering near the exit. "Or maybe it happened at exactly the right time."

"So, are you two in biiiiig trouble now?" Carter asked, waggling his eyebrows with a ridiculously exaggerated movement.

"Sorry to disappoint, but no," Landry said dryly. "He actually *knew*."

"You weren't exactly subtle, at literally any point," Deacon teased. "I had you two pegged from the moment you both showed up." He nudged Landry. "I think I even told you a few times that you should make a move."

Riley laughed. "I'm glad he listened."

"Imagine wanting to have sex with the same person for the rest of your life," Carter said mournfully. "Even someone as hot as you two are."

"Thanks, I think?" Riley said, chuckling.

Landry hadn't told anyone this was for forever—not even Riley—but clearly Carter was right on the money because nobody looked shocked. Not even his boyfriend.

Maybe he should be more surprised that it wasn't a surprise, but instead, Landry just felt...calm and at peace.

"Everyone ready for tomorrow?" Jem asked.

Carter grumbled. Riley looked vaguely nervous. But Landry nodded with confidence he wanted to feel but didn't quite believe in. "Sure, the Riptide won the Super Bowl last year, but that doesn't mean we can't come to their stadium and surprise them. Every team is capable of losing every game."

"That's right," Deacon said, nodding approvingly. "We've got this. Even without Rex."

"Even without Rex," Carter echoed, though he didn't have any of Deacon's certainty. "Desmond *almost* stopped me in practice yesterday."

Nobody wanted to say that on his best day, Carter was *almost* as good as Chase Riley.

"Hey, we're always looking for a challenge, right?" Jem asked and looked around at each of them, meeting their gazes one by one. "Playing last year's Super Bowl champs without our starting corner isn't going to be easy. But if we wanted easy, we wouldn't be here, doing this. We wouldn't be on this team."

Jem's words turned out to be painfully true.

If they'd wanted easy, playing the Riptide, who'd won the Lombardi trophy for the second time in four years, with their high-powered offense and *without* one of the Condors' best defensive players, wasn't it.

"Well," Riley said matter-of-factly as his butt hit the bench midway through the third quarter, "this sure could be going better."

He could've sounded despondent—the fact that they were down by three touchdowns would've made anyone feel despondent, honestly—but he didn't.

"Hey, we scored on our last drive," Charlie reminded him, settling down on Riley's other side. "That pass was a beaut. We're not going to just roll over and play dead. Not yet. Not ever."

Riley met Landry's eyes for a moment. He knew Riley had wanted to throw it to Landry and get him another touchdown, but Landry had been pressed into service as a blocker all day because not only did the Riptide have one of the best quarterback-receiver combos to ever play the game, they had a dominant defensive end in Spencer Evans, who was currently making Riley's life difficult on every single play. As a result, Evans was now making *Landry's* life difficult on every single fucking play because the offensive line had struggled with keeping him contained almost from the very beginning of the game.

Which meant Landry was way less available to catch passes.

This last touchdown had gone to Carter.

Landry had to give the guy credit. He might've toned down the celebration because they were currently losing 31 to 10, but he hadn't. He'd showboated like they'd just scored the go-ahead touchdown.

And why shouldn't he? Moving the ball down the field and into the end zone wasn't all that easy, considering who the Condors were playing.

"Of course not," Riley said. "We're going to come back, next drive, and do everything we can to try to even it up."

He didn't say that coming back from three touchdowns down was basically unheard of. Or that it would probably be *four* touchdowns because, smartly, the Riptide had targeted the receivers Desmond was covering—or *trying* to cover—pretty much every play.

"We need a new corner," Landry said.

It was a common refrain he'd heard about a dozen times today already.

"Right now, we're focusing on this game," Charlie reminded them and pulled out his tablet, flicking through the last series. "That's a problem for Monday morning."

On the field, Deacon made a tough stop, evading the center and reaching through the line, tackling Sam Crawford before he could throw another pass—and probably another touchdown—to Chase Riley.

"Come on," Charlie said, "I think I've got a way we can maybe get you another second or two, Riley."

"You got another tight end up your sleeve?" Riley joked.

He had a surprisingly positive expression on his face as Charlie went over the game plan for the next drive.

Of course, it wasn't like there were many people who believed the Condors were going to win this game. Even if Rex's leg had remained unbroken and his gambling unexposed, they would probably have lost.

But they'd come here and put on a good show anyway.

With another touchdown in the remaining quarter and a half of play, maybe two, even Riley's stats would be undeniably impressive.

It wasn't as good as a win, but it might mean he'd get more chances.

And Landry was all about giving Riley every chance he deserved.

"Yeah," Landry said as Charlie finished. "I think that might work, actually."

"Let's give it a shot," Riley said.

They jogged onto the field for their next drive.

Deacon, Jem, and Beck looked exhausted on the sideline. Exhausted and undeniably grim, yes, but they also didn't look like they'd given up.

If they hadn't given up yet, then Landry wasn't going to either.

Riley wasn't giving up. He was still holding his head high, ready to finish this game out, despite the score and all the odds stacked against them.

He called out the play.

Landry took his spot on the line. At least this down, he didn't have to try to grapple with Spencer Evans. Carter and Darius had the joy of getting to do that during this particular play design.

Landry knew he wasn't going to get a lot more chances to catch the ball, so he needed to make the most of this one.

The whistle blew and Cole snapped the ball to Riley, and Landry pushed off, driving hard down the field, legs working, lungs bellowing with the effort as he sprinted down the sideline.

He didn't normally run these deep routes, but Charlie had said he was hoping to take the defense by surprise.

They looked surprised, all right. The safety changed direction and started crossing over to try to intercept Landry's route, but he kept churning. Ten yards down, twenty, thirty, then he crossed mid-field, and then he turned, watching as Riley unloaded the pass.

The ball arced through the air, and Landry caught it mid-stride, instinctively tucking it away right before the safety attempted to tackle him. He pushed out his arm, catching the other player on the chest, and he shoved him down, continuing to keep running.

Only five yards til the end zone. Landry's lungs burned, and his legs were so exhausted the best way he could describe them was numb, but he crossed over the line, adrenaline surging through him.

One last touchdown for Riley's stat line and another one for them to share.

Riley caught up to him then, laughing behind his helmet, and jumped up in his arms again, the crowd going wild, even though they'd just scored against their home team.

Everything, Landry decided, wasn't terrible after all.

Even if they lost.

Football and Riley combined could never be terrible.

Half an hour later, the pain was finally over, and Landry met Chase at mid-field to shake hands and, since this was Chase, *hug*.

Carter was already there, hanging back, and the two players eyed each other before finally giving in and sharing one, too. It was quick because it was Carter, but Landry thought it was good he'd done it.

Landry knew Carter would rather die than ever admit it, but he both hated and loved being compared to the other receiver.

I'm nobody's best version except my own, he'd boast, but Landry knew he wouldn't bring it up if it didn't sting somewhere deep down.

"Great game," Landry said when he reached Sam Crawford. They shook hands, then Sam laughed and pulled him into a quick hug. He didn't know Sam well, but he'd always admired him.

Sam nodded. "That TD in the fourth was a thing of beauty. Give you guys a year or two together, and you're going to be blowin' up all my records with Chase."

"I don't know about that," Landry said, though he actually loved the sound of it.

"Rough luck about Rex," Sam said but didn't exactly sound torn up about it. "You guys goin' after another corner?"

Landry just shrugged. "I guess we'll see."

"Y'all really should," Heath Harris said. He was the quarterbacks' coach for the Riptide and also Sam's longtime partner.

"Trust me, I'm trying to convince our new owner," Deacon said as he walked up to their group.

"You like the guy?" Sam asked. "I know, well, I know the last guy was a piece of shit."

"Understatement," Deacon said.

"Yeah, we really like Davis around here," Heath said casually, but there was an undercurrent of dead seriousness in his voice. An intensity that hadn't lessened from when he played and had competed against Sam for the starting quarterback spot on the Riptide.

It was clear which side *he* had come down on when it came to the old Condors team.

"I do, too," Riley said.

He'd been chatting with Chase Riley, and he reached out to shake hands with Heath. "Good to meet you," he said.

People were always telling Riley that he shouldn't meet his heroes; that he'd be inevitably disappointed by how regular they were.

But it seemed like Heath Harris was a pretty cool guy in real life, not just in the rare sound bites and interviews he gave anymore.

When Riley had been growing up, it had been easy to idolize him because Heath had been incredibly good at everything he tried. He'd seemed so in-control and in charge of the game. Like it always ran at *his* speed and not anyone else's.

Then had come the year when Heath had battled a lingering injury, the Riptide had traded for Sam Crawford, they'd battled for the same starting spot, and then to everyone's shock, they'd ended up coming out *at* the Super Bowl by kissing over the Lombardi trophy. Nobody had quite believed it could be true, not about *Heath Harris*. But Riley had only admired the guy more after that. Even more when he'd retired to coach Sam, finding the best version of himself.

Riley wanted to find that version of himself, too, and more than anything, he hoped he was on the path to finding him.

Heath and Sam had even invited Riley to hang out at their place, but he'd already planned on meeting Paige.

It turned out some heroes were just as cool as you'd always assumed they were.

"I can't say this place makes the best tacos in the city," Riley said as he brought a tin bucket full of beers and ice to the table Landry was already sitting at, "but it's convenient to the place Paige works."

"It seems nice," Landry said, spreading out his legs under the booth table.

A week ago, Riley had asked Coach if he could stay behind for a night in LA and take a flight home Monday to see Paige while he was in the city, and Coach had agreed. Landry had decided to stay, too, when he'd found out that Riley was meeting Paige.

He'd wanted to meet her, too.

"Maybe she'll tell me some really embarrassing stories about you," Landry had teased.

No doubt she would tell him all about Riley's very embarrassing past crush, but then Landry already knew most of that, anyway.

"So, how did you two meet?" Landry asked.

"We went on a date. One single, terrible date," Riley said. "Some mutual friends thought we'd be the perfect couple."

Landry looked surprised. "Why?"

"Because we're the two prettiest people they knew." Paige appeared at the head of the table, and yep, Landry's jaw fell a little. Because Paige *was* gorgeous. Riley could admire the way she looked because he liked beautiful things, but he'd never been attracted to her. And he knew her feelings enough to know that had been mutual.

She sat down and continued, "Unfortunately for them, we didn't hit it off well enough to have two point five stunning children and a very aesthetic Instagram feed."

"I think," Landry said, reaching out to shake her hand, "I'm pretty grateful for that."

"Me, too," Paige said with amusement. She let go of Landry's hand. Riley could see her cataloging every inch of him, from the carelessly pulled-back hair, to the warm, kind eyes, to the big build barely concealed by the tabletop. "Though I guess we can't say now that Riley settled."

"Thanks," Riley said dryly.

"Hey, just speaking the truth," Paige said. "Honestly, it's great to meet you, Landry. Riley's only been telling me about you for...well, only for five years now."

"*Only*," Riley muttered.

"Yes." She fixed Riley with that steely-edged dark stare. "I'm sure if I'd known you when you were fourteen, you could've been waxing rhapsodic about this one for *far* longer."

Landry laughed. "I like you."

But Paige eyed him speculatively still.

That was Paige's way. She took her time making her mind up about people and wouldn't just approve of Landry because Riley loved him.

"And yet you *also* like Aidan," Paige said.

"That's true," Landry admitted, reaching over and grabbing a beer from the bucket. He popped the top off, and to Riley's surprise, set it in front of him instead of taking it for himself. Then he proceeded to do the same with a second and placed it on the coaster in front of Paige before going back for a third bottle, which this time, he kept, taking a long drink.

Paige's eyebrow shot up as she observed Landry's actions.

Yep, Riley thought smugly. *He's totally a gentleman. He's thoughtful and kind and always putting me first.*

Even if he was friends with Aidan before we ever hooked up.

"I suppose I should explain that Aidan used to be different, but then I have a feeling you already know that," Landry said. "Just as you know how much shit he's given Riley over the years."

Paige leaned back in the booth, still acting aloof and like she wasn't even remotely convinced by Landry's words, but Riley knew her better than that.

He could see the astonishment lingering in her dark eyes.

"I certainly do," Paige said. She turned to Riley. "Did you order for me?"

"I sure did," Riley said. "Your usual."

"Ah, good."

"So Riley said you work near here. What do you do? On a…" Landry paused. "A Sunday night?"

Paige tapped her flawless nails on the table. "I work on one of the big soaps in the costume department. Yes, yes, it's ridiculous. But it's a job in LA and good experience. We were filming a movie late tonight, so I had to be on set."

"Glad you escaped so I could see you," Riley said, reaching over and squeezing her hand. He'd missed her. Phone calls were good and all, but it wasn't the same.

"Same." He caught a glimmer of how truly happy she was to see him, in the upturned corner of her lips, in the joy she wasn't quite hiding in her eyes.

He knew her better than to accept the walls she put up for everyone else.

"You tell Aidan to fuck off yet?" she asked archly.

Riley chuckled. "Well, about that..."

He and Aidan hadn't talked since their phone conversation two weeks ago. But soon, their enforced silence would come to an end, with a few million people watching, when they met in Toronto a week from today.

Riley was both looking forward to it and dreading it in equal measures.

"No," Landry inserted with a tough look in Riley's direction. "No, he has not."

"And you want him to?" Paige really sounded surprised now.

"I told you, he was different when we met, and I've been...not exactly ignoring how he could be because I called him on his bullshit plenty of times, but I wasn't aware of how crappy he was to Riley until now."

"And now?" Paige asked.

"And now I told him I didn't like it, and I'm encouraging Riley to set some healthy boundaries," Landry said. "I want Aidan to know the kind of guy his brother is, and I want Aidan to show Riley his true self, the one he keeps under wraps. But I can't force that to happen. I can only encourage him to be the better man."

Paige shot Riley a look. It said, *Holy shit, keep this one. He's not only gorgeous, he's literally ride-or-die for you.*

But while Riley was glad of Paige's approval, he hadn't needed it to fall in love with Landry. He'd done that all on his own.

"In fact, we're planning on telling him about us next week," Riley said casually. Even though Paige would *know* that was not going to be a very casual conversation.

She knew he'd never introduced a significant other to Aidan before; he'd never even wanted to.

Of course, he didn't really need to introduce Landry. But it was *still* a very big deal that he was prepared and ready to tell Aidan the truth about what his relationship with Landry had evolved into.

"That's a big step," Paige said.

Landry's expression was open, and he didn't seem particularly bothered by the fact she kept testing him. "When something's right, it's right," he said firmly. He reached down beneath the table and squeezed Riley's knee. "And I know Riley's the right person for me."

"Speaking of that," Paige said crisply. "Congrats on coming out."

"Thanks." Landry paused. "You gonna ask me next if Riley's just an experiment or a detour?"

"I wouldn't do you the disservice," Paige said. Her expression had softened considerably. Maybe Landry didn't know what that meant, but Riley did. "After all, we're all queer here. I know how tired I get of being asked if dating a woman is some kind of temporary, passing interest."

"I guess I have that to look forward to," Landry said.

She raised an eyebrow. "Guess you do. Besides, if I thought Riley was an experiment for you, I'd have already flown out to the east coast and beat some sense into you."

"Not just kicked my ass, huh?"

Paige's gaze narrowed. She leaned forward. "No. I'd make sure you understood the situation. You two are right for each other, and if you didn't see it, you wouldn't need an ass-kicking to scare you off. You'd need me to remind you of what you had."

Riley was surprised. He shouldn't have been. But he was.

"Seriously?" he asked incredulously.

Paige just shrugged. "Listen, I've been hearing about Thor crossed with Superman over here for years. I already knew you were waiting for him. It was only a matter of time before he opened his eyes and saw what was right in front of him."

Landry's hand squeezed his knee harder. "Wish I'd seen it earlier."

"Nope. You saw it at the perfect time," Paige said, and there it was—her approval. Usually so hard-won and stingily dished out, she'd given it as easy as that.

Like she'd already approved even before this moment.

And Riley had a feeling that maybe she had.

Chapter 18

"I was worried you two wouldn't be back from your LA love fest in time to join us," Carter said as Riley and Landry walked into the Pirate's Booty hand-in-hand.

They were still being circumspect, but it wasn't like they hadn't done *way* more obvious things within this bar's walls.

But now that they'd told Landry's parents and his siblings, Coach Kelley, Mr. G, and a few of their friends who happened to be players about their relationship, there was only one person of note left to tell: Aidan.

Landry couldn't lie to himself or to Riley; he was worried about it.

It wouldn't be the first time Aidan had been pissed off at him, and he could handle it, but Landry hated when Aidan was shitty to Riley, and he could already imagine how this was going to go.

"When you texted and said you were doing this, we caught an earlier flight," Riley said, letting go of Landry's hand and pulling Carter into a quick hug. "You doing alright?"

"Me, oh, I'm fine," Carter said with a lazy grin. "Nobody expected us to win that game anyway."

"Doesn't mean we didn't try to win it," Deacon said with a snort from his spot at the bar. He was resting his elbows on the smooth wood surface, his expression wry. "I don't know about you, but I'm hurtin' today."

Yeah, Landry had definitely been feeling the number of times he'd grappled with Spencer Evans when he'd woken up this morning.

Waking up with Riley in his arms hadn't changed that, but it had sure made it worth it.

Plus the fact that when Landry asked, Riley said he hadn't heard a peep from Aidan.

For the first time after a game, Aidan hadn't sent an email detailing everything he'd done wrong.

He knows what's coming. Maybe not the shape it's gonna take, but the idea of it, Landry realized. *He knows he's fucked up.*

Except because he was Aidan freaking Flynn, that didn't mean he was going to do a damn thing about it.

"Yeah," Riley said ruefully. He stepped up to the bar.

"Sparkling water with lime," Kieran said without even asking Riley what he wanted.

Riley nodded.

Kieran glanced over at Landry. "And a beer for the big guy."

Deacon slid the pitcher over the bar towards Landry. "Feel free to share my misery," he joked.

"This is supposed to be a party to celebrate losing, not a *pity party*," Carter argued.

"Yeah," Beck said, "that doesn't feel any weirder the more you say it."

"The plane ride home sucked. Sitting there today thinking about it sucked. I didn't want to do it anymore," Carter claimed. "And I don't think I'm alone."

"You're not, but it's still weird," Deacon said. He let out a heavy sigh. "We need a fucking corner. We have Rex, or someone better than him, we're in that game. Against the fucking Super Bowl champs."

Landry nodded. They'd only lost by two touchdowns. Take away one of those easy gimmie TDs to Chase Riley, and they'd have been right in the thick of it.

"Well, then," Jem said, as he approached the group, "tell your Grant to get you a fucking corner then."

"He's not *my* Grant, Jesus," Deacon retorted. "And you think I haven't told him? He knows. He was there yesterday, wasn't he?"

"Anyone check on how Desmond's doing?" Riley asked as Kieran poured his drink and handed it over. "I texted him yesterday, but he didn't reply."

"Probably licking his wounds somewhere," Jem said quietly. "He'll be fine. He knew we were asking too much of him. Frankly, asking *anyone* to cover Chase Riley is a lot. But I'll check in on him, too." He patted Riley's shoulder. "You're a good guy for trying."

Riley nodded, and the group fell quiet.

"I know someone who could do it."

The whole group looked at Beck.

"What?" He threw his hands up. "I do."

"I thought you didn't want to talk about Rose," Jem said.

"Trust me, I don't. But it's the truth."

Landry always paid special attention to the Piranhas since Logan had ended up there two years ago, and he knew Micah had struggled there at first, but towards the end of his rookie year and the first few games of this season, he'd found himself again.

Which was why Landry had thought it was weird he'd asked for a trade.

When he'd texted Logan about it, Logan had said Micah wasn't necessarily unhappy but that he wanted a fresh start. A clean slate.

Logan wasn't usually cagey about things, but he had been about this. There was something he wasn't telling Landry.

"Well, I guess we'll see," Deacon said. "He's the best corner on the market. If he's actually on the market, anyway. I know he asked the Piranhas for a trade, but if I was them, I wouldn't want to lose him."

"Seriously, we know what it's like to be limping along without a good corner," Jem agreed.

Carter stuck his hands on his hips. "You are being *very* depressing, and that's not allowed here. Who's gonna go dance with me?"

Riley tucked himself into Landry's side. Gazed up at him. "You wanna dance?" he asked.

"With Carter?" Landry asked, raising an eyebrow.

Carter grinned. "I would totally dance with you, Landry. Name the time and place, and we'll do it."

"I think..." Deacon stood slowly, stretching out every muscle as he went. "I think we should *all* dance."

Riley raised an eyebrow. "You do realize it's Disco Night, right?"

Landry realized that the only other time they'd come to the Pirate's Booty for Disco Night, most of their group had stayed away from the dance floor.

But what was a celebration without a little ass-shaking?

Deacon grinned. "You afraid of gettin' down tonight, Flynn?"

"Never," Riley said. "Come on, let's go."

That was how Landry found himself in a group of ten or so football players, grooving to the mellow rhythms of KC and the Sunshine Band.

Carter grabbed Deacon's hands and tugged him into some kind of move that might've been a two-step as they crossed the dance floor.

"Deacon's got moves," Riley said to him as Landry caught him by the waist, pulling him in closer. "Who knew that he could get down?"

Landry thought maybe he was terribly biased, but nobody danced like Riley. The way his hips shifted, smooth and sinuous, was a fucking sin, and Landry wanted to indulge all night long.

"On the other hand," Riley said, smirking, "Beck could use some pointers."

Beck was trying to find his own groove next to Charlie and Jem, and yeah, Landry had a feeling he wasn't used to hanging out at Disco Night. His movements were awkward and off-kilter.

But then, Landry didn't think he was all that much worse than him.

"I think," Landry said, tilting his head down, breath grazing Riley's ear, making him shiver, "your crush is still showing."

Riley grinned up at him. "Maybe a little."

Carter switched partners with them then, pulling Riley into the center of their group and the two of them together? It was obvious they could really dance, and Landry discovered the jealousy he'd once felt towards Carter had evaporated completely.

It was easy to see why when he knew, deep down, in a place he never doubted, that Riley cared about him.

Riley turned in his direction, and the joy on his face was everything.

Landry wanted him to look like this—laughing, carefree, and more than anything else, *happy*—for the rest of his life, and he'd do anything, conquer any obstacle, including Riley's brother and his own best friend, to make sure that happened.

His apprehension about telling Aidan faded away.

It didn't matter what Aidan said or even what he did.

He and Riley were together, no matter what.

The song segued into a slower number, with the singer begging the object of his affection not to go, and Landry caught Riley's hand, pulling him in close.

Riley tilted his chin up towards Landry, and he couldn't help it—he kissed him.

"Awww, really?" Carter cried out.

"It's alright, Maxwell, I'll dance with you," Deacon teased him, and the moment before all of Landry's attention got stolen by his guy, he spied Deacon and Carter moving into an exaggerated slow dance.

"You're gorgeous like this," Landry said, leaning down and brushing another kiss across Riley's mouth.

Riley chuckled. "Sweaty and in the clothes I wore to fly home?"

"Yes," Landry said.

He wasn't much of a dancer—much more like Beck than Riley—but he could do a pretty good slow dance because his mom had made sure before they went to any middle school dances the Banks brothers knew how to do right by whatever partner they chose.

They danced for a minute, just swaying back and forth, and Riley's eyes flickered closed as he lost himself in the music and in Landry's touch.

He opened his mouth, and the words were right there. He wanted to tell Riley exactly how he felt. Yes, they were at Disco Night and surrounded by their friends and teammates. Yes, this was new. Yes, they had no idea how much shit Aidan was going to give them. But his feelings weren't going to waver. He already knew it because he'd never felt like this before.

But before he could speak up, finally, his phone dinged. Riley's phone did the same. Then Deacon's actually rang.

Landry glanced over at Deacon and watched him look at the screen then wave at the rest of them as he disappeared off the dance floor.

"I wonder what that is," Riley said.

Landry wanted to say fuck it to the whole world, but his curiosity was undeniably piqued.

Riley pulled his phone out of his pocket, and it was definitely something because Riley's eyes widened in astonishment.

"The Condors," Riley said, gazing up at Landry, "just traded for Micah Rose."

Landry couldn't help it. He looked straight at Beck, who looked like he'd just been hit by a truck.

Beck turned on his heels and walked off.

"I should…" Riley trailed off.

"Let me," Landry said. "I'll talk to him."

It wasn't hard to find Beck. He'd ducked off the dance floor and was leaning against one of the brick walls lining the passageway to the main bar.

He looked up as Landry approached, his face totally—and Landry suspected, *carefully*—blank.

"Hey," Landry said. "You okay?"

"I'm assuming you saw the news," Beck said bitterly.

"Yeah, it was kinda hard not to," Landry admitted.

"I'm sure that was Mr. G calling Deacon, telling him he got the deal done."

"Clearly, something happened between you two, but maybe this is a chance to mend fences? Mend your friendship?" Landry suggested cautiously.

Beck scrubbed a hand over his face. He had a few days of dark brown scruff, heading into nearly-a-beard territory. "It's complicated."

"Seems like it," Landry said. He leaned against the wall next to Beck. "If you want to talk about it, I'd be happy to listen."

"Not much to say."

Landry knew he was lying. But he wasn't going to force the guy to talk about it.

"He's a great player. You two are great together. He'll be an amazing addition to the team."

"*Were* great together," Beck said.

"Ah." Landry was beginning to wish he'd sent Riley instead. Riley could get blood from a stone with just one of his charming grins.

Or maybe he should've sent Jem. Landry knew they were pretty close.

Well, it didn't matter. He was here now.

"We'll still be fine on the field," Beck said quietly after a very long silence. "So you don't need to worry about that."

"You didn't…" Landry trailed off, unsure of what to say and *how* to say it. Beck had come out after college, but he'd never heard even a whisper of rumor about Micah Rose being queer.

"No," Beck said with absolute finality. "No, it wasn't like that."

"Alright." Landry wasn't going to tell him that in the weeks after Pittsburgh, when Riley had rocked his world for the first time, he'd have given the exact same answer in the exact same way.

"I just…" Beck made a noise. "Want to be alone for a minute."

"Sure, of course. We just wanted to make sure you were okay."

"I'll be fine," Beck said.

"Alright. Well, we're here for you, no matter what," Landry said, patting him on the shoulder.

"Thanks," Beck said, and for a second, there was a flash of something on his face—was it happiness or maybe even relief?—but then it was gone.

When they'd gotten home from the Pirate's Booty, Landry had said he was taking a shower, and for a moment, Riley had considered joining him, but then his phone had gone off, with Charlie asking a question about tomorrow's schedule, and he'd told Landry he'd join him in the bedroom in a minute.

Landry had nodded distractedly and headed off to his room.

Everyone at the Pirate's Booty had been both excited at the possibility of a new player joining the team and understandably concerned about Beck, who hadn't rejoined the party before they'd eventually broken up to go their separate ways home.

Riley answered Charlie's text, then after brushing his teeth and stripping down to his briefs, headed down the hallway to the bedroom he was essentially sharing now with Landry.

He'd never even hooked up with a roommate before—never mind ended up in a relationship with one—and he was continually surprised at how easily they'd fallen into the pattern of two people living together. And not just how easy it was but how effortless and right it felt.

It made perfect natural sense for Riley to walk down the hallway to *their* bedroom.

Made perfect sense for him to set his phone on the charger on what had become *his* side and settle into bed as he waited for Landry to finish up in the bathroom.

Then Landry walked in, naked and totally at ease with it, striding over to the bed, and Riley swallowed hard.

It was more than comfortable.

It was also hot as hell.

"Hey," Landry said, sitting down on the edge of the bed next to Riley. His hand curled around Riley's neck, warm and a little damp just like his hair.

Just like his whole fucking body. Gloriously right there.

Riley struggled to get his suddenly uncooperative brain on the right page. The *easy and relaxed romance* page. It just kept wanting to land on the *fucking til they couldn't even think, couldn't even breathe* page.

Leaning over, Landry gave Riley a quick peck on the lips.

Not what you really wanted, Riley's mind screamed. Right along with his cock. For once, they seemed to be in perfect accord about this particular craving.

"You look surprised," Landry said, pulling back. "Everything okay?"

"It's…" Riley stuttered. He wasn't used to having so much trouble vocalizing what he wanted. Of course, he'd never wanted it this much before.

Needed it.

Landry's fingers tightened on his neck. "What is it?"

"You said…before…that you wanted me to…uh fuck you. Is that still something you'd want?"

It was still unbelievable to watch as Landry's eyes dilated. Going from a warm, loving brown to a dark, hot pinpoint. "Yes," he said. "*Yes.*"

"We don't have to do that tonight or…"

But Riley didn't get the last of the words out before Landry was kissing him, hard and fierce, pouring his own kind of need into Riley's mouth.

It didn't take long for their kisses to grow even wilder or for Landry to end up on top of Riley, grinding his bare cock against Riley's still-clothed one.

"Fuck," Riley said breathlessly as he broke off, fingers digging hard into Landry's bicep.

"Yeah, I think that's the idea," Landry said, chuckling.

He rocked back onto his heels and reached out to tug Riley's briefs down, but Riley squeezed his eyes shut for a brief moment, searching for control. This was Landry's first time bottoming, and he wanted him to enjoy it. Wanted him to *love* it.

That was much less likely if he was ready to go off like a rocket.

His hand caught Landry's before he could get him totally naked.

"Not yet," he said.

Landry raised an eyebrow.

Riley patted the bed next to him. "Lie down," he said.

Well, *ordered* was more like it, but he was the resident expert here, wasn't he?

Landry must've had the exact same thought because he went easily, shooting Riley a smirk as he lay down. "What am I supposed to do?" he asked. "Just lay and look pretty?"

"Just lie there and *enjoy* it," Riley corrected. He found the lube in the drawer and, for a second as he moved back towards Landry's naked body, took time to really enjoy the view.

It was a serious, control-ruining view.

Every inch of Landry was big and thick and muscled, his legs and arms and even his chest dusted with a fine layer of golden brown hair, same color as the tumbled waves on his head. His eyes were drooping and languorous as he moved his hand down to where his cock sat, just as big and thick as the rest of him.

"No," Riley said, batting his hand away again. "That's *mine*."

He wasted no time wetting his fingers and then crouching low, flicking his tongue out, licking up the underside of Landry's cock as he explored lower with his fingers.

Landry groaned as Riley pressed the pad of his thumb against his hole, swirled it slightly, getting him used to the idea of Riley touching him there. "Shit," he said, voice rough. "Shit, that's good."

"Yeah?" Riley ducked his head, sliding more of Landry's cock into his mouth as his thumb finally penetrated him.

He kept up a regular sort of rhythm, alternating short, teasing sucks of his cock with his thumb pushing and then receding, again and again until Landry was begging him and his cock was leaking against his tongue.

"God, please, give me more," Landry pleaded. His voice was a slur like he was drunk on the pleasure of it.

Riley pressed the hard heel of his hand against his own dick so he wouldn't do something crazy like lose his mind and just rut against Landry's big, muscled thigh. He wanted inside him, but the control needed was a big ask, especially when he felt like this.

Landry would do it for you, he'd do anything for you, so you can do anything for him.

It was just the reminder Riley needed.

He returned to his task, sliding a finger in along his thumb, carefully stretching Landry out one agonizing movement at a time.

"Shit," Landry moaned. "So good, so fucking good. God, give it to me now. I want you inside."

"I'm gonna make it good for you." Riley's own voice wasn't exactly even as he lined up a third finger. Landry's cock twitched as he slid it home and began pumping in and out, slow at first and then with more force, more speed, until Landry was nearly fucking back on his fingers.

Riley had thought he was gorgeous before, but like this, sweat beaded on his forehead and on his collarbones, hard, leaking cock making a mess of his abs, eyes squeezed shut, head thrown back with how pleasurable it was, he was a vision.

And all yours.

His hands were shaking with the force of the thought as he tore open the condom packet and slid it on.

Landry had been his before this, of course, but the moment he slid into his hot, wet tightness, he felt it more strongly than he ever had before.

Landry's hands scrabbled against Riley's arms, trying to pull him in harder, tighter.

Riley half-groaned, half-laughed, as he tried to control his movements, resisting with every bit of self-control he had not to just thrust wildly.

To take his own pleasure.

It was undeniable now, swirling inside him, building up as he carefully slid in one inch at a time.

When he was finally fully seated, Riley panted. It felt so good, it was almost impossible not to just *move.*

"Jesus," Landry said roughly. "Come on, I know you want to."

"I want it to be good for you," Riley said stubbornly, though with the way Landry's hot, tight body was sucking him in, he wasn't sure he could hold off much longer.

And if Landry's still rock-hard cock was anything to go by, he wasn't exactly hating this.

Which...didn't that light a whole other fire inside Riley?

"It's good, it's *so* good." Landry was slurring again and then thrashing as Riley reached down and wrapped his fist around Landry's dick.

"Yeah?" Riley asked, giving a careful experimental thrust. Precome bubbled out of Landry's slit, and *yeah,* it was so good.

So fucking good.

"Come on." Landry was full-on trembling now. "I can't...I won't..."

Riley wasn't going to last much longer, either. He was overwhelmed by the tight squeeze of Landry's body, every tremor, every bit of pleasure magnified around Riley's cock.

But before he came his brains out, he was going to make it good for Landry.

Well, even *better* for Landry. He started thrusting, working his hips the way he knew would send Landry into the stratosphere.

Less than a minute later, Landry was babbling, coming in his fist, and that was all it took for Riley to follow him.

It felt like an endless orgasm, both sharp and mellow, and also all-encompassing.

He pulsed and pulsed, knees straight up shaking as he came down from the overwhelming pleasure.

He collapsed next to Landry, and the first thing Landry did was turn towards him. His eyes were big and wide, and that was all Riley saw before Landry was kissing him over and over again, mumbling a long litany of somethings Riley couldn't quite catch.

But it didn't matter, Riley thought hazily. Nothing else mattered now. Just the two of them in this bed.

Sex had always been good for him. Varied and pleasurable and fun.

It had never felt like that before, like he'd been scooped out, but not empty, because someone else filled in the gaps before he could think to miss anything.

I love you, Riley thought, and for now, for tonight, that was enough.

CHAPTER 19

RILEY WAS HALFWAY THROUGH his workout, trying and mostly failing not to check out Landry's biceps as they flexed through his set of reps when Coach Kelley ducked his head into the weight room and said, "Hey, you got a minute, Riley?"

It had been two days since the announcement the Condors had traded for Micah Rose, but Riley had yet to meet him.

He had a feeling that was about to change.

"Yeah, sure, let me finish this up," Riley said. "Give me twenty?"

"Good. Then you can meet us in the big conference room."

Riley nodded and went back to his reps.

When he was just about finished, Landry came over. "You think he's here?"

"Yeah, probably." He lowered his voice. "Beck's over there trying to bench press the entire weight room, so it seems likely."

Beck was—straining and red-faced, as Jem spotted him with something that looked a lot like concern.

"Well, I guess you're gonna get to meet him."

"I kinda thought I wouldn't 'til practice, that maybe Deacon would get called in, but I guess they want me."

"You're the leader of this team," Landry reminded him. "Coach knows that."

Riley knew it, too, but it was a good reminder.

He wiped his face, took a very quick, cold shower, and then headed up to the conference room on the second floor of the building.

When he entered, Mr. G, Coach Kelley, and Coach Rufus—the defensive coordinator—were gathered at one end of the long, burnished wood table, along with a guy with light brown skin, close-cropped dark hair, and a hesitant smile as Riley walked over to where they were sitting.

"Hey," Riley said, extending a hand, "you must be Micah. I'm Riley Flynn."

Micah took his hand and shook it. He had a nice, firm grip, one hundred eighty degrees from the apprehension lingering in his gaze.

"Nice to meet you. You're the quarterback here now?" Micah asked.

"Yeah," Riley said as he took a seat next to him. "Brought in a couple weeks back when Nelson Perez tore up his knee."

"Riley is proving to be an excellent pickup," Mr. G said, speaking up for the first time since Riley had entered the room. "A great player and a leader, on and off the field."

Something flashed behind Micah's gaze. More than apprehension now. But...terror?

Riley did a double take.

Then Micah said, haltingly, "I didn't get off on the right foot in Miami. I made mistakes there that I'll regret forever. I don't know what you've heard..."

"Nothing," Coach Kelley said kindly but firmly. "The guys in Miami had nothing but great things to say about you. Which is why I was so surprised to hear you'd requested a trade."

"Yeah," Micah said, chuckling self-consciously. "I appreciate they spoke up for me, but I didn't always do the right thing. *Say* the right thing. I fucked up plenty...didn't listen at first. Made some enemies. But—" He took a deep breath. "But I'm not gonna do that here. This is the fresh start I wanted, the one I asked for, and I'm not gonna screw this up."

"Nobody thinks you will," Coach Kelley said reassuringly.

"Yeah, I'm not so sure about that," Micah said bluntly. "What I'm saying is I did all this wrong the last time. That won't happen again. No matter what you've heard."

"Good." Mr. G was nodding.

Riley wasn't sure what to say. He'd known there had to be *something* because why on earth would he and Beck have fallen out so completely? Course, it could've been Beck at fault, but Riley knew whenever a friendship fell apart like that, it was usually way more complicated than one person fucking it up.

"And," Micah added, looking more terrified and yet more resolute than he had before. He met Riley's eyes, lifting his chin like he was challenging *Riley*, or maybe, Riley realized, he was challenging himself. "And I don't want this fresh start to begin under any kind of misapprehension." He paused. "I'm gay."

It was amazing what just saying those two words did to Micah Rose.

He let out a gust of breath, and his shoulders relaxed. It was like Riley was seeing the *real* Micah Rose for the very first time.

Riley smiled at him. He knew how that felt, the first time you told someone—and Riley would guess, too, that this might be one of the first times Micah had said it at all—and the intense relief you felt after when nobody called you a name or denounced you or even worse, looked at you like you were an alien in a man's body.

"That isn't a problem at all," Mr. G said confidently. "Riley here came out after college, before the draft, and we have several other queer players on the squad. And as for me...well, I intend to run this team as open-minded as I can. Coach Kelley agrees. That's one of the reasons I hired him."

Landry had speculated the other day that Mr. G might be queer himself, even though he was notoriously private, but Riley hadn't gotten that particular vibe from him, not until now.

"You definitely aren't alone, and while we appreciate you telling us," Coach Kelley said, nodding, "I don't care one bit who you see off the field. Just how you play on the field."

Riley watched as Micah's face lost even more tension. Like he'd been holding it back this whole time.

"I'm sure you'll want to catch up with your old teammate, too," Mr. G said, smiling. Like he had no idea that Beck didn't want to see *him*. And, Riley realized, he probably didn't. Maybe nobody knew that they weren't friends anymore. He certainly hadn't.

Micah, who'd just been relaxing by significant degrees, tensed up.

"Beck?" he asked cautiously like he didn't know if he was even allowed to say his name.

"Yeah," Riley said. This was not good. Beck had said his personal feelings wouldn't intrude on the field, but one of the reasons he and Micah had been so dynamite together, so unbelievably good that the

Condors were so eager to reunite them, was that they were always on the same page.

What would they be like if they weren't?

Riley wasn't sure, and that was bad news, especially considering what the Condors probably had been forced to trade for Micah. Mr. G was gambling that this would work and work well.

What if it didn't?

What if everyone was wrong about Beck and Micah?

"We've got your locker all set up downstairs and equipment assigned to you," Coach Kelley said. "But whatever you need, let me or Coach Rufus know." The defensive coordinator nodded. He looked eager, probably to put the defensive disaster of the last game to rest and to see what his two famous backfield players were going to play like now that they were back together again.

"Or me," Riley offered with a smile. He didn't want to interfere with whatever had passed between Micah and Beck, but Landry was right; he was the leader of this team.

It was his responsibility. It was Deacon's responsibility, too, as captain of the defense.

But Riley had every intention of doing his part to help them mend fences. And if that failed, to be not only a friend, but a friendly ear. Micah might need it. Beck might, too.

"Yes, absolutely," Coach Kelley said. "Or Deacon Harris, who's the defensive captain. He's been around here a long time, and he knows the ropes well. We haven't always taken care of rookies here, but we're turning over a lot of new leaves this year."

"You and me both," Micah said wryly. He didn't have to say he meant it—it was written on every part of his face that he wanted to make the most of this. That he wanted to put whatever had happened in Miami behind him. Start fresh.

"Riley, why don't you take Micah down to the cafeteria, get him some lunch before practice?" Mr. G asked.

"Sure," Riley said, standing. He'd been about to offer anyway.

Micah trailed after him out of the conference room but didn't speak until they were in the hallway, waiting for the elevator to go down to the cafeteria.

"Lots of people think the Piranhas are gonna win a Super Bowl," Riley offered as the elevator dinged open.

"Yeah," Micah said. But he didn't sound regretful or sad at all that he might miss the chance at a ring. This was not a guy who'd been traded away against his wishes. This was someone who meant exactly what he said: he'd been looking to start over. "The coaching staff's great, the players are good, they work hard."

"I've always heard Asa Dawson is...different," Riley said cautiously as he pressed the button for the main level.

"He's great. He's..." Micah wet his lips. "Coach Dawson and Coach Scott, they helped me a lot. Made me a better player, despite my attempts to tell them to fuck off. Made me a better man, even."

"Yeah?" Riley grinned. "That's great. But you still wanted to leave."

Micah sighed. Shoved his hands into his jeans pockets. "You ever mess up so bad you can't forget it, can't leave it behind, no matter how many times you apologize, no matter how many times you try to make it right?"

"No," Riley said wryly. "Actually, I have the opposite problem. I'd never fuck up because I'd be too worried. Too cautious. Not even when I need to step out of line. Everyone thinks I should tell my brother to fuck off. They think I should've told him that years ago, but I just...can't."

"Your brother's Aidan Flynn?"

Riley nodded.

Micah smiled. "I've heard some shit about him. Maybe you should."

"Maybe I should," Riley said with a chuckle. "So how about this, we make a pact with each other. You messed up, but you made it right. Then you came here and wanted more than anything to start this new experience with honesty and transparency, and so far, you've done it. So let yourself off the hook, okay? And I'll try to work up the nerve to tell my brother to fuck off. Or at least mind his own business."

"Work up the nerve or *actually* do it?" Micah asked, raising an eyebrow.

Riley couldn't help it. He laughed. "You're tough."

But Micah just shrugged as the elevator dinged open again. "Here's the thing," he said as they walked down the hallway towards the cafeteria. "You can have all the best intentions in the world, but it doesn't count for shit if you don't act on them."

"True."

Micah turned to him. "Don't have regrets. I'm here to tell you they really fucking suck."

Riley nearly asked if those regrets included Beck, but before he could, Deacon appeared in front of them.

"Hey, man, it's great to meet up again and great to have you here. The famous Micah Rose." They shook hands.

Micah shrugged. "Not *that* famous."

"Hey, famous enough we'd have loved to have you last week to cover Chase Riley," Deacon said dryly. "Beck said you can."

"Beck did, huh?"

"He sure did. Was really boasting about your skills," Riley said, which wasn't exactly true—he hadn't exactly *boasted* about it, but Beck was quiet enough, rarely offering his opinion on anything, so Riley just had to stretch reality a little bit.

"Yeah?" Micah looked pleased.

Really pleased.

See, Riley could do this leadership thing. *Fuck off, Aidan,* he thought to himself.

Of course it didn't actually count unless he said it to his brother, but Riley figured he was already practicing for this Sunday, when it was inevitable he'd say something irredeemably shitty either about Riley's play or his relationship with Landry.

"Yep, he sure did," Deacon confirmed. Riley figured they were both on the same page. Deacon had been around a long time. He knew how to read the players on his defense, and Beck hadn't been exactly subtle about his chilly feelings.

"Cool."

"We've got a table over here," Deacon said. "If you want to go through the food line with Riley."

"Sure thing," Micah said.

He was quiet as they both picked up several different plates of food, but when they were heading towards the table Deacon had pointed out, currently occupied by Landry, Jem, and Carter, Micah asked out of the blue, "He really said that about me? And not anything else? Not anything…"

Riley knew what he was fishing for, but what could he say? *He's not happy you're here. But that doesn't mean you can't fix it.*

Doesn't mean we can't fix it together.

"Yeah, he did. I think that's the only time you came up, actually…" Riley trailed off. That wasn't one hundred percent accurate again, but he felt weird stretching the truth even more than he already had.

"Ah." Micah didn't have to say anything else; there was a wealth of meaning in that single word.

He set his food down on the table and greeted everyone, shaking hands all around.

Riley poked at his chicken salad, popping a grape tomato in his mouth as Carter waxed rhapsodic about how he was going to have a *real* challenge now at practice. Landry was nodding along with him, and Riley was free to just watch as Micah got folded enthusiastically into their friend group. He had a feeling that had been Deacon's intention all along, and he was happy to do his part to help out.

But Riley also knew the exact moment Beck appeared in the cafeteria.

Next to him, Micah stiffened, his face freezing into a completely neutral expression.

Deer in the headlights had nothing on the way Micah was currently staring at Beck as he also hesitated in the doorway.

Then Beck walked towards them like it was inevitable and there was no point in putting it off.

He was right about that. If they couldn't even say hello to each other over lunch, how were they going to play together?

"Rose," Beck said, his voice even as a thousand different emotions flashed in his eyes.

This morning, when he and Landry had been talking about Beck's reaction to the trade news, he'd mentioned Beck had said they were *complicated*. From both of their reactions to meeting again, that seemed to be the most accurate description.

"West," Micah said, tipping his head. "Good to see you again. But even better to play with you again."

Something Riley couldn't identify flashed across Beck's face, and then it was gone, tucked away like it'd never existed at all. "Yeah," he said. "That was always the dream, wasn't it?"

But there was an edge even to those innocent words. Like it *had* been the dream, but then something had corrupted it.

Riley didn't know what it was. It probably wasn't any of his business. But if it impacted the team, then it *had* to be his business.

"Yeah," Micah echoed. "Yeah, it was."

Then Beck turned away. "Gonna grab some lunch, then head to a meeting," he said shortly.

Micah opened his mouth and then snapped it closed again.

Carter, gazing between the two guys—one sitting at their table and the other practically running away—said with a forced cheer that made it obvious he hadn't been oblivious to the undercurrents, "Must be nice to be reunited."

"Sure," Micah said and returned to his lunch like it was the most interesting plate of food he'd ever experienced.

Riley and Landry exchanged looks across the table, but neither of them even tried to protest when Carter started in on a lengthy description of the *date* he'd been on over the weekend.

Later, when Carter finally left and Deacon and Jem took Micah on a quick tour of the facilities and locker room, Landry looked over at Riley as he finished up his salad. "Well, that was awkward," he said.

"About as awkward as I expected," Riley agreed.

"I guess Beck wasn't exaggerating when he said things were complicated."

"Guess not." Riley considered telling Landry what Micah had said in the conference room about being gay. It had been on his mind all during lunch, not because he had any judgment for the guy, but because now he knew that both Micah and Beck were into guys, it was not an insane possibility that whatever had happened between them was *very* personal.

Maybe this wasn't a broken friendship but a *breakup*.

"You sure Micah isn't into guys?" Landry asked as they headed towards the locker room to get ready for practice. "I know a couple of nights ago Beck said it was *not* like that, but the way they looked at each other today..."

Riley had seen it, too. Had *felt* it. The longing in the air.

"Well, uh, about that..." He still felt awkward sharing. Micah hadn't told him explicitly that he could. But he'd also said he was starting his time with the Condors open and free. "He might be."

"He might be?" Landry's eyebrows shot up.

"Okay, he is," Riley said with a grumble. "He said so when I met him this morning."

"They're exes then," Landry said. He sounded relieved now that he'd finally figured it out.

But Riley wasn't so sure. They didn't seem like exes. Instead, they felt like…Riley didn't know exactly. But they were absolutely something.

Something he was really fucking praying wouldn't intrude onto the field.

Riley shrugged. "Maybe," he hedged. "Who knows what actually happened between them. I'm more concerned about what happens between them when they get on the field today."

"You want *The Wall* back."

"That's why Mr. G brought him here," Riley said. "And we need it. Maybe not every opponent we have this season is going to have a receiver like Chase Riley, but we gotta be better. I can't…*we* can't let them score like that, at will, no matter how good you are, or how good Carter is, or how many yards Darius gets for us on the ground."

"And no matter how good *you* are," Landry reminded him, reaching out and squeezing his hand.

"Yeah, yeah, that, too," Riley acknowledged. "We need a good defense if we're gonna be the team I think we can be, and Micah and Beck? They're an integral part of that. That's why Mr. G spent the draft picks to get him. He wouldn't have come cheap."

"No," Landry agreed. "It's gonna be fine, though. I feel like it *has* to be. They're both pros. They'll make it work."

Halfway through practice, Riley was more than a little relieved that Landry had been at least *half* right.

Whatever you wanted to say about what had or hadn't happened between them, nobody could deny Micah and Beck were both trying.

Coach Kelley announced again that for today's practice, the starting offense would be running plays against the starting defense.

"Yes!" Carter had announced immediately, clearly very pleased that he'd get the chance to test his skills against the reunited Wall.

So far, they'd been *mostly* cooperative, and yes, they had given Carter—and Landry, too—a run for their money.

Riley could see, even as it exasperated him, even as the offense stalled again and again in the face of their tight coverage downfield, flashes of why they'd been called *The Wall* back in college.

But only flashes.

"Goddamnit." Carter spiked his gloves on the ground after yet another play when Micah had covered him tight and close, his timing impeccable as he turned at precisely the right time to leap up and bat the ball away before Carter could even *dream* about catching it.

"You're good at that," Riley said to Micah as they took a break, forcing his tone to stay even and friendly.

"Yeah," Beck said. "Your timing was good before, but it wasn't always *that* good."

Micah shot the safety a look. It was like Riley wasn't even there, which...he got that. Wished he didn't, but he did.

"Howard gave me a bunch of pointers," Micah said, referring to Sebastian Howard, who before he'd grown older and slower, had been one of the top corners in the NFL. Maybe one of the top corners to ever play the game. Now he was a safety for the Piranhas, and it made perfect sense that he'd taught Micah everything he knew.

"Surprised you were willing to listen," Beck said.

Micah shot him a look but didn't say anything back.

Like he didn't believe, Riley realized, he had a right to defend himself against the accusation.

Maybe he didn't feel like he did.

But before the next play, Riley stepped across the line and said, in a low voice, "Remember our deal?"

Micah stared at him incredulously.

"You learn how to forgive yourself," Riley said pointedly, "and I'm going to tell my brother to fuck off."

"Can I be there when you do it?" Micah joked weakly. "That would be something to see."

"Maybe," Riley said with a shrug. "We *are* gonna be in Toronto next week. Gonna be facing him."

"Gonna b*e beating* him," Landry chimed in. "He's not even gonna know what hit him."

"I hope so," Riley said with a grin, returning to where the offense was gathered together. "Come on, let's get this first down."

The play called for Landry to run his crossing route, which was quickly becoming something he was not only *really* good at but kind of a trademark of his time with the Condors.

It took absolutely perfect timing, which Micah could have easily broken up, but instead, this time, Micah ended up biting on Landry's fake, and as Riley dropped back to pass the ball, he let it sail long, Landry's big strides eating up the grass on the practice field.

Easy touchdown.

"What the fuck was that?" Beck demanded to know.

Micah threw his hands up, but he didn't say anything.

"You can't let him behind you," Beck continued. Riley had never heard him be so insistent. So impassioned.

Usually, he kept his head down at practice other than a few necessary exchanges.

But he wasn't doing that now.

He was practically getting into Micah's face.

"Hey, it's cool. Landry's tough to cover in the best of circumstances," Deacon said, wandering over. "You'll get there. It's what practice is for." He patted Micah on the back and shot Beck a pointed look.

"*I'm* not the one who's worried about it," Micah said quietly but with quiet, determined confidence.

He wasn't smug or cocky. He just acted like he could get the job done.

Landry had said in college that he'd run his mouth, boasting that he could cover anyone, at any time, even calling out certain receivers they were going to be playing against on social media. But it seemed that whatever had happened last year with the Piranhas, whatever he'd gained from the coaches and players there, he'd learned to keep his mouth shut.

Like he'd finally realized that what mattered more than anything else was what you did on the field and in a game, not what you said before it.

Still, as practice drew to a close, Riley couldn't deny he was worried. He stopped by Deacon as he stood by the sideline on his way back into the locker room.

"Should we do anything?" he asked, wondering.

Deacon didn't ask what he was referring to; he already knew. Of course he knew. Riley had rarely played with anyone, offense *or* defense, who was as wily and smart as Deacon Harris.

"They'll sort each other out eventually," Deacon said, not seeming as confident as he sounded.

"Really?" Riley couldn't help his skepticism.

Maybe Deacon hadn't heard all the potshots Beck had taken at Micah. The shit he hadn't even bothered to return, like it glanced right off, but you didn't have to be particularly intelligent to see he'd taken some of it to heart.

"Yeah, and if they won't, I don't know, I'll lock them in a closet or something." Deacon grinned.

"That's not a solution," Riley argued.

"Well, what's your suggestion, QB1?" Deacon wondered.

That was the problem, wasn't it? Riley didn't have one of those. And unfortunately, the one person he'd always been able to go to about these sorts of team leadership questions was the one person he really wasn't looking forward to talking to again.

However, he also felt a *deep* and *desperate* need to go to Toronto this Sunday and beat his brother at his own game.

Blow him right out of the water so effectively, so completely, that Aidan never doubted him again.

Riley knew Aidan and knew there was only one way to truly convince his brother the right path for him was this one. It was to kick his ass.

Then tell him to fuck off for good measure.

Then maybe they could eventually settle into a semi-normal brotherly relationship.

None of that was a possibility if the defense played like crap again. If they couldn't cover receivers downfield.

"Not sure," Riley admitted.

"Well, when you have an idea…" Deacon trailed off.

"You'll be the first one to know," Riley promised.

He considered the problem through his shower and getting dressed.

Charlie said he was going to grab them a few sandwiches from the cafeteria before they went over the tape from practice.

"You heading home?" Riley asked Landry as he loitered by Riley's locker.

"Yeah, was thinking about it," Landry said. "Have some laundry to catch up. Want me to throw a load of yours in?"

"Aw," Riley said. He glanced around, saw that almost all the players had left, and he leaned in, dropping his voice to a low murmur. "You're adorable."

Landry flushed. "Is that a yes?"

"Sure," Riley said. "It's in my hamper."

"Why do we have two hampers again?" Landry asked, very matter-of-factly, like this was something he'd genuinely wondered about.

"I don't know, I hadn't thought about it," Riley answered, mostly honestly. He had thought a few times that it was weird he'd sleep every night in Landry's room, and then all his stuff was still down the hall, in the bedroom he barely spent any time in.

"Well, I did, and I think it's stupid. I have plenty of room. The closet's huge, and you didn't come with that much stuff," Landry said. "You might as well move it into my room." He paused significantly, flashing Riley a smile he wouldn't ever forget. "I mean *our* room."

Riley took the risk no one was watching and pressed a quick kiss to Landry's cheek. "I'd love to," he said honestly.

"Sounds good," Landry said, still pleasantly flushed. "I'll see you at home."

It was the thought that Landry was waiting for him at home that ultimately made Riley's decision for him.

He could call Aidan because Aidan couldn't hurt him anymore, not the way his over-solicitous care and worry had always cut him.

Riley had a life, a damn good one now, and he didn't need Aidan if he chose to be an asshole.

"Hey, stranger," Aidan said when he answered Riley's call. "I thought you might've dropped in a hole."

Riley rolled his eyes as he leaned back against the wall in the QB room. Charlie wouldn't be here with dinner for another five minutes. Plenty of time to ask Aidan about this problem.

"We didn't have anything to say," Riley said pointedly.

His brother was quiet for a moment.

"What do you want then?" Aidan asked finally.

Riley wasn't happy about it either, but if this was what they were reduced to—at least for the time being—then so be it.

He just had to tell himself that their difficulties wouldn't last forever. Someday, he'd stand up for himself, and Aidan would simply accept the new version of reality.

"You ever have two guys on your team that wouldn't get along?" Riley asked.

"What are they fighting about?" Aidan asked, not really answering the question.

"Not sure, actually. They won't talk about it."

Aidan hummed. "Well, hard to give advice then. Sometimes two guys just don't see eye-to-eye, and you've got to hope that it won't impact the game you're playing."

"Just accept it?" Riley was incredulous. That was an ambivalent attitude completely opposite to his brother's typical control freak tendencies.

"I don't know what you want from me, Riley," Aidan said testily. "A magic wand?"

"What is wrong with you?" Riley retorted. "Yeah, you can be an asshole, but you usually have to work up to the worst of it."

Aidan was quiet for a very long time. Then finally, he said, in a frustrated voice, "They won't trade for Mo."

The Toronto Thunder hadn't re-signed Aidan's favorite receiver last season, letting him go to another team for a big payday, and Riley had heard his brother gripe about it for months. Then, he'd abruptly stopped, and when Riley had asked why, he'd said he had a new plan.

Apparently, the new plan was to convince the Thunder to trade for him.

"Then throw to someone else. You've been doing that for twenty games now," Riley reasoned.

"It's not...you don't get it." Aidan broke off. "It's not that simple."

"What do you always tell me? *Make it simple, Riley*?"

"Yeah."

"So that's your grand advice then? Tell them to fight it out and hope the blood doesn't end up on the field?"

"Sometimes," Aidan said in a hard voice, "shit doesn't work out, Riley. You've got to face that fact. I gotta go."

Charlie came in the room, and Riley, who actually *wanted* to keep talking to Aidan to figure out what the fuck was going on with him beyond the normal BS, had to agree that, yes, he had to go, too.

"It'll be okay, I promise. See you Sunday," Aidan said, his tone softening. "It'll be good to see you. And Landry."

"Yeah," Riley said. *About that. I'm kinda in love with your best friend, and he's crazy about me, too. Surprise!*

But he didn't say it because the news was going to go over badly enough in person, nevermind over the phone when his brother was already in a tizzy over Mo.

Aidan hung up, and Charlie shot him a look as he unloaded sandwiches and drinks onto the table. "Everything okay?" He asked.

"Oh, the usual Aidan bullshit," Riley said because he didn't particularly feel like confessing to his backup that he'd gone running to his brother for leadership advice.

Leadership advice he hadn't even gotten, by the way.

"You need to—"

Riley laughed and finished the sentence for him. "Tell him to fuck off? Trust me, yeah, I know."

But he was less tempted to do it now than he had been before. Something in the lost way Aidan had sounded.

Like more than ever, he needed not just a friend, but a brother.

Chapter 20

Landry remembered when he'd finally chosen to sign with the Condors and the first thing Aidan had said to him when he'd heard the news was, *"Circle the third Sunday of the season on your calendar. It's on, Banks."*

At the time, he'd just thought it would be cool to finally play *against* his best friend. But now, shading his eyes against the late Toronto sun as he took the field for the Condors' warmup, there was so much more riding on this game.

Riley didn't have to say out loud how much the outcome of this one mattered. Landry *knew*.

Then, totally separate from the game, was the inevitable discussion they needed to have with Aidan. A discussion that, if Landry knew Aidan at all, wouldn't start off very well—or at all, probably. He hoped, with time, Aidan would come around to seeing Riley and Landry together as a good thing, but he wasn't naive enough to believe he'd be happy about it at first.

"You ready for this?" Riley jogged up next to him. He was still in shorts and a tank, hair falling over his forehead, blue eyes bright. He looked young and confident, ready to tackle whatever this day brought.

He didn't want to say, *I'm freaking out about this—not for me, but for you*, but it was true.

"You look like you're about to vomit," Riley answered for him. Patted him on the shoulder. "And I know it's not for you. Don't worry. I'm ready for this."

It was impossible to pretend any longer. Riley knew him better than that.

"You might be, but maybe *I'm* not," Landry said. He shaded his eyes with his hand, and yep, there was Aidan Flynn, in the flesh, jogging over to where they stood.

"Here we go," Riley said under his breath.

He's gonna know the moment he sees us together. The shit is about to hit the fan.

But he didn't because Aidan's smile was totally normal, not a molecule out of place.

"Riley," Aidan said, and they briefly hugged before he turned to Landry. "Good to see you, man, as always," he said to Landry as they embraced.

His greeting and their response were exactly as they should have been.

"See you found a new corner," Aidan said, taking a step back, hands on his hips. "He gonna be causing problems for me all day?"

"I sure hope so," Landry said.

Aidan raised an eyebrow. "When did you become so competitive, Banks?"

"Since, forever, you idiot," Riley retorted. "He's *your* best friend. You think he just wants to roll over and play dead in front of you? He doesn't. Neither of us do."

For a single moment, Landry held his breath. Had Riley gone too far? Was it too weird? Was the next thing Aidan was going to say, *What the fuck is going on between you two?*

But he didn't.

He just laughed. "And there's the kid I know." He ruffled Riley's hair, and underneath his touch, Riley made a face. "Seriously, though, you look tense, Landry. You okay?"

If Riley answered for him again, Aidan would be suspicious.

He was going to have to say something to dispel the tension. Not even the tension between them, the tension *inside* himself.

"You're really committed to that nickname," Landry said mildly. "Maybe you'll rethink it after today. Actually, I *hope* you rethink it after today."

"We'll see," Aidan said, which was code for, *not in a million years.*

Riley looked over at him. Unlike Landry, he apparently wasn't terrified to even glance over in his direction. *You're telling him after the game. It's not like he won't know the whole truth sooner rather than later.* "Maybe we need to come up with a good nickname for him. It's *his* turn."

"Oh, I can think of several you could call me. The GOAT, for starters."

Landry rolled his eyes. "That's Tom Brady, you asshole."

"Aidan the Asshole kinda has a nice ring, don't you think?" Riley mused.

But Aidan just laughed, like it was all one big joke to him.

Maybe it was.

Landry had hoped several things would come out of this meetup. *One,* that he could relax enough in Aidan's presence to not tip him off before they could pull him aside after the game and tell him the truth. *Two*, that Riley's confidence would only grow. And *three*, that he could put his mind at ease about some of the weirdness he'd witnessed from his best friend over the last few months.

Riley had told him about the odd conversation they'd had about Mo, and it had only worried Landry more.

Now that Aidan was in front of them, in person and with that casual, dazzling smile deployed like it was a weapon, it was painfully easy for Landry to see that he *was* off.

Something was up with Aidan, and if Landry tried to ask about it, he'd brush any of his concerns away.

"How about you?" Landry asked anyway because he had a feeling after today, they wouldn't be talking for a while.

Aidan would eventually come around, but Landry didn't know how long the *eventually* would take.

It could be weeks. It could be months. It could be a year.

He just didn't know, and if he let it go now, he'd worry.

"I'm fine," Aidan said with a shrug. "Not happy about Mo, but you know, shit happens in the NFL."

"Yeah, it does," Landry agreed.

The media crew for the Condors chose that moment to arrive on the scene, and they asked for some photos and video of Aidan and Riley and Landry greeting each other.

They all put their game faces on and redid their greetings.

There hadn't been many sets of quarterback brothers who'd played each other. In fact, Landry knew of only one pair who'd faced each other: Peyton and Eli Manning.

These photos would show up everywhere in the next week.

Probably everywhere for the rest of time if the Flynn brothers ended up being as impactful as the Mannings had been.

Landry was happy to step aside and watch as history was being made for a second time.

They'd take more pictures after the game, the crew said, and then they finally disappeared, leaving the three of them alone again.

"Well, that was fun," Aidan said sarcastically.

"Hey, I think it's pretty damn cool," Landry retorted. "You're playing your brother. It's an amazing accomplishment that you're both in the NFL and both starting quarterbacks."

"It's alright, Landry. I know he didn't want me playing at all, nevermind playing against him," Riley said coolly. He was eyeing Aidan with a casual confidence that Landry didn't think he'd possessed even a few weeks ago. He'd come a long way since arriving in Charleston. As much as Landry could help him continue to grow, he would.

"What's that supposed to mean?" Aidan frowned.

"It means," Landry said, final realization dawning, "that you're afraid Riley's gonna beat you."

"What? Are you serious?" Aidan said, and he might try to laugh it off, but the fear was there in his eyes. Landry could see it now.

Aidan was used to being number one. Used to being the Flynn everyone looked at and looked up to. He counted on it.

That, Landry knew, might no longer be the case.

Riley had arrived, and he was going to continue to not only deliver but to demolish every single person's expectations of what he could do.

"Yeah, I'm serious," Riley said.

"Well, I guess we'll see then," Aidan said, trying to laugh it off again. Landry was sure he thought he was convincing, but he'd known Aidan too long and seen through too many of his charades to believe it.

"Guess we will," Riley said matter-of-factly. "See you out there."

Aidan just made a face, turned, and walked away.

"He's afraid of you," Landry said in total awe and astonishment as soon as he was out of hearing.

"Yeah," Riley said. "I've wondered for awhile if that was the case. I wasn't sure, but now I am. But I think there's more going on with him than he wants to say."

"Well, that Mo thing was ridiculous. He signed with the Raiders. He's going to play for them now, under that huge contract. Why would the Thunder trade back for him? Why would Aidan even want them to?"

"I mean, part of me gets it," Riley said seriously as they began stretching out on the sideline. "Of course, I'd rather throw to you than throw to anyone else. But I'm not turning myself inside out to make it happen. A good quarterback can throw to anyone. It doesn't matter who it is. It doesn't need to be Mo Jeffries."

"Really? You'd rather throw to me than anyone else?" Riley hadn't ever said that out loud before, though the brightness of his smile when Landry caught one of his passes had been pretty good evidence it was true.

"Of course I would," Riley said with a laugh and a shake of his head. "You're my boyfriend."

Then he froze.

So did Landry because he must've had the same impossible, improbable thought.

"No way," Landry said. "*No way.*"

"I know it seems crazy," Riley said.

"Crazy is an understatement. Your brother has *never* been involved with Mo Jeffries. He'd have told me. He'd have told *you*."

"Maybe," Riley said. "Maybe not. Maybe they're not involved, maybe he just has...I don't know...feelings."

"Feelings? For Mo Jeffries?"

"If it's true, that kinda sucks for him, doesn't it?" Riley questioned.

Landry sank into another stretch. "It would, but I still don't buy it. It's just not possible. Aidan was *so* against you coming out. He talked about it nonstop for weeks."

"You think it just lasted weeks? Try *months*. Try a whole fucking year." Riley laughed humorlessly. "Aidan's got weird ideas in his head sometimes. Ways he needs to be. How he has to live. The worst part is I could see this actually being true, and he's hidden it, maybe even from himself, this whole time."

"It would explain how strange he's been." Not that Landry believed it. He still didn't. Aidan *would* have told him. He knew he would have. Landry wasn't just anyone. He hadn't just been a teammate or a passing acquaintance. He was Aidan's fucking best friend. They'd been through everything together.

"It would," Riley agreed.

"What are you two arguing about over here?" Carter appeared in Landry's view. "You already have the big PR meetup with Aidan? Is that the problem?"

"Yes, and no," Landry said.

He wasn't going to share Riley's theory with Carter. It would be all over the news in a week. Of course, Carter had been surprisingly close-lipped about their own relationship. But he had some kind of loyalty to him and Riley. Carter had zero loyalty to Aidan Flynn—or Mo Jeffries, for that matter.

And if it was really true, which seemed impossible to believe, but if it was, then this needed to be handled...gently. Carefully. Cautiously.

"Landry thinks the last meetup between two QB brothers was the Carrs, but they never played against each other," Riley said.

Clearly, he also didn't feel like sharing his theory with Carter.

"No way. David's way older than Derek. They didn't play each other. But the Mannings did, three times."

"You know who won every time?" Riley asked.

Carter and Landry both shook their heads.

"I know," Riley continued, "because I paid attention. I knew it would be us out here one day. Didn't know when or how, just that it seemed inevitable. Peyton, who was older, won every single game he played against Eli. But now? I think it's time for the big brother win streak to come to an end."

Carter slapped Riley's hand in a high-five. "Fuck yeah, it is," he said.

The game did not start with the offensive explosion every media pundit had predicted.

It was both easy and predictable for them to say it, Landry thought as he stood on the sideline, watching as Aidan dropped back to pass and had to scramble out of Deacon Harris' way almost immediately. There'd already been so much freaking emphasis on the fact two brothers, both playing quarterback, were facing off against each other.

But instead of the offenses shining in the first half, the defenses had played lights out, keeping the scoring to a minimum.

Even Micah and Beck, who were still giving each other a mutual cold-shoulder, seemed to find a fraction of the groove they'd once occupied, smothering the back half of the field so that Aidan couldn't make any of his trademark deep passes.

It was currently three to zero, and across the field, Landry could see Aidan pacing back and forth on the Thunder sideline, talking to his offensive line, exhorting every player on his team to work harder, do better, do *more*.

Riley had been doing the same thing, huddled up with the rest of the offense, but now they were getting ready to head back onto the field after the Thunder punted the ball back to the Condors.

"You ready?" Riley asked, grinning at Landry. He still looked as breathtakingly confident as he had on the first drive. Even though the Toronto defense had been stifling, he'd come back to the bench after each drive with his head held high, determination clear in his gaze as he'd rallied everyone around him to plan for their next chance.

"Never been readier," Landry said.

Coach Oscar called in a play, and in the huddle, Riley repeated it back, meeting everyone's eyes once as he clapped to break up the group.

Landry took a breath and lined up, readying himself to run. They'd been using him to block almost exclusively since the game started, but clearly during halftime, the coaching staff decided that while that was sort of working, if they didn't move the ball down the field, they weren't going to be able to lengthen their lead.

The ref blew the whistle, and Cole snapped the ball to Riley. Landry wasn't running his deep running route this time, but crossing over into the soft part of the zone, hopefully just under the eye of the safety. The plan was to just get enough yardage to gain another first down.

Landry pushed off, running around the edge, moving in a slant pattern towards the middle of the field.

He watched as Riley dropped back as he glanced down the field, starting to go through his progressions. He spotted Landry, and their eyes met. He was technically the first choice on the play, but Riley wasn't going to telegraph his actions and leave himself open to a batted ball or worse, an interception.

Riley turned his head, taking in Carter, who was streaking down the sideline. He was double-covered. Landry could see it. Riley could see it. It was tempting, though, a really tempting throw that would almost certainly end in disaster.

But Riley was too smart of a quarterback to make that throw.

Aidan had taught him better than that.

Landry knew now that Riley's exceptional decision-making was something he'd gotten from his brother. And now he was going to use everything Aidan had taught him to beat him at his own game.

Without even looking at Landry, Riley threw across his body, letting the ball fly.

Landry grabbed it out of the air and then turned upfield.

He took in the safety moving fast across the field to intercept him, and he took what he believed was a great angle. At the same time, he braced himself for a collision and the inevitable tackle, so he stuck out his arm, legs churning hard as he attempted to push the safety off his course.

A smaller guy wouldn't have been able to do it. As it was, it took every bit of Landry's not-inconsiderable strength, but he managed it, the safety glancing off him, falling to the turf, and he kept going.

One of the two corners covering Carter downfield spied him and moved to intercept next.

Ten yards down.

Twenty.

Then thirty.

Landry was breathing hard now

He wouldn't go down without a fight; he'd already proven that.

But this corner was clever and tangled their legs together, Landry landing with a hard *oomph* on the turf.

His blood was buzzing as Riley and the rest of the offense caught up to him, Carter holding out his arm as he took it to help leverage himself upright.

"Fuck yes!" Carter yelled, hands pumping like he was the one who'd caught the ball.

Landry bumped fists with him and shot Riley one last reassuring look before he took to the sideline to catch his breath.

"Great play," Coach Kelley told him as he passed by, patting him on the back.

"Thanks," Landry said, grabbing a Gatorade bottle from an assistant. He poured half of it down his throat while his eyes never left the field.

Riley called a running play and handed the ball to Darius. After pushing through the defensive line, he got about five yards.

Landry went to rejoin the field, but Coach Kelley held up his hand, telling him to wait. That he could rejoin next series. Landry made a face.

He'd gotten them to mid-field, hadn't he?

But he settled back to wait, not very patiently, as the Condors' offense lined up for another play.

This one was passing, and Landry felt his heart plummet all the way to the ground as Boyd, the left tackle currently protecting Riley's blind side, slipped on the turf, and the pass rusher went right by him, totally unblocked. Riley wasn't going to see the hit coming, he was going to get absolutely demolished, and there was nothing Landry could do to stop it.

His fists clenched.

Nothing he could do but just stand here and watch it happen.

The guy drove Riley right to the ground, knocking the ball loose, and even though Cole, the center, landed on it, saving the fumble from turning over to the Thunder, Landry only had eyes for Riley.

The players moved, then, and there was Riley. Lying on the field. Motionless.

Landry's heart didn't just plummet.

It fucking stopped.

He didn't think, and he certainly didn't hesitate.

He ran right onto the field, shucking two sets of hands that tried to hold him back.

He wasn't going to stand by and just watch. Not any longer.

He reached Riley a few moments later, falling to his knees next to him. "Riley," he called out, "God, Riley, are you okay?" He didn't touch him, even though he wanted to more than anything else on earth, because he knew if Riley did have a spinal or brain injury, moving him right now before he was prepared could make it worse.

But Riley didn't move.

"Riley, God, no, you can't…I can't…" Landry panted. "I never even told you."

"Never even told him *what*?"

Landry looked up, barely able to tear his eyes from Riley's motionless form to meet the irate, baffled, concerned gaze of his older brother.

Aidan must've come from the opposing sideline to make sure Riley was okay.

"Nothing." But the muttered response wasn't from Landry. It was from Riley, who'd just moved and was now struggling to sit up. "He didn't need to say anything."

"Riley, come on, don't move. They gotta check you out," Landry said, fretting as Riley groaned and levered himself into an upright position.

"I'm fine," Riley said. "Just got the breath knocked out of me for a second."

"It looked bad." That was from Aidan, sounding curiously flat.

Riley held up a hand. "If you say for the millionth fucking time I'm too small to take the hits, I'll hit *you*."

Landry laughed because if he didn't laugh, he was probably going to do something insane like bawl like a baby all over Riley's shoulder.

"Guess you're fine."

"Guess I am," Riley said, and Landry helped him up. "Too bad for you."

Aidan made a face, and Landry turned back to him as two trainers took Riley's arms to lead him to the sideline to get checked out.

Landry couldn't deny it; he wanted Riley to be okay because he loved him. But he also wanted him to be okay because he wanted them to beat Aidan in this game.

He wanted *Riley* to beat Aidan.

"What the fuck was that?" Aidan hissed under his breath, grabbing Landry's arm and not returning immediately to the Thunder's sideline.

"What the fuck was what?" Landry retorted, but he knew what Aidan was asking about. He'd raced out here without a single concern about intruding on the field of play, without caring about any possible flags thrown by the refs.

He'd only wanted—no, *needed*—to make sure Riley was okay.

Because he loved him.

"You ran out here like you were possessed or something, and your face..." Aidan cleared his throat. "What's going on between you and my brother? Did you...you *wouldn't*."

Oh, but he would. Happily and many, many times.

But this was not the way he'd wanted Aidan to find out.

Not only because it was literally in the middle of the game but because now it looked like he and Riley were trying to hide it from him.

Aidan would not take that well. Not at all.

"I wouldn't what? Care about your brother? You know what, Aidan? Go fuck yourself." Maybe it wasn't Riley telling Aidan to fuck off, but it sure felt good anyway.

"Are you actually serious right now?" Aidan sounded angry and also incredulous.

"Very," Landry said in clipped tones and turned and walked back to his own huddle.

Charlie came out, not giving an update on Riley, but they'd all get one as soon as they scored a touchdown on this drive—and a touchdown it had to be because Landry was more determined than ever to win this game and show Aidan just how wrong he was.

"You guys good to go?" Charlie asked, glancing down at his armband with its listing of plays. "Good, 'cause we're gonna score here. Darius, you ready for the ball?"

Darius nodded. "For Riley," he said, and the whole huddle chimed in with a variation of the same chant.

For Riley.

It turned out that Darius didn't score on that play, but on the next. Charlie handed the ball off, and he just took on the line, pushing through it with a bruising force Landry knew he'd be feeling tomorrow.

But he wasn't feeling it right now. None of them were.

Landry knew, even as they celebrated the touchdown, they were all really thinking about what they'd learn when they returned to the Condors' sideline.

Would Riley be playing? Or had that hit knocked him out of this game, one of the most important of his young career?

But Riley was waiting for them on the bench, already out of the medical tent.

"I'm all good," he promised as the team crowded around him. "Promise. Now, let's talk about how we're gonna score again and finish the Thunder off."

"You actually good?" Landry asked under his breath as they got ready to take the field again, the Thunder readying for another punt when Beck and Micah, apparently on the same page, batted down a ball together that a receiver nearly caught for a thirty-yard gain.

"I'm fine," Riley said firmly. "As for what you said on the field..."

"After," Landry promised. "We'll talk about it after." He meant it. After that scare, he wasn't going to let another day go by without saying how he felt.

Sure, they were both guys who put more stock into actions than into words, and Landry knew they'd both been *living* like they loved each other for awhile now, but he'd realized it was important to say it, too.

Riley needed to know, beyond a shadow of a doubt, how he was now the most important person in Landry's life.

The smile on his face.

The reason he got up in the morning.

The brilliance in every single day.

"Come on then," Riley said with a confident smile. "Let's do this, then."

"Riley," one of the reporters asked him when he'd finally gotten to the microphone for the after-game press conference, "what does it mean to not only beat your brother, but to now have two wins under your belt?"

Riley took a deep breath.

So much had happened in the last two hours that it was hard to even process it. He'd played against the Thunder, against his *brother*—and won. He'd nearly been knocked out of the game. Landry and Aidan had apparently gotten into it right after he'd gone down, and Landry was being close-lipped about exactly what had happened, but Carter had told him, right before he'd walked in here, that it hadn't sounded good from where he'd been standing.

"I'll tell you one thing to start," Riley said. "Did you know that only one set of quarterback brothers have ever played against each other? Yeah, you probably already know that. It's all anyone's been talking about all week. The one set of brothers was the Mannings, of course. And all three times, Peyton beat Eli. But today, I got a little payback for all the younger brothers out there."

"More than a little," the reporter retorted lightly. "You beat him twenty-one to three."

"Felt good," Riley said. "Felt real good. Especially because there was a time when nobody was sure I'd be able to hack it as an NFL quarterback. But those days are gone. That conversation is closed.

I'm here, and I'm ready to play. And not only that, but I'm planning on playing *my* kind of game."

"What about the injury you sustained in the third quarter?" Another reporter asked.

"Just got the wind knocked out of me. Some rib bruising. No breaks. I'm sure I'll be hurting tomorrow, but I'll be back to practice Tuesday."

"Do you have anything to say about the way Landry Banks came onto the field when he saw you'd been injured and weren't getting up?" This was from the first reporter, a dark-haired woman, clearly tenacious, who both fortunately and unfortunately reminded him of Paige.

"No," Riley said shortly. He knew the press would get more out of his simple denial than a lie that Landry was just a friend and he'd been worried, but he wasn't going to make up some story. Not when Landry was right outside the door, waiting for him to finish so they could go tell Aidan the truth.

He never wanted to lie about him and Landry and what they meant to each other, but he sure wasn't going to do it right now.

"Any more questions?" Nikki asked, speaking up no doubt to deflect any additional attention from the question he hadn't answered. But then, it wasn't like the reporters hadn't already taken note of his brief *No* and run with it.

He fully expected to see a few speculative stories in the press about them, but that was okay. As Coach had said, it was up to them how they chose to engage. If they didn't want to talk about it, they didn't have to.

Another reporter asked one last question about a running touchdown he'd made late in the fourth quarter to finally put the game away, and he commented some on that, but then, thankfully, he was done.

Landry was waiting for him outside the media room.

"You could've said," Landry observed under his breath, "that I was worried fucking sick about you because you were just *lying* there."

"Yeah, I could've," Riley said, shrugging. "But I didn't want to. It's…it's okay that this is just for us, for now, yeah?"

"Yeah." Landry put an arm around Riley's waist. Tucked him into a tight embrace. "And I wouldn't want to do or say anything that might downplay or take away from what you accomplished today. You did good. Correction…you did *fucking amazing*."

"Thanks, so did you. You really kicked us off with that pass you caught and ran with in the third," Riley said. He paused because he wasn't sure how to put the question. "What happened between you and Aidan? Carter just said you got into it after the trainers helped me off the field."

Landry stopped, turned, and faced Riley. "I'm gonna be honest," he said. "I freaked out. You weren't moving. I was losing my mind. I said—"

"I *know* what you said. You said, *I never even told you.*"

"Yeah," Landry acknowledged, nodding. "I know."

"And Aidan heard."

"Aidan…" Landry shook his head. "He might've guessed. I don't know. He was pretty angry. Said something typical asshole-Aidan, and then I told him to fuck off. *God,* I told your brother to fuck off, and now I'm going to have to tell him I'm in love with you."

Riley's heartbeat accelerated. Had he heard correctly? Or had it just been his imagination—no, his *fantasy*—filling in the gap with what he most wanted to hear?

"Did you just say you *love me*?"

"Yeah," Landry said, eyes never leaving Riley's. "I did."

Landry's gaze was so warm on his face. So loving. Riley had known this was love; it couldn't be anything else. They'd been showing it for weeks, but neither of them had said the words until now.

He'd even kinda believed the words weren't entirely necessary since they were both more men of action.

But now that Landry had said it, he knew the words were exactly what he needed. He wanted to hear them every day for the rest of his life.

"I love you, too," Riley said, "so fucking much." But before he could get any other words out, Landry had scooped him up and was twirling around with him in his arms, like they were some kind of rom-com pair, and then Landry kissed him, and nothing, really *nothing,* else mattered.

"God, you're incredible," Landry said as he finally set him down. "I know I messed this up with Aidan, but we're gonna fix it. We're going to tell him, and it's going to be..."

Landry trailed off, and Riley, still caught up in the way Landry was looking at him—though frankly it wasn't like he hadn't already recognized that particular look, he *had*—didn't figure out why Landry had stopped talking until he finally tore his eyes away from his boyfriend, and saw what he'd seen.

Aidan, stalking towards them, a frown on his face.

"Care to explain what the hell is going on here?" he asked, his glare encompassing both of them.

Riley hadn't quite been able to decide how Aidan was going to handle this.

Would he blame Riley for seducing his best friend?

Claim it was Landry's fault for taking advantage of a young and naive Riley?

But the way Aidan looked now, it seemed like they were both currently on his shit list.

"Surprise," Riley said weakly. "We're together now."

"You mean, this isn't a joke?"

"Does it look like a joke?" Landry's voice was still even. But it had a core of steel. "I wouldn't ever joke about this. Riley's very important to me."

"No," Aidan said insistently. "Riley's very important to *me*."

"Then you have a funny way of showing it," Landry said quietly, resolutely. "I want Riley to succeed. I want him to find the ceiling of his capability. You just want to shove him down so you don't look bad. So you continue being the top dog. Well, today was a real awakening for you, wasn't it? You're not. Not anymore."

Aidan's face went white.

Riley had always wondered if he could actually tell his brother to fuck off, but here Landry was doing it instead. Instead of cheering, all Riley wanted to do was to wrap his arms around his brother and shield him from all the uncomfortable truths he needed to hear but wasn't ready to listen to.

But if he did that, if he walked back everything Landry was saying, Aidan wouldn't ever grow. He wouldn't ever learn.

He'd be treating Aidan the same way Aidan had always tried to treat him, and Riley knew he couldn't let that happen.

Every inch of the way, he'd fought against Aidan's instinct to coddle him, to protect him from anything bad, and he couldn't deny that was part of why he'd succeeded when everyone else had predicted he'd fail. Now that the tables were turned, Riley wasn't going to subject him to the same bullshit.

That wasn't what family did.

That wasn't what *brothers* did.

"Riley, you need to talk to me," Aidan demanded. "What the fuck is going on? You're with *Landry*? And he's..." Aidan fumbled the rest of the sentence like he couldn't believe the most loyal friend in the universe, Landry Banks, had transferred that loyalty to someone else. Aidan didn't realize it now, maybe he never would, but Riley knew that the only reason Landry had was that Aidan no longer deserved it the way he once had.

"He's right," Riley said.

Aidan did a double take. "Excuse me?"

"I said," Riley repeated, "that he's right. I don't want him to be, Aidan. I know it sucks to hear. You wanted the best for me, but only as long as I wasn't as good as you were. I can't do that, put a cap on my own ability because you're afraid of feeling irrelevant."

Aidan's face hardened. "Riley—"

"No," Riley said, holding up a hand. "No. This is how it is. I'm a quarterback in the NFL. I'm a *starting* quarterback in the NFL. I'm not too weak. I'm not too small. And Landry and me? We're together now. I know that's going to be hard to face, but we love each other. We found each other, and we love each other, and I don't want to hear a damn word about it except that you're happy for us. As for today, as for the game, I know, deep down, in a place where you're not hurting, you're happy for me, too. So just say it. Just say you're happy about it."

But Aidan didn't say anything. Not for a very long time.

Long enough that Riley couldn't help but despair that he wouldn't.

Was he going to have to walk away from his brother because he wouldn't do the right thing? He might have to.

Landry's hand found his own and squeezed it hard. He knew it, too. He might lose his best friend over this, at least temporarily.

It had always been the potential cost, and they'd both willingly paid it, but was it so wrong to hope anyway that Aidan might come around?

"I..." Aidan finally spoke. "I'm sorry you thought I might not be happy for you." He'd said it quietly, in a voice unsure and very unlike Aidan Flynn.

"I hoped you would be," Riley said.

"Well, I am. And I'm sorry too that I was so tough on you. I..." Aidan hesitated. "I do want the best for you. I guess I always thought I knew what that was. But maybe I don't."

Riley nodded. "Maybe you don't. But maybe...maybe we could start over. Not as Aidan and *the kid*, but...Aidan and Riley? Then you'd get to see it firsthand. Learn it for yourself what the best thing is for me."

Impossibly, Aidan's face softened. He looked, Riley realized, almost like he had during those awful days when their parents had freshly divorced, and it felt like nobody was looking out for them—when nobody looked out for *him* except for his older brother.

"Yeah," he said. His voice was rusty, like he hadn't tried any of this in a long time.

Riley figured he hadn't.

"Good." Riley let go of Landry's hand and caught a glimpse of shock on Aidan's face right before he hugged his brother.

He might drive him crazy, he might dislike so many of thc things he did and said, but deep down, he was always going to be the brother Riley loved. No matter what.

After a second, Aidan hugged him back—tightly, fiercely. Then he turned to Landry and said, "If you hurt him..."

"Don't worry," Landry said. "I'll be the first to punch myself in the face."

"Sounds good," Aidan said. "I suppose you've got a plane back to Charleston to catch."

"Yeah," Riley said and discovered he was actually reluctant about that.

"Well, when the off-season arrives you won't be able to run off so easily." Aidan's smile was uncomfortable, but Riley could tell he was trying. "Maybe I'll even come to you."

"I'd like that." Riley paused. "*We'd* like that, actually."

With one last awkward smile, Aidan turned to walk away, but then, suddenly, he turned back halfway down the hallway. "And if I didn't say it," he called out, "hell of a game today, little brother."

Riley laughed, leaning against Landry as his brother disappeared from sight.

"Well," Landry said cautiously, "that went pretty well, actually. All things considered."

"I didn't tell Aidan to fuck off."

"No, you did even better than that. You made him understand, in a way telling him off never would've accomplished. I'm just so proud of you, Riley. For how you played, for standing up to him, for handling yourself like a pro. You're just..." Landry gazed down at him. "I keep saying it because I can't stop saying it. You're fucking incredible. And I love you."

Riley reached up and cupped Landry's cheek, feeling the scratch of the stubble under his hand. How many years had he imagined doing this exact thing? He couldn't count, not anymore, but in the end, none of them mattered. He knew what it felt like now, and if he was very lucky, he'd never be able to forget it because he'd be able to do it whenever he wanted. "I love you, too," he said. He *didn't* say he couldn't have done it all without Landry because he knew he could've. But instead—"And thank you for always believing in me."

"Always," Landry vowed. "Now, let's go home, okay?"

Riley smiled. "Okay."

CHAPTER 21

Landry should've expected it was coming.

Should have seen it from a million miles away.

But Monday afternoon, a little over twenty-four hours after he and Riley had confronted Aidan, his best friend called him.

Didn't just call him. *Facetimed* him.

Right, of course, as Landry was watching as Riley moved his stuff from the guest room closet to his own closet from the bed.

He'd hoped to christen the closet after, before they had to be at Carter's for a Monday victory party, but then, his phone had rung.

"You gonna take that?" Riley asked as he folded t-shirts.

Landry stared at his phone's screen—at the picture of Aidan he'd taken ages ago, with a silly expression on his face, his tongue sticking out, looking lighter than he ever looked these days.

"Yeah," Landry said, sliding off the bed. "I'll be downstairs."

"It's my brother, isn't it?" Riley asked, but he didn't give Landry a chance to answer. "Be easy on him, okay?"

Even after all the shit Aidan had given him, Riley still wanted the best for him.

If Landry needed any additional evidence that his boyfriend was the best guy in the world, there it was.

"Hey," he answered as he took the stairs down, a few at a time. He settled against the kitchen island as Aidan's face popped up on the screen again. This time, it was easy to see the stark differences between the old Aidan and the new.

The new looked weary and tired, gray circles under his eyes. Like he'd spent too many late nights soul-searching.

Landry discovered that he wasn't even angry anymore. He just wished he could find that old Aidan again and bring him back.

"I've been a dick," Aidan said bluntly.

But then, that was Aidan's way, wasn't it?

"Yeah, kinda," Landry admitted.

Aidan sighed. "I'm sorry."

"What was that? Should I record it and play it back for you every once in a while?" Landry teased.

He saw a flash of the old Aidan in the way he smiled.

"Fuck you," Aidan retorted lightly.

"Did you call to point out any other obvious observations or give me the shovel talk or..."

Aidan laughed, the sound rusty, like he didn't do much laughing these days.

"No shovel talk necessary. I meant it yesterday. You're a good guy. The best guy. I wouldn't want my brother to be with anyone else. And he's pretty cool, too. I'm happy for you two."

"Thanks," Landry said. Meaning it. "I'm really happy for us, too."

"I can tell, you know? You look it."

"You guys are gonna get your shit together," Landry said, changing the subject. He knew the Thunder's loss to the Condors was probably still smarting. Would sting for a lot longer than a single week. "And then you're gonna be a force to be reckoned with."

"Yeah, yeah," Aidan said, rolling his eyes. "Maybe not this year. But soon. I gotta just…figure out my shit. The shit with this offense. These new guys can't catch the ball worth a damn."

"They'll get there. They're just young." And Landry knew Aidan was still missing Mo. In what ways? Landry wasn't sure, but even if it was only on the field, that would suck.

"Guess I'll have to find some patience," Aidan said wryly.

"Good luck with that."

"Hey," Aidan said in mock outrage. "I *can* be patient."

"If you wanna win, you better look real damn hard."

"Yeah."

For a long moment, they just looked at each other.

Was Aidan thinking the same thing Landry was? *Will we ever be okay again? Will you be angry with me forever for what happened with Riley?*

"I want things to be solid between us," Aidan said after clearing his throat.

Landry couldn't deny it; he was more than a little shocked. He hadn't actually expected Aidan to tackle the elephant in the room.

"I want that, too," Landry said and knew, in his heart, it was true.

"Good. Good."

"And if we both want that, then we'll make it happen," Landry said confidently.

"You think so?" Aidan sounded unsure. So unlike him. Landry's hand tightened on the phone because, no matter how frustrated he could be with his best friend, he never wanted him to be lost. Not like this.

"Would you bet against us?" Landry challenged.

Aidan's expression broke into a bright, fierce grin.

There he is.

The old Aidan.

The Aidan I'd follow anywhere.

"No fucking way," Aidan said.

And Landry knew then that they *would* be fine.

Riley got out of Landry's car and couldn't help the shocked expression currently crossing his face.

"Are you sure this is the right address?" he asked Landry as he closed the door behind him.

"Yeah," Landry said, nodding. "It's right. I just never expected..."

"For Carter to live in a place that looks like an actual *home*? Me, either."

It was confirmed then because the front door swung open, and Carter walked out onto the wraparound porch, shading his eyes from the setting sun.

"I told you," Carter said as they approached the stairs. "Deacon was full of shit."

"Unless you're hiding a bunch of dead bodies in the basement, your house is most definitely not a mausoleum," Riley agreed. "But I'm surprised."

"That I live in an ordinary house?" Carter chuckled.

"So normal," Landry said under his breath, clearly just as mystified as Riley was.

The further they'd driven out of downtown, the more surprised Riley had become, but even then, he'd not expected this big rambling farmhouse, painted a cheery, *normal* yellow, with white trim and white plantation shutters, and then there was the wraparound porch.

It did *not* look like the house of a guy who routinely indulged in threesomes and more.

"Well, come on in. I got pizza," Carter said. "And hot wings, which Deacon and Jem are attempting to demolish by the dozen."

The inside of the house was just as normal as the outside, filled with comfortable-looking couches, warm walls covered in brightly colored artwork, and Jem and Deacon, a growing pile of chicken wing bones on a plate on the coffee table in front of them.

"Food and beer's in the kitchen. There's pop, too, if you're not drinking, Riley," Carter said, and he sounded self-conscious. Like he wasn't used to hosting his teammates at his house.

"This is actually *really* nice," Riley said, reaching over and patting him on the shoulder. "It's a very nice house. We just didn't expect it."

"Us either. I asked him if the basement was where the orgies were, and he just laughed at me," Jem said, sounding mildly outraged.

"Like I'd bring any of those hookups here," Carter said, rolling his eyes. "To my personal space. Where they could stalk me anytime they wanted. Please."

"Sex with you leads to stalking?" Deacon asked, raising an eyebrow. "What kind of sex are you having?"

"The best kind of sex, baby," Carter said, winking at him. "You wanna try it sometime?"

"And become enthralled to you for life? No, thank you," Deacon retorted.

There was a knock on the front door. "Oh, must be Beck or Micah," Carter said, standing up.

"You invited both of them?" Riley was surprised. Yes, they'd played together well on Sunday. But in the locker room after the game and on the plane ride home, it was clear from their mutual silence, nothing else had changed.

But since they *had* performed well on the field, Riley had decided it was up to them to handle it.

Clearly, Deacon had had other ideas.

Or maybe this was just more of Carter's bullshit.

"Carter said he invited them," Jem said, lowering his voice, "because he wanted them both to be our friends. That we weren't going to pick between them. So they'd have to get used to being around each other."

"That's..." Landry hesitated next to Riley, coming back into the living room with two plates piled high with pizza slices and wings, "actually kind of sweet?"

"Don't let Carter hear you say that. He'll go on a week-long Bacchanalian tear, and now that our record's two and one, we need him to keep his dick in his pants at least long enough to play," Deacon said with an affectionate huff.

"Whose dick in whose pants?" It was Micah who asked as he and Carter came into the living room.

"Carter's. Who else?" Deacon said. He wiped his face and hands with a wet wipe and stood, pulling Micah into a quick embrace. "Good to see you, man. So glad you came."

"I was real glad to be invited," Micah said, looking like he was still surprised he'd been included. He greeted Landry next, then turned to Riley. "How you doing?" he asked after he'd carefully hugged Riley. "Your ribs okay?"

"They're okay," Riley said. *Actually, they hurt like a motherfucker.* But he didn't say it because he wasn't focusing on that today. He was still living in the thrill of having beaten the Thunder and his brother. Nothing hurt whenever he thought about that.

"He's tough, tougher than anyone imagined," Jem said approvingly.

"Go sit down. I'll grab you some food," Carter told Micah.

Landry patted the spot on the couch next to him. "Yeah, seriously, come sit. You just missed Carter propositioning Deacon, who turned him down flat."

"At least he didn't laugh at me like Beck did," Carter said, then froze. Like he realized what he'd just said.

Shit, we were doing so well, Riley thought mournfully.

"You hit on Beck?" Micah's eyebrows were nearly to his hairline.

Carter shot him a speculative look. Then, clearly decided it was worth owning. "Yeah," he admitted.

Riley was about to intervene and say, *Don't worry about it. Carter does it to basically everyone. I'm sure you'll be next.*

But before he could, Micah just chuckled darkly under his breath. "Well, Beck's a good-lookin' guy," he said. "Don't blame you for trying."

Landry's knee nudged Riley's, but Riley had caught all the undercurrent. You'd have to be blind and deaf to miss it.

"Yeah," Carter said brightly. "See? I'm not such a horndog."

"You are the worst kind of horndog," Jem said with a grin. "But we love you anyway."

"Aw guys, you're the best," Carter said. "I'd yell *group hug*, but Jem's covered in hot wing sauce, and Riley's ribs probably couldn't take it."

"Probably not," Landry said.

He'd been one of the few to see them in their full mottled black-and-blue-with-even-a-few-fun-shades-of-purple-thrown-in-for-good-measure glory. The concern in his eyes had told Riley everything he needed to know about how bad they were.

But he'd be okay. The pain had been better this morning, and by the time next Sunday's game rolled around, he'd be in good shape.

"So if you don't hook up with anyone here," Jem said, "where *do* you hook up with them?"

"Hotels, *duh*," Carter said. "Isn't that what y'all do?"

"Deacon here's going for a record level of abstinence," Jem said dryly, "Riley and Landry don't need to worry about it because they're way too in love to ever consider anyone else, and as for me, I'm apparently less of a sex god than you because nobody's ever stalked me in order to repeat the experience."

"It's alright," Carter said, patting Jem affectionately on the head as he passed by. "Not everyone can be me."

"Thank god for small mercies," Micah said with a laugh. "You guys are really interesting. Different kind of interesting than my old teammates in Miami."

"Yeah, what were they like?" Riley asked, genuinely curious.

"There's some young guys, some older guys. We even had a coach who hung with us sometimes. Pax's guy," Micah said. "Davis. He's a good dude." It went unspoken that the Condors had fucked him over—at least the previous version of the Condors.

"Did you know Mr. G extended him an invite to come back here and play? As sort of an apology?" Riley spoke up.

Micah shook his head. "I didn't know that, but I can't imagine Davis would take it. He's crazy about Pax. Well, they're crazy about each other." His voice went wry. Not envious, not exactly, but something like that. "And there's these two rooks, well, I guess they aren't rookies anymore, but they fucked *constantly*. Like Carter here level of fucking. We had to knock on every single freaking door to make sure we didn't walk in on them. I sort of expected you two to be like that at first," Micah said, gesturing towards Riley and Landry. "But then I remembered your bro and his boyfriend, Dylan. They're not much for PDA either, which…"

"Thank God," Jem said. "Imagine if we had two Carters floating around."

"You'd only be so lucky," Carter retorted.

"But yeah, they were good guys. I was lucky to play with them. Now, I'm lucky to play with you," Micah said.

"And we're lucky to have *you*," Riley said.

Micah flushed at this compliment, looking pleased.

"Thought y'all would've invited Beck to this. He's normally your go-to guy, yeah?" Micah asked self-consciously.

"We did," Deacon said kindly.

"Oh. *Oh.*" Micah licked his lips nervously and reached for the open bottle of beer Carter had handed him. "Yeah. Makes sense."

It made sense that Beck had skipped this get-together because he'd figured Micah would be invited? Ouch, Riley thought, that sucked.

"I think," Jem said, speaking up, "that we're *all* very lucky you're here. Lucky to be together, lucky to be doing something about this team that isn't just running it into the ground." He raised his bottle of beer. "To the Condors. May we always fly high!"

"This place is so nice," Riley said as he relaxed against the edge of the wraparound porch. "It's peaceful out here."

"You ever want to live out here like this, in the country?" Landry asked as he wrapped an arm around Riley's waist, pulling him against him gently, still clearly worried about Riley's ribs.

"Maybe someday," Riley said. "But for now, I like your house."

"Enough you aren't going to move out?"

"No," Riley said with a smile. "I think I've found just the right place."

"Right next to me?" Landry sounded hopeful. But not only that, confident, too. Like he not only knew what Riley meant, but that he believed in it just as strongly as Riley did.

"Yeah," Riley said.

His phone dinged. And then dinged again and again and again, like a flood of texts were coming through.

"What's that?" Riley asked, feeling a bit of apprehension washing over him. He dug his phone out of his pocket, hoping nothing terrible had happened.

But he didn't think so, as he stared at the screen.

All the texts were from Aidan.

It wasn't his normal format—he hadn't emailed, he explained, because that was what he used to do, and they were starting over, fresh—but in the texts was his usual breakdown of the game.

Well, *not* in his usual way, Riley realized as he read through each and every message. He did give a few helpful pointers, but there was plenty of praise. A *lot* of praise, in fact.

Aidan rounded out the last message with something Riley could barely believe and might not have believed if it wasn't right there on the screen in black and white.

I'm sorry I tried to get you to quit. **I'm sorry I tried to control you. But I'm most sorry that you thought I wouldn't be happy for you.**

Not everything's great here, but we're fighting, we're working, and I think I let some of that strain ruin me and you because I was so afraid you'd beat us. Well, you did, and it was well-deserved.

But I'm sorry I made you think even for a second that I wasn't happy for you. I am. I'm even happy you're with Landry now. At least I don't ever have to worry about you finding the great partner you deserve because he's the best. Talk to you soon. A

"Wow," Landry said, his head hooked over Riley's shoulder as he read each text right alongside Riley.

Riley couldn't believe it. It was everything he'd ever wanted from his brother and nothing he'd ever expected he'd get. Aidan must have done some real soul-searching to send this.

"Did you..." Riley trailed off.

Because Aidan and Landry *had* talked earlier today. Privately.

"No," Landry said firmly. "No, this is all him. Well, other than you schooling him very firmly yesterday."

"I guess that really got through to him."

"That, and," Landry added, squeezing Riley gently, "this is the Aidan I knew existed all along. I thought maybe he was lost. Maybe even gone forever. But not so much."

"Not anymore," Riley said. He was smiling so hard it hurt.

"What are you gonna say to him?" Landry wondered.

What *could* he say? Riley thought he had a million responses and no responses at all, both at the same time.

"I don't know," he finally said slowly. "I think...I think it's pretty simple, isn't it?"

"What?" Landry said.

Riley typed it out one word at a time. **I love you, too, big bro,** he sent back.

It was all he needed to say. All he *could* say.

Landry brushed a sweet kiss against the top of his head. "Every time I think I know you," he said with wonderment in his voice, "I see a new side of you, and I fall in love all over again."

"Seeing me in various states of undress doesn't count," Riley teased, even though he knew what Landry meant.

"Oh, it counts," Landry said. The next kiss he pressed to Riley's mouth wasn't so sweet. But Riley couldn't deny it was satisfying.

"What are we gonna do now, now that your brother doesn't hate us and isn't giving you shit?" Landry asked, and Riley knew his question was probably rhetorical, but he answered it anyway.

"Be happy and stupidly, ridiculously in love for the rest of our lives," Riley said firmly. "How does that sound?"

Landry grinned. "Nothing's ever sounded better."

Craving more Condors? Don't miss the bonus scene, which you can download here.

Check out the next book in the Condors series — Micah & Beck's book — *The Game.*
Much to Beckett West's dismay, Micah Rose arrives in Charleston and The Game is on.

INTERESTED IN READING MORE OF
BETH'S BOOKS?

CHECK OUT A FULL LIST OF TILES
BY SCANNING THE QR CODE
OR VISITING HER WEBSITE

WWW.BETHBOLDEN.COM/BOOKLIST

WANT TO FOLLOW BETH?

MAKE SURE YOU NEVER
MISS A RELEASE?

SCAN THE QR CODE BELOW
OR VISIT HER WEBSITE
FOR A SOCIAL MEDIA LIST,
NEWSLETTER SIGNUP,
AND SO MUCH MORE!

WWW.BETHBOLDEN.COM/ABOUT